The Credit Crunch

Conspiracy

By

Dominic Varadi

authorHOUSE®

AuthorHouse™ UK Ltd.
500 Avebury Boulevard
Central Milton Keynes, MK9 2BE
www.authorhouse.co.uk
Phone: 08001974150

First published by AuthorHouse 10/19/2009

ISBN: 978-1-4490-3553-2 (sc)

This book is printed on acid-free paper.

Contents

'There is no such thing as society':

Margaret Thatcher

This novel is dedicated to all who disagree.

Although this novel is based on real events
it is not intended to be historically accurate
and all the main characters are fictional.

Act 1: FEAR

Scene 1: From Wallsend to Wall Street

'Shit' exclaimed Dan candidly as he surveyed the pink pages of the Financial Times.

Dan took immense pride in being able to predict the fortunes of blue-chip companies. It was a talent that had taken him from a Tyneside flat to a Manhattan penthouse via a succession of increasingly lofty positions at an American private equity firm.

Now, sitting in the business class departure lounge at Heathrow he could scarcely believe his eyes. He re-read the cover story just to make sure the coke he had snorted last night wasn't causing him to hallucinate. It wasn't. One of the oldest and most widely respected banks in the world, Polmont had filed for bankruptcy!

Polmont had been founded by a Scottish aristocrat in the nineteenth century and was named after the small Scottish town near Falkirk that he had left in search of even greater riches in the colonies. It had grown into one of the biggest companies in the world. In the 1990's it made a million dollars a day and some of its staff had remuneration packages that were enough to make premiership footballers green with envy.

Dan was not in that league, at least not yet, but he was climbing the ladder fast and had a ruthless ambition to reach the summit. He measured success by his bonus cheque and his last one gave him one hell of a thrill; not bad for a black kid from Wallsend!

What really freaked Dan out was that he had got his blue-print for success from the whizz-kids at Polmont. Until the 1980's, banking had been a stuffy, conservative profession. That all changed with the neo-liberal monetarism of Thatcher and Reagan. *'Greed is good'* inspired a new breed of banker where bright sparks from diverse backgrounds were encouraged to be innovative, risk-takers that bet on the stock-market to maximise returns.

Freed of effective state regulation, fortune favoured the brave and Polmont led the world in developing complex products such as embedded derivatives, hedge funds and short-selling that its own Board didn't fully understand. Now, Polmont had taken one risk too many and millions of people around the world were about to pay the price.

Dan steadied himself and decided to check the FTSE for how his latest investments were faring in the wake of Polmont's demise.

'Holy Shite', he vented.

'Sorry Father' he added as he looked up to witness a priest sitting opposite him.

Suddenly, Dan was not looking forward to the meeting with his boss back in New York. He got the feeling his next apology would not be received as gratiously.

*****

Back home in Newcastle, Dan's elder brother Kyle was also having a bad day. Crouched apprehensively in front of a small screen he waved and goaded his steed on to no avail. The 28:1 shot was performing true to form and Dan's fiver was becoming a distant memory.

'Go on', he urged timidly as he gestured the grey stallion forward with his hands. A few faces turned disapprovingly at his meek encouragement.

'Howay, you grey bastard' he clarified more assertively. The faces turned away re-assured.

Kyle regretted his outburst as far from staging a late rally for a place, his chosen horse faded badly and came in a distant sixth. He screwed up his betting slip in disgust and looked out of the betting shop window. The rain was beating down with a vengeance from a dark, foreboding sky. Kyle was clad in traditional Geordie attire of jeans and t-shirt with no puffy jacket or coat. Although the station was merely 5 minutes away down Pink Lane he realized he would be soaked through if he left the bookies now.

'So much for global warming' an old man in the corner declared.

Kyle, a passionate environmentalist, thought momentarily about pointing out that a monsoon on Tyneside was in fact sound evidence of climate change but thought better of it.

'Aye, its shit isn't it?' he affirmed.

The old man had already looked away. The screen had switched to the 4.10 at Wincanton and he obviously had an interest in the race that was unfolding. Kyle's mind wandered philosophically. He was about to turn 42, the statistical half-way point, and he pondered where his life had gone. If anyone was describing him now, they would probably see him as a typical, middle-aged man with a nagging wife and morose teenage son who took solace in football, beer and the occasional flutter. He had a steady job as a performance analyst for the Police Authority, with responsibility for ensuring the accuracy of crime data. He lived in a 1930s semi in Wallsend, the working class suburb where he had been brought-up.

When Dan teased him about his age, Kyle responded positively about 42 being *'the answer to everything'* (a *'Hitch-hikers Guide to the Galaxy'* reference) and '*twenty-one, times two*'. However, he was not looking forward to the milestone.

Things had been so different when he was 21. Nobody would have described him as typical or conventional then. He shunned the normal choice of economics graduates of accountancy to fulfil his childhood dream of saving lives as a fire-fighter. He was the fire brigade's first black fire-fighter and the women loved him when he paraded down the Quayside. He was witty and confident with a strong circle of friends and spent much of his spare time participating in extreme supports.

He fell passionately in love with a feisty red-head called Helen. They married and had one child (Nathan) who was now 15. They were very happy. He loved his job, his wife, his kid and wouldn't want to live anywhere else but Newcastle. The toon was buzzing with the return of the Messiah, Kevin Keegan, and anything seemed possible.

So, where did it all go wrong, Kyle asked himself? Well, firstly he got moved to another watch in Sunderland and he got racially harassed. The watch system is a clique, which is great when you are on the inside basking in camaraderie, but torture when you are locked out. One fascist thug of a crew manager singled him out for criticism, shouting at him and abusing him on a daily basis and harmless banter soon crossed the line into hurtful racial slurs. The watch followed like sheep and for all their fine policies on equality and diversity, management chose to turn a blind eye.

Kyle's confidence was shattered and when he sought sympathy at home all he got was more criticism about how he should be a man and stand up for himself. In any case, why did he have to be a fire-fighter and not choose a more lucrative career like his brother? When Helen had vowed to love honour and obey she hadn't expected to be stuck in a depressingly mundane neighbourhood with a pile of ironing and dirty nappies. She expected more. She deserved more, because for all her insecurities she knew deep down that she was beautiful, sexy and intelligent and she could make men go weak at the knees with a flash of a smile and a glimpse of cleavage.

Eventually, Kyle made a formal complaint about the crew manager. The Chief Fire Officer revealed he had a zero-tolerance approach to bullying and promised swift action. Three months later, Kyle was taken off the watch and given a desk job in performance management. He kept his uniform, but he lost his pride. He spent the next 4 years trying to escape from the brigade that had let him down so badly and eventually he secured a similar role at the Police Authority.

The raindrops zigzagged down the window pane and a howl of wind and rain entered along with a soggy man as the door of the bookies swung open. Kyle wondered if he was going to get an earful when he finally got home. He had gone into town to take back a dress that Helen thought was too tight. He thought it looked great on her, exposing every curve of her hour-glass figure, but Helen had been distraught because it was a size 8 and she realized she needed a size 10. They didn't have any 10's so Kyle was returning empty handed with a refund, minus £5 on a useless nag at Chepstow.

A hen-party of giggling, scantily-clad girls with bunny head-pieces sauntered past in the rain. In any other town, in any other city the girls would have attracted a wolf-whistle or two as they passed the bookies but not in Newcastle. This was an every-day sight in Europe's party capital.

The rain seemed to have eased a little bit and Kyle opened the door to test the theory. A gust blew some torn ticket stubs through the door and a line of Shane McGowan's entered Kyle's mind:

'Torn ticket stubs of a 100, 000 mugs,

Washed away like dead dreams in the rain'.

Kyle had always been a dreamer. It was something he shared with his brother. However, whilst Dan dreamed of making millions and living in luxury, Kyle dreamed of Newcastle United winning a trophy and making love to Natalie Imbruglia in a toon shirt.

The old man's horse had failed on him as well and he exited the open door in disgust.

'At least the rain's dying down' he remarked as he stopped beside Kyle and looked up at the sky.

'Yes. I better head for the Metro', Kyle nodded.

'Same here'.

The two new acquaintances walked briskly off down Pink Lane, resisting the tempting aromas from the chippy on the corner of Clayton Street. Central Station was almost in sight now, but the rain had got a second wind and they had to walk past the Forth, a cosy local hostelry that served a fine pint of Workie Ticket.

'Fancy a swift one' the old man enquired with admirable telepathy.

'Go on' said Kyle. *'Another half hour won't hurt'*.

*****

Dan peered through the small oval window of his transatlantic jet and watched the circuit-board of lights slowly disappear from view. He was worried about what lay ahead of him when he got back to New York and he didn't do worry.

'Dam' he uttered under his breath as he felt the birthday card to Kyle that he had intended to post before setting off. It would probably get there late now, even if he posted it as soon as he touched down in JFK.

Kyle was on the metro now, hoping Helen hadn't cooked him tea. He would not hear the last of it if she had broken with recent convention and decided to cook him and Nathan something for supper. It would be just his luck, he thought.

And so our story begins: two brothers embarking on journeys, each fearing what lay ahead. Neither knew that their lives were about to change forever.

Scene 2: All those channels and nothing on

By the time he reached New York, Dan had regained his swagger. He lived by the motto *'every crisis is an opportunity'*. At both Heathrow and JFK, newspaper boards relayed the same story. The financial world was in chaos, shares were tumbling and investors were panicking. Little old ladies were withdrawing their life savings and hiding them under mattresses feeling they were more at risk of their banks going under than getting burgled.

Dan knew that every time someone was desperate to sell there were bargains to be had. Great riches were on offer for those that held their nerve and played the long game. On paper he had lost his firm millions on his recent deals and he was due a severe bollocking. If he went into his meeting defensive and apologetic he was finished. His reputation as the black Geordie with the Midas touch would be tarnished. No, he had to be bullish and positive and convince his bosses the losses were peanuts compared with the future profits he would bring them.

The strategy was simple. Sell the huge array of diminishing assets he had built up. Shares, mortgages, debts, securities –everything must go. Then when the price got low enough, buy them all back at a knock-down price so when the market returned to normal levels they could be sold at a huge profit.

Would the bosses buy it? You bet they would. They had grown rich by trusting smart-arses like Dan who sounded like they knew what they were talking about. The 90's were testament to the glory of recklessness. The more risky and hare-brained a scheme seemed, the greater the rewards when the chips were cashed in.

Polmont going under was good news. They were a major competitor and now there were fewer kids at the table when the birthday cake was handed round. When the administrators sought buyers for Polmont's financial instruments Dan was determined not to miss out.

Dan congratulated himself on being so smart. He swaggered swiftly along Madison Avenue towards his office, projecting his chest like a peacock on display. He didn't notice the frail beggars on the church steps or the mad preacher bellowing out about Armageddon as he weaved expertly in and out of the throngs of sharp-suited commuters. He was focused and there was something about New York that made him feel as tall as one of the skyscrapers that graced the Manhattan sky-line. He sucked in the polluted City air and considered which high-class escort he was going to take back to his penthouse and give a right good seeing-to tonight. He was living the capitalist dream. He didn't care about the bankers at Polmont that had lost their jobs or the investors around the world who had seen their pensions vanish overnight. There were losers and there were winners and he knew which one he was.

*****

Helen had not cooked dinner but she was not happy. She didn't ask where Kyle had been all afternoon. Kyle rather wished she had, because she never seemed interested in what he was up to any more. Instead she started a long lament on what an awful day it had been. She had got her hair wet on the way back from the hairdressers, her mate had cancelled on their night out and her PC had crashed losing a spreadsheet she had promised her bosses for Monday morning. On top of that, Nathan had been giving her Foul-mouthed abuse all day (Kyle really had to have a word) and now Kyle had come back from the shop empty-handed. Nothing was going her way.

Kyle put his arm round her on the sofa and tried to install a sense of perspective into her Prozac-dependent world. It never worked but it made him feel better for trying. She reached for the remote control and switched on her beloved 42 inch plasma TV. She scanned down page after page of channels, occasionally pausing to read the information only to move on saying things like *'seen that'* and *'that sounds rubbish'*. Eventually she settled on a trashy makeover show and sighed *'all those channels and nothing on!'*

*****

Dan's boss was a rotund man in his late 50's who wore colourful glasses and a vivid, pink striped shirt. His Burberry trousers were held up by big navy braces that he toyed with annoyingly. He shook Dan's hand in the ferocious way he always did, as if he was competing in an arm-wrestling contest and simultaneously slapped him on the back saying:

'Dan, good to see you. I'm relying on you to cheer me up. All I've heard all day is gloom, gloom, gloom. Have a seat.'

'That's music to my ears. There's panic out there and people are behaving irrationally. It's a great time to trade. I want you to be the first to hear my strategy.'

'Go on – I'm hooked!' Dan's boss stated leaning forward and clasping his sweaty palms together.

5 minutes of glorious bullshit later Dan's boss was again shaking Dan's hand like his life depended upon it, slapping his back and sending him out to take more reckless risks and add more noughts to the liabilities on the company balance sheet. Dan's plan had worked like he knew it would.

At one point the boss was having doubts. He roared *'Buy Polmont's debts? I heard they were toxic.'*

'That's what makes them attractive. No-one is interested so they are available for a song and some of them really aren't that bad. In fact, their credit ratings are almost identical to some of ours, but I reckon I could get them for half the price'.

That did the trick. Like most investment bankers, Dan's boss couldn't resist a bargain. He liked Dan's style. He had big plans for him if this all worked out the way he said it would. Sure, it was a big '*if*' but Dan's record spoke for itself.

You could only use the recent past to predict the future and the recent past was an unprecedented period of economic growth, especially in the UK. Under Blair and Brown an economic miracle of low inflation, low unemployment and high growth had been achieved and British economists had returned to favour. Dan's boss worshipped Tony Blair, having met him once at a function and been swept off his feet. '*He'd make a great president if only he was American*' he gushed. Dan didn't have the heart to tell him it was actually the rather dour Gordon Brown that masterminded the British economic miracle. Instead he told him how Blair was a Geordie just like him and supported the same soccer team.

Dan left the office in triumphant mood. Some gorgeous young girl was going to prosper from his good mood. He used to hang around bars and clubs stalking his prey before drawing them in with wads of cash. Sometimes it worked and sometimes it didn't but it often led to emotional fall-out he really hadn't got time for. Once he spent five long months courting a girl and spent several thousand dollars on fancy dinners, flowers, gifts and drinks and at the end of it she turned him down. It was then that he discovered escorts.

In the three Cities he spent most of his time (New York, Newcastle and London) there were some excellent agencies a world away from the sleazy image of prostitution. For a little over £100 an hour, beautiful, intelligent girls from all over the world would cater for his every whim. They were all regularly screened, treated well and clean of drugs. Dan often asked them why they did it and their answer was always the same. '*It's not a career, just a way of getting some money to set me up for what I really want to do in life*'. Many had student debts to repay; others needed capital to buy a house or business. It was a short-term thing.

Dan quickly realized that these escorts cost him no more than the average night at the trendy pick-up joints he had frequented and the outcome was guaranteed. The sex was '*no strings*' and although the girls pleasure might have been fake the quality and variety of the sex was unbelievable. He couldn't be arsed with relationships and escorts were the perfect outlet for his inflated ego.

Tonight, he had selected Daniella, a stunning 19 year old Ukrainian with measurements of 34DD; 24; 34. She was coming to his penthouse in a French maids outfit and he was turned on just thinking about it.

*****

Kyle and Helen rarely made love these days. They were both too tired and one tended to retire to bed before the other. In their early days they had been at it like rabbits and Helen had taken as much pleasure in turning on

Kyle as in her own satisfaction. Tonight Kyle was lying in bed mildly aroused when Helen got in beside him in a skimpy night-dress and her soft, warm skin cradled against him. He caressed her hair and traced the curve of her spine until he gasped at the touch of skin. Her nighty had risen up and exposed her peach of a bottom. His hands wandered lower and his body was coiled like a spring ready for action.

'Go to sleep, Kyle', Helen said pushing his passionate hands away. Kyle turned over disdainfully. So, there was to be no early birthday present. More importantly, he felt his marriage was sliding away from him and he didn't know what to do. He had been loyal and faithful for 17 years, but he was sick of the rejection. He lived in hope that the old Helen would return and kiss away the blues but with every passing day the happy memories grew more distant.

An hour later he was still tossing and turning, unable to sleep. The heat from Helen's body was no longer a turn-on. He wished he could open the window without getting shouted at. He went down stairs and sipped a long, cool glass of water. He switched the TV on and switched channels a myriad of times. There was still nothing on.

Scene 3: What goes up!

Kyle was enjoying a quiet Saturday at home alone in his Wallsend garden. Helen had taken Nathan to buy some new school shoes; his feet had grown again. This afternoon Kyle was taking Nathan to St James' Park to watch the latest instalment in the soap opera that is Newcastle United. Kevin Keegan had returned briefly for a second stint as Manager only to find the millionaire Chairman only wanted him as a figurehead and didn't trust him to manage after so long out of the game. King Kev had stormed off leaving the hot-seat vacant just weeks into the new season.

An apple prematurely dropped from the tree. Autumn was coming. The apple turned Kyle's thoughts to Isaac Newton and how his scientific theories explained so much about the ups and downs of life. Kyle turned to silently address an imagined audience with his philosophy:

"Gravity quite literally helps us keep our feet on the ground. Our planets survival depends upon it. It is a benign force more powerful than the greatest Army. Many have tried to defy gravity but they have all come crashing down to earth like a bruised apple in September.

Economists have long studied the endless cycle of boom and bust. The cycles are of variable lengths but the end result is the same. After every boom, there's a bust. After every bust, there's a boom. It is nature not economics. That is not an excuse for the do-nothing economics of the 1980s. Politicians can do much to prolong the boom and shorten the bust but they are fools if they think the good times can last forever. They can't.

Just like a squirrel does not wait to winter to search for food, the canny politician should use the autumn of the economic cycle to replenish stocks ready for more austere times ahead. The trick is reading the signs that the good times are nearing an end and putting more away for a rainy day.

Unfortunately, in the early part of the new Millennium, governments around the world suffered from the delusion that they had finally defeated boom and bust. The boom had gone on too long to be part of a cycle. Economists had found El-Dorado!

We were ill-prepared for the credit crunch. The economy was built on credit and America had become so dominant in the world of international conglomerates that when it sneezed the whole world caught a cold. Millions of American debtors defaulted, the lenders stopped lending and the life-blood of a credit economy was switched off. Suddenly people that had invested in property and shares as if they were guaranteed highways to wealth and happiness found that what they had been taught as kids was still true today. What goes up; must come down.

Many people believe that our emotions follow cycles as well. They are called biorhythms and firms market computer models claiming to predict your fortune based on your date of birth. There may be some truth in it. We all have up's and down's. When we are happy and content we want things to stay like that forever but before we have tasted the fruits of our labour, life's roller-coaster has hurtled on once again; on into oblivion. Life doesn't come with a pause button on it. You just have to hold on tight and enjoy the ride."

Dan had also read Economics at Newcastle University but he wasn't interested in political and philosophical debate. For him, economics was about buying and selling, supply and demand and making money. He had started his own business at University, joined a Newcastle stock-broking firm upon graduating and within five years been poached by a London investment bank. Two years later, it was taken over by an American giant and he was promoted. Another two years and he was promoted again but this time it meant working out of Wall Street.

It was easy to see why Dan expected the good times to continue. It had been one success after another for the 15 years since he graduated. He was yet to experience a down-turn in his fortunes and he felt impregnable. Impregnable was a word often used about Polmont as commentators likened the bank to the infamous Scottish prison that shared its name. Now Polmont was no more and no doubt the prison will be gone one day as well.

Dan's plan was not going as well as he expected. He couldn't give away some of the complex financial packages he had so lovingly assembled. Investors were scared off by their similarity to Polmont and were asking questions that they never used to ask. He was left holding on to financial instruments that were losing value on a daily basis and all the time the company's paper losses were growing. He wasn't the only one. The office was full of glum, perplexed faces and the talk around the coffee machine was of redundancies, not bonuses.

Kyle looked forward to spending some quality time with his son. If Kyle was a typical middle-aged man, Nathan was a typical male adolescent. Since his voice had broken, he used it sparingly in a staccato of grunts and expletives. Teenage boys were under constant pressure to prove how hard they were, to hide any hint of softness and convince their peers that they were not in any way gay. It had always been like that but somehow it seemed more extreme these days. Nathan was a molotoff cocktail of raging hormones, teenage angst and spirited rebellion.

Football was one of the few things that brought them together, united for two hours of painful solidarity with 50, 000 similarly oppressed disciples. Gone were the halcyon days where the three of them went out as a proper family. It was no longer cool for Nathan to hang out with Mum and Dad and besides he could sense the tension between Mum and Dad and it made him sad.

Kyle recalled how he had caught Nathan watching a video a few days ago; shot with the camcorder he had bought when Nathan was born. It was a compendium of happy scenes of proud, loving parents who couldn't keep their hands off each other and looked at their offspring with glowing eyes. Embarrassed by his Dad's presence Nathan had gone out for a kick-around, leaving Kyle to reflect tearfully on how much he wished those days could return.

The crowd was in an angry mood as they converged upon the cathedral like structure of St James Park. Even the lady busker who sat in Gallowgate sounded ready for a fight today. The protest outside the Milburn stand got louder as kick-off approached but then the majority took up their seats to watch the inevitable catastrophe unfold.

Kyle and Nathan trudged back to the metro station, lambasting the Chairman, the referee, the overpaid foreign mercenaries and Joey Barton. Back in the days when the video that Nathan had been watching had been set things had been different. Sky TV christened Newcastle the entertainers and they were everyone's second favourite club as they challenged Manchester United for the title. It seemed only a matter of time before the silverware came back to Tyneside. Then it all unravelled.

Packed like sardines on the metro, the fans were in sombre mood. There was the occasional outburst of anger but for the most part there was an air of resignation that came with years of disappointment. A defiant chorus of the 'Blaydon Races' broke out as the crowd shuffled off the metro at Wallsend and went their disparate ways. United through adversity, each fan felt stronger and more able to face up to Monday morning than they had done upon leaving the ground. The Magpies were going through troubled times but their fans understood Newton's Law better than economists and politicians all over the globe.

Scene 4: Bankers and Barmaids

Kyle had a torrid week at work. He had a lengthy to-do list at the start of the week and despite diligently completing tasks, he kept adding new ones. He didn't get home till seven on his birthday and by the time they had eaten, washed up and he had opened his presents it was half past nine. The plan was for Helen and him to go to a pub quiz that kicked off about half eight, but with that idea blown Helen was not in the mood for the compromise solution of a couple of pints before closing time.

At least Kyle had Friday night to look forward to. He was meeting the lads for a session in town and the crack was always good. As usual he was first in the pub and staked out a free table and a couple of spare stools. He speculated on the order his mates would arrive in but gave up when Elton John arrived first.

No, not that Elton John! This Elton John was a painter and decorator from Darlington. A few years ago he spent the fortune he had accumulated in the boom on a posh new pad in a village near Stockton called Elton and so he became Elton John. This was partly to distinguish him from the other John in the group, John Medburn and partly to annoy Elton John, who was notoriously homophobic.

'*How are you doing old man*? Elton enquired predictably.

'*Can't complain*', Kyle responded shaking Elton's outstretched hand. '*How's business. Are you feeling the credit crunch yet?*'

'*Credit crunch? What's that? Is it a type of biscuit*?' Elton laughed. '*No. Trade is down a bit on last year but I'm normally turning people away this time of year as there's a mad rush to get outsides done before the winter. Here, let me get you a whisky chaser to go with that pint*'.

Before Kyle could express a preference for his favourite single malt Elton had left for the bar. '*Shit*', Kyle thought, '*Bells it is*'.

While Elton was forcing his bulky frame to the bar, Mattie arrived. Kyle thought Mattie was great. Everyone thought Mattie was great. He was a debonair charmer and his anecdotes held an audience captive like Ronnie Corbett used to do in his solo bit on the Two Ronnie's. Mattie was intercepted before he reached Kyle. Kyle could see him chatting to a couple of strangers just back from the bar and within seconds they were both curled up with laughter. He left them immediately, spotted Elton getting served and gestured for a pint with one hand, whilst shaking Kyle's hand with the other.

'*Your never guess what happened at the station*' he said cleverly wetting the appetite for an anecdote. '*No, wait till the others gets here*' he said before Kyle had a chance to respond.

Next up was One Word. One Word was so called because he was a listener rather than a talker. He used words as if they were an endangered species and answered most questions with a simple yes, no or maybe. Mattie did a brilliant impersonation of One Word and it often provoked him into a two-word response. The second word was *'off'*.

'Hiya', said One Word.

'Hiya mate. I haven't seen you for ages. What you been up to?' quizzed Kyle.

'Busy' shrugged One Word.

'What busy at work?'

'No'

Fortunately, Elton got back from the bar with the drinks and an inappropriately loud commendation on the barmaids tits.

'I think I'll get the next round in' Mattie volunteered altruistically.

John Medburn appeared wearing a rather loud shirt. *'What the fuck is that?'* asked Elton. *'So that's where my ironing board cover went'* added Matt. John was the only single member of the crew and he might as well of worn a sign on his chest saying *'I'm desperate to pull'*. He was always too obvious, too needy and that's why he was still single. Even One Word had a wife. Mattie said that his misses made a special trip to the vicars the night before the wedding to ask him to accept *'Aye'* in lieu of *'I do'*.

The final member of the gang was Dobbo. Dobbo was an enigma. Sometimes he could be the life and soul of the party, pulling childish pranks, daring his mates to match his outrageous behaviour. Others he could be quiet and vacant, as if his body was present but he had left his mind at a party somewhere in Fenham in the eighties. Kyle had known him since his days as a fire-fighter. Dobbo had been through Fire Service College with him and joined the same watch. He had stayed with the Service and had risen to District Manager. He was a good, public-spirited man and Kyle was pleased for him.

When they were all seated with pint glasses in hand, Mattie embarked on his story.

"You have all been through Morpeth station haven't you? It's a lonely, desolate place. It's on the East Coast main line, but all the drivers slam on the accelerator when they go through it so the tourists aren't able to read the station sign and identify where the hell it is. Well, very occasionally an express train does actually stop there. I was waiting patiently for my train to Newcastle when one such train came to a stop on the opposite platform. The public address system crackled into life with something inaudible, probably about fag-ends on the line or something and out stepped a man in a suit.

He looked disapprovingly up and down the shabby platform with brambles growing up through the tarmac at one end and a group of teenagers at the other playing rugby without the ball. 'Excuse me' he bellowed across the line to me in a cut-glass accent 'Could you direct me to the first class lounge?'."

Everyone laughed raucously. 'What did you say' asked Dobbo.

'I replied in my best Home Counties accent: Yes sir, if you come over here and get on the next train to Newcastle I can take you there myself'.

Mattie asked Kyle how his big-shot banker of a brother was faring with the credit crunch. 'I don't know', replied Kyle. 'He didn't even send me a birthday card. I haven't spoken to him in weeks'.

'He always was a tight git' stated Elton. 'If I had my way, all the bankers that started this credit crunch thing would be forced to give up their bonuses to the people that can't get credit any more'.

'You're an economist Kyle. How do we get out of this mess?' Mattie challenged.

'Well, there are two lines of attack: a monetary policy and a fiscal policy. Firstly, the Bank of England will slash interest rates. The difficulty in getting credit will be negated by the cheapness of the credit that is available and so the same amount of money will be flowing through the system. Secondly, there will be a Keynesian stimulus to public spending. The Government will need to move in to compensate for the lower private sector spending as firms and households become more cautious than they have been for years. If the spending is targeted at the right areas that create extra public sector jobs and subsidise spending in areas where British jobs are most at risk, a major recession could yet be avoided'.

'Sounds good to me' said Elton. 'I hope you've told fucking Gordon what to do'.

'My worry' said John Medburn 'is whose going to pay for all this extra government spending in the long-run? OK for now they might be able to borrow more money, but I reckon sooner or later they will be coming back to you and me asking for more taxes'.

'Maybe, but as Keynes once said: In the long-run we are all dead', Kyle explained.

'So do you think we should withdraw our savings from the banks? They said that Polmont couldn't go under and it's sunk like the Titanic', enquired Dobbo.

'No. Definitely not! The more people that panic and withdraw their money the worse the banks liquidity becomes. It's a self-fulfilling prophecy. Look what happened to Northern Rock. Robert Peston goes spouting off about how the bank is close to going to the wall and immediately there are queues of *lemmings trying to close their accounts. The queues are televised and more people panic and the next day the queues are even longer. Eventually, the bank was finished, thousands lost their jobs and the toon lost its main sponsor.'*

'But did anyone with savings left in the stricken bank lose money. Of course not, I left my savings there knowing the Government would not, could not; let a British bank go to the wall. Of course a nationalised bank is as safe as houses. If you want to move your money, move it to Northern Rock.'

'Aye and if enough of us do it we might be able to pay Michael Owen's wages for another year', joked Mattie.

'Thirsty work, this intellectual discussion' said Elton, tilting his glass to prove that it was empty.

'Ok – what's everyone want' offered Mattie. As he repeated the orders he glanced over at the bar where the barmaid had bent forward to open the cellar hatch in the floor as if goading the lads with her ample cleavage beneath her tight, low cut vest top. 'In the words of Captain Oates, I may be gone some time' Mattie said as he set off on his latest conquest.

Two rounds later, Kyle got to his feet and ventured to the bar, nervously checking his watch and seeing that the bell was about to toll. He had really enjoyed the night and he didn't want it to end. However, he didn't fancy going clubbing with John and One Word.

He managed to position himself and time his shout well. He had attracted the sexy barmaid's attention. She was well-spoken with a slight accent, probably Yorkshire. A student, Kyle deduced, which probably made her roughly half his age. Still she had a beautiful smile with big kissable lips and a face illuminated by big brown eyes. Kyle observed a stud in her nose and a purple streak in her jet black hair. She smiled warmly at Kyle as she handed him the change and whispered quietly in his ear 'thanks for not leering at my tits'.

Kyle wished he was 21 again. Well, 21 but as worldly aware as he was now and with a decent hair-cut. The barmaid was lovely. In a few brief minutes Kyle had already assessed her personality as a perfect match for him: cheeky, feisty, wild, unconventional, intelligent, fun-loving and fantastic in bed. In fact, she reminded him of Helen when they had first met. He wanted to try his luck but she was so young and he was so married. In any case, she had moved on to the next customer and his mates were baying for their drinks. He didn't know the barmaid's name and would probably never see her again but for a few brief minutes she had made him feel special and he hadn't felt special for a very long time.

Scene 5: Pass the Panic

Dan was perched at a New York bagel bar with a Jewish Journalist friend of his called Lucas. Lucas came here habitually for breakfast on his way to work so there was no need for Dan to arrange a rendezvous. The fact that he had done so suggested he wanted something.

'*Lucas*', Dan said after the foreplay had run out of steam '*I want the Press to tone down their coverage of the Credit Crunch. You've seen the queues outside banks around the world. The media are spreading hysteria and your rag is the worst of the lot.* '

Lucas took a long sip of espresso and picked up 2 papers from the table beside him. '*Ok Dan. Just for a minute try being me*', he said with an accent so like Woody Allen's it was untrue.

"*Exhibit 1: Suppose this paper has the headline: 'The banks are safe' followed by an article saying Polmont was a one-off. There's nothing to worry about.*"

'*Now*', Lucas continued holding up the second paper.

"*Exhibit 2: Suppose this paper has the headline: 'Polmont gone. Is your bank next?' followed by a big photo of queues forming outside banks. Now, Dan the Man which paper would you buy?*"

Dan was irritated by this reaction. '*Sure, but don't you see, you have crossed the line from reporting news to creating news. There really was nothing to worry about until the media started spreading hysterical scare stories. If people carry on panicking the way they have been then more banks will go the way of Polmont.*"

Lucas was undeterred and tried a different tact that might appeal to Dan's love of soccer:

"*Exhibit 1: Suppose this paper comments on England losing a soccer friendly to the good old US of A with 'Disappointing friendly result for England' followed by a picture of the coach looking disinterested*".

"*Exhibit 2: Suppose this paper's headline is 'Clueless England Coach on the Brink' followed by a picture of the coach looking stressed and a damming character assassination.*" Again, you would buy the second paper and it's my job to sell papers. If the story starts a campaign to oust the England coach, so much the better as it will give us many more stories for the days ahead and we can claim to have been first with the news*".

Dan wiped his brow with a napkin and looked at Lucas with puppy-dog eyes. '*Lucas. I'm appealing to you as a friend. My deals have lost a shed-load of money. I need to sell quickly and people are too scared to buy. My job could *be on the line, but not just mine. Millions of financial jobs around the world could be at risk if this panic goes on much longer. You are a great financial journalist. You know that if the banks are allowed to fail then capitalism will fail and we will enter a Depression like the 1930's. You don't want to be responsible for the misery that would cause do you?'*

'Wow!' exclaimed Lucas. 'This story is bigger than I thought. Do you really think this could be the death of Capitalism!'

'I do. What would you have to write about then? No Wall Street, no Dow Jones, and no London Stock Exchange: we all stand to lose from this Lucas'.

'If I don't cover this someone else will Dan. You are wasting your time. Bad news sells better than good news. Thanks for the coffee and bagel but I've really got to get to work. Call me. We will do lunch some-time"

Dan bid farewell to his friend feeling even more concerned than when he got to the office yesterday to hear of the firm laying off 300 staff world-wide. His job was safe, for now, but some good colleagues who had made enemies with the wrong people were going along with many back-office workers.

He picked up one of the papers that Lucas had played with and read the real cover story. It was all gloom and doom. It had been like that on a daily basis since that day in Heathrow when the news of Polmont's demise had reached him. That was 10 days ago. He could see no sign of it abating. The media were certain other financial institutions were to follow and they were like a pack of hounds chasing a wounded fox. Dan feared it could be his job on the line next. He was surviving on his reputation alone and he could see no way out.

*****

Kyle was also reading a newspaper but he was giving his pet subject of the economic crisis a rest and reading about something closer to home: clinical depression. The statistics were shocking. Ostensibly, one in four British people now suffer from emotional disorders. The mind boggles about how many people are suffering in silence, with identical but undiagnosed symptoms. You are 10 times more likely to be suffering depression than you were 50 years ago. More repeat prescriptions are written out for anxiety and depression than any other illness.

Kyle was also struck by how much higher the rate of depression is in rich, English-speaking countries was than in the rest of the world. The World Health Organisation found the rate was 6 times higher in America than it was in Lagos and Shanghai. Millions of working days are lost through stress but the highest rates of severe depression and anxiety are found in professions where workers are too important to be off work sick and lunch is for wimps. Successful New York business people were more at risk than any other group. Kyle found this hard to believe as he couldn't imagine his ultra-confident brother suffering from stress.

Helen on the other hand had been on anti-depressants for years. He wished he could do something to help her. It made her irritable, snappy and self-obsessed. He had to tread on egg-shells around her and her negative, lugubrious mood was infectious. Kyle had suggested counselling countless times but Helen was too proud. She preferred to think of stress as a physical illness, a serotonin imbalance that needed drug treatment rather than a mental illness that could be traced back to a troubled childhood.

The drugs didn't work for Helen. They gave her an initial high, two to three weeks after starting on medication but the temporary euphoria soon gave way to a numbed state of despondency and lethargy that made it difficult for her to get out of bed on a weekend. When she was not at work or in bed she spent most of her time watching TV and reading about the glamorous lives of A-list celebrities in trashy magazines. She knew it was a terrible waste of a brilliant brain that had got her a first class honours degree and that's what depressed her most!

Helen's main hope of escaping from this drug-filled hell was winning the lottery. She hated being unable to afford things that she wanted. She was an advertisers dream as she found herself wanting more and more after every ad-break. Helen looked enviously at richer neighbours and work-colleagues and repeatedly asked herself what they had done to deserve such wealth. She was oblivious to the fact that Kyle and her earnings as a couple were significantly above the regional average.

Helen found a work: life balance impossible. She yearned for the glittering prizes in her career and saw hard work as the best way to reach her goals. However, she also yearned for the simple days of her parent's generation when gender roles were clear and hers would have been to raise her child. She felt she had to work because her useless husband had made the wrong career decisions and didn't bring home a big enough pay cheque to support her life-style. Kyle felt her disappointment in him every day.

Helen shared a deeply entrenched view of men with many women of her generation. *'All men are bastards'* she would remark nonchalantly in front of Kyle, but not directed at him. During her youth she had been teased about being fat and suffered an eating disorder that left her emotionally scarred but with the figure of a glamour model. Suddenly, the boys were crazy for her and would say or do anything to try and get into her lacy, size 8 knickers.

Now Helen was approaching 40, she spent a fortune on beauty products trying to postpone the signs of ageing. Every new wrinkle was a crisis, every crease in her skin an abomination. She lived in fear that once her youthful, extrinsic beauty went there would be nothing left and none of the bastards would look twice at her any more.

Kyle did his best to re-assure Helen that he would still love her when she was 64, but it was difficult when the depression made her so difficult to live with. Helen sensed his dissatisfaction with her and erroneously assumed it was because he wanted to trade her in for a younger model. In fact, he did want the youthful Helen he had fallen passionately in love with back, but not because she had been the most stunning women he had ever cast eyes upon but because she used to be great fun to be around. He would give anything to get that Helen back.

Whilst Kyle was lying on his sofa contemplating his marriage, the TV programme was interrupted by some breaking news. Despite millions of pounds in state aid, a British high street bank had announced it could not survive without a massive further injection of funds. One year after Northern Rock had been exposed it seemed the Credit Crunch had claimed another scalp.

Kyle listened intently to the City experts giving their verdict ebulliently on the latest shock-wave to reverberate around Thread-needle Street and Canary Wharf. The Government are going to have to nationalise the banks, he concluded almost in disbelief at his own synopsis.

Kyle got up and placed the late birthday card from Dan up on the mantle-piece. He had already taken all his other cards down but he didn't have the heart to put his brother's card straight in the recycling bin. It stood rather pathetically on its own between Helen's assorted ornaments.

At that very moment the phone rang and it was Dan from New York. Once they had exchanged the usual pleasantries about the different time zones and the weather, Dan did something he didn't do often, he apologised. *'Sorry, I missed your birthday broth'* he said quietly. *'I meant to post it from Heathrow when I was last in the UK but I realized too late and then with this Credit Crunch blowing up I haven't had any peace'*.

'That's ok Dan. I've just put it up on the mantle-piece. It's not much to celebrate when you get to my age'.

Kyle couldn't help noticing that Dan sounded different. He sounded like a child who had just learnt that Dad filled his stocking every Xmas rather than Santa. He was not his usual bullish, high-octane self. His tone was measured, his voice unsteady. He wanted someone to talk to but had forgotten how to open his soul.Kyle reflected on how unfamiliar his brother had sounded. He normally contested Kyle's Keynesian economic prospective but now he almost sounded resigned to the failure of monetarism. Dan worshipped the market place and believed individual self-interest drove successful economies and not state intervention. Kyle argued that people were not robots and their irrational behaviour often confounded expectations.

Polmont had developed a computer model called the 'crystal ball' that predicted the impact of loan and investment decisions. It had hundreds of variables each with historically based probability estimates. The 'crystal ball' indicated that bankers would profit from taking greater risks with lending. Most rejected mortgage applicants could have met their liabilities. Moreover, rising real estate prices meant that the banks could have re-possessed the properties of the others without incurring any losses. Longer-term models confirmed that ability to repay was often irrelevant to the profitability of a loan. The 'crystal ball' paved the way to 110% mortgages and self-declaration of income. President Bush spoke wistfully of the day all Americans would own their own home. The generous bankers at Polmont were heroes of the American dream and regulators that urged caution were the enemy of the poor.

Dan convinced his bosses to buy the 'crystal ball' and enter the lucrative world of 'sub-prime' lending. In 2003 this was still a fringe activity but the eye-watering profits and bonuses created a strong second-hand market for lucrative sub-prime debts. Many banks wanted the profits of sub-prime debts with lower risks. By mixing together sub-prime debts with safe bonds and giving them the comforting title of securitised debt, every bank in the World bought into Bush's pipe-dream.

Kyle winced when his brother explained that by 2006 it was no longer possible to tell how contaminated financial instruments were. The banking system depended on a single computer model and its assumption that house prices would continue rising. It was a rational assumption based on supply and demand and years of data. However, it was an economic view not a sociological view and demand is based on human emotion, not dollars in wallets.

As millions of American homes were re-possessed and the home ownership dream turned sour, a Geordie bank became the first casualty of the Credit Crunch, but still the reckless lending went on. Suddenly in mid-2008 demand sunk, prices crashed and debts rocketed. No bank would touch sub-prime debt but securitisation meant the toxic debt was no longer transparent. Banks stopped lending. The life-blood of the economy was switched off. Dan's faith in the market place was destroyed. What good is a market without any customers?

There was one thing Kyle didn't understand about the Credit Crunch. One man had the power and brains to stop it all but didn't. In Britain, decisions on interest rates are made by the Monetary Policy Committee of the Bank of England, monthly decisions are debated and the minutes published. In America one man makes the decision. That man was Alan Greenspan. Greenspan was revered by politicians from all sides and by both Monetarists and Keynesians as an economic genius. So why did he keep interest rates low when the World was awash with cash and all other reputable economists agreed they needed to rise? It just didn't add up.

Scene 6: The Bitterest Pill

Kyle had gone off to sulk in the shed at the bottom of the garden. Nathan had seized control of the TV to watch some sport and Helen had sought her husband to recover the remote control. He had asked politely, he had shouted at Nathan and he had tried to physically wrestle the remote from him, but in the end he had to surrender to his son's greater will-power.

Helen took Kyle's tame resistance as a personal insult. He wasn't man enough to control their son. He didn't love her enough to keep fighting her corner. There was a time when Kyle revelled in being set challenging tasks by Helen and he proved his love for his princess with knightly prowess. Now he pulled a face if she asked him to go to Tesco for some milk.

Normally the shed was an oasis of calm and tranquillity where Kyle could count to ten before re-entering the fray. Today, some bastard was drilling a hole in the road behind the garden fence and it felt like someone was trying to drill through Kyle's skull. He got tension headaches easily these days but not as frequently as Helen. She took almost as many painkillers as she did anti-depressants.

He went back inside and upstairs to the bedroom, ignoring the stone-faced truce that had broken out between Nathan and Helen in the living room. He knew that the communal paracetamol supply in the medicine cabinet was exhausted but Helen kept a secret supply in the drawer on her side of the bed.

'*Fuck*' he said when he opened another empty box. There was a paper chemist's bag peering out from beneath some papers so Kyle rummaged inside hoping there might be some strong painkillers inside. Maybe she had some codeine or ibuprofen. It had been a stressful week, even by Helen's standards.

What he found horrified him. They were contraceptive pills! It had been 10 years since Helen had talked him into having the snip. He had little choice. She wanted to come off the pill because of the increasing health risks as she got older and she didn't trust condoms. It was a case of vasectomy or abstinence. Recently, Kyle felt like he'd ended up with both!

Kyle tried to think of alternative explanations but swiftly concluded there were none. He had to face facts. His wife was having an affair. He had been suspicious a few months ago about a male friend Helen had at work. Her mood had briefly picked up and she was spending an inordinate amount of time exchanging text messages and chatting on her mobile. The conversation started off with work but seemed to get more personal and left Helen laughing and blushing. Kyle had suggested her work colleague's intentions were dishonourable but Helen had always replied with the line '*He's just a good friend*'.

Kyle had trusted her, scolding himself for being so paranoid. Now he felt a fool, let down by the person who mattered most to him. How long had she been deceiving him? Has he shagged her in the very bed he was now sitting on? What other secrets and lies did she have? Was he better in bed than he was? Is that why she had gone off sex with him? Was he so good that a full ten years after first deciding she was too old to be on the pill she was willing to throw caution to the wind and pump yet more chemicals into her blood-stream? So many questions, Kyle's head felt like it was full of exploding hand grenades.

Kyle left the pills out on the bed and stormed downstairs, flinging the front door open and shutting it loudly behind him.

Kyle arrived at his local trying to hide the tears he had been spilling on his journey. *'A pint of bitter'* he said croakily. The barman poured without intruding into his customer's private grief and Kyle sat silently in the corner of the pub, looking for answers through a tower of empty beer glasses.

By the fourth pint Kyle had stopped wallowing in self-pity and started to think about what to do next. He couldn't sleep in the same bed as her tonight. He did not want to see the betrayal in her beautiful big green eyes. He didn't see why he should be the one to sleep on the uncomfortable sofa. At 5 foot 7 she could just about fit on it but at 6 foot 2 his feet dangled well over the end.

He wanted to go back to ensure she knew that he knew. However, he didn't want a slanging contest. He still loved her deep down and he was worried about pushing her over the edge. He could not live with her suicide on his conscience and there was Nathan to think about as well. Kyle needed to explain things to him.

Ultimately, he decided to ask John Medburn if he would put him up for a few days. John lived alone and had a spare room. He would probably appreciate the company. Kyle reached for his mobile and his friend did not let him down. *'Just till I get my head straight'* he said. *'No problem. Stay as long as you need'* John responded.

Helen argued desperately that she hadn't gone through with her planned infidelity because she realized how much she still loved her husband. Kyle didn't know what to believe but he knew he had to get out so he packed his suitcase in silence.

He went up to tell Nathan where he was going. Nathan wanted to know why and Kyle couldn't resist telling him to ask his mother. *'When are you coming back?'* Nathan asked fearing the worst.

'I don't know son. I need some time alone. We can still go places together. I will try and get tickets for the next home match.'

Nathan, the big hard teenager was welling up. Instinctively, Kyle put his arms round him. *'You'll be fine son. You're a good lad'*, his father said.

Kyle paused as he put the case in the boot of his Mondeo. He wondered if he would ever sleep with his wife again. He took a deep breath and slammed the door shut. A luggage label from their last family holiday caught in the door so he had to open it and shut it again. He looked back at his house. Downstairs Helen was looking out from behind the net curtain but she disappeared upon realizing that she had been spotted. Upstairs the curtains were open and Nathan was standing at his window.

As he drove off, Kyle looked back and saw Nathan sobbing. It immediately brought him out in floods of tears. He had only gone about 400 yards when he had to stop because his driving glasses were all steamed up. He reached for the CD rack and something to make sense of his misery. He selected the *'Best of the Smiths'* and put it straight on to track 14.

Kyle drove on turning *'There is a light that never goes out'* up to full volume and crying out the words with all the pain and isolation that Morrissey must have felt when he originally penned the song. Kyle could recall the video with the band cycling round Salford in the midst of the last big recession. The desolation of the bleak landscape was magnificently in tune with the dark, despairing lyrics. However, the tune finished with hope, a light in the darkest hour of the darkest night.

'There is a light that never goes out' Kyle sang mournfully long after the track had finished. He drove past Swan Hunters. The lights had gone out at the shipyard long ago.

Scene 7: The Very Expensive Jacket

Kyle was off sick the next day. He hadn't meant to be off work but he hadn't slept well and when his alarm rudely awoke him at 7 a.m. he switched it off in favour of another half hour's snooze. The next thing he knew his mobile was going off and his boss was asking him where he was. Bleary eyed Kyle noted the time was ten past 11 and he decided it was time to come clean about his domestic crisis. His boss was suitably understanding and told him to take the day off and see if he was feeling up to work the following day.

'I will be fine. I'll see you tomorrow' he assured his boss.

'No you won't. Remember you agreed to stand in for me at the Police Authority Networking Meeting in London tomorrow', his boss reminded him.

Kyle had completely forgotten. He had agreed weeks ago to deputise for his boss at a meeting of colleagues in charge of performance management at other Police Authorities, when his boss had discovered a diary clash. With everything going on, his memory loss was understandable. He was looking forward to the luxury of first class train travel, a perk not normally open to such underlings. However, the meeting didn't excite him. It was basically a meeting about meetings.

He had been to a similar networking meeting when he was with the Fire Brigade. It had been a complete waste of time and money. The gushingly nice Chair had spent much of the time justifying the event by saying how good it was to talk and share ideas and what a good idea it had been to organise the event. She thanked everyone for their contribution and everyone felt compelled to say something to justify them being there. The meeting finished two hours early with the Chair stating what a good meeting it had been, partly because it had finished two hours early.' *Thank you everyone for being so efficient'* she declared.

Kyle sighed as he recalled the painful experience. About 20 people had travelled from all over the country (many of them first class) to talk about how good it was to talk. Nothing had changed as a result of the meeting, no actions had been agreed and Kyle never saw the promised minutes. The public purse was bankrolling many such meetings and some managers didn't have time to manage these days. They were always in meetings!

The next day Kyle reluctantly arose at 6.00 a.m. and walked up the steps from the Quayside to Central Station. Legend has it that a dog had once leapt off the top of the steps and survived, giving the curious name *'Dog Leap Stairs'* to the ancient steps beside the castle keep. If the networking meeting was as bad as his last one it would be Kyle leaping off the top tonight.

Kyle had a coffee in the first class lounge, recalling Mattie's anecdote about Morpeth Station as he did so. He would have to arrange another lad's night out. Maybe he would have another crack at that gorgeous barmaid now he was a single man. The 7.00 a.m. train was packed with commuters in their smart suits, already on their mobile phones to work colleagues and itching to get on board and open up their lap-tops. There were nearly as many first class coaches as standard class ones and the price on Kyle's ticket read an astonishing £300.

Kyle noticed the businessman opposite him had a suit very much like his. He looked and sounded far too posh for it to be from *'Next'* like his one was and Kyle was sure he saw an Armani label. That must have cost him a grand or two, Kyle decided.

The businessman's mobile went off and he sprang to life. He spoke obstreperously, completely unperturbed that the whole carriage could hear his conversation. His accent was Old Etonian with the occasional Geordie twang.

'Have you heard the latest from Japan?' he enquired. *'The Nikkei is down 140. Yes.... that's what I thought. I think when the market opens in London we should sell big-time. '*

His contact was clearly less convinced but the Armani clad Geordie got very excitable and even louder. He littered his London office with damming statistics and emotive language. *'It's all going tits up'* he yelled down the line. *'Sell, Sell, Sell!'* If his contact wasn't worried before, he certainly was now. Indeed his outburst prompted other brokers to relay the same message back to their firms. By the time the train had reached Newark, panic had set in and mobiles were going off every few seconds.

Kyle watched this spectacle with the fascination of a foreign tourist discovering a new culture for the first time. He thought of his brother in New York and wondered if this is what his life was like. Sure, it brought in big bucks, but was it worth the strain it must have on your heart?

The trolley came round and Kyle helped himself to more free coffee and biscuits. He was determined to make the most of this experience. Besides, he thought, the caffeine might come in useful to stop him falling asleep at the meeting. All the coffee made him need a trip to the gents and he waited patiently for the vacant sign to show.

When he emerged from the loo he was surprised to see Mr Armani standing alone in the vestibule whispering into his mobile. As Kyle passed he heard one word that caught his attention. That word was *'illuminati'*.

Last night, Kyle had enjoyed the rare experience of being able to watch what he wanted on the TV. There had been a documentary about a clandestine, elitist clique called the *'illuminati'*. Kyle enjoyed programmes like this, combining history with wild speculation and theories of orchestrated conspiracy on a global scale. He had heard some of it before via the popularity of Dan Brown's Robert Langdon novels. However, this programme went to new levels implicating the likes of Dennis Healey and Sir Keith Joseph in a 400 year old cult.

Kyle assumed that Mr Armani must have seen the same programme, but why was he whispering about it outside the loo when earlier he had been installing panic in a whole carriage with inside information on the stock market? It didn't add up and Kyle looked at him suspiciously through the remainder of the journey to Kings Cross.

The Westminster meeting was much as Kyle had feared. It was an ego trip for some performance managers who wanted to tell the world how superbly they ran their Police Authorities almost single-handed. Nothing was achieved and Kyle had to resist the temptation to throttle the person next to him and scream *'you are talking bollocks'.*

Back on the train, Kyle was surprised to find that his seat was in the buffet car and still more surprised to find that Mr Armani was sitting opposite once again. He was clearly pleased with himself as many of his calls on the journey back were conveying good news of a successful day's trading. He disappeared with his mobile a few times but generally seemed more relaxed than before. The free copy of the Evening Standard told of millions of pounds wiped off shares. He had been right, so I guess he had earned the right to look smug.

Just past Doncaster, the stock-broker fell asleep and snored as loudly as he had talked. His head dropped onto the shoulder of his adjacent passenger; an incongruously attired platinum blonde who looked like she was just off to a night on the Bigg Market. Her skirt was much too short for her age and physique and the two of them made an unedifying spectacle. She was clearly wealthier than she looked as she was having the full 3 course meal.

The food on National Express was Michelin Star but it was served with a visible contempt for the rich customers. A steward went along the carriage almost throwing the deserts across the tables. *'Cheesecake'* he yelled on a first trip through the carriage. Next he made it down the carriage even quicker spinning plates and yelling *'Crème Brule'.* Finally he came back with a solitary plate for the lady opposite.

'Tart' he yelled. Kyle laughed out loud spluttering coffee across the table. She was not amused but Mr Armani slept on.

Finally, the train crossed the Tyne and rolled into Central Station. Mr Armani was still deep in a power nap. Kyle was getting out and retrieving his belongings wondering if he should wake him. Maybe he intended to go on to Edinburgh. Finally, half way to the exit, he turned back and woke him up. *'Newcastle?'* he quizzed.

'Gosh' said Mr Armani and quickly packed away his lap-top, snatched his jacket and got off the train in the nick of time.

As he walked back to John's pad down *'Dog Leap Stairs'* Kyle noticed his jacket seemed a bit large. Maybe all the stress had made him lose weight, he deliberated. Then a shuddering thought stopped him in his tracks. In the hurry and confusion had he taken the Armani jacket by mistake?

He looked nervously at the label. It was just as he had feared – genuine Italian designer-ware. For a brief interlude he laughed as he imagined Mr Armani's reaction, looking at his own label only to see '*Next*': made in Singapore!

As he rang the intercom at John's flat he searched inside the jacket but there were no business cards or receipts. There was a memory stick and a scribbled note with a name and number on. He doubted whether either would provide the answer to Mr Armani's whereabouts. Why would be scribble his own number and name on a bit of paper? In any case the name was Agnes!

Maybe National Express would be able to trace him but as he hadn't retained his ticket he couldn't even tell them his own seat number and the reservation was made via '*Train-line*' along no doubt with half the other passengers. '*Oh well*' Kyle concluded. He had obtained one half of the most expensive suit he had ever owned.

Scene 8: One Pensioner's Prison

Back at John's flat, Kyle placed the memory stick in his computer and found to no great surprise that it was encrypted. Without a password, there was no hope of ascertaining if it revealed any information that would help Kyle re-unite it with its owner. He unfolded the piece of paper. It read Agnes Stephenson - 0191 (the code for Tyneside) and then 7 digits.

Uneasily Kyle dialled the number on his mobile. It rang a dozen times and just when Kyle was about to hang up a lady answered:

"*Hello*" the lady said timidly.

'*Agnes Stephenson?*' Kyle asked gently.

'*Yes*' the lady confirmed.

'*I'm sorry to disturb you but I accidentally picked up another man's jacket on a train back from London and he had your number in his jacket pocket*'

'*Yes?*'

Bloody hell thought Kyle pausing. It's not One Word's Mum is it? '*Can you think of anyone who might have your name and number in their pocket?*'

'*Well there's my daughter Elizabeth, her husband Eric, my grandchildren, my home help, someone from the housing office. Lots of people I guess.*'

'*Do any of those people make business trips to London and wear Italian designer suits?*' enquired Kyle without a hint of sarcasm.

'*An Italian gentleman you say. No I can't think of any Italian's that have my number*'.

This was proving frustratingly hard work. '*No not an Italian, a Geordie businessman who wears very expensive designer suits*'.

'*No. I don't think I can help you. Sorry what did you say your name was*'.

'*That's ok Mrs Stephenson. I'm Kyle Forster. If you think of anything please can you give me a ring because I really want to get this jacket back to its rightful owner as it must cost over £1000*'

'*Goodness*' remarked Agnes.

Just as Kyle was about to give her his mobile number she interrupted:

'*Now wait a minute I have been ringing financial advisors. You see I have taken my savings out with all this worry about the banks and I wanted some professional advice on where to put it.*' She sounded anxious again as she got to the end of her sentence. *'I don't have a lot of savings you know, just a little bit I've put aside from my pension for the grand-kids',* she qualified. *'Do you think your businessman could be one of the advisors?'*

'Yes. I do' stated Kyle. *'Have you got any business cards for the advisors you rang?'*

'Oh! I don't know about that. My daughter organised it all. I've got one coming tomorrow at 6.00 p.m. but so I guess you could come and see if that's your man.'

'Thanks Mrs Stephenson. You've been a great help', Kyle said relieved and wrote down the details of the elderly-sounding ladies address. He would visit her straight after work tomorrow.

*****

Agnes did not have the most salubrious of addresses. She lived on the Cowgate Estate, which was a sprawling council estate surrounded by moorland a couple of miles to the North West of the City Centre. Kyle knew from his job that it had been a crime black-spot in the 1990's, but crime had fallen dramatically in recent years as millions of pounds of regeneration and community safety money was put to good effect.

There was no hint of deprivation as Kyle parked his car in an ordinary looking street of bungalows. Most had well-tendered gardens but one was more overgrown than the others and contained the rusty shell of a car. Kyle opened Agnes' garden gate and proceeded up the gravel path to her recently painted front door. He was aware of net curtains twitching and a neighbour's dog barking aggressively.

There was no bell so he knocked loudly on the door. He could hear Agnes coming and she opened a succession of locks before finally opening the door just enough to peer out from within her fortress; a chain securing the door. Immediately she saw Kyle her eyes leapt out of her sockets and she slammed the door shut panting loudly as she did so.

Kyle knocked again and called gently *'Mrs Stephenson. It's Kyle Forster. We spoke on the phone. We had an appointment for 6.00 p.m.'*

After what seemed like an eternity, Agnes opened the door and said *'well, you had better come in. But I think you are wasting your time. The advisor cancelled and he knew nothing about the suit'.*

Kyle's heart sank but he smiled and followed Agnes' snail-like walk down the hall.

'Would you like a cup of tea?' She asked.

'That would be lovely Mrs Stephenson'.

Kyle sat in Mrs Stephenson's front room and listened to the sound of an old-fashioned kettle whistle. He surveyed the scene. There was a small oak-leaf table with a lace tablecloth and an antique dresser with a large collection of ornaments set out meticulously. Above them hang a small portrait of the Queen! In the corner of the room there was a small mahogany unit with a portable TV resting on it unobtrusively.

The old sofa creaked as he adjusted his position to look towards the door. Mrs Stephenson entered with a jangling tray of pretty tea-cups and pots plus a small floral plate of digestives. *'Thank you'*, Kyle said as he poured the tea. *'I'm sorry if I startled you when I came to the door'.*

'That's all right. You don't come from around here do you?' she asked. Kyle didn't rise to the bait. *'No, I'm from Wallsend'* he said.

'Wallsend?' Agnes looked puzzled.

'Yes. By the river where the shipyards used to be.'

'I know where Wallsend is young man. It's just I don't go out any more and last time I went to Wallsend I was a wee lassie not much older than you. They didn't have people like you in Wallsend back then'.

Kyle sensed she regretted the social progress of the last 30 years and the more cohesive, diverse community on Tyneside that it had created. He observed how her frail hands were visibly trembling and the more he looked at them the more they shook until the tea spilled over the rim on to the saucer below.

'Where's the jacket you were talking about on the phone?' she said accusingly.

'It's in my car. Have you found the list of financial advisors that your daughter rang?'

'No. Elizabeth must have taken it with her. I will ring her when I have had my tea. She might not be back from work yet'.

'It's a nice place you've got here' Kyle said as he sipped the weak tea.

'Thank you. It's small but it's big enough for me and the Council send someone round to help with the chores. This is a nice quiet street. Not like the rest of the estate. I don't know what the country's coming to. There's crime everywhere. When I was your age we could leave our front doors unlocked and nobody ever got burgled.'

'Well, crime is coming down. Things probably aren't as bad as you think?'

'Not that bad, you say. Try living around here young man. There are gangs of kids hanging around everywhere and the language on them is terrible. They swore at Mr Cartwright the other day as he was putting his rubbish out and

31

then set fire to his bin. Then when the firemen came to put it out they showered them with stones'.

'That's terrible. I work for the Police Authority but it's easy to forget there's a human tragedy behind all the crime statistics.'

'A policeman you say. Well, I should have guessed. You are so tall. I know you are all doing your best but there aren't enough of you. When I was young, there were Policemen patrolling every neighbourhood and we all new them by their first names'.

This sort of misunderstanding was common and Kyle wasn't going to waste time explaining that he actually worked on checking crime statistics and he knew not only that crime had fallen to its lowest level since the 1970s but there were more Police Officers now than there had ever been. Faced with a daily diet of crime reports in the paper and on the TV, a chasm had opened up between people's perception of crime rates and the reality. At least the fact that Agnes thought he was a copper seemed to relax her a bit.

Kyle finished his tea and biscuits listening to Agnes reminisce on the halcyon days of child labour, slavery, capital punishment, half the population being denied the vote and a tacit acceptance by the poor that they had no right to expect a decent standard of living. Well, maybe she wasn't old enough to remember some of those things but Kyle was sure that growing up in the Great Depression of the 1930's was not the bed of roses she remembered it as. Perhaps, in 70 years time people will look back fondly on the days of the credit crunch!

Kyle stood up and lifted the tray of empty pots from the coffee table. Agnes coiled up into a ball like a hedgehog with her arms outstretched as if she expected Kyle to throw the tray at her. 'What are you doing? She demanded.

'I'm just taking the tray back to the kitchen' Kyle explained.

'Don't. I will do that. I will do that after you've gone. Now if you don't mind you will sit down whilst I ring my daughter and then you will go, locking the gate behind you.'

'OK'.

Agnes had one of those old fashioned phones where the numbers were holes around a clock-face and she struggled to move some of the digits all the way round. She put the receiver down and started again four times before she said 'that's done it'. There was no answer.

'You've got my number if you find anything out that can help when you do get to speak to your daughter', Kyle said standing up as slowly as he possibly could.

'I will. Please could you put my newspaper in the bin on your way out? I don't like going outside if I can help it. You can't be too careful can you?'

'*No problem*' Kyle said taking the Daily Mail from her on his way out and depositing it with relish in the recycling bin.

'*Don't forget to shut the gate*' she called from behind her partially closed door with the chain already back on.

'*What's the point?*' Kyle asked himself out loud when he got back to his Mondeo. He wasn't referring to the aborted trip to locate the owner of the Armani jacket, although that was frustrating as well. He was referring to his day job. He spent every day validating crime data and producing reports and charts for managers, for politicians and for the general public. They all told a good news story about falling crime and safer communities. Even the anti-social behaviour that Agnes had described had fallen recently in Northumbria. Yet people like Agnes were convinced the Government was lying, the Police were lying and he must have been conned. No number of fancy bar charts could allay the rising fear of crime that gripped the Nation in the 1990's and never relented.

Kyle checked the jacket was still in the boot and laughed at his own paranoia as he confirmed its presence. It's catching he thought! He got back in the car and turned to direct his thoughts at an imaginary audience again:

"*Fear has taken away the freedom our forefathers fought so hard to win us. Children today grow up wrapped in cotton wool, their parents scared they have been abducted every time they pass out of view. Many pasty-faced, obese kids sit goggle-eyed staring at computer screens day after day. They are unable to play the daring outdoor games their parents played when they were their age.*

The massive difference in traffic volumes in the school holidays tells us how many parents drive their kids to school these days. They are too frightened to let their offspring walk or cycle to school. Statistically more kids will get run over by the Chelsea Tractors these paranoid parents drive than will ever get abducted. But people no longer trusted statistics.

Properly validated statistics can be summarised with one word – facts. They are not open to manipulation or distortion. They tell the truth, the whole truth and nothing but the truth. Regrettably, facts and figures make a transient impression on most people's memories. They are soon replaced with vivid, dramatic accounts of real-life tragedies that grow ever more colourful every time they are re-told.

The number of these tragedies matters less than the frequency with which they are reported and boy were they reported a lot. The internet spreads a web of fear, the 24 hour news bulletins repeated the same news on every hour and the papers battled each other for the most shocking tales of a broken society.

No wonder we were becoming a nation hooked on Prozac. Anxiety was everywhere and the bogeymen lurked on every street corner. It was ironic that

New Labour was now being destroyed by the very spin that it had employed so expertly in its first term. Like a spider caught in its own web, people had got so used to heavy PR and cynical spin that when their policies actually started to work and services started to improve nobody believed them.

Just like in a marriage, once the trust has gone the love affair is over. The public's love-in with New Labour ended long before Gordon Brown entered Downing Street. Whatever the rights and wrongs of the disastrously managed Iraq War, the blatant lie about weapons of mass destruction proved the nail in the red rose coffin. Blair may have improved Britain. Let's face it after Thatcher and Major things really could only get better, but proving it well that was another matter. Evidence could not break down the walls of Agnes's prison. Fear held people like Agnes captive in a prison of their own mind."

Scene 9: Ducking the bullets

Kyle told John about his encounter with Agnes over a pint in the timber-framed splendour of the Cooperage. John preferred to talk about a potential date he had lined up with a lady from Pity Me, which was an aptly named village in County Durham rather than a description of John's date.

Walking back along the Quayside to the flat, John's mobile went off and he answered excitedly, immediately putting on a slower, softer voice as he spoke to his new acquaintance. Suddenly, Kyle recalled that he had switched his own mobile off when he went in to see Agnes and had forgotten to switch it back on again.

9 missed calls and 3 messages! Someone was keen to get hold of him. Most were from a number he didn't recognise but one message and 1 call were from Helen and 1 call was from Dan. He read Helen's message first:

'A man has been urgently trying 2 find you. He thinks you've picked up his jacket by mistake. I gave him your moby number. I hope you don't mind.'

After recovering from the dismay of receiving a text from his wife without a kiss, he rejoiced in being finally able to return the jacket. Sure enough a voice-mail from the persistent caller turned out to be Mr Armani from the train.

Kyle checked on John. He was still chatting away like a teenager with his first crush. He returned the call on his phone. Mr Armani picked up instantly. No rings. It caught Kyle off guard.

'Thank God I found you. Have you got the memory stick that was in the jacket pocket?'

'Yes. I put it back in the pocket'

'Did you read the memory stick?'

'No.'

'Good. Right here's what I want you to do. Tonight at midnight meet me at Unit 5c on the Team Valley Trading Estate'

'Can't it wait till tomorrow? I've just had a pint and I'm ready for bed'

'No. Be there'.

He hung up. How odd Kyle thought. He must be really desperate to recover his property. What was on that memory stick that made him ask about that instead of one half of an Armani suit? Also, why ask if he'd read the memory stick. Didn't he know it had been encrypted?

Team Valley bustling with activity in the day was dead at night. Kyle roamed the soulless avenues laid out in parallel, ordered lines looking for Unit 5C. He found it and immediately checked his watch. It was five to mid-night. He looked around. There was nobody to be seen. There was an eerie silence, broken only by the distant sound of an alarm. This unit looked like the shutters were permanently closed; an early victim of the economic down-turn. Kyle didn't like this choice of venue, not at this time of night. He liked it even less when he noticed this yard seemed to be the only part of the estate not covered by CCTV.

He kept his driving glasses on and got out of the car to look around. No, the yard was just as he had thought it was - deserted. He got back in the car and checked the time on the car radio. It said 11.57. He synchronised his watch.

Suddenly, there was a noise behind him. He shivered and turned to look out of the rear windscreen. It was pitch black. Once more he got out of the car but this time he walked in the direction of the noise. Suddenly Mr Armani emerged from the shadows dressed in dark jeans and a black leather jacket, Kyle's jacket draped over his shoulder.

'*Where's the jacket*?' he demanded curtly.

'It's *in the car. I will get it*'

A distant clock struck 12 as Kyle retrieved the jacket and walked back into the shadows to exchange it for his.

A screech of brakes, the jackets exchanged, the memory stick falling at Kyle's feet, a car turning the corner, Kyle bending to retrieve the memory stick and '*Fucking hell!*'

A single bullet was fired and Kyle hit the deck his heart thumping; another screech of breaks; silence.

Two bodies lay motionless on the tarmac for more than a minute. Then one raised his head, looked around and seeing that the coast was clear got to his feet. The other lay in a pool of blood seeping out from beneath his leather jacket. The bullet had whistled past Kyle's ear as he bent to retrieve the memory stick and plunged straight into the other man's chest. He was dead, face down on the cold, wet tarmac.

Instinctively, Kyle picked up the memory stick and run for his car. He tore away through the night looking anxiously in the rear mirror every few seconds. He was not being followed. The assassin had fled the scene as quickly as he had arrived. The question that haunted Kyle all the way back to the Police Station was who was the bullet meant for? If he hadn't bent down it would have pierced his arteries and left him dead and alone in an industrial estate in Gateshead.

Scene 10: Dan's Last Cocktail

Dan entered his boss's office to face the music. He had run out of excuses. He had tried everything to sell the packages of financial instruments he had acquired on his company's behalf. Sure his Boss had authorised the transactions but he knew the score. He had been pulling the shots, making him risk millions he didn't really want to risk. Now he was on his own and there was no plan B.

There was another man in the office. It was not a good sign. Dan reckoned he worked for an outsourced HR firm that they used to hire and fire. His Boss still shook his hand vigorously but this time Dan was sure he tried his utmost to break it. He was right about the guy from HR.

'Dan. This is a sad day' his Boss started. *'You have been a real asset to this company but you got cocky. You thought you could beat the system. You risked a lot of money on some toxic assets; our money. Now we are going to have to write it off. Our shareholders want blood. You know the score. I want your desk cleared in 5 minutes and your security pass left with my colleague here who will escort you off the premises.'*

'I'm sorry it's come to this but you left me no choice. Maybe when this hell is over we will work together again. You've got balls I'll give you that. Good luck'.

He offered his hand but Dan walked straight out of the office. He didn't wait to clear his desk. His colleagues stopped working and wondered what to say. Someone coughed nervously. Dan made for the lift as quickly as his feet could carry him and flung his security card in the direction of the axe-man whose job it was to see he walked away from the building empty-handed and never came back.

'Wait' yelled the axe-man as he just made it to the lift before the doors shut behind Dan. *'You've got to sign this. It's a standard confidentiality agreement.'*

The document was the size of a Dickens novel but Dan signed regardless. He was finished. His penthouse dream was over and to make matters worse the lift overshot the ground floor and plunged into the basement. Dan had never been down to the basement in all the years he had worked in New York. Why would he? It was a horrible, smelly place with rats in the store-room, rats in the boiler-room and manual workers from Harlem everywhere.

'Good-bye Mr Forster' the kind security guard said as Dan by-passed reception and stepped out into the damp October air. He didn't reply. He just wanted out.

Suddenly Dan felt lost in the Big Apple. He didn't know what to do and where to go. He hailed a cab and made the driver wait whilst he pondered his destination. Eventually, he settled on a cocktail bar he knew, which served some lethal drinks that were 90% spirits and 10% fruit juice; liquid dynamite with a cherry on top.

Dan had been so used to winning he didn't know how to lose. His life was built around work. He breathed and slept work. Most of his social life revolved around business lunches and after work drinks at jaunts like this one. He didn't mind the long hours and the tough deadlines as long as he was continually told how brilliant he was and his remuneration reflected this brilliance.

Now, alone in a crowded New York bar in the middle of the morning he felt small and impotent. He had drowned in a sea of ambition and greed and now he was drowning his sorrows like he did everything – big style.

He rang Kyle but his phone was switched off. He couldn't even be bothered to work out the time back home but he knew it must be afternoon. Part of him wanted to talk to someone. Part of him was too ashamed.

After a few hours of serious drinking he staggered outside into the rain. *'Shit'* he said as the rain beat down on him. He passed an internet cafe and fifty yards further on an idea came to him and he turned back.

He had a coffee to help sober him up and he logged on to the site of his favourite escort agency in New York. He needed a lot of cheering up so he plumped for two bi-sexual American girls: one blonde, one brunette; both stunning. They listed girl on girl, toys and bondage amongst their interests. Dan decided he needed the lot and then he would round the evening off by shagging them both. He had to wait an hour and a half for them to become available so he went back to his penthouse and snorted some coke.

The coke perked him up and made him glad he could afford top-class escorts. Then he remembered he had been fired and this might be the last time he could afford them. Bloody hell, they better be good, he told himself counting out the dollars their services would require.

Ramona and Marie arrived bang on time and immediately set to work pleasuring each other's cosmetically enhanced bodies with their tongues. It wasn't Dan's first Lesbian experience with the agency and somehow the mystery had gone. Ramona went to her carry-bag and produced a huge black dildo. For the first time in his life Dan felt insecure about the size of his own big, black toy soldier. Ramona plunged it deep into Marie and Marie gasped with pleasure. *'Oh hit me baby'* she cried.

Dan was only mildly aroused by all this. It felt staged. He decided it was time for him to get involved. He would take Ramona from behind whilst she continued to pleasure Marie. Unfortunately, his toy soldier would not stand to attention. Ramona abandoned Marie and gave him a blow-job but there was still nothing. After 20 minutes of oral, hand-relief and even breast-relief from Marie the two girls abandoned their efforts.

'I'm sorry. Your cock is not hard enough' said Ramona in a Mexican immigrant accent. *'Have you had too much booze maybe?'*

'There's no discount' Marie added more sharply.

Dan went to his wallet and paid the girls off. He had never felt this crap before. It was as if all the angels in Heaven were pissing on him.

*****

Kyle was at the Police Station for two hours. The Police had already found the victim's body following an anonymous tip-off and initially they seemed to have Kyle as their number one suspect. His story did seem a little far-fetched. He was locked in an interview room and told to get a solicitor. Forensics had been on the scene and confirmed that Kyle could not have fired the bullet. It was fired from some distance. Kyle had the victim's blood on his clothes and fragments of shrapnel in his hair.

The Police had a new theory. The bullet was meant for Kyle. The meeting was a set-up for a planned racist killing. A similar incident had happened in Team Valley six months previously and the victim had previously been to the Police with a death-threat from a white supremacist organisation. Mr Armani transpired to be a fully paid up member of the BNP. No doubt, he thought Kyle had stolen his jacket and only agreed to return it when he had tracked him down. In the eyes of a racist psychopath, Kyle had signed his own death warrant.

Kyle didn't buy the link but he was too relieved to be alive and free to try to trash the theory. In the other Team Valley shooting the Police Officer informed Kyle that the victim had been there to exchange drugs when he was shot. Did the Police reckon that their performance analyst was a drugs dealer?

Upon leaving the Police Station, Kyle reflected on what a shocking month it had been. He had:

- found out his wife was having an affair;

- moved out of the family home;

- stolen an Armani suite;

- witnessed a man being shot dead;

- escaped with his own life by a hairs breadth; and

- spent two hours convincing his employers he wasn't a murderer.

It was 3.00 a.m. when he finally got to bed. He was just dropping off when his mobile rang. He could hear it but couldn't see it in the dark and it rang off before he could answer it. He didn't recognise the number so he went back to sleep with the mobile on his pillow.

Suddenly there was a noise outside the window. Kyle froze with fear. It sounded like a man scaling the drain-pipes. Then there was silence. Kyle's ears pricked up like a startled rabbit.

Crash!

A thick-set man dressed all in black came somersaulting through the window. Kyle instantly focused on the glint of his gun. The intruder stood up and towered over Kyle, who pulled the bedclothes up to his chin as if they could shield him from the imminent bullet. The man was huge and masked. He recovered his breath and steadied his aim. The gun was pointing at Kyle's chest. Kyle prepared for excruciating pain and shut his eyes.

There was nothing but the howl of the wind through the shattered glass. Guardedly, Kyle opened his eyes and was shocked to see the masked man's body shape had changed. He looked smaller now: more feminine, more vulnerable.

The gun was still directed at his heart but it was visibly shaking, sending shadows dancing up and down the wall by Kyle's bed. The intruder put his other hand to his face and slowly removed the mask. It was Helen!

Kyle shook himself awake. It was a nightmare. It was just a nightmare. The curtains were still and the window pane was intact. The only sound was the sound of John snoring in the adjacent bedroom. Kyle lay back down feeling cosy and safe and buried his face in the soft shield of the pillow but he was wide awake now and it was nearly dawn. After 10 minutes he was on the verge of falling back to sleep when his mobile went off, still on the pillow next to him.

'*Hello*' he answered apprehensively.

It was his Uncle and he sounded sombre as if he was reading a prepared statement:

'*Hello Kyle. We've had some terrible news.*' His Uncle paused and sounded crackly and fragile.

'*The NYPD were called to Dan's block yesterday evening. It appears he jumped from his balcony.*' He paused again, this time longer than before. It was clear that he was struggling to get the words out.

'*They say he would have died instantly on hitting the ground. We are awaiting the results of the post-mortem. '*

With that he lost his composure and broke into a tearful apology. *'I'm sorry to wake you but I thought you should hear it from us rather than wait till the NYPD rang you in the morning'.*

Kyle was speechless. Dan was dead? Suicide? He was the last person Kyle would have expected to commit suicide. He was so confident, so strong and so successful. Nothing bothered him. Perhaps Kyle really didn't know his brother that well after all.

Kyle got up and went into work early. He wanted things to return to normal. He was not cut-out for all this chaos and danger. He was a normal bloke with a normal job; not fucking James Bond! He was an organised man who liked order and hated things he didn't understand.

The day passed serenely and he went back to John's as early as he could. However, if Kyle felt his life would return to normality he was very much mistaken. Things were about to get even more extraordinary and dangerous!

ACT 2: Seeing the Light

Scene 1: Opening the Books

In the canteen at Police HQ, Kyle was describing his adventures to his colleagues. He could tell that most of them preferred to believe the official Police line of a racist act of revenge than a conspiracy theory.

'So! Let me get this straight' said Dave, a burly Police dog handler. *'You think that the bloke who got killed was so desperate to recover an encrypted memory stick that he was prepared to arrange a shooting and put himself in the line of fire just in case you might have guessed the password and read it!'*

Kyle shrugged. *'I don't know. It just seems odd that he was so worried about getting the memory stick back and that he thought I might have read it if he knew it was encrypted.'*

'Could it be that the victim had a high-powered job and was worried about his BNP membership coming to light and ruining his career?' asked Rachel, a young criminal psychologist. *'Maybe the memory stick contained neo-Nazi propaganda, showing him parading about in a Nazi uniform like Prince Harry'.*

'I guess it could be', the petite girl in a dark pin-striped trouser suit might have a point, thought Kyle.

'No. I reckon Kyle's the son of God and he's been sent down to Earth to warn us about global conspiracy' mocked Dave. *'Anyway, where's the mysterious memory stick now'* asked Dave.

'The DI took it away to see if the computer boffins could crack the password' revealed Kyle.

'Sorry mate but they probably think you are nuts', said Colin, a bearded estates manager who Kyle had known for years, with typical curtness.

'Ah, don't be horrible Colin' laughed Sam, a plump young girl from Kyle's section and then respectfully *'his brothers just died you know'*.

'Yes. Sorry mate' said Colin *'Terrible news about your brother. You hear these horror stories about the pressure driving bankers to jump out of skyscrapers in the papers but you never think it could happen to someone you know.'*

'It puts things in perspective' said Kyle.

'I guess we better get back to the grind' said Dave, standing up to leave.

At that moment one of the uniformed officers from another table came over. *'Excuse me. Kyle Forster? I thought I'd update you on progress re the incident at Team Valley. We spoke to the victim's girlfriend. It sounds like it was just as we thought. He'd fallen in with a pretty unsavoury crowd and a few loose words about the nigger who nicked my Armani jacket probably led to one of them deciding to try and shoot you'*

'They are probably devastated they took out the wrong guy but in my experience they won't come back for seconds. I know it must have scared the life out of you and I really think you should talk to Victim Support but you can relax now.'

'Thanks officer'

'Oh', the officer said as an after-thought reaching inside his pocket. *'You might as well have this back. We managed to hack into it; just soft-core porn really. Anyway chuck it if you want to. We've left it encrypted so it's useless.'*

Kyle felt stupid but relieved. Dave, Colin and Sam added comments that were along the lines of *'I told you so'* and left. Rachel sipped the last drops of her black coffee before standing up to follow them out. *'The officer was right. You ought to talk to someone. Losing your brother, problems at home and being shot at all in a few days. You are only human. If you don't want to talk to Victim Support, you could always talk to me'*, she said with a delicious Geordie lilt and genuine concern.

'Thanks Rachel', he said smiling.

'Take care Kyle', she replied as she left the canteen.

Kyle sat for a moment fiddling with the memory stick. He contemplated his life returning to normal and decided he would have to book his flight to New York for Dan's funeral on his way home from work. He wondered if he should ask Helen if she wanted to go first and then thought better of it. This was a private, family event and he didn't want his domestic situation to complicate things. It was funny how Rachel had got to hear about his domestic circumstances. Gossip travels fast in this place. He had only seen Rachel about 3 or 4 times before, mainly in meetings involving a large number of people, but it was good of her to offer to help.

His mobile went off and it was John asking after him. Another person who cared, thought Kyle. He had rung Helen to tell her about the shooting and Dan's suicide this morning and she hadn't offered him any crumbs of comfort. She almost sounded angry with Kyle for bringing more misery into her already intolerable life.

Kyle booked the flights after work. *'Going anywhere nice'* the travel agent had said at the Bureau de Change. *'Not really, a funeral'* Kyle had replied taking the wind out of her sails.

He changed into some casual clothes and tossed the memory stick into the bin. *'Good riddance'* he said as he did so. He recalled the desperate sound of his racist nemesis as he asked about the memory stick. *'You haven't read it, have you?'* he quizzed Kyle.

Kyle retrieved the stick from the bin and plugged it into the USB slot. Sure enough, the *'enter password'* box came up as before.

'pass-word' Kyle input laughing.

'pass-word incorrect; access denied' the red message flashed up on the screen.

Kyle entered the Victim's name. Again *'password incorrect; access denied'* flashed up.

Kyle thought for a moment. Most password systems only allow 3 guesses. Nothing really came to mind. Then he remembered the hush tones of the victim as he whispered into his mobile phone outside the loo on the National Express train.

'Oh fuck it' he said and typed in *'illuminati'*, taking great care to spell the ancient Latin word correctly.

To his astonishment the whole screen went blue, flashed away for a bit and a large file opened up.

In a large Gothic font the heading came up on the screen *'The Books of the Illuminati: An introduction'* by Charles Reynolds, Dittmer Forsberg and Professor Hugh Lyons. There were hyperlinks to five books sequentially numbered from *'the first phase'* to *'the fifth phase'.*

Kyle felt deeply uneasy. Why had the Police lied to him? Had they even bothered to try and hack into the files? One thing was for sure. This was no soft porn!

Kyle poured himself a glass of single malt whiskey and stood at a distance from the memory stick as if it were a ticking bomb. The potent, peaty spirit allowed him to crystallize his thoughts. He decided that he didn't want anyone to know that he had hacked into the dead man's files.

He briefly considered reporting his discovery to the Police. However, they had told him the files were innocuous, if a trifle embarrassing. He had worked for the Police Authority for long enough to know it doesn't pay to call a uniformed officer a liar.

Besides, if this dangerous sect found out he was on to them, he might need more than Northumbria Police's finest to protect him. Ideally, he wanted to get the memory stick back to the sect, without drawing attention to the fact that he knew what the file contained.

He began to formulate a plan and searched for a pen and some paper. He wrote a note to the grieving girlfriend of the memory stick's owner:

'Dear Madam,

I am sorry to hear about your tragic loss. I didn't know your boyfriend but was with him when he died. The Police believe the bullet may have been intended for me and your boyfriend may have been killed as a result of a terrible accident. My heart goes out to you in your time of need.

I enclose a memory stick that I was returning to your boyfriend on the night he was shot. I don't know what it contains as it has a password restricting access to the files. The Police suggested I threw it away, but I thought that should be your decision as your partner seemed very concerned to get it back.

The Police say that your boyfriend kept some unsavoury company who might have been involved in the shooting. I urge you to go to the Police if you think they could have been in any way responsible for your loss.

I would be grateful if you let your boyfriend's pals know that I have returned the memory stick that I inadvertently acquired. I have no interest in seeking retribution and the Police are minded to drop the investigation.

I am sorry again for any part I played in this terrible outcome.

Yours sincerely,

Kyle Forster.'

Kyle sealed the envelope and walked to the post-box. It was a fine evening and he felt confident that he had done the right thing and this would put an end to the affair. In two days time he was off to America to pay his respects to Dan. He was due back in the country just in time to take Nathan to the next home game. He had been through a hellish few weeks but slowly things would get back to normal.

However, Kyle was far too inquisitive to put the memory stick straight in the envelope after finishing his whiskey. He had copied the files across to his laptop and planned to make the '*Books of the Illuminati*' his next read.

Scene 2: An Illuminating Read

'The Books of the Illuminati' comprised of 6 files entitled:

- introduction and history;

- the first phase;

- the second phase;

- the third phase;

- the fourth phase; and

- the fifth phase.

The former was massive because it contained embedded links to all the other files. The 5 phases were also large acrobat documents, remarkably with identical file sizes. Kyle decided it was going to be a long read and out of respect for his dead brother he would not take his PC with him to New York. Thus, he would read the introductory file and the others would wait until his return.

Eagerly, Kyle clicked on the first file and watched the egg-timer whirl into life before finally the page cleared to reveal the secrets that Kyle believed a man had lost his life protecting. The text is reproduced in full.

Introduction and History

The illuminati – manifesto
for a New World Order

Illuminati is Latin for 'the *enlightened ones*' and the movement has its origins in the Age of Enlightenment that spread through Western Europe in the 18th Century. Forward-thinking intellectuals and philosophers rebelled against the primitive notion that power should be inherited or the reward for religious sacrifice. Enlightenment is about rewarding rational thought and not faith, superstition and inheritance. The brave pioneers challenged '*The Divine Right of Kings*' and the power of the Church.

Throughout the previous 100 years, great thinkers such as Descartes had advocated greater freedom from the tyranny of the Monarchy and the Church. Great scientists like Galileo, Newton and Darwin had dismantled the theories on which these outdated institutions were based. Science had proved that creationism was a sham, the Earth was round and human beings were just animals, especially intelligent and developed animals, but still animals all the same. We now know that we share over 99% of our DNA with primates. We do not have some mystical right to rule this planet, we must earn it through the one thing that makes us different; the size of our IQ.

The enlightened realized that in time science would explain everything and make the impossible possible. We needed to worship science, not some mystical being. We must nurture the great scientific minds of our generation, investing in real people, not gods and legends.

Eventually around 2000 of the enlightened joined the '*Illuminati of Bavaria*', a peaceful brotherhood in Southern Germany who shared the vision of a fairer and more logical world, where the brightest human beings would be given the greatest rewards along with roles at the head of business and government. The brotherhood was crushed within 20 years by the might of the Catholic Church and the Bavarian aristocracy.

However, their ideas lived on in many new organisations that sprung up over the World. First to take on the baton was the Freemasons, then the Skull and Bones Society of Yale University and finally the Bilderberg Group, all of which survive today thanks to their secrecy. They are our associates but none of us are mutually exclusive. The day of enlightenment will come in the 21st Century and our associate members will have to decide whether to join us and help establish a New World Order or remain elitist debating societies.

Some scholars point to the reformation of the Illuminati in the 1950s when the Bilderberg Group first met. In truth, we never went away. We existed underground implementing the first phase for hundreds of years, generation after generation. Our founders always knew it would take hundreds of years of scientific and educational advance to make the time conducive to a New World Order. Many got impatient and embarked on doomed totalitarian projects to fast-track many of our principles. Thus, we had followers form the National Socialists in Germany and the Communists in Russia. We were never extremists like these parties. They owed their power to military strength, not intellect.

Don't believe half of what you hear about us. Conspiracy theorists have linked us to everything from shooting JFK to faking the moon landings. Hitler was not a member, neither was Stalin. Many of their early followers were but they were later suppressed and persecuted for not backing their extremist ideologies. We are men and women of reason, where high intellect is a condition of membership. We are not neo-Nazis and we welcome members from all faiths and racial backgrounds.

Our beliefs have remained unwritten for hundreds of years through fear of persecution and an acceptance that the time for a new World Order hasn't yet arrived. I am writing this as we enter the new Millennium because the conditions are almost right to put our plans into practice. Science has at last enabled us to spread our secrets throughout the world without being detected by our enemies. We must rejoice at the *Illuminati's* greatest achievement, the greatest invention of all time – the internet.

If you are reading this, then you have been singled out by an existing Member as someone of high intelligence and talent with potential to lead the New World Order. Welcome. We hope you join us on our great crusade. We already have 750, 000 members world-wide, the cream of our generation. Our coup will be bloodless, our triumph universal and in time the world will thank us for having the enlightenment to intervene before it was too late.

*****

There followed an exhibit showing a pyramid with 12 steps. The exhibit was called '*The 12 Pillars of the Illuminati*'. Each one was then explained in the text below.

1. meritocracy;

2. freedom;

3. internationalism;

4. technology;

5. environmentalism;

6. hierarchy;

7. confidentiality;

8. investment;

9. birth control;

10. safety net;

11. regulation; and

12. unity.

1/ Meritocracy

We believe that power and wealth should be awarded on merit. The cream should always rise to the top. Impediments such as racism, sexism, nepotism and snobbery should be eliminated. There should be a ladder of intellect with those of exceptional talent throughout the world given leadership roles appropriate to their greatness.

In business, successful companies do not select their senior executives through a vote of their customers. They are selected on merit, normally characterised by a high IQ and practical business acumen. The selection process for the top jobs will involve a series of challenging tests designed to measure competencies and the successful candidates will be given huge rewards to buy their loyalty and motivate the exercising of their great minds.

In education, nobody would seriously suggest that the pupils elect their head-teachers. Throughout the world the most successful schools test pupil intellect either as a means of selection or a means of setting. Mixed ability classes do not work. The schools heading league tables allocate the best resources to the brightest pupils rather than wasting them on those of low IQ. Pupils are regularly tested and promotions and demotions are made annually to reflect the fact that intelligence develops at different rates, especially during adolescence.

Why then do we not select governments on merit? Government is simply one powerful organisation charged with running a country, a state or a local authority just like a board of executive directors runs our top companies or a head-teacher runs a school. Government is too important to entrust with the whim of an electorate, many of whom will be of low intellectual ability. Talent should be the key, not popularity and pledges that rarely get fulfilled. Democracy is the enemy of meritocracy. How many elected leaders leave office as popular as when they were elected? Time after time elected leaders let us down. It is a time for a New World Order; one based on merit.

2/Freedom

We believe that freedom is not only intrinsically a good thing which encourages blue-sky thinking but it is essential for the long-term survival of a government. Totalitarian governments of both the extreme right (fascists) and extreme left (communists) have used the power of the state to crush free thought and deter resistance.

However, history tells us that this never lasts. Eventually, the oppressed masses will lose their fear and take to the streets and even the loyalist and strongest army will be forced to surrender. Witness the spontaneous uprising in the Communist block at the end of the Cold War; the Spanish Civil War; the overthrow of apartheid in South Africa.

Totalitarian states squander vast resources on clinging on to power. Eventually the elite are more occupied with preserving power than using it. What is the point of power if it is not used to efficiently manage? Accordingly, totalitarian countries are inherently inefficient and a means to an end becomes the end itself.

We believe citizens should be free to challenge everything and anything. They are the real scrutiny committee; exercising checks and balances to stop abuse of power.

3/ Internationalism

'Imagine there's no Countries' wrote John Lennon in his classic ballad *'Imagine'*. In this respect, Lennon, was indeed enlightened. Millions of lives are lost throughout the world due to wars fought over border disputes and misguided nationalism. In many countries the populations starve because their governments are always at war. The loss of talent; the waste of resources; the destruction of the environment is scandalous.

The notion of separate countries, states and local authorities all with disparate objectives and policies is primitive and dates back to tribal loyalties. It is an obscenely inefficient way to run a planet. Successful international companies may have national or regional structures but their business plan is the same throughout the world and management co-ordinates policy globally. Government should be no different. Economies of scale exist with global government and wasteful protectionism is avoided. Policies that affect the planet such as measures to tackle climate change and pandemic flu are more effectively co-ordinated.

The United Nations is a noble concept but it has no teeth. We believe that there should be one government made up of the greatest talent from around the world. They should be the guardians of our planet and shallow national interest should be set aside to advance the common good and achieve efficient implementation of international policy.

4/ *Technology*

Science and innovation are the catalysts of progress. We must champion science like never before. There is a rational explanation for everything, a solution to all the World's problems. Half of what is possible today was thought impossible a generation ago. However, throughout history scientists have been persecuted rather than encouraged.

The luddites that preached creationism over evolution and told us the World was round are still alive today. The Roman Catholic Church is still just as much an enemy of progress as in the days of our Jesuit pioneers. They are against the issuing of condoms in Africa to stop the spread of HIV; they are against stem cell research that is our best hope of eliminating other fatal diseases and genetic mutations. They are against abortion when mothers have the chance of stopping these defects before birth.

Science is a triumph of logic and reason over fear and superstition. It is why we are here and the way of ensuring that we are still here in generations to come. Scientists should be our Gods. We should spend more on technology than anything else but a miniscule proportion of international GDP is actually spent on it. We believe unless we act quickly and collectively to find scientific solutions to the challenges we face, within a few generations, our time on this Planet will be over.

5/ Environmentalism

We were the first to tell the World about the dangers of Climate Change and although there is now political consensus that global warming presents a clear and present danger, there remains a lack of will to take the radical action required to address it. We are the true greens, committed to using technology and international action to cut carbon emissions to 1975 levels by 2025 and capping them thereafter. Our top scientists, many of them *Illuminati,* have told us this is what is required. We have to trust them.

The only way to radically reduce carbon emissions simultaneously to allowing developing countries to grow and make poverty history is for the other pillars of our manifesto to be implemented. Democracy and tyranny have failed. Famine and war have vandalised our environment. We are our Planet's guardians and we have a responsibility to our children and our children's children to jettison our prejudices and trust the brightest minds on the Planet to lead us to a better world.

6/ Hierarchy

Every successful organisation requires a structure; a pyramid with a Chief Executive at the top and a management team who take all the key decisions. It is the way that order is kept, leaders are held accountable and people understand their roles and responsibilities. The tragedy of the great western democracies of the last century is that as people got richer, they got more miserable. This is because people don't currently understand their roles and responsibilities and have unrealistic aspirations. A janitor doesn't join a company hoping to reach the Boardroom but the masses with low IQs have grown to believe that they should get the same rewards as the intellectual elite.

The original '*illuminati*' was organised in three classes. These classes have been reformed over the years to place less reliance on inheritance and wealth and more on skills and ability. Now we propose that every child will be assessed for a range of competencies at the ages of 11 and 16. They will be provisionally and then finally allocated to a class for which there is an internationally recognised role description and pay ceiling. Every 10 years, adults will be re-assessed to ensure that they are still in the most appropriate class. The 3 classes are:

Class 1 – 'Executives *and Innovators*'.   This class is effectively the management team, the scientists and trouble-shooters. The elite will be within the top 10% in terms of intellectual and practical skills and will get the top 10% of earnings.

Class 2 - 'Professionals'. This class includes all those performing jobs requiring a reasonable standard of intellect and additional skills that not everyone with a reasonable IQ would be able to supply. Some degree of specialism and adult learning plus continuing professional development will be required.

Class 3 – 'Generalists'. The lowest class will be reserved for those with a low IQ or other disability that will prevent them doing any specialist jobs. They will be instead expected to do tasks, primarily manual, which class 1 and 2 people would be quite capable of doing if they had the time. They will need to be totally flexible, moved around the World and between jobs to meet demand.

7/ Confidentiality

We are often described as a secret society as if secrecy is sinister. We believe confidentiality is essential to allow the executives and innovators to speak their mind without fear of what citizens will think. Leadership requires difficult and unpopular decisions to be taken. Controversy is an unnecessary distraction.

Citizens do not need to know the details of internal debate within the ruling class. Freedom of information should be on a need to know basis. We believe the pendulum has swung too much in favour of access to information.

8/ Investment

Democracy encourages myopic decision-making and deters investment in the longer-term. Typically, elected Governments know they must face re-election every 4 or 5 years and few Governments last longer than 2 or 3 terms. This paralyses investment and creates instability. Why spend on a project that won't have an impact until after the next election? The incentive is for quick fixes to complex problems that need long-term planning and guaranteed funding levels.

Thus, all plans should be for a period of 65 years, reflecting average life expectancy in the World today, with an annual re-fresh. Expenditure and funding should be planned to balance the books over a 65 year period, borrowing in the slumps and saving in the booms. 65 years may seem a long time but it is hardly a dot in time in the history of life on Earth.

9/ Birth Control

The global population is growing at an unsustainable rate. Moreover, it is growing fastest in poorer regions where the infrastructure is least able to cope. We must not live in denial. Birth control should be promoted everywhere but especially in Africa and parts of Asia. We should provide condoms free so poverty is not an obstacle to family planning.

10/ Safety Net

We should not reward failure but we must enable those of low intellect and ability to survive humanely. The safety net of an international welfare state should be in place but welfare should not be generous enough to make it possible for a generalist in one part of the world to enjoy a better standard of living than a professional in another part of the world. Incentives to work must operate globally.

Over time we should use education, science and technology to ensure everyone of working age has a job or is subscribed to the Army and given a role supporting voluntary and charitable organisations throughout the globe. The dream of full employment will become a reality.

11/ Regulation

Without rules and standards, chaos erupts. Annual targets will be set globally and cascaded down to each individual citizen. Everyone no matter what their class will be able to see how they contribute to the Global 65 –year Plan. Performance against these targets will be published on the internet each year so the ruling class can be judged fairly and accurately. They must prepare and publish an action plan for all missed targets.

The Global Regulators will monitor each work-place for how well they are performing on a 10 year cycle and if by the time of the next inspection inadequate performance has not been addressed the responsible executives will be demoted from class 1.

12/ Unity

The *'illuminati'* are a bother-hood. We must all swear an oath of allegiance to the ruling class. We must trust them to do what is best because of their superior intellect. All class 1 brothers must work together, without any regard for selfish interest or ego-mania. Unity is strength. Arguments must be in private and support for the Global Chief Executive and the management team that elects him or her absolute.

*****

Kyle looked up from the computer screen and quickly shut the file. He was shocked. He was not so much shocked by the content of what he had just read but by his reaction to it. Yes, it was radical. Yes, it was revolutionary. Yes, it was incredible. However, it was well-written and logical, not at all like he had imagined it. Indeed he probably agreed with the majority of it or at least had an open mind.

It did not seem the sort of poisonous conspiracy to justify attempting to kill him to stop him reading it. Perhaps, after all the Police were right. The victim in the Armani suit might have been worried about the pillar of confidentiality being broken but not worried enough to arrange an assassination. His racist friends had done that and he had been the unlucky recipient of their stray bullet.

Scene 3: Behind every great man!

Dan's funeral was quiet and respectful; the polar opposite of his life and the nation he came to call his home. The word suicide was never uttered and friends and work colleagues kept a distance from the grieving Forster family.

Kyle recalled the funerals of his Mum and Dad both struck down by cancer in his youth. His parents had a good marriage. There had been rows and hushed conversations that Kyle recalled from his childhood but he never doubted that they loved each other and they would honour their wedding vows. When they grew old and cantankerous they had nagged and wined regularly but never argued and they had lived their lives like they were joined at the hip. They had given up expecting each other to change in mid-life and instead tolerated their weaknesses and rejoiced in their strengths.

One man introduced himself to Kyle as they stood in the crematoria car park. *'Kyle. I've heard a lot about you. I'm Lucas Barowski of the New York Times. I was a great friend of your brothers. He was a great man. Indeed the NYPD say I was probably the last person to speak to him. He rang me from a bar. He didn't sound himself. I wish I had seen the signs and done something'.*

'Thanks Lucas' Kyle said. *'I'm sure you couldn't have prevented this. I just couldn't imagine it of Dan, no matter how bad things got'.*

'I guess we never really know what's going on in other people's heads, do we?' Lucas replied rhetorically.

With that, Kyle shook his hand and got back in the car waiting to take him to the Airport.

'You all right Uncle?' Kyle asked as they stood next to each other on the transit bus at JFK.

'Don't worry about me Kyle' he replied with a tear in his eye. He turned and looked at his Aunt who had a far-away look in her eyes.

'That's us' he said as the bus stopped and she remained seated in a world of her own. She accepted his hand as he helped her to her feet.

The jumbo jet seemed to take an eternal time to leave the tarmac. At times Kyle felt the Atlantic must have been covered in tarmac and the pilot had decided to drive home. Eventually it was air-bound and the 4 of them travelled quietly home together; Uncle, Auntie, Kyle and the burnt embers of a man who had scaled great heights only to jump from them to a premature death.

*****

Kyle made it back to Newcastle in time to take Nathan to the match. An embarrassing home defeat to Blackburn was not what either needed in their present state of mind. Somehow it didn't seem so important given the recent turn of events. Nathan had been unusually chatty on the way to the game, happy to see his Dad again. On the way back home they were both silent. At one point, Nathan had asked when Kyle was coming back. Kyle had said *'let's not rush things. We both need to think things over and decide if we are going to try again or make the separation permanent'*. Nathan seemed satisfied with Kyle's honesty.

Helen was sitting on the sofa watching TV when they returned. *'The kettles' just boiled if you want a cuppa'* she said without looking up. Nathan went upstairs to replay the match on his games console. Kyle thought 2 things:

- firstly, I bet Newcastle don't lose that one; and

- secondly, this gives Helen and me a chance to talk.

Helen barely raised an eye-brow as he told her about the *'Books of the Illuminati'*. At the end of his expert summation, Kyle asked *'Well?'*

'Well what?'

'Do you think they sound like a dangerous cult that ordered my execution or are they a radical solution to today's problems?

'I think you've been watching too many Michael Moore films. You could have been shot for any number of reasons. He might not even have been shooting at you. As for whoever wrote that trash he sounds as daft as you are.'

Helen returned to watching the *'Eastenders Omnibus'*. She hadn't always been like this. They used to talk about politics and philosophy and all the great novels. Now, the works of Hardy and Austin were gathering dust in the garage and been replaced by a vast library of chick-lit in the book-case. Helen never bothered to vote any more. *'They are all as bad as each other'* she would say. If the New World Order did take control she would probably give them the benefit of the doubt as long as they didn't take *'I'm a Celebrity'* off the air!

Kyle wanted very much to talk about the separation and whether or not they should try marriage guidance for Nathan's sake but her lack of interest in his dice with death and his brother's funeral made him certain marriage guidance would be a waste of time and money. It was at this point that he realized his marriage was almost certainly over.

Kyle drove back to John's flat thinking of all the happy times Helen and him had enjoyed together. A photo album of family holidays, birthdays, Christmas' and nights out as a couple flashed through his mind. It was terribly sad that it was all over but he couldn't made excuses for Helen's behaviour any longer. Depression or not, if she had been like this when they first started courting they never would have got past the first few weeks. It was time to accept fate and move on.

The next day Kyle found it really hard to retain focus on work. His mind kept drifting off to what the five phases might be. He didn't tell anyone in his office about his latest reading material and after they had exhausted talking about the funeral, New York and the football the three older ones in the office knuckled down to work.

There were 5 in the office. Kyle was the section manager and Brenda, a frightfully efficient woman in her 50s his right hand woman. Then there was Keith. Keith was about Kyle's age and was very thorough but had the charisma of a wet fish. He could bore the office to tears and he rarely bothered these days.

Then there were the 2 girls: Sam and Donna. Sam was a bubbly, vivacious girl in her early 20s who was curvaceous on a good day and plump on a bad one. She was a talented data analyst but incurably indolent and whenever Kyle looked over her shoulder she seemed to be surfing the web or sending private e-mails. Donna was the same sort of age as Sam and worshipped her. She would follow her every move and Sam loved it. She was skinny with a boyish figure, small features and short, jet -black hair. Kyle was sick of being asked if his two office juniors were lesbians. Having worked with Sam and Donna for five years he had not seen one shred of evidence to suggest this and he didn't think adult movie producers would be queuing up to offer them a starring role either.

Besides, Sam had a boy-friend, who was staging a 25th birthday party on Friday and the whole office plus several other staff at Police HQ were invited. Needless to say Donna was going and Brenda and Keith were not. Kyle hadn't made up his mind yet. A party with a load of 20-somethings could either reinvigorate him or make him feel depressingly old. He was also unsure if he would have finished reading the five phases by Friday.

Sam tried to convince Kyle as she started her daily routine of tidying her things away at 4.00 p.m. that he needed to get out and meet other women now he was separated. Donna added mischievously *'Alicia will be there'*. Alicia Bell was the pin-up of Police HQ. The 24 year old HR Assistant was always tanned, fresh-faced and immaculately presented. She had big brown eyes that contrasted deeply with her long-blonde hair. She was slim, 5 feet 6 and according to rumour an impressive 34DD. She delighted in teasing her many admirers with a tantalising array of figure-hugging work outfits. She always had a boyfriend but they rarely lasted more than a few weeks. Maybe a caring, older man was just what she needed fantasised Kyle.

Kyle left the office soon after Sam and Donna, hoping his boss wouldn't come by and spot the office practically deserted by half past 4. He planned to read the first phase tonight. However, when he clicked on the hyperlink to open the file he was faced with an unexpected message:

'Please enter your personal password for phase 1'

'Oh sugar!' said Kyle.

More in hope than expectation he entered *'illuminati'*, *'phase 1'* and *'the first phase'* in succession. On the 3rd failure a message was displayed:

'You have been locked out. If you have forgotten your password please contact your recruiter who authorised you to read this file'.

'Great!' commented Kyle ironically. He had been naive to think that a single guessable password could gain him access to confidential material. Now it looked like he was going to be left in the dark regarding the secret machination of the enlightened ones to take over the Earth. Maybe he should just try and forget he ever took that Armani jacket and get on with a normal life, starting with going to Sam's boyfriend's party on Friday night and having a bloody good piss-up.

Scene 4: Sunrise over Sunniside

Kyle welcomed the fact that the rest of the week passed fairly uneventfully. He decided that he had overstayed his welcome at John's flat and moved into a flat in Gosforth. He struck lucky for the first time in ages. A banker made redundant from Northern Rock had decided to supplement his income by letting part of his house in this up-market area and Kyle had been first to view it. The poor guy was desperate and took Kyle's deposit there and then. Two days later he heard that he had secured a temporary job in London and thus Kyle was going to have the run of the whole house for 6 months at a bargain rent.

Sam had told Kyle he could take a friend to the party and Kyle had asked John as a kind of going away gift. They each brought a bottle at the off license and boarded the bus to Benwell. John joked that they should take a bulletproof vest; such is Benwell's notoriety as Newcastle's answer to Brixton. It used to be an ordinary student area with rows of terraced houses sloping 'Hovis-fashion' down to the North bank of the Tyne, but then years of neglect by landlords led to such a state of decline that even students found the properties too scruffy and less reputable tenants moved in.

In the dying years of the last Conservative government, Benwell's fall from grace was complete. Half the houses were boarded up and vandalised. Some were set alight, some were stripped of slates from roofs and others were daubed in threatening graffiti. Stuck in this hell-hole were a few privately owned houses. The terrified owners had bought their houses when the area was decent, but were now barricaded in night after night. The Council rescued them from negative equity by buying the houses up and selling them for the princely sum of 50 pence to anyone willing to renovate them. The idea worked. The area is still a world away from salubrious Gosforth but the houses are now fetching over £100, 000, making a mockery of those that said investors were mad to buy property in a war zone.

Sam lived with her boyfriend in a large refurbished terraced house that had been converted into four flats with a communal lounge, kitchen, bathroom and back yard. The noise of people shouting at each other over the top of thumping club tunes could be heard all the way up the street to the West Road. A stranger opened the door already looking vacant and let them in without challenge. They squeezed past an old bicycle and a young couple French-kissing in the hall and found Sam and Donna laughing raucously in the kitchen. Sam swigged from a plastic bottle of cider and hugged Kyle and John warmly. She took their bottle and led them to the beer. Kyle tried not to look disappointed at the choice of cheap lager on offer. John was already checking out the talent.

As expected, they were the only people that looked over 35 and worse still the vast majority were probably under 25. *'Wow. Great party'* said John, his eyes fixed on two teenagers in mini-skirts and very little else. *'Howay man'* said Kyle disapprovingly before adding *'They're young enough to be our daughters'*.

The lager tasted like fizzy piss and the music sounded like the stereo had got stuck on the drum and bass bit and just kept repeating it without anyone noticing. Worse still there was no sign of Alicia and there was hardly anyone from work there. Kyle went for a wander and found Will from Finance, who greeted him and introduced him to some other guests. A few beers later, a fight broke out in the hall and a skinny skinhead went crashing over the bicycle. He got to his feet and the scrap spilled out on to the street with a crowd gathering, some as peacemakers; others egging them on.

Kyle retreated into the back yard and breathed in the fresh October air. A half moon lit up the sky and a cool wind blew rotten leaves along the dirty alley that separated this terrace from the next one. He looked at his watch and wondered whether he was too late for the last bus to Gosforth. It read 11.15. He might still be able to get a bus into town and then a metro to Gosforth. However, when he found John he was set on staying. *'I think I'm in there'* he said with an inane grin. *'I wouldn't be so sure'* Kyle replied seeing that Donna was the target of John's courtship.

Kyle found the bottle of red wine he had brought was still unopened and searched for a cork-screw. A huge biker with a goatee beard and tattoos everywhere obliged with a Swiss army knife.

'That was good timing' said Alicia as she glided into the kitchen. Kyle was intimidated by her beauty and couldn't get his words out but she just smiled and held out an empty glass. She was wearing a short, see-through, shoulderless dress ordained with sequins and despite the cold weather her gorgeous brown legs were naked. Kyle decided that this beautiful vision had vindicated his decision to stay for another drink.

Time seemed to fly by after that. Kyle began to acclimatise to the party scene and imagine he was in Ibiza, young, free and single. He always did have a vivid imagination. John had given up on Donna and walked straight on to his next victim, who looked too pissed to notice his clumsy directness. Alicia had chatted to Kyle long enough to make him feel special before talking even longer to Sam. *'Were they talking about me?'* Kyle deliberated. A car alarm went off and half the party went outside to chase the thieves only to startle a fox that had been raiding the bins and had probably set the alarm off.

An ugly girl dragged Kyle on to a wild dance floor where people were being flung round crashing into furniture to the sound of *'Come on Eileen'*. *'The old ones are the best'* declared Kyle laughing as he was pushed into the middle of a circle that breathed in and out, round and round until rising to a crescendo in which everyone fell in a heap on the sticky floor.

Kyle thought he'd go and find Alicia again. Maybe he wasn't too old after all. She was being flagrantly chatted up by a tall man in a torn white t-shirt. Kyle stood and took on his rival; the two of them exchanging combative looks like knights before a dual. Alicia was charming as usual but Kyle began to realize he was losing the battle to his younger opponent and when he came back from the bathroom he found them kissing on the stairs. John thought he looked a bit too rough for Alicia but earlier Alicia had told Sam and Donna *'Core. He's a bit of rough'*.

Alicia always got her man. Earlier she had given Kyle hope by telling him about her split from her useless boyfriend who was only after one thing. It's strange how they always are with you Alicia, Kyle had thought. *'Bastard'* he had said.

Kyle looked at his watch. It was exactly 2.00 p.m. on a Friday night. He tried booking a taxi but the earliest one could promise to get there for was 3 in the morning. *'Don't worry mate'* said Sam's boy-friend. *'You can crash out here'* and he went and got a sleeping bag and showed him to a room where six bodies were already stretched out in the land of nod. Kyle thought Sam's boyfriend looked a lot older than 25. He had a world-weary face, pale skin and sullen eyes. Kyle wondered if he did drugs.

He lay on the floor watching the walls and ceilings spin round and feeling the humiliating taste of sick in his mouth. He held his hand over his mouth and made it to the loo. If he hadn't felt sick before, he certainly did now. If someone had drawn him in the puke stakes they were in for a disappointment. The bathroom reeked of fresh puke and there were remains on the toilet seat and the rug. Kyle emptied his guts and emerged furtively from the bathroom. He briefly lost his sense of direction and wandered into the wrong room. A girl screamed and Kyle said *'sorry'*, amazed to see that the startled girl was Donna and she was sitting on the bed in just her knickers next to a naked bloke. She covered her chest instinctively but Kyle thought she needn't have bothered. She was just as he had imagined; flat as a pancake. Kyle fell asleep chuckling to himself about the gossip he could send round HQ on Monday. This will put an end to those lesbian jibes he thought. However, in the morning when he got out into the fresh air and sat on the wall drinking tap water from a pint glass he thought better of it. She was one of his staff and deserved some privacy. Besides the blokes would probably just decide that Sam and Donna were bi-sexual! Kyle wondered whether Alicia had shagged that rough bloke. There was no sign of them this morning.

He turned his head and looked south over the Tyne to the hills of Whickham and Sunniside. The sun was rising above the hills and the grey clouds and Tyneside was slowly waking with a hangover. Kyle's head was thumping and he concluded that he was too old for this hedonistic life-style. It had seemed fine when he was 21 but now he was 42 he would have to look for new ways of meeting someone special. Lonely but enlightened he began the ascent of the street back to the hustle and bustle of the West Road and a date with a greasy spoon and a tin of Red Bull.

Scene 5: Professor of History

For a secret society there was an incredible volume of public information about the *'illuminati'*. Kyle playfully typed the word into Google and was staggered to get almost 10 million hits! A wet Saturday in October disappeared as he diligently researched the topic. Sure, there was copious speculation and hyperbole but there were enough sound facts and data to triangulate the historical accuracy of the *'Books of the Illuminati'*.

Kyle typed the names of the 3 authors into Google and found that one was an American businessman, one a German scientist and the third Professor Huge Lyons was a Professor of History at Cambridge University. Kyle's curiosity was aroused. The Professor was also a prolific writer with a fascination for American history and 19th Century politics. Kyle obtained a number for the publisher of these weighty books and picked up the telephone.

'Sorry to trouble you but I'm trying to track down an old University chum, Professor Hugh Lyons. I know you published his works, would you happen to have a contact number?'

'I'm afraid Professor Lyons got diagnosed with Parkinson's Disease last year, Sir. He hasn't been in touch for some time. I might be able to get you the name of the hospice where he last wrote to us from. Hang on a minute.'

A good three minutes later the lady returned: *'Yes. If you try St Francis' Hospice in St Neots they might be able to help you.'*

'Thank you. You've been very helpful'.

Kyle obtained the address of the hospice and set his alarm to drive down the A1 first thing on Sunday Morning.

The hospice receptionist was extremely suspicious of Kyle arriving unannounced at 11.00 on a Sunday morning. She went away and returned shaking her head. *'I'm sorry. Professor Lyons does not wish to see any visitors today'.*

'Wait' said Kyle as she turned away to return to some filing. *'Tell him I need to see him urgently about the brotherhood'.*

That did the trick and 5 minutes later he was ushered through a maze of corridors for an audience with the Professor of History. Professor Lyons sat propped up with a pillow peering over some small-rimmed spectacles at a crossword puzzle. He looked well into his 70's, frail but alert and slightly eccentric.

'Come into my office Mr Forster' he beckoned. *'Id offer you a pew and a drink but alas I am not as agile as I used to be'*

'*Can I get you something Professor*', Kyle said looking at the jug of water at his bedside.

'*Thank you Mr Forster. That's very kind. I will have a bottle of Hobgoblin please*'

Kyle looked at him quizzically, unsure if he was joking.

'*In the cupboard methinks. Help yourself to one my good man*'

Kyle opened two bottles of the potent, dark beer and poured them expertly into two pint glasses beside the water jug.

'*Ah that hits that spot*' the professor said. '*Tell me Mr Forster do you like your real ale?*'

'*Yes. Rather too much*'

'*What do you think? Roasted malt with a hint of spice and dark berries?*'

'*Yes. It's full of flavour. I'm surprised they let you bring alcohol in here but!*'

'*Nonsense! Alcohol won't kill me. It's this dam disease that will account for me. Anyway, I hear your business is urgent so you'd better crack on before I pop my clogs.*'

Kyle told him how he had come to read the books and said that he wanted to join the '*Illuminati*' and to read more. The Professor roared with laughter.

'*My dear fellow; you can't apply to join the Illuminati. They choose you; not the other way round*'.

'*How will you ever get enough members if you don't encourage people to join?*' asked Kyle.

'*Quality not quantity is the key. Tell me Mr Forster; are you a senior politician, a brilliant scientist or a mover and shaker in the business world? Do you have a few million in a Swiss Bank account or maybe your best friends with a top civil servant?*'

'*No, but the New World Order is about skills and intellect, not power and money*'.

'*True, but there won't be a New World Order without influencing the movers and shakers be and a huge wad of cash will there?*'

Kyle thought for a moment and came back with a different tact, whilst the Professor rubbed his chin in contemplation at his cross-word.

'*I would like you to tell me the passwords for the 5 phases'. I hate only knowing half the story*'.

'I see! You know about the pillar of confidentiality; the great risks involved with passing the secrets on to the unworthy; but you thought a senile old man might let you have them anyway.'

'No. You are far from senile. You write beautifully and I want to read more'.

'Thank you but things are not that simple. The plan is at a delicate stage. There has been a power struggle within the brotherhood and I'm sorry to say my views are not flavour of the day. User passwords are changed 4 times a year and mine have expired. I couldn't help you if I wanted to. I am worried where things are going to tell the truth. It was a noble cause. We took such care to avoid splits and represent all views as long as they agreed with our core aims. At our policy making forums we had equal numbers of liberals and conservatives and time after time logical argument won the day. Now with the fifth phase nearing by the day there are dark forces at work. The forces believe the end will always justify the means no matter how vile those means are.'

'Don't you have influence within the brotherhood now as a co-author of the Books?'

'My force is to keep alive, inspiring the true enlightened ones to stay loyal; a mere figurehead now Mr Forster. I'm no longer within the circle. I, like you, can't make history. We are history'.

'So, who is making the history?'

'There is a hierarchy in place in every region of every westernised nation with a Chief Executive at the top pulling the strings. You'd be amazed if you knew the names of some of these people. I can't tell you but there are some very famous names. As Disraeli once said it's amazing where the power truly lies. One thing is for sure, it's not with the electorate. Democracy is a lie'

'Are you still in touch with any of these power brokers?'

'No. I am in touch with a few people at a lower tier in the hierarchy. Good people who want a fairer world, but some of them are getting cold feet about the whole thing.'

'Could you put me in touch with one who might be able to help me get the passwords?'

'Possibly, but it would be very dangerous, especially if you have been already targeted by an Illuminati hit-man, which is certainly possible. I would need to sound them out first. I'd hate to put old friends at risk. I'm sure my calls are monitored.'

'Use my phone'.

'Wait outside. I need 5 minutes. No promises but.'

'*Thanks Professor*'.

Kyle paced the corridor until a nurse beckoned him back. '*Well*', he said impatiently.

'*Dougie Lawton would like to meet you. He's a lecturer at Edinburgh University. You will like him as he loves his real ale almost as much as his single malts. He will be in touch. Now before you go would you pass me that Good Beer Guide over there?*'

Kyle thanked him and passed him the Guide. The professor produced a pen from his pocket and ripped a small piece of the Times off, looking up over his glasses. He wrote something down and put it inside the Guide before adding:

'*I would like you to take this Guide and a top tip on where to get an excellent pint of Bitter and Twisted as a present for coming all the way from Geordieland to see me*'.

'*That's very kind but I couldn't possibly*'.

'*I insist. I'm not likely to get to see any of these places and I've read it cover to cover several times. Besides, Dougie loves his wee pint of Bitter and Twisted*', he said with a lifting of the eye-brows.

Kyle took the Guide and bade his farewell. The old man raised his glass and winked. Just as he was exiting the old Professor called: '*Think carefully before your next move. I am dying a long, slow painful death. I am 79 next week. With a fair wind and the excellent care in this place I might make it to see my 80th. But you, my friend; you are not long for this world*'.

Kyle peeled open the Good Beer Guide. It opened on Northumberland and on the small torn piece of newspaper were the words:

'*Dougie. Wednesday at 3. Half-way, Edinburgh.*'

Kyle solved the riddle instantly. Half-way to Edinburgh there must be a pub selling Bitter and Twisted ale that Dougie has agreed to meet me on Wednesday afternoon in. The words '*Bitter and Twisted*' leapt off the open page. There was a pub in Berwick upon Tweed listed in the Guide that sold this fine Scottish ale. Looks like a half day on Wednesday, decided Kyle as he embarked on the long journey back up the A1.

Scene 6: Half-Way House

Kyle had planned his half day off work meticulously. The train crossed the Tweed at altitude and glided into Berwick Station on the Scottish side of the historic border. He had an hour to spare and his research suggested the *'Barrels Ale House'* was the intended rendezvous and stood by the river on the main road through the town. It was a fine October morning with a cold Easterly breeze swirling off the North Sea.

Something troubled Kyle as he stepped off the train. A gust of wind added to his discomfort and stopped him in his tracks. It was true that Berwick was half way between Newcastle and Edinburgh and the Good Beer Guide had opened at the page describing 4 pubs in the town, only 1 of which served Dougie's favourite tipple. However:

1. how did the Professor know Kyle actually lived in Newcastle? He had never mentioned his address and although he had a strong Geordie accent there were Geordies living all over the world; and

2. the Professor hadn't inserted the cryptic note carefully in the Northumberland section of the Guide. Kyle couldn't recall if he even looked at where he was placing it as he handed the Guide to him.

The last of the train doors shut and the Guard scanned the platform before raising his flag. Instinctively, Kyle turned back to the train hoping the central locking hadn't kicked in. He was just in time. One of the doors half opened and got jammed. The Guard's whistle blew. Kyle managed to lever the door open and jump on just as the train resumed its journey to Edinburgh.

Kyle frantically flicked through the Good Beer Guide until he found the 20 pubs listed under Edinburgh.

'Yes' he declared aloud.

There was a pub selling *'Bitter and Twisted'* called *'The Half Way House'*! He looked again at the Professor's note and suddenly it made sense.

There was a comma between *'Half Way'* and *'Edinburgh'* nor the word 'to'. The Professor had not been testing Kyle's geographical knowledge but merely stating the name and location of the meeting. Kyle laughed at his own stupidity as he settled back in the chair. Thankfully, there was an hour to spare and the pub was near Waverley Station. Barring leaves on the line at Dunbar he should just about make it on time.

*****

Kyle strolled purposefully out of Waverley Station and sucked in the fresh air. It tasted more like mountain air than the air of a Capital City. As he turned left to the sound of bagpipes the sight of Arthur's Seat disappearing into the clouds confirmed his senses. He fought his way through the throngs of tourists on Waverley Bridge and past the Edinburgh Dungeon searching for the steps that led up to the Royal Mile.

Half way up the steps stood the cosy Scottish inn known as the Half-Way House. Kyle checked his watch and admired his perfect timing. There were half a dozen people perched on stools at the bar and a family in the corner by the juke-box. Suddenly it dawned on Kyle hat he had no idea what Dougie looked like and he could not be sure that Dougie knew him from Adam either. As there was no instant acknowledgement of his entry he bought himself a pint of Bitter and Twisted and went and sat in the opposite corner of the bar facing the entrance.

The bar was small enough for him to compare the colour of his pint to others being quaffed and he identified one possible match. He put the Good Beer Guide on the table with the Professor's note visible and made eye contact with the Bitter and Twisted drinker. He looked back discomforted and turned to the lady next to him. She looked over at Kyle, said something and the two of them resumed their conversation, leaving Kyle feeling embarrassed.

At that moment Kyle's mobile went off and he hunted for it in his pockets. He got the call just in time. It was Elton John on the line.

'Hi Elton' he said trying to hide his disappointment.

'I'm in the toon. Do you fancy a bevy after work?'

'Sorry. I'm not at work. I've taken a half day. I'm in Edinburgh'

'Edinburgh! What the fuck are you doing there mate?'

'It's a long story. Another time maybe'

'Yes. No problem. I'll arrange something with the lads. Bye'

'See you Elton'.

Kyle returned to his pint. It wasn't bad: a bit light and hoppy for Kyle's taste. He certainly wouldn't have travelled 100 miles for it! At that moment the door swung open. However, it was an old man who looked like he had been in every pub in the Guide. Kyle checked his watch again. Fifteen minutes late! Maybe Dougie had been scared off. The Professor had indicated he would be putting himself in danger by discussing Illuminati business with an outsider.

A barman brought some cutlery out for the family by the juke-box and one of the kids started playing up throwing beer mats at his sibling, much to their mother's embarrassment. Kyle swirled the bottom of his pint around and wondered if it was worth getting another.

At that moment one of the men at the bar came over and pointed at the Guide.

'This pub has been in that Guide for 25 years you know' he said in a pleasant Scottish twang.

'Aye, it's a canny little pub. Serves a good pint of Bitter and Twisted.'

'Does indeed! Can I get you another one?'

'Thanks. I'm Kyle', Kyle said holding out his hand.

'Dougie' the man replied shaking Kyle's hand and returning to the bar.

He returned with a pint for Kyle and a double whiskey for himself. *'I thought the Professor said you were a Bitter and Twisted man'*, Kyle said pointing at the whiskey.

'Charming! I've been called many things but never bitter and twisted before'. They laughed and he added more quietly *'Walls have ears. Please whisper anything about the Professor and his works'.*

'OK.'

'I can't stay long so a wee dram suits me better than a long pint.'

'Did the Professor tell you why I wanted to see you?' Kyle whispered.

'Aye that he did'.

'Have you got the passwords?'

'What do you want them for? The books are not something you can order from Amazon you know.'

'It's a personal interest. I came across the introduction and found it compelling. However, I believe someone tried to shoot me to stop me reading them and I want to find out what's so bad about them'.

'Compelling, you say? Are you sure you are on your own, not reporting back to the any higher powers or any media?'

'I'm on my own. I'm a junior manager in the public sector. I don't have any power or influence. You are my only hope of learning about the Illuminati secrets.'

Dougie took a big swig of whiskey and pondered his dilemma.

'You do realize what you are asking puts yourself and your family at great danger. Are you sure you want to do this'.

'Yes. I know the risks'.

'*And you will never disclose your source?*'

'*Definitely not*'.

'*I don't know how much you know but there is a big power struggle within the brotherhood. I've backed the wrong horse. I'm having grave reservations about what I used to believe in the closer it gets to the day of reckoning. Those that have spoken out from within have met mysterious deaths. Just by talking to you I fear for my life. I wonder if my phones are tapped. I wonder if my movements are tracked. I am here because the Professor was a hero of mine. He taught me history at Cambridge and now I lecture myself at Edinburgh. I am his protégé. I also half hoped you would be acting for the Government or the Secret Services, but in my heart I know it is too late to stop the New World Order. Que Sera, sera*'!

'*What is the power struggle about?*'

'*We have always believed that the New World Order should not be about left and right, liberals and conservatives. That is why we try and keep the number of liberals and conservatives even and advocate reasoned consensus. However, that's easy when you are a theoretical debating society; not so easy when the prospect of power is real. As the day approaches the right wing of the Illuminati have taken control and developed policies I find abhorrent. Liberals like the Professor and I have been side-lined*'.

'*I see. And you think the New World Order will happen and be dangerously right-wing?*'

'*It's not a question of if, it's a question of when and that's the other split in the ranks. The books teach us to be patient and wait for society to be so broken that our takeover is not challenged and the coup is bloodless. The leadership have now decided that the coup must happen in January 2009 and the end justifies the means. There will be violence almost on World War 3 scales if necessary. Peace has gone out of the window*'.

'*Why must it happen in January?*'

'*Ever since the settlers conquered North America the Illuminati and its associates have dominated American politics. Roughly 9 out of 10 presidents of the USA have either been members or sympathisers. The exceptions like Kennedy on the left and Nixon on the right have been promptly removed from office in suspicious circumstances. The brotherhood dominates the Republican and Democratic parties, the CIA, the FBI, and the Pentagon. All the power is with Masons and former members of The Skull and Bones. Normally the American people don't decide their president, the Illuminati do. This time the chosen one looks to have lost out. The Illuminati thought they had both the Republican and Democrat nominations sewn up. They hadn't counted on Barack Obama.*'

'*Correct. Obama is ahead in the polls and I assume January is when he gets sworn in.*'

'Aye. Obama could wreck centuries of planning. I wouldn't rule out an as-sassination but the official line is the plan will be fast-tracked and the New World Order will be sworn in the day before the new President is due to take office'.

Dougie suddenly shivered and dried up. He had got swept away by his own need to get his concerns off his chest and now felt guilty for being more candid than he had intended. He looked around furtively and finished his whiskey.

'That's a fine single malt' he said. 'A 25 year old Laphroaig. I recommend it. You might need it!'

'Thanks. I might try one before I go'.

'I will leave you some tips for more malt whiskies to assist your stay' Dougie said loudly handing Kyle a bit of paper and getting to his feet.

'It's been canny meeting you. Take care, Kyle' he said as he left.

'You too!'

Kyle went to the Gents and unfolded the piece of paper. There were several complex codes mixing numbers, letters and alpha-numeric characters in a way that could never be remembered. He put the piece of paper in his pocket congratulating himself on getting the passwords for the five phases. How-ever, one thing confused Kyle. There were 6 passwords!

*****

It had got dark when Kyle left the convivial ambience of the Half-Way House. The stars lit up the sky above the New Town and the waters of Leith. A few revellers had gathered outside and were smoking and drinking in a stone walled beer terrace. Ahead of him down the steps a tramp sat with his blan-kets and his trusted, canine companion and a hat set out for small change.

Kyle started his descent of the steep steps. Suddenly, a foot came out of the shadows. He tripped and was hurtling forward head-first towards the hard stone steps. Kyle prepared for excruciating pain. Thud! His head hit the steps. There was pain. There was blood. He fell unconscious.

However, the pain was not as bad as he had anticipated. One of the revellers told the Police as he was carried into the Ambulance:

'He just seemed to lose his footing as he came out of the pub. He must have had one too many, but with amazing reactions the old tramp chucked out his rags and bedding to soften the impact. That tramp probably saved the drunks life!'

Scene 7: The Five Phases

Kyle sat propped up with huge pillows in his hospital bed transfixed by the second hand of the clock. The ward was stuffy and silent. Every bone in his body seemed to ache. Why, he thought, does time move so much slower when you are waiting for something. Still, he consoled himself, only another 45 minutes and he could call the nurse for another injection of painkillers. Then, for at least two glorious hours, the pain will be numbed.

Kyle had come round in the middle of the night and called out for attention in the dark. A consultant had seen him and he'd been to x-ray and for a brain scan. A kindly nurse with a moon-face had contacted Helen and Nathan and kept them informed. She had also made enquiries about the tramp. Kyle had been eager to thank him personally but apparently he disappeared when the Police had arrived and started interviewing people. Kyle knew they wouldn't take any action. He remembered being tripped but nobody would believe it wasn't an accident; just another Sassenach who couldn't handle his scotch.

Kyle's ears pricked up at the sound of heels on the hard, polished floor. The sound got louder but then quieter again as the person passed by along the corridor. Kyle realized he could not turn his head to observe the stranger pass and once more his eyes fixed on the clock.

Every movement was painful. He shuffled on the bed to reach into a pocket and confirm the note he had been given in the pub was still there. It was. The note contained six cryptic passwords, which hopefully unlocked the 5 files on his lap-top in Gosforth. Kyle deliberated on what the sixth password could be for but thinking was painful. Suddenly, there were more footsteps and two doctors and a nurse arrived in his ward, all with papers. Kyle's head hurt and he feared the worst.

'We've got the results of your brain scan, Mr Forster' the most senior looking of the three medics announced.

'*It's not good news is it?*' Kyle responded.

'*Well, there is some damage*' continued the surgeon as if he was commenting on the weather rather than Kyle's brain tissue. He held out the scan and pointed at a slight variation in the shading.

'*However*', he said with a wry smile. '*The good news is that part of the brain is barely used tissue. I'm pretty confident you will make a full recovery. You've been pretty lucky. All being well we will discharge you tomorrow and suggest your GP refers you for a check-up in a month's time*'.

'*Oh, thank God!*' said Kyle, breathing out audibly.

Almost by magic the pain eased and the last half an hour wait to his next dose of codeine passed relatively quickly.

The doctor was true to his word. He was discharged at noon the following day with a week's supply of painkillers and a note for his GP. Kyle re-traced his steps in the Old Town and shuddered as he found the place where he fell. There was no sign of the tramp that had saved his life, but Kyle bought a copy of the Big Issue on his way back to the station to ease his conscience.

He made several phone-calls on the way home and his friends and family sounded genuinely relieved for him, but he had to keep them brief as the battery was running low. Kyle still felt numb all over as if the events of the past few weeks had been some elaborate dream and he was only just beginning to get his senses back. However, reality hit him as soon as he turned into the leafy avenue where he had recently taken up residence.

*****

The flashing blue light on his burglar alarm sent a shiver down his spine. He put the key in the door but the door opened without turning it. There were papers strewn in the hall and an eerie, hollow feeling throughout the house. Kyle reset the alarm and surveyed each room for missing items. The intruders had made a mess but they had not taken any of the usual spoils. The TV, DVD, Hi-fi, digital camera, MP3; they were all still there. Even the car keys that Kyle had carelessly left on display in the kitchen were untouched. There was only one thing missing. The thieves had stolen Kyle's PC!

Kyle called the Police and was impressed with their quick response. Maybe they knew he recorded statistics on their response time or maybe they were just in the neighbourhood and having a quiet day. Anyway, they took down all the details, could not find any prints and decided that the robbers were probably kids stealing lap-tops to order and had fled on foot as soon as they had found their booty. Kyle didn't have the energy to try and convince them otherwise, especially after the young copper had remarked on Kyle's nasty blow to the head, evident from the bandages and swelling.

Kyle contacted his insurance company and confirmed that he was covered. He tidied up and left the house. He felt sick knowing his enemy had already located his new abode and could return to finish him off at any point. He walked up to Jesmond Dene, a beautiful wooded valley less than 2 miles from the heart of the vibrant city, and sat for a while by the waterfall. For a moment he contemplated going back to the safety of his Wallsend home, hugging his wife and forgiving her affair. He thought of Nathan smiling and he smiled too. He considered abandoning political meddling and living a normal life again.

It started to rain and he sheltered under the tall trees considering his next move. If he could be sure that the Illuminati only wanted to scare him off he would have headed east and caught a bus along the Coast Road to Wallsend. However, he could not be sure. They had tried to kill him twice. He was sure of that now. He suspected they would count on it being third time lucky and if he went home he would endanger his family. Reluctantly, he held his head up high and turned West towards Gosforth.

He almost expected to see the alarm light flashing again when he got back but all was quiet. He took the car and went to buy a new PC. The Illuminati had under-estimated his gumption and resolve. In one pocket he had a note handed to him by a Scottish lecturer. In the other pocket he had a memory stick. He took a back-up of his PC religiously every week. The secrets of the five phases were about to be revealed.

*****

Kyle opened each file to ensure the passwords worked and read the titles of each phase. They were:

1. infiltration;

2. globalisation;

3. communication;

4. economic collapse; and

5. taking control.

There was no clue as to the purpose of the sixth password, which did not unlock any of the phases or the introduction. Each file was a book in its own right and Kyle decided he would need to take his time to read the secrets that the Illuminati had been so determined to protect. He did not know if he would live to read the final phase and part of him no longer cared.

Kyle spent most of the weekend reading about the first phase. Each hour that passed he grew stronger and more confident that his assailants were not about to return. The pain in the final hour before the painkillers were due became less acute. The house became less threatening and lonely. He was absorbed in his reading and he made copious notes.

In total he listed 20 key findings about the Illuminati's plans for infiltration:

1. infiltration would take several generations to achieve so parents would need to pass the message down to their enlightened off-spring;

2. all wealthy and powerful institutions would be infiltrated. Political parties, major companies, banks, armies, senior police officers and civil servants; they were all fair game;

3. power-bases would be built through associates such as the Free-

masons, the Round Table and other secret and elitist organisations;

4. eventually, associates would become so dominated by Illuminati that boundaries would become blurred;

5. the New World (by which the books seemed to mean the USA) would become a pilot scheme for the New World Order;

6. right from the start the Illuminati would set up two apparently rival parties, one liberal and one conservative and thus whichever party the people chose to elect the Illuminati would retain control;

7. the New World would use commerce and science to exert power and influence over less advanced and rich nations;

8. huge wealth would be used to buy favours and secure a network of people that owed their own fortunes to the brotherhood even if they did not wish to become members;

9. countries with rich natural resources would be targeted and coerced into allegiances with the New World;

10. each member would be tasked with recruiting at least 1, 000 new members in their life-time by targeting the rich and powerful and the intellectual elite;

11. newspapers and mass media would be gradually bought up by Illuminati tycoons so public opinion could be shaped;

12. science would be advanced to develop huge sticks and carrots in the form of inventions that could destroy or save the planet depending on whether the people embraced the New World Order or not;

13. annual meetings would be held of some of the most influential members of the generation to review progress and decide on the next steps;

14. secrecy would be maintained at all times and detailed plans would be known only by a chosen few;

15. allegiances would be formed and broken in order to exploit changes in political thinking around the world;

16. science would be used to crush the influence of religion in the developed world, disproving many of the gospels and playing one religion off against another;

17. threats to the brotherhood would be removed in whatever way was expedient, noting that the noble aim of world peace and prosperity justified the means, however unpleasant that was;

18. advertising would be used to create an insatiable demand around the world for brands backed by Illuminati industrialists;

19. corporate mergers and takeovers would be used to develop friendly international corporations and infiltrated regulators would be used to block unfriendly ones; and

20. universities would be used to groom future leaders and form bonds between the geniuses of each generation.

Kyle read about how the brotherhood had already achieved phase 1 by the 1930's and a split had opened up between those that felt the time had come to take control on the back of the Great Depression and those that disagreed. Eventually the leaders felt that both fascism and communism were too obsessed with nationalism and suppression of freedom to provide a Trojan horse to power. It was not until Pearl Harbour that the USA and thus the Illuminati finally took sides and postponed the New World Order.

The economic success of the 50's and 60's led the brotherhood to return to the shadows, gradually expanding influence but not seeking to rival the social democratic consensus that was bridging the Atlantic. Then they infiltrated the Unions and stirred such militancy that the consensus broke down in chaos and stagflation. The conservative reaction of the 1980's was inevitable; as was the failure of their laissez faire economics.

The trust of right-wing governments in big business and unregulated profit-seekers was music to the brotherhood's ears. They began to get a stranglehold on a new breed of financial institution, which was mutating and infecting the world's major economies. Centuries of infiltration were matched by a single decade of unbridled growth and innovation in the Illuminati-dominated world of private equity firms and investment banks. By the time of Bush and Blair, phase 1 was well and truly complete.

Scene 8: A safety-net with holes

Normally Kyle would have ignored his doctor's advice to take it easy and have a few days off work. However, phase 1 had wetted his appetite to read the remaining 4 books and so he through a sickie and got down to some serious reading.

Phase 2 commenced with a long justification for the New World Order. It was as if the authors had realized the long thesis on infiltration might have scared off potential recruits and decided to remind readers why it was necessary. The horrors of war were portrayed graphically and the case for one world, one government and one peace-keeping army put quite persuasively. The argument was that as long as different nations existed there would be dangerous nationalism and self-interest that led to territorial disputes, hatred and conflict. Only a united takeover by the international elite could end the spiral of misery, war, destruction and hunger.

Graphs charted the environmental Armageddon the world was heading for and the grave consequences of unchecked population growth. The question was asked – why would developing super-powers like China and India stop the industrial and population growth that Europe and America had made long before global warming was proven? The answer was they wouldn't unless they were forced to by a United Nations with teeth or rather a brotherhood with control of the nation's economy and nuclear scientists.

The case for globalisation was put in the context of Earth being a small planet in a vast solar system without a divine right to be blessed with life. If an alien invasion ever happened they would find our planet insular, parochial and divided. There would be no agreed response or co-ordinated defence and the aliens would soon gain control and establish the sort of global meritocracy that the Illuminati advocated. Borders were created by young bucks stamping out their territory and they made no sense in the modern world. They were a sign of a primitive, tribal society that allowed suspicion and mistrust to defeat the progress possible through co-operation.

The final part of phase 2 focused on the extent to which the World was already globalised. Multi-national companies had come to dominate trade and most sizeable businesses had changed hands many times often ending up as one branch of some international conglomerate. Virtually every City around the world had branches of McDonalds, Pizza Hut and Starbucks. American and European TV, film and music had long replaced indigenous cultures and English had become the international language of the cultured and intellectual.

Kyle hadn't realised that Esperanto had been an Illuminati initiative to stimulate internationalism. They soon realized it was too complicated and through their weight behind English instead, funding English language classes throughout the World and suppressing rival languages in developing countries.

Kyle realised that phase 2 had been largely achieved during his lifetime through the Americanisation of the World and he saw the advantages in terms of efficiency, security and peace. He would not mourn the loss of national autonomy and identity but he found all that power resting in one government disturbing. He also had a romantic side that enjoyed travelling and exploring different cultures, rejoicing in diversity and deploring familiarity. It was quite a leap from promoting a New World Order that was united in defeating poverty, hunger, disease and climate change to one where individuality was destroyed and everywhere was the same. It was a leap of faith that Kyle was not prepared to take.

*****

Phase 3 told the story of how scientists had spent centuries trying to develop a global system of communication, which could spread the word over thousands of miles to millions of people in seconds. Without this breakthrough a bloodless, worldwide coup would be impossible. In the 1930's an Illuminati faction argued that all the 5 phases were in place so the time was right to seize power. They were defeated because phase 3 was quite clearly not yet in place. Communication was slow and easily intercepted. Radio signals were blocked and channels had limited reach. The plan was jettisoned.

The position was improved by TV; especially with the advent of satellite TV owned by global entrepreneurs and media magnets, many with Illuminati links. However, there were still many nations where TV was state-controlled and the masses could not be reached.

The Eureka moment came when Illuminati scientists made their greatest discovery; the internet. The internet was the Holy Grail that made stage 5 feasible. It was impossible to suppress. Rebellion could be organised without fear of retribution. Combined with control of most of the World's press and TV, control of the internet allowed the Illuminati to shape world opinion in whichever way it wanted. When the day of reckoning arrived, the message to spill out on to the streets would be sent simultaneously around the World and armies and governments would soon realize that resistance was futile.

As an economist, Kyle found phase 4 engrossing. As far back as 1999 the brotherhood were plotting the economic crisis that was now unfolding and had taken his brother's life. They recognised that the leaders of business and commerce could hold Governments to ransom by threatening to take their wealth, trade and jobs abroad if they were ever regulated or taxed. They embarked on a global charm offensive at the same time as the global economy was on an up-turn and convinced gullible politicians that low regulation and low taxes created the right incentives for wealth creation. The politicians were told how brilliant they were for recognising this link and having the foresight not to meddle.

Of course, Kyle knew that bankers and billionaires who preached the virtue of the free market couldn't give a toss about the state of their host nation's coffers. It was pure greed that motivated them. Yes, they were all for wealth creation - theirs!

Every time a politician became squeamish about the rising inequality of tax havens and pandering to big business, the super-rich pulled out their trump card. Does it matter that we are getting obscenely rich if the whole country is benefitting? What would happen if we moved away and took our businesses and jobs with us?

Of course it did matter. Happiness is more connected to relative than absolute wealth. Inequality breeds envy, crime and depression. The World had never had it so good but it had never been more miserable. The Illuminati knew this and nurtured it. Some members of the brotherhood were among the super-rich and became convinced that the ancient pillar of regulation was no longer part of the brotherhood's manifesto.

In fact, they had been duped. Deregulation was a temporary step to pave the way for phase 4: economic collapse. The enlightened leaders knew that like a fat kid left to run a sweet shop the super-rich would feast on deregulation until they were sick. They couldn't resist the temptation of turning billions into trillions, taking reckless risks with other people's money. They were addicted to greed and believed their own bullshit about being able to out-smart the markets. They surfed on a sea of credit and the waves came crashing down when the poor started defaulting on their loans. Bankers had become so divorced from reality that they didn't understand how anyone could fail to keep up instalments of a few measly dollars a week. The Illuminati knew this. They orchestrated the whole credit crunch from the start.

It was the easiest phase to achieve. Once the World's wealth became concentrated in a few thousand hands it was easy to manipulate. Ensure a few banks go under and the rest come crashing down like a pack of cards. Panic spread through the financial sector, banks stopped lending to each other and the price of credit soared. The press spread disaster stories and queues of old grannies were soon forming to withdraw savings and plunge banks further into debt.

The Wall Street Crash had shown how precarious capitalism is once people stop trusting each other and their banks. Now, with globalisation and communication achieved, a crisis was much easier to engineer. No government could afford to let its banks collapse. All fiscal restraint would go as public money was poured in to keep banks afloat. It wouldn't matter if a Government was an elected democracy or a totalitarian state as their coffers would still be ransacked to save the banks. Rich nations would be brought to the brink of bankruptcy and all the time the Illuminati would be getting richer and stronger; preparing to take control.

The final phase was about using the previous 4 phases to take control through a bloodless coup. A senior management team would agree when the depression was close to bottoming out and despair was at its highest. The model predicted early 2010 but the precise time would depend on economic events and the extent of revolt. At that time, the Illuminati would emerge from the shadows with a plan to save the World.

A summarised version of the books would be published on the Intranet, respected entrepreneurs, scientists and celebrities would appear on TV and in the Press giving a human face to the secret society. All opponents would be silenced or ridiculed and blamed for the misery of millions. The Illuminati plan would be advertised to the extent that people became desensitised to the fear of a secret society taking over the World and began to see it as the only alternative to the failed politics of the early twenty-first century.

Then the internet would be used to tell every citizen in every nation to take to the streets and demand the transfer of power to the management team that was already waiting serenely with a clear action plan. Millions of ordinary people would do so catching the incumbent powers off guard and the next day after seeing the protests on media non-stop for 24 hours there would be millions more. Gradually, Governments would surrender as many of their own members come out of their Illuminati closet to call for change. Centuries of infiltration would at last reap its rewards. There would be no election, no war and no bloodbath. Resistance would crumble. The people would be so desperate for change that they would trust the greatest minds on the planet to work together to solve the crisis, blissfully unaware that it was a crisis of their own making.

Scene 9: Friend or Foe

Kyle yawned and focused his bleary eyes on the small luminous screen of his digital alarm clock. It was 4.30 a.m. and he had set the alarm for 7 to return to work. He lay down and contemplated changing it to half 7 but before he could summon up the energy to do so he dropped off into a deep slumber. He dreamt of chasing Illuminati leaders on a jet-ski up the Tyne, foiling them just as they were about to set off a nuclear bomb near Wallsend and having Helen and Alicia fighting over him in bikinis on the beach at Whitley Bay.

The day at work was a real struggle. There was a deluge of e-mails and paperwork to catch up on and he had a long one to one with Sam, who was in tears about her boyfriend not wanting to go out anymore and just sitting around the flat in Benwell getting wasted. He could have done without it but it sounded like she had been waiting all week to get it off her ample chest.

He was just preparing to leave the office when Helen rang. Recalling his dream, Kyle imagined her jogging along Long Sands in a red bikini and his whole body ached with sexual frustration. She sounded softly spoken and horny and wanted to meet Kyle at the weekend for a chat. Kyle suggested Long Sands and wondered if his luck was about to change! Maybe she was going to plead for him to come home and apologise for her affair, saying she would do anything to make it up to him, including a threesome with Alicia.

Kyle knew before they reached the Coast that there was a chasm between his dreams and reality. Helen looked anxious and aloof and he had to make all the conversation on the Metro. There was an icy wind blowing in off the North Sea as they walked from Tynemouth Metro Station to the Coast. Helen declined his invitation to hold hands and her beautiful big, green eyes were fixed on the cold, grey horizon.

The beach was clean and deserted as they strolled across the golden sands from the Priory rocks towards Whitley Bay. To the right, Kyle watched the huge, swirling, foam-topped waves come crashing in from Norway. To the left, the cliffs rose steeply to meet the elegant Victorian buildings that looked out to sea. Then suddenly Helen stopped in her tracks and said five words:

' *Kyle, I want a divorce*'.

Kyle didn't know what to say so he walked away towards the sea and stood alone in the wet sand until the icy water reached his trainers and drove him inland. He hated failure but in the one thing that mattered to him most, he had failed. His marriage and his family life were over. Helen was so wrapped up in a thick winter coat and woolly scarf that he hardly recognised her from a distance. Eventually, he took a deep breath, approached her and said:

'*Fine!*'

Helen smiled and squeezed his hand. *'I want to do it amicably. If we say we've been living apart for two years rather than two months we can get a quick, no-fault divorce.'*

'And not even mention your affair!'

'Why? Is that what you want; Nathan growing up hating his Mum?'

'No. I know it's best for him to keep things civil.'

'You can still see him every weekend you know. Providing, you give me advance notice that won't be a problem.'

'Are you seeing that bloke from work again?'

'That's none of your business.'

'Let's go. It looks like rain'.

'OK. You should find yourself a girlfriend you know. You're a free agent again now.'

Kyle felt the first spots of rain and lengthened his stride. He didn't feel very free. He was being monitored by a clandestine cult that had tried to kill him twice and knew where he lived. Furthermore, now he was all alone and his lonely heart was running on empty.

*****

Kyle reminded himself that he was a middle-aged, middle manager from Tyneside and not 007. He needed to take the Books of the Illuminati to the appropriate authorities and let them save the world. However, who were the appropriate authorities?

The generations spent infiltrating powerful Western organisations meant there were Illuminati members and sympathisers everywhere and rather inconveniently they didn't wear name badges identifying themselves. Kyle could not be sure if he could trust his employer Northumbria Police. It was easy to imagine the Chief Constable and Deputy Chief Constable exchanging dodgy handshakes with local dignitaries. Kyle did not know if he could trust MI5, MI6, the government or the Opposition. He knew he couldn't trust the Americans!

Moreover, Kyle reckoned he might be dismissed as a conspiracy nut who had written the books himself. He couldn't take that risk, at least not with his own employer. He needed advice and he needed his friends. It was short notice but Elton John agreed to meet up providing Kyle could make it down to Yarm.

Yarm is where Smoggies go to forget that they live on Teesside. Its cobbled High Street is packed with rowdy revellers every Friday, Saturday and rather more curiously every Tuesday night. The coaching inns have long beer gardens stretching down to the Tees; many warmed by efficient garden heaters and lit by Victorian lamps. In one such garden Kyle opened his soul to a painter and decorator called Elton John.

Elton understood divorce and relationship breakdown well. *'Women don't know what they want mate'* he claimed. *'They want jobs; then they don't want jobs. They want kids; then they moan about how tough being a mum is. They want a sensitive man in touch with his feminine side; then they want a hard bastard who makes them feel safe. You can't win, mate'.*

Kyle and Elton spent a whole pint lambasting the female race and the next pint eyeing up top Teesside totty. Meanwhile, gangs of glamorous girls sipped large glasses of rose' and lambasted the male race with the normal *'all men are bastards; they are only after one thing'* refrain. Kyle knew he wasn't a bastard and he wasn't just after sex, although he was finding chastity bloody difficult!

Eventually Kyle felt brave enough to raise his dilemma about the Illuminati. Elton listened with one eye on the girls at the next table.

'So what do you think?' enquired Kyle.

'Don't know mate.'

'I mean, should I report what I have read and if so who to?'

'I'd keep out of it. If this thing is as big as you make out, there's not much you and me can do about it. Besides, it sounds like they've got some canny ideas'.

'Elton, they want to take over the world.'

'So! A bunch of Arabs want to take over the Toon. They might be good news; they might be bad. Only time will tell'.

'Doesn't it worry you that an unelected secret society will have the power to run the planet as they please?'

'I don't vote anyway. Politicians are all as useless as each other. If I were you, I'd go home delete the files and forget you ever read it. It's probably all bollocks anyway. They will get nuked if they try and take over the world. Bloodless coup my arse! Do you think the Chinks and the Russians and that are going to hand over power without a fight? No. It's pure fantasy'.

'Aye, you might be right'.

'A pint says I am'.

'Elton, you're impossible! You want to bet a pint on the future of the planet.'

'Why, Aye, man. A pint says it's all bollocks'.

Kyle laughed. Elton was not the sharpest tool in the box but sometimes he made a lot of sense. However, when Kyle changed trains at Darlington station he remembered something in the Illuminati books about them infiltrating the Round Table. *'Shit, Elton is a Round Table member'*, he recalled. Then he laughed at himself and his ridiculous paranoia.

Scene 10: Black Friday

Fancy organising a fire drill for a day like this, mused Kyle as he watched the torrential rain beat down from black, heavy skies. It was five to eleven and any moment now the deafening, shrill alarm would ring and he would have to shepherd his whole floor out into the rain for some infuriating charade. He only got nominated as fire warden because he used to be a fire-fighter but a fire in this downpour would be extinguished long before the Fire Brigade arrived. The alarm sounded. The office groaned.

He managed to evacuate the floor within 5 minutes, although he practically had to drag Steve from IT away from his computer and out into the rain. He accounted for everyone under the woefully inadequate cover of a laurel tree and waded out gingerly onto the partially flooded car park where the other wardens were comparing notes. The Deputy Chief Constable was there giving orders and looking important. He thanked everyone and as if by magic the alarm went silent.

'Oh' moaned Sam. '*I thought we were going to see some hunky firemen in their little red engines*'. Donna whispered something in her ear and they giggled.

Kyle ushered his colleagues back in the building and went to get himself a hot chocolate.

'*Great minds think alike*'. It was little Rachel from criminal psychology.

'*Yeh. What a day for a fire alarm!*' remarked a soggy, bedraggled Kyle.

'*Are you going to your bosses silver wedding bash*' asked a slightly more pristine looking Rachel.

Technically, the Director of Policy and Performance was Kyle's boss's boss, but he wasn't going to argue at a promotion.

'*I don't know. I suppose I better put in an appearance but a black tie buffet is not really my scene. What about you?*'

'*Mine neither but my Boss insists it will be good for networking so unless I go to Edinburgh, have one too many and fall down some steps I guess I'll have to go.*'

'*Ha! Ha!*' laughed Kyle sipping his hot chocolate cautiously. '*It was no laughing matter, you know. I could have died if it hadn't been for the razor-sharp reflexes of a tramp*'.

'*Yes. I heard. Did you track him down to thank him?*'

'*No. I tried, but he was nowhere to be seen*'.

'*Ah well, maybe I'll see you Saturday. Take care, Kyle.*'

'*And you Rachel*'.

Kyle returned to his office thinking up excuses for the Directors silver wedding. He had bought tickets months ago to go with Helen. He felt certain he would be out of place. Firstly, nearly everyone going seemed to be taking a partner. Secondly, nearly everyone going was much more senior in the organisation than he was. Kyle much preferred a few pints with his mates than champagne and crudités with the big-wigs at Jesmond Cricket Club.

Back in the office he found Alicia had come round with the month's sickness statistics and was gossiping with Sam over a glossy magazine.

'*Come on Sam, the excitement's over. Back to work now*' he said and smiled at Alicia, who was playing seductively with her blonde pig-tails.

'*How's the sickness looking Alicia?*' he asked softly.

'*Uniformed is up a bit but it's not too bad for the time of year*', she replied in a strong Geordie accent. Kyle looked at the figures as a way of disguising his glances at Alicia's figure. She was almost bursting out of her white blouse, which contrasted vividly with her all-year tan. Kyle thought of that rough bloke she was snogging at the party in Benwell and wondered if it had been more than a one-night stand. '*Lucky bastard*', he uttered under his breath.

'*Sorry?*' asked Alicia her Bambi-brown eyes looking up at him hurt.

'*Nothing*' he said signing a sheet.

'*It's the first sign of madness Kyle, talking to yourself*'

'*Oh, I'm past redemption Alicia. Are you going to the anniversary bash at the weekend?*'

'*No. I'd love to. It sounds like it's going to be dead posh. Half the top floor is going, but nobody from HR is going.*'

'*I've got a spare ticket. Why don't you come with me?*'

'*Wow! Thanks Kyle!*' Alicia said flashing a smile. '*I will let you know. I will have to check with my boyfriend.*'

Kyle's hopes were raised and crushed as quickly as a wave at Long Sands. He felt foolish for thinking that a stunning 24 year old would be interested in him and wondered if he had looked silly in front of his colleagues, but nobody said anything and he tried to get back to work and forget his loneliness and unquenched desire.

*****

Friday came round quickly. It was Kyle's first trip to London since the day he had first stumbled across the Illuminati. He was off to a benchmarking meeting and this time he had to slum it in standard class. Nevertheless, the coach was full of executives on their mobiles frantically negotiating, organising and trading. He wondered if the ones sounding terrified were outside the brotherhood and the ones sounding excited were inside! He kept a close eye on his jacket throughout his journey.

It was a cold, sunny morning when he left Newcastle but as soon as the train passed the Emirates, the sky went dark and the first few spots of rain appeared on the train window. It was pissing down as he left Kings Cross for the meeting venue in Euston Road and he broke into a jog, adeptly weaving between the brolly waving commuters. The meeting was reasonably interesting and Kyle made a few salient points. More importantly, the lunch was good and Kyle went back for 2 plate-refills.

It was drizzling when he emerged and walked back to Kings Cross. The billboards read *'Evening Standard: Black Friday'*. The newspaper vendors repeated these words in coarse cockney accents. He procured a copy to read on the train. The World's stock markets had experienced their biggest crash since the 1930's. Millions had been wiped off shares. In America, one of the World's biggest insurance companies had crashed and another bank had followed suit. The White-house were reluctantly bailing banks out and trying to stop a run on the banks, following the model already adopted in Britain.

The paper had a huge debate about the rights and wrongs of bank bail-outs, which Kyle knew to be purely academic. Even the most fervent advocates of sink or swim economics couldn't afford to let the banking sector collapse. It would be political suicide.

The train was sombre on the return journey. There were no more excited phone calls. People looked sullen and sounded like they were at a funeral and in some ways they were. The death of blue-blooded capitalism can be traced back to Black Friday, October 2008. Kyle knew the World would never be the same again.

Act 3: Darkness Descends

Scene 1: The Director's Wedding Anniversary

Such is the nature of office gossip that everyone in his office knew Kyle was taking Alicia to the Director's Wedding Anniversary before Kyle did. Alicia had told Sam the news in the lift and she had passed it on before Kyle came back from his meeting. Brenda stared at him disapprovingly and Keith stared at him in awe.

'Alicia's really looking forward to it. She showed me the dress she's planning to wear on the web' said Sam.

'I can't imagine her boyfriend's too keen on the idea' Kyle responded.

'He's a dick. He's really getting on Alicia's nerves coming over all clingy and possessive after a few dates. You'd be much better for her', Sam declared.

Kyle's interest grew. Alicia and Sam were quite close. Maybe she fancied him after all and she wasn't just using him as an admission ticket. He looked out for Alicia at lunch-time but she seemed oblivious to him. However, Colin came bounding over to greet him:

'Kyle! You dark horse! Is it true you're screwing Alicia Bell?'

'Colin. Don't be daft. I'm taking the lovely Miss Bell to the Director's Silver Wedding Anniversary party but there's no more to it. She's got a boyfriend so don't go around saying things like that or I might get my head kicked in'.

'It would be worth it mate.'

When Friday arrived without any direct word from the human resources heart-throb Kyle decided he would have to go looking for her. She was on the phone, flirting with a police officer. She played with her little blonde plats and varnished her nails as she egged on his sexist banter. It must have been a good 5 minutes before she finally put the receiver down and directed her big brown eyes up at Kyle.

'Are we still on for the party tomorrow Alicia', Kyle asked?

'You bet' she replied. *'I've got this lovely new ball-gown. I can't wait to wear it'.*

'What time shall I call for you?'

'I've ordered a taxi for half 7 so be at mine about twenty-five past I guess.'

'You only live about half a mile away from Jesmond Cricket Club. What's wrong with walking?'

'Kyle. You cheap-skate! Surely, I'm worth a taxi fare!'

Alicia looked at him seductively and he knew this was not open for negotiation. It meant he would have to get the metro to Jesmond, walk away from the Cricket Club to collect Alicia from her Sandyford flat and then get a taxi back over the route he'd just walked. However, if this gorgeous minx was really interested in him it would be well worth the effort.

*****

The cheap-skate comment stuck in Kyle's throat. He treated himself to a new suit and decided to take a taxi to Alicia's. He also got a hair-cut and spent an unusual amount of time grooming. She cancelled her taxi and texted him to tell him to wait in his cab until she was ready. Kyle looked nervously at the meter as the adjacent clock showed 7.42. Suddenly the light in Alicia's flat went out and she hurried to the taxi. She had also had her hair done and sported a loose perm. Kyle leant to kiss her softly on her cherry lips and whispered *'You look stunning'*.

She smiled and strapped herself in. Her long, cream ball-gown swept down to some sparkling stilettos and the slit exposed her slender, tanned legs as she sat beside Kyle in the back of the cab. The dress was strapless and held up by a long zip up the back, which Kyle imagined undoing later. The dress barely rose high enough to cover her large, natural breasts, which were bursting out from the frills and silk. A gold necklace dangled above her cleavage as if it were advertising her assets with the message: *'Look at me. Aren't my tits fantastic?'*

The taxi arrived in leafy Osborne Avenue and Kyle did the honours with the fare. *'Have a good night'* said the taxi driver with a tone that suggested he wanted to add the words *'you lucky black bastard'*, but he didn't want to prejudice his tip. The Director and his long-suffering wife were there to greet the guests in a queue like the royals at a cup final. Most of the greetings were brief but he lingered on Alicia much longer than the rest, his face beaming and his eyes transfixed on her chest.

Inside they were offered champagne and stood looking around the hall at the three or four clusters of early arrivals. All the gents wore bow ties and suits and most of the ladies had dresses that looked like they were from Fenwicks or John Lewis. Apart from Alicia, Kyle looked about the youngest person there.

'Isn't it wonderful' said Alicia.

'It's a bit stuffy. I'm going to get some fresh air on the veranda. Are you coming?' asked Kyle.

'No. I'm going to mingle' replied his glamorous date.

There was a beautiful view over the cricket pitch from the romantically lit veranda and the cool evening air was spoilt by a man in a white suit puffing on a huge cigar. Kyle sipped his champagne and tried to think of some witty repartee to woo Alicia. However, when he returned Alicia was engaged in conversation with the Deputy Chief Constable. Kyle joined them but neither acknowledged him and he struggled to find a route into their conversation.

'*Kyle*' a voice said as he felt a tap on his shoulder. It was the Director. '*What a charming girlfriend you have. You really must come and have dinner with us some-time*'

'*Oh, I'm not his girlfriend*' Alicia said suddenly noting Kyle's presence. '*We're just friends*' she added fluttering her eye-lids. Kyle felt shit. Something told him he wasn't going to undo Alicia's zip and watch her gown tumble to the floor tonight as he had fantasised. He stood awkwardly as the Deputy Chief Constable and the Director battled for Alicia's attention and she lapped it up. Occasionally, he managed to add a comment to remind them of his presence but he sunk the pint the big cheese had bought him before the rest of his group had reached half-way with theirs. They declined his offer of a round so he went to get himself a pint at the bar. When he returned Alicia was no-where to be seen so he hung around near the Deputy Chief Constable and the Director waiting her return.

His ears pricked up with the word '*Illuminati*' coming from the Director's lips.

'*I'm worried what might happen if Obama gets in*' said the Director.

'*It's not what we expected*' replied the Deputy Chief '*but who knows it might work out for the best*'.

'*How do you work that out? They are talking about bringing the date forward to before his inauguration. That gives up less than 3 months. It's not enough time. Besides if he wins next week he will be seen as the answer to all the world's problems. We will be redundant.*'

'*You worry too much. Firstly, I can't believe the yanks will vote a black man into the Oval Office. It is one thing to say you will do it but another thing to put the cross on the ballot paper. Secondly, his election would cause such vile from the South that I would be surprised if he made it to the inauguration*'.

'*You think we might bump him off?*'

'*Heavens no but there are plenty of other groups who will try to do it. We have members with a key role in protecting the President, but with so many enemies that role might prove impossible.*'

'*I get it and then with the great black hope assassinated, the demand for a New World Order will be even higher*'.

'*Voila!*'

'*Do you think we will be ready by January?*'

'*I only know what I'm told. Batman reckons we will be*'.

'*How is Batman? I thought he'd be here tonight but apparently he's a no-show*'.

'*Being Deputy Chief Executive of the North East Illuminati is taking up all his time now. He's had to mothball his business and charity interests and so I guess he's got no time for a social life*'.

'*I guess not. I heard that he has seen the sixth phase*'.

At that moment Alicia returned from the loo and they expertly changed the subject. Kyle recapped what he had just learnt:

- the Deputy Chief Constable and his own Director were both Illuminati members;

- the brotherhood would be less than rigorous in protecting the President should Obama win as expected next week;

- a bloke called Batman was second in command in the region; and

- there was a 6th phase, which explained the 6th password he had got from Dougie.

Suddenly, a dull evening was becoming a lot more interesting!

Scene 2: Surprises

The Deputy Chief soon pulled rank in the quest for Alicia's attention and the Director bored Kyle about work for the next 5 minutes. Kyle did his best to appear interested but he was continually glancing over his shoulder for someone more interesting to talk to. Ultimately, he recognised an Accountant from Police HQ called Tony and managed to escape for a conversation on the dire state of affairs at St James Park.

Local band '*The Baghdadi's*' came on stage to perform an electric mix of Latin-sounding instrumentals fresh from the World Stage at Glastonbury. Most of the audience were unmoved but Kyle gave them his attention for a couple of tracks and put his pint down to clap them politely. Alicia glided over serenely to join him.

'*You managed to drag yourself away from the Deputy Chief then*' stated Kyle.

'*Oh. Nasty man! He gives me the creeps. He couldn't keep his eyes of my tits and then he went and spilt some beer on my new dress!*'

Kyle consoled her and started talking about musical likes and dislikes, managing to focus on her big brown eyes. The conversation was pleasant but their tastes were very different. Kyle bought Alicia a drink but by the time he got back she was deep in conversation with a rugged, fit looking copper.

He went out once more on to the balcony. It was empty apart from two shadowy figures talking slowly at the opposite end. It was the Deputy Chief and the Director. Kyle went back inside the curtains but moved close enough to hear their conversation without being seen.

'*Something I've always wondered. How did Batman get his nickname?*'

'*It's nothing exciting really! His real name is Jon Bateman. John without the H. Bateman without the E gives Batman*'.

'*That is dull. I thought it must be because he had a mask and a cape and lived in a cave*'.

'*No. He lives near me in Darras Hall, but he does have a dog called Robin*'.

'*I'd heard that. He lives alone in a big mansion with just Robin for company*'.

'*He's happy enough living that way. He has lots of lavish dinner parties where anyone who is anyone is invited. It's a good recruiting ground for the brotherhood*'.

'*And you really think he's seen the sixth phase*'.

'That's the rumour. It's all top secret but'.

'You've no idea what it's about?'

'No. It is a plan for after we've taken power. That's all I know'.

'I better go and catch up with my wife. I think she's feeling neglected and after all I guess she's the reason we are all here'.

'Yes. I better find mine. I don't think she's too pleased that I've been ogling at the lovely Alicia from HR all night'.

'I had noticed you old devil. I think she blew you out after you spilt your beer all over her mind'.

'It was only a drop and she went mad. She didn't seem to appreciate my kind offer of helping her out of her dress.'

'How very uncivil of her! See you later.'

With that, Kyle returned to the bar for another pint. He looked at his watch. It said 9.30. He wondered how much longer Alicia would want to stay and if she would want to share a taxi back with him. Observing the body language between her and the copper he thought the answer was probably negative.

*****

Kyle scouted round for anyone he recognised and eventually he noticed Rachel from criminal psychology sitting alone nursing a pint of Guinness.

'Hiya Rachel. I didn't notice you here. Have you been here long?'

'No. I've only just arrived. I was just thinking this is going to be hell as there's hardly anyone I recognise so it's a relief to see you Kyle.'

'Mind if I join you?'

'No. Please do'. Rachel smiled shyly and looked genuinely delighted at Kyle's company. Rachel wore a shoulder-less top and smart, grey trousers. Her mousy, straight brown hair swept both sides of her shoulders, which were pale and freckled. Kyle had never seen her with her hair down before or in anything other than a business suit. He liked the change. It made her look less serious and more girly.

'I never know what to wear at these things,' she said in an intelligent Geordie accent. 'Most of the women are wearing dresses but I'm not really a dress person. Alicia looks gorgeous doesn't she?'

'Aye and doesn't she know it? I've had to put up with her flaunting herself at the great and good all night.'

'Oh dear! Your date isn't going well then?'

'It's not really a date Rachel. I'm more like her chaperone'.

Rachel laughed and sipped some Guinness, gently wiping the froth from her lips. She wore no make-up and her skin was pale, punctuated with frequent beauty spots but she was quite pretty in a quirky sort of way. Her features were little and her forehead high, conveying the impression of intelligence, which her conversation confirmed in a down-to-earth sort of way. Kyle and Rachel chatted easily about many things and indeed Kyle did so much talking that Rachel finished her pint first and got to her feet to go to the bar.

'No. Let me' said Kyle, but Rachel insisted he could get the next one and turned to head to the bar. As she did so, Kyle noticed for the first time what a sexy bottom she had. Her trousers clung tightly to a rounded peach of an arse that was totally unexpected. She always kept it covered up with jackets and coats in the office. Kyle surprised himself. He had met Rachel a few times and thought she was a nice girl, if a little quiet and sensible, but he had never thought of her in a sexual way before. She was very petite, probably a foot shorter than Kyle and skinny. However, as he watched her at the bar he assessed that whilst she was very narrow from the waist up and her top looked loose on her, she had relatively thick thighs and her trousers looked tight on her. She was probably wearing size 10 clothes that were a bit loose on her top and a bit tight on her bottom.

'The Baghdadi's' came back on as Rachel returned with the drinks. They agreed they were pretty good but not really their type. They both preferred Indie bands and Rachel surprised Kyle with tales from Glastonbury and the Isle of Wright festivals. Kyle made sure he finished his pint first and got Rachel another pint. He asked her where she put it, given that she was so tiny and yet seemed to be able to knock back the pints. She just said she had always been little and it didn't seem to matter what she ate or drunk or how much exercise she did. She asked Kyle if it was a new suit he was wearing and he commended her observational skills.

When Rachel went to the loo, Kyle once again admired her shapely rear and began to wonder if she had a boyfriend. He really didn't know her well enough to know one way or another. She was 29 years old and had worked at Police HQ since graduating but Kyle had only seen her to speak to probably a dozen times in those 8 years and certainly in the early years she earned a reputation for being shy and studious. When she returned she asked him about his encounters with the Illuminati and he was sufficiently inebriated and relaxed to tell her pretty much everything to date.

She didn't laugh at him or suggest he was a conspiracy nut. She looked at him with caring deep blue eyes, the pupils dilating in the dim light and said: *'I'm worried about you Kyle. You can't expect to stop a new world order on your own and they won't think twice about killing you if you continue to be a threat to their plans'.*

'You don't think I'm making it all up'.

'No. I've read enough about the Illuminati to know what you say makes sense. They will probably fail to take over the world so we just have to let things run their course'.

'You are probably right Rachel.'

'I'm going to have to go now. I'm staying at a friend's house in Jesmond and I don't want to keep her up.'

'Ok. It's been a nice evening. See you Rachel.'

Kyle looked around the room and there was no sign of Alicia or the copper. In fact, there weren't many people left now at all. He bid farewell to the Director and his wife, now looking every bit the happily married couple this event was supposed to celebrate. As he walked to the Metro he had competing emotions inside his head. There was curiosity to find out about the 6th phase and there was a desire to stay safe and follow Rachel's advice. He was torn both ways and unsure which emotion to follow.

Scene 3: Red Sky in the Morning!

Kyle woke fresh as a daisy to witness a beautiful sunrise. He counted seven different shades of red and orange as the sun inched up to wake the Party City from its Sunday morning slumber. He collected Nathan and they had a kick-around on some waste land near the Tyne Tunnel. A group of teenagers joined in and soon they were into a full eleven-a-side game. Kyle surprised himself with some silky ball skills that took him past 3 lunging tackles before tapping the ball past a timid goalkeeper. This prompted someone to shout *'Hey Mister. My Mate thinks your Tino Asprilla'.*

This case of mistaken identity was the highlight of Kyle's football career. Glowing with confidence he found that everything he tried worked and only his fitness let him down against his teenage rivals. He set up a couple of goals for Nathan and father and son finished the day muddy, exhausted but happy.

When Nathan got back to Gosforth he reflected on his dilemma. He did not wish to risk his life defending democracy. He had received two near fatal warnings but nothing for weeks. As far as the Illuminati were concerned his threat had been neutralised with the theft of his PC. They did not know he had a back-up. Sure, he could go blabbing to the authorities about the greatest conspiracy of all time but who would believe him without any compelling evidence. Providing he lay low and let fate unfold he should be safe to enjoy many more days like this with his son.

Monday morning came round all too quickly. There was no red sky to wake up gradually to. The alarm went off and it was still pitch black. Kyle forced himself up and went into work. Donna was in making coffees and as she brought his she had a twinkle in her eye. *'How did it go with Alicia'* she enquired directly.

'I didn't see much of her. She had men round her all night like bees round a honey-pot and last time I saw her she was all over some copper'.

'Oh. We had high hopes for you two.'

At lunch-time Kyle bumped into Alicia on his way to the canteen. She apologised for leaving early and thanked him for a lovely evening. Kyle didn't mention the CID bloke. Alicia looked less captivating than normal. The make-up looked a bit over-done, the hair a bit too obviously bleached and her clothes a bit ordinary. She was still beautiful but in a rather too obvious sort of way. Kyle looked at Alicia in the way he did as a child when he opened a Christmas present that he had known for months he was getting. He found it much more fun to un-wrap a complete surprise and find it was just what he wanted but hadn't thought to ask for.

As Alicia walked away sexily swivelling her hips in a grey mini-skirt Kyle recalled how he had went to bed on Saturday night with a vivid vision of her wriggling out of her cream ball-gown to reveal her perfect naked body. He had imagined himself taking her from behind and was close to climaxing when the object of his sexual fantasy changed and suddenly he was making love to Rachel. This had shocked him as he could probably have asked 100 men who was the belle of the ball and he would have got the answer Alicia from 90 of them, providing their wives or girlfriends weren't within earshot. In fact, at least half of them had probably gone home and shagged or masturbated to a vision of Alicia. However, it somehow felt right with Rachel. It felt real. He only wished it was.

*****

Kyle stayed up to watch the American election results. He recognised the huge impact that the result would have on world events. America was so powerful that their President shaped the future of the entire planet. Accordingly, it was highly undemocratic that only Americans were allowed to cast a vote. The World would never have elected George Bush over Al Gore and it was a ludicrously selfish act for the Yanks to do so. Mind you, thought Kyle, that Bush victory was probably the lowest point in American democracy as the result of the election was changed on the basis of a few spoilt ballot papers in a state run by the President's brother!

In 2008, long before Florida declared, it was obvious that this time America had made the right choice. It had matured as a nation and looked beyond the colour of a candidate's skin. Barack Obama had come from nowhere to win because he was clearly the best candidate for the job; a man with outstanding leadership qualities capable of inspiring any organisation. It was a triumph both for democracy and meritocracy.

So then, Kyle thought, the Illuminati are going to have to hurry through their plans and rely on some bigoted redneck to assassinate the inspirational President-elect. He wished he could get details of the Illuminati plot to Obama without fear of being intercepted but he knew that both the Republican and Democrat party machines were infiltrated to the core with members of the brotherhood and its associates. He remembered his promise to himself to stay out of it.

Then Obama spoke and he spoke with such dignity, such hope and such clarity that Kyle was visibly moved. As a black man, Kyle had faced racism on many levels and knew how difficult it was to overcome stereotypes. He never thought he would witness a black President of the most powerful country in the world. Obama's delivery was evangelical but measured and respectful. He was the first politician Kyle had ever fully warmed to and believed in. When he said '*Yes, we can*', Kyle found himself agreeing.

Kyle went to bed feeling that democracy was not dead and it could yet deliver a better life for the citizens of Planet Earth. The New World Order was unnecessary and it would be tragic if Obama was murdered before he had a chance to deliver on his promises. Someone had to stop the Illuminati. What rotten luck it was that it seemed the only person who could do so was him!

Scene 4: One night in the Crown Posada

It was 7.00 on a Friday night and throngs of beautiful young people were converging on the Quayside and the hills winding down to it from the City Centre. There were roughly even numbers of male and female groups each numbering around half a dozen. Most were dressed for Ibiza in August but it was November in Newcastle. Each new train pulling into Central Station brought new groups of young people from all over the country. There were stag parties, hen parties and people just looking for a carefree, wild night without the expense of a flight.

Kyle, John, Dobbo, One-word, Mattie and Elton John met for a pint under the ornamental ceiling of the Centurion in Central Station and when they were all present and correct downed their pints and continued to the Crown Posada. Kyle liked the Crown Posada. It hadn't changed since his student days. It was a long, thin bar with snugs and wood panelling. The wide range of real ales was consistently well-kept. The clientele was a wide range from old men in flat caps to the young and glamorous taking a break from the standing-room-only, disco-bars where bouncers monitored the queues and most beer was served in bottles.

Elton John was first to the bar. He'd wanted to follow a hen party to a bar called the Lounge but been out-voted. He drank lager so much of the appeal of the Crown Posada was lost on him.

'Here, I hear you've just been on a stag-do in Amsterdam, One-Word' said Mattie.

'Aye' said One Word.

'It's a fantastic place; beautiful canals, beautiful women, beautiful attitude, beautiful women. I could live there. It's like Newcastle, except you have to pay for it', Mattie continued.

'How much does it cost One Word?' enquired John Medburn.

'50' shrugged One Word.

'How do you know One-Word? Is there something I should tell her indoors?' asked Mattie laughing.

'No' replied One Word looking insulted.

'When I was there I met a joiner from Shields who told us his wife let him go to Amsterdam once a year with the lads. I asked him whether she knew what he got up to and he said she didn't mind because each year he returned with a new lease of life and the sexual prowess of a 20 year-old. That's great I said.

You're a lucky man. He laughed and said well I was until one year I came back with the clap!'

Elton returned as everyone was laughing and Mattie had to re-tell the story. It was often difficult to tell when Mattie was recalling a genuine anecdote and when he was telling a joke, but it didn't really matter. He always made people laugh and it was a skill which helped him punch above his weight with the girls and stay popular with the lads.

They all managed to get seats around a table and compared the quality of their assorted pints. Then John Medburn revealed that he had a date. Mattie slapped him gently on the back and shook his hand. *'Fuck!'* said One Word. Dobbo asked him what she was like and whether she had a guide dog. John got embarrassed and described her in less than enlightening detail. He had taken her to the pictures and spent the whole film wondering if it was ok to put his arm round her. Then as the titles came up she grabbed him and kissed him on the lips. He revealed that they were meeting the next day in Tokyo, a trendy bar near the Station.

Kyle said it was great news and it was about time he broke his duck. Elton asked Kyle how long it had been since he had last tasted the pleasures of the flesh. Kyle worked it out and said *'Six months'* to much derision from his friends. *'Well after your wife has been unfaithful to you it kind of puts you off sex for a while'.*

'Bollocks' said Elton. *'I bet if that girl in the gold boob-tube made a pass at you, you'd soon forget about Helen tonking around.'*

'Thanks Elton', Kyle said unimpressed.

Diplomatically, Mattie intervened with a joke. *"Have you heard about the Mackem who promised his wife at New Year that every time she gave head he would put £20 in a jam-jar to save up for their next holiday?'*

Everyone shook their heads so Mattie continued: *'At Easter he had a look in the jam-jar and counted £1, 000. How did you manage that, he said. We've only had sex five times since Christmas. I know she replied but not everyone's as stingy as you are.'*

'I've heard that one' said Dobbo. *'Turning to John here Mattie, you're the master of the chat-up line, what advice would you give John on his date'.*

'Chat-up lines can be really cheesy. I'd advise you to stay clear of preparing anything. It's best to just ad-lib', replied Mattie.

'Some of us don't have the gift of the gab like you Mattie'.

'OK One Word. Ignore all those people who tell you to be yourself. Well, in your case that's the worst thing you could do'.

Even John laughed, although he added the comment *'you bastard'* as he did so.

The conversation switched from women to crime. Kyle's job as a crime statistician came under the microscope. Kyle couldn't convince his friends that crime was falling and had been for years. Elton John wanted to bring back hanging and National Service. He said we were far too soft and understanding with louts these days and that's why the streets were unsafe. Dobbo explained that he had been caught by a stray glass in a bar and gone to A&E but had not reported the crime and that was the problem with Police statistics.

Kyle agreed that drunken City Centre violence had increased but argued violence was only criminal if it was reported. Recording fights would distort the success the Police were having driving down serious crimes like burglary, rape and arson.

The debate was becoming quite heated but as usual Mattie diffused the tension. *'Did I tell you about when I reported a burglary at my neighbours?'*

Everyone shook their heads.

'I knew my neighbours were on holiday and their alarm was going off at night so I rang the Police. They said they didn't have any patrols free so could I go out and have a look through the windows. I thought for a minute and then thought fuck that. I'm not getting dressed and going out in the rain doing the cops job for them. That's what I pay my council tax for. So I rang the Police back'.

'Did you tell them to send a patrol round immediately' asked Kyle.

'No. I told them not to bother because I'd just shot the buggers'

'The fuck you did!' said Elton.

'I did. They were round in five minutes and they caught the bastards redhanded. The DI had a go at me for lying about shooting them, but I just said wait here, you told me you didn't have any patrols free and you send four around! Who's the liar?'

More laughter followed and it was time for Kyle's round. The stress of Kyle's battle with the Illuminati seemed half a world away.

Elton brought up the subject of Kyle's conspiracy theory. Initially, the others found it hilarious but when it became clear that Kyle was being serious and he had nearly lost his life twice the mood changed. All agreed that he should not intervene. Ordinary people couldn't take on and beat the establishment. The establishment had become too powerful and if the Illuminati had infiltrated and taken over the establishment their victory was inevitable.

Kyle explained how he had been inspired by Obama's speech and feared for the life of the President-elect. All the friends welcomed Obama's victory but opinions varied from *'after George Bush, anyone will be an improvement'* to *'I think he might be the only one able to sort this financial crisis out'*. However, none of them seemed over perturbed about the prospect of his assassination. Dobbo didn't think it could happen. Elton thought if it's going to happen, it might be worth a bet.

Maybe it was the alcohol, but Kyle couldn't believe their apathy. He said he had been broken into and had his laptop stolen. Now, he planned to get revenge on the Illuminati. If the sixth phase was as frightening as he expected he would reveal their secrets to the world. Mattie urged caution as he prepared to leave. Elton left with him to catch the last train to Teesside. The other four stayed for one last pint returning to the safer subject of Kyle's *'date'* with Alicia.

*****

Kyle was last to leave the pub. He found a newspaper left on the Metro with an opinion poll on the front page which showed the Tories with a big lead and collapsing support for Gordon Brown in the aftermath of the credit crunch and gloomy news on the economy. Kyle wished for a British Barack Obama to give the nation hope. Instead all we had to look forward to was David Cameron!

He turned to an imaginary audience and reflected on where New Labour had gone wrong:

'Don't get me wrong. New Labour should be commended for doing what was urgently needed and spending much more on public services. Billions more! Public services were in a sorry state at the end of 18 years of Tory rule. Schools were decaying and waiting lists were making a mockery of the NHS. Something had to be done. Public services improved significantly. The statistics speak for themselves.

It is a shame people are so cynical. If you ask them if their local school and hospital had improved nearly all would say yes, but the majority did not think the NHS and quality of Education had improved nationally. Things are great here, but not there. However, 'there' was a mythical place that didn't exist. Everyone's 'there' was someone else's 'here'!

So far so good! We are living longer, waiting lists are much shorter, exam results are much better, school and hospital buildings modernised. Yes, and crime really is down! Things could only get better and they had done.

However, looking back on it now it is impossible not to conclude that a great opportunity has been squandered. The public were more willing to fund investment in public services than for a generation, the coffers were boosted by privatisation sales and North Sea Oil revenue and the economy was booming with a consequent dip in expenditure on welfare and peak in tax revenues. New Labour had huge public goodwill behind them and they could have transformed public services, not just improved them.

Unfortunately, for every billion that delivered improvements another billion was spent without any tangible benefits. The waste was criminal. Sniffing the cash, rapacious public servants seized much of the bounty. Weak management and a Government obsessed with making the public sector more like the private sector compounded the problem.

I have worked all my life in the public sector. I didn't choose this path for the money. I did so because I believed in public service. Most of my contemporaries were similarly altruistic. However, recent recruits have looked enviously at private sector salaries and demanded parity. This fails to recognise the benefit of working for the public good, the generous pension scheme, flexible working hours, good holidays and a short working week. In the public sector the likes of Sam get away with doing not a lot and keeping their jobs as long as they are popular with their colleagues and the harder workers compensate for their idleness.

I witnessed the FBU demand a 50% pay award when inflation was below 5%. Many of the fire-fighters I worked beside really believed that they were a special case that deserved such a rise. They couldn't understand why the Government might expect efficiency savings in return. We pay them to spend most of their night shift sleeping and give them beds to make them more comfortable. I'm surprised the FBU didn't demand a bed-time story along with the 50%! This was the most extreme case of greedy public servants forgetting that their purpose was to serve the public and not bleed them dry. However, it was not the most significant.

Quite rightly, most of the new money went into the NHS. Quite deplorably, most of that money was spent on dramatic pay rises for NHS staff. The big problem with the NHS is it is not managed by managers. Doctors run the NHS. They always have done. All political parties talk about devolving yet more power to clinicians in the NHS and teachers in schools. It is a recipe for disaster. You don't improve the management of a football team by devolving power to the players. It happened once at Newcastle United. They got relegated.

We need strong managers who are experienced at running multi-million pound budgets, freeing doctors to treat patients and teachers to teach. Instead when the Government re-negotiated consultant's contracts to try and reduce the amount of time they spent on private medicine their salaries almost doubled and their NHS workload hardly changed. Family doctors felt left out so when their contracts were re-negotiated their pay almost doubled as well and many cut surgery hours! They got more for doing less. Patients benefitted from New Labour, but not half as much as their doctors.

You didn't have to earn £100K per annum to prosper from the NHS pay bonanza. Nurses and finance staff did well too and when Agenda for Change tried to even out pay inequality it was so mismanaged that most of those with reduced pay had it re-instated on appeal and a cost-neutral exercise added yet more billions to the NHS pay-bill.

Managers simply didn't think carefully enough about how the extra resources should be spent. Police forces competed with each other to recruit the most new coppers and NHS trusts did a similar thing with nurses. In fact, many of the extra constables and nurses would have been better replaced with lower paid staff able to take the paperwork off coppers and the manual tasks off nurses. Nurses successfully campaigned to be paid like professionals but half their job still involves cleaning bed-pans, changing sheets, bathing patients and other tasks that in any other employer an East European immigrant on the minimum wage would do. The NHS needs care workers to support nurses and allow them to become dedicated professionals. Instead it pays them £25K a year and expects them to wipe arses!

Talking of arses, management consultants have focused on making the public sector more like the private sector. They have come up with structural change after structural change. Each change costs millions and achieves sod all. Consultants have pocketed big fees and Chief Executives of merged organisations have seen their salaries rocket to reflect their increased responsibility. Managers showed uncharacteristic innovation thinking up new jobs to stop having to make the redundant staff redundant.

New Labour bought into the idea that market principles could improve public services. If schools and hospitals were structured like private sector firms, with power devolved to the most local level they would start operating like private sector firms. Of course it was bollocks. The people were still the same: they just wore different name tags and sat in different offices. There were still lots of weak managers who wouldn't last 5 minutes in a large private firm. There were still lots of Sam's who were awfully nice but lazy and really rather crap.

Perhaps the saddest indictment of public sector inefficiency is the mass of capital works programmes funded by the Private Finance Initiative and Building Schools for the Future. Billions followed billions but it was all piecemeal. Schools built in the last 40 years and extended through PFI schemes in Millennium projects were suddenly earmarked for replacement. The paint was barely dry on the gleaming state of the art sports hall and music block when the plans were approved to demolish the whole site and start again on a new site up the road. This is what happens if you devolve spending decisions to teachers and doctors. They will spend your money on Rolls-Royce when they already have an Audi with low miles on the clock.

I often wonder what would have happened if structures had been left alone and power retained by health authorities and local authorities. I think the same results could have been achieved a lot cheaper. Wise investment in dynamic new managers with experience of managing huge budgets efficiently could have left a New Labour legacy of world-class public services. Instead their legacy is a mountain of debt and a cemetery full of red roses and crushed dreams.'

Scene 5: Batman and Robin

Darras Hall is Newcastle's most exclusive suburb. Set in the green belt near Kyle's office it is home to footballers, film stars, bankers, doctors and lottery winners. Many of the mansions are invisible from the road as electronic gates, tall shrubs and long drives cocoon the residents from prying eyes. The mansions come in two broad types; either with swimming pool or without swimming pool. Almost all the children are privately schooled, despite the fact that the houses lie in the catchment area of one of Northumberland's best schools. There are no pavements but plenty of helicopter pads.

Kyle had parked in a lay-by and found the grand entrance to the bat cave. There were CCTV cameras everywhere and Kyle was unsure if he had managed to evade them as he stood beneath an oak tree and peered through a gap in the conifers. The bat-mobile was parked at the head of a long gravel drive, a gleaming black Aston Martin. An old man on a sit-on lawn-mower came in and out of view and dodged between the rotating sprinklers. The house had CCTV cameras and an alarm system and there were floodlights near the stone lodge just inside the gates. A break-in was going to be tricky.

A car came up the road and Kyle knelt down beside the tree, disturbing a red squirrel searching for nuts. Maybe this was a stupid idea. The risk of getting caught was too high and the consequences for a Police statistician would probably be career-ending. He rose to his feet to return to the car but as he did so the Aston Martin headed off down the drive. Kyle crouched again and observed the tinted electric window on the passenger side open and a man call out to the gardener. The gardener turned off the mower and came to talk to the passenger and after a few words the window shut and the car drove off down the drive.

The gardener returned to his work and the car passed quite close to Kyle before the driver opened the gates and the car drove off towards Ponteland. The driver was immaculately dressed in uniform; a chauffeur Kyle deduced. The bulky passenger was in his 50s with a grey beard, jeans and a satin jacket. A large Labrador sat in the back-seat and looked Kyle right in the eye as they passed.

Kyle re-assessed the situation. Batman and Robin lived alone and he knew they were out. As the gardener was still present there was a chance they wouldn't have locked the mansion or set the alarm. If Kyle kept to the perimeter of the garden he might be able to dart between the conifers and approach the house from a blind spot just round the corner from the CCTV cameras and the gardener. The sound of the mower would drown the sound of broken glass. This was meant to be a reconnaissance mission but if he was going to break-in, the opportunity was now!

Sixty meters from the mansion there was a 5 metre gap between trees. Kyle dashed for cover but was certain a camera had flashed him. He looked up and observing the strong, setting sun considered it might have been a chink of sunlight. He continued on and panted as he stood back against the fine sandstone edifice of the mansion. He could hear the mower but not see it, which was a good sign. He produced a rock from his pocket and smashed the glass. It cracked enough for him to make a small hole and reach inside to undo the latch and open the window to the library. He climbed in and tipped some books off the shelf as he scrambled down to the floor. An alarm light flashed at him but there was no sound. He had been right.

He searched the ground floor for a computer. There was nothing. The study was cold and bare with a fire that looked like it hadn't been lit for ages. The centre of the house was a huge entrance hall with a grand staircase, bordered by murals and fine art. The stairs were so thickly carpeted that Kyle felt like he was wearing slippers as he mounted the staircase.

The first door he came to was locked and the second was a beautiful guest room that looked like it was permanently on display and the bed was never used. Third time lucky; the master bedroom was huge and the en-suite alone was bigger than any of the rooms in Kyle's house in Wallsend. The four poster bed was unmade and there were objects everywhere. By the bay window in a corner of the room Kyle saw a computer table with a large desk-top computer.

Kyle looked in the desk drawer hoping Batman had written down his passwords. There was nothing but a packet of half-eaten biscuits and a dog lead. Kyle switched on the computer just as the lawn mower noise ceased. As he waited for it to boot, Kyle hoped the gardener was not going to check on his master's property. The computer took ages but eventually opened up with a password screen. Kyle tried *'batman'*. It didn't work. He thought for a moment and tried *'robin'* with the same result. One chance left! Think!

There were so many possibilities.' *Illuminati'* might do the trick or maybe *'phase 6'* or *'sixth phase'*. He was so deep in thought he hardly noticed the sound of an engine. *'Shit'* Kyle said. The Aston Martin was reaching the end of the drive where the gardener was waiting. Kyle quickly logged out and watched the computer slowly begin to shut down. *'Quick'* he begged it with one eye on the window.

Batman and Robin got out and Batman chatted to the gardener with the engine still running. The gardener climbed into the car and Batman waved as his chauffeur drove him away. Batman turned and led his dog to the door. The computer screen turned off at last. It was too late to escape. Batman was in the hall. Kyle noticed a huge walk-in wardrobe and climbed inside. Hiding between the clothes he peered out through a little glass window in one end of the wardrobe just as a dog bounded into the bedroom barking.

Robin had smelt the scent of a stranger and leapt up, his front legs hitting the wardrobe doors. *'Shut up Robin'*, yelled Batman entering the room cautiously and looking confused.

'What the devils got into you?'

He came over and patted the dog but Robin was still agitated. He took his lead and led him away to the bathroom. Kyle heard the sound of piss and wondered whether to run for it but his knees were trembling and weak. The chain flushed, the tap run and Batman returned holding a water bowl. He placed it on the floor and said *'There you go. Is that what you wanted,'* Robin lapped the water and wiggled his tail. Phew thought Kyle.

Batman switched the answer-phone message button and a voice said *'Hello Batman, its Tristan. We need to discuss the sixth phase. Please give us a ring back'.*

'Tosser' was Batman's riposte and he took off his jacket and walked across the bedroom towards Kyle. If he hangs the jacket in this wardrobe I'm finished thought Kyle. He tried to bury himself in the dark between the clothes and hold his breath but it was too late. The wardrobe door swung open and Batman stood looking Kyle in the eye.

*****

Kyle instinctively curled up and blinked, preparing for the blow. Batman may be knocking on but he was a big man and he had a big dog. Batman's fist came towards Kyle's face and he ducked. Batman took out a hanger and placed his jacket on it rather awkwardly and put it back on the rail. He was no longer looking at Kyle and he shut the wardrobe door and staggered to his computer desk. It was then that it dawned on Kyle. Batman was as blind as a bat!

Robin came to his master and Batman patted his faithful guide-dog on the back as he logged into the computer. He reached down and fumbled for a button that Kyle hadn't seen. It was voice activation software. It didn't matter that Kyle could not read the password because an electronic voice repeated it: *'batman&robin23'*

Batman opened up his e-mails. There was one from someone called the Chief who wanted to know when Batman was going to produce a regional business plan for the first 100 days. The others were spam and were quickly deleted. It was clear that planning for the New World Order was well-advanced and Batman was in the thick of it.

Batman logged off and sighed deeply. He got up and walked to the window. After standing for a while looking out into the Northumberland dusk he pulled the tall, thick curtains and the room became quite dim. Robin lay on his tummy moaning like he was playing dead. *'Come on now boy'* said Batman and patted him again once he'd worked out that the dog was lower than anticipated and almost fell over him.

He stood up, leaned back and unzipped his jeans. Kyle's mouth opened wide as Batman pulled out his dick and stood holding it like he was having a pee in the middle of the room. Robin stood up obediently.

'*No*', thought Kyle and shut his eyes in horror. He opened them to see the ghastly sight of a guide dog's tongue licking a blind man's penis. '*Oh God*', Kyle said almost aloud as the sound of the lapping got louder. Batman stood closer and more of his tool entered the Labrador's jaw. One bite thought Kyle and he shivered at the thought. He couldn't believe what he was witnessing. He was standing in a wardrobe in Darras Hall watching Robin give Batman a blow-job!

'*How the hell did I get here?*' he asked himself as the noises and motions became more frantic. He turned away out of respect as this sick act reached its climax. Batman went to the bathroom and Robin spat out the semen in several stages, before curling up in front of the unlit fire.

'*Come on Robin*', Batman said almost apologetically and the loyal dog got up and followed him out of the room and down the stairs. Kyle waited a minute and heard a distant TV or radio. He tip-toed to the computer and switched it on making sure the voice recognition was switched off. He entered the password and searched for the file.

'*Yes*' he said as he found phase 6. He inserted his memory stick. The machine was encrypted and the start-up password didn't work. He tried '*batman&robin*'. It worked. There was a bang downstairs which froze him in his tracks but then silence again. He copied the file to his memory stick and logged out.

Kyle crawled down the stairs and out of the front door. He was so relieved to be out that he forgot about the CCTV camera and darted straight for the trees across the newly-mown lawn. A dog barked. Kyle broke into a sprint. He didn't look round until he reached the road. There was no sign of a pursuit and he could see his car in the distance still parked in the lay-by. The secrets of the sixth phase were about to be revealed.

Scene 6: Secrets

The sixth phase warned its readers what to expect. The introduction explained that it was a plan for the first 100 days when the World will be in a state of emergency and radical measures would be needed to maintain security. A constant theme was that the noble end would justify the means. The author conceded some of the contents were shocking and would appear incompatible with the key Illuminati pillar of freedom. However, the people of the World would look back upon the first 100 days as regrettably necessary like the atom bombs that ended the War in Japan.

The importance of the pillar of confidentiality was stressed. The sixth phase was to be released only to Chief Executives and Deputy Chief Executives in the brotherhood and other nominated individuals on a need-to-know basis. They would be trusted to guard its secrets with their lives.

Kyle was hoping that this top secret text would name names. It didn't. However, it was clear that the Illuminati felt that they had control of many of the World's leading armies and Governments. The author revealed that 40% of the World's nuclear weapons were within Illuminati control. Their scientists had developed nuclear weapons in the first place and had retained their grip on the technology even when hostile governments were elected. More importantly, they already had the technology to shoot down any nuclear weapons launched against them; technology that even NATO had failed to implement yet. Thus, they had the ultimate weapon to combat resistance. Nuclear weapons would be used as a last resort and warning would be given so the populous could choose to free the country and join the brotherhood or be nuked.

The Illuminati predicted that there would be massive resistance but it would be primarily uncoordinated akin to that in Iraq and Afghanistan. It was here that nuclear weapons were most likely to be necessary. Work had already commenced on building 60 new eco-prisons in remote parts of the World. Designs were complete and local labour recruited. They were due to reach practical completion in March 2009 and would hold 1, 000 in-mates each. Initially, they would be almost exclusively used for prisoners of war. However, in the long-run they will be necessary to support the Illuminati's three strikes and out policy on law and order.

Murderers would receive automatic life sentences but other criminals would be given two chances to redeem themselves. On the third offence they would be given a life sentence. Thus, all sentences would be for life. Trying to rehabilitate prisoners was a waste of time. Instead the probation service would focus on first and second time offenders. The criminals would be electronically tagged and given community service. Second-time offenders would be under curfew outside the working day and arrested every time they left their homes. For the first 100 days existing laws would apply, whilst the new leadership developed an international system of law, which would know no borders.

Existing armies would be headed by nominated Illluminati generals. Their role would be as World Police. The numbers would be dramatically increased by immediate international service for anyone without either a full-time job or place in full-time education between the ages of 18 and 25. The international school leaving age would be 18 with immediate effect. Any mutiny within the Army would be dealt with by a firing squad.

Within the first 100 days every single one of the World's citizens will be required to register at their nearest executive office. Registration will involve a series of skills, health and intelligence tests and completion of a form outlining income, wealth, qualifications and special abilities. Every citizen will have their DNA taken and be given a card, colour coded to show the merit points awarded. The top 10% will be given gold status, which will award them extra freedoms and a guaranteed minimum income throughout the World. There will also be silver and bronze classifications. All those with low intellect, no skills, qualifications or jobs will be unclassified.

The unclassified will be immediately neutered to stop them breeding. They will be moved to shanty-towns around the World, where they will be reliant on charitable aid and begging. Benefits would end. Residents of shanty-towns who achieve gold, silver or bronze status will effectively swap places with them. Thus, throughout the developed world there will be full employment. In time, a minimum income level will be set for all silver and bronze residents so poverty will be confined to shanty-towns and these will disappear within a generation. It will effectively be fast-tracked evolution.

Any 'silver' mother who has already had three children will be sterilised as will any 'bronze' mother who already had two children. Anyone aged 25-65 with disabilities that prevent them working will be hospitalised. Abortion will be extended to terminate all pregnancies with a high risk of abnormality. Voluntary euthanasia will be offered on an annual basis to all those expected to live their lives in shantytowns, prisons or hospitals.

Medical advances by the scientists of the brotherhood will allow designer babies and conception from laboratory created sperm. These services will be available to all gold parents and will be rationed to assist mothers without children in the silver and bronze categories to conceive with or without a male partner.

One of the main selling points for the New World Order in the first 10 days will be the cure for cancer that Illuminati scientists have found. Further medical miracles are still being trialled but will be announced on a monthly basis to help keep the people on-side. The media will sell the advantages of the New World Order such as medical breakthroughs, full employment, low crime and no more wars. The downside in terms of conditions and death-rates in shantytowns, prisons and hospitals for the mentally and physically disabled will be downplayed.

Only the gold elite will be entitled to pre-book air travel, own more than 1 car, own any cars with Co2 emissions above 150 and pass on any assets with a value > $100, 000 to beneficiaries. All citizens must carry their registration cards at all times and random checks will be performed to monitor compliance.

Each Chief Executive must develop a detailed business plan for the first 100 days in their Region. It will aim to keep services running as normal, whilst maintaining security and implementing the emergency measures described in the sixth phase. At the end of 100 days there will be a convention on each continent at which Chief Executives will collectively assess progress made and agree plans for the next 100 days.

The sixth phase ended with a statement that its top secret contents were due to be discussed at a meeting of the Bilderberg Group in June 2008. If approved, each Chief Executive and Deputy Chief Executive will be given an action plan to complete and will be put on full alert in 2009 ready for an announcement of the day of reckoning.

*****

Kyle looked at the clock and yawned. It was 2.15 a.m. and he had read the book continuously without a break. No wonder I'm knackered, he thought. He went to the loo and stripped to his underwear ready for bed. As he brushed his teeth he reflected upon the magnitude of what he had read. A cure for cancer was momentous enough, but he had also read about genetic and social engineering on a scale he could scarcely imagine. It was extreme Darwinism and it scared him.

There was a howl of wind in the trees as he rinsed his toothbrush and the windows rattled. He started to go downstairs to turn off the computer when he leapt out of his skin at the sight of a silhouette of a man with a gun in the hall. He froze unable to move forward or backwards, shaking like a jelly with vertigo. It was no nightmare, no vision brought about by extreme fatigue. A masked man, dressed in black came into view and shouted up at him. Kyle didn't hear what he shouted but he instinctively put his hands up.

Another man came round the corner similarly dressed holding Kyle's laptop. '*He's seen it*' he yelled at the other man in shock. The man held the gun to Kyle's face and Kyle closed his eyes expecting it to be for the last time.

*****

Instead of a bullet in the chest Kyle felt a sharp stab in the arm. He then felt himself falling and drifting away, almost floating down the stairs. Suddenly he realized he was being carried and looked up at the masked man struggling with him towards the front door. Everything was becoming fuzzy and blurred and the voices sounded like they were far away. Then he felt at peace, like the stresses and traumas of his life had evaporated away into a November night. Then there was nothing. No voices, no vision, no pain; just a dark void like he'd been carried through his front door and fallen into a black hole.

Scene 7: The eternal night

It's a strange feeling not knowing if you're dead or alive. Kyle regained consciousness but he was lying down in the pitch black, silent and alone. He could see and hear nothing and he felt numb. He tried to sit up but he could hardly move. Just as he was wondering if he had been sent to hell he realized that his mobility was restricted by ropes and metal cuffs. He was tied to a bed and his hands and feet were cuffed together. He turned his head and felt the discomfort of a knot beneath his head. He was blindfolded.

He recalled the events of the previous day. He had broken into a blind man's house and hacked into his computer. He had watched a vulgar performance of depraved, sexual acts and escaped to learn the shocking shape of the New World Order. Then two masked men had broken into his home, seized his computer and pointed a gun in his face. Then there was a sharp stab in the arm and increasing numbness. Gradually, it dawned on Kyle that he had not been shot or stabbed. He had been given a general anaesthetic and now he was being held captive, tied down to a cold, hard bed.

Kyle called out and was disappointed with the volume of his tentative cry. Thus, he took a deep breath and screamed out for attention. This time he heard a distant echo but there was still no reaction. He lay back down and reflected on the terrible downturn in his fortunes. After a while he fell back to sleep, exhausted by his own self-pity and his fruitless search for an escape route from the eternal night into which he had fallen.

Kyle shrieked in the dark. He felt like his feet were on fire and they throbbed with pain. A shot of steam greeted his fading scream and his eyes watered as the pain reverberated around his body. Kyle was instantly awake and although he still could not see, he was aware that someone was standing at the foot of the bed with a red-hot iron in their hands.

'*You have been a naughty boy, Mr Forster*' the stranger said with a deep Belfast accent. '*Breaking and entering, trespass, theft of data and from a blind man too, a pillar of the community well-known for his charitable work and business acumen. The decent thing to do would be to hand you into the Police. You would probably get 6 months inside and lose your job and your reputation. I don't think Northumbria Police would want to employ a statistician who had just added to their crime statistics would they? No, a criminal record is a terrible stigma to shake off. I should know.*

 Hand you in to the cops, Mr Forster, would you like me to do that now? Like I said, it would be the decent thing to do. Unfortunately, for you Mr Forster, I am not decent.'

Kyle screamed as the iron scolded his already blistered skin and he felt the extreme heat penetrate his feet.

'*Who are you? What do you want?*' Kyle asked.

Kyle felt the man's presence close to him and then he whispered in Kyle's ear '*I am Satan*' and spat on Kyle's face. He longed to wipe the saliva from his stubble and put his feet under a cold tap, but he couldn't move. He was tied down. Satan left the room and he heard him climbing stairs and then silence again. He must have been imprisoned somewhere deep in a basement in a remote area, because there was no sound to suggest a world outside the walls; no birds singing, no traffic noise, not even the sound of wind or rain. Nothing!

It was impossible to ascertain how long had passed before Satan returned and thrust a plastic cup of water in Kyle's face saying '*Drink*'. Kyle was dying of thirst and lapped up the tepid water like a puppy. He hoped food was to follow but Satan just went away and left him feeling much more hungry than before, his taste buds teased with unfulfilled expectation and his stomach rumbling.

A similar length of time passed and Kyle's hunger had almost overtaken the pain in his feet as his prime cause of distress. This time Satan had an ac-complice. They silently went about unscrewing his bed and lifting it with him still tied to it. '*Got it*' one said. '*Yes. You lead the way*' the other replied. Kyle felt himself being carried into another room and manoeuvred on to an even more uncomfortable bed. He struggled to get free as his arms and legs were untied and then locked again at full-stretch. However, it was 2 against 1 and his feet were still in agony.

After a brief pause for breath, Satan interrogated his prisoner: '*Who are you working for, Mr Forster?*'

'*No-one*' Kyle replied. '*I'm on my own*'.

'*Liar!*' Satan yelled angrily and turned some cogs. Suddenly there was a creak-ing sound and Kyle felt his feet and hands pulled apart. He realized instantly that he was being tortured for information and the instrument of torture was one of medieval origins. He was in the rack!

'*Why would a pen-pusher start poking his nose into the plans of world lead-ers and entrepreneurs unless he was working for a more important group? Where would he get all the passwords from to access the files? Do you think I'm stupid? I'll ask you again. Who is paying you to spy on the Illuminati?*'

'*I came across the books by accident. I guessed the password and was fas-cinated by what I read. I'm not working for anyone. I just needed to find out what the New World Order was all about*'.

Satan turned the screw again and this time the pain was unbearable.

'*You take a memory stick from a businessman on a train and just happen to guess that his password is 'illuminati' with no outside help. I don't believe you Mr Forster.*'

'*I overheard him use the word on his mobile when I was in the loo. He was standing outside when I came out and looked shifty. I'd seen a TV programme about the Illuminati so it was the first thing that came into my head. It all just led from there.*'

Kyle braced himself for more pain. Satan tapped on the contraption and then said '*Wait there*' and left the room. Given that he had locked Kyle in the rack it was a superfluous instruction.

When he returned, he had company; a man and a dog. Kyle recognised Batman's voice immediately:

'*How did you know where to find the 6th phase?*' he enquired gently. Kyle explained his eavesdropping at the Director's party and his trip to Scotland.

'*Um! And I guess you over-heard me type my password into my desktop when I disturbed your break-in?*'

'*Yes. I hid in your wardrobe when you came back unexpected*'

'*Who else knows?*'

'*About the sixth phase? Nobody. I had just finished reading it when I was kidnapped. I told a few friends and family about the first 5 phases but they all thought I was making it up. Even the Police didn't take me seriously. So, as I told Satan, I am on my own.*'

'*He's lying boss*' said Satan twitching at the levers.

'*Maybe he is but his story checks out. Bring him some food and water and leave him here for now*'.

With that the two exited. Satan brought some bread and water and Kyle demolished it in seconds, tearing at the bread with his teeth and his one free hand, the other still in the rack. He could not think of Batman and Robin without images of the dog's blow-job coming into mind. His feet still throbbed but at least the hunger pains had subsided. He dropped off to sleep several times only to wake in pain.

It seemed like eternity till Satan's next visit. He was wheeling another piece of machinery into the room and Kyle shuddered at the prospect of more torture but he said nothing and went away. More time passed. Kyle started to hear noises in the room. At first, he thought that it was his mind playing tricks on him. There were shuffles and moans and sniffles. They were coming from the direction of the other piece of equipment.

Kyle shouted out: '*Is someone there?*'

'*Aye! Where the fuck am I?*' came the reply in a strong Scottish accent.

Kyle couldn't answer that question but the sound of approaching footsteps ended the conversation. The two prisoners were about to be introduced.

Scene 8: Mind Games

'*Forster. We've brought you some company*' Satan bellowed as he entered the room and marched purposefully towards Kyle. He roughly propped up Kyle's head and unfastened the blindfold. For the first time in ages, Kyle could see but it took several minutes for his eyes to focus. The room was a kaleidoscope of shifting colour and shape and eventually the pattern settled on a muscular, dark-haired man about Kyle's age but with a more lived-in face. He was bearing down on Kyle and as he grinned a large gap in his front teeth became visible. They were in an ancient torture chamber, possibly in a castle, given the dust and stone walls. To his right lay a man blindfolded, gagged and bound and frantically fighting to free himself.

'*Recognize him?*' enquired Satan.

'*No*' Kyle answered noting the man looked scruffy and disturbed and recalling his rough Scottish accent, more Glaswegian than the soft lilt of Dougie's Lothian twang.

'*I'm disappointed in you. This tramp saved your life when I thought I'd killed you. He's a bloody nuisance. He's a pest that needs swotting; a scrounging parasite that contributes nothing.*'

The tramp shouted something back that was unintelligible but sounded aggressive. Kyle thanked the tramp for saving his life. The tramp fell quiet and then howled like a wolf.

'*He's mad*' said Satan. '*I can't wait to see his head in that basket*'.

Kyle looked in horror at the contraption his saviour was in. High above his neck was a black axe, suspended by a system of pulleys to a lever on the other side of the room. A basket with an old navy blanket lay waiting to catch his head when the axe fell.

'*No*' said Kyle instinctively.

'*This is your chance to return the favour Mr Forster. You can save the tramp's life but only if you tell me everything about your plan to resist the Illuminati, who is involved and how much they know.*'

Kyle squirmed. '*I told you I'm working on my own. I haven't formulated any plan. Until I read the sixth phase I was even contemplating joining you. I agreed with much of what you said. I am just as insignificant to you as my Scottish friend over there. If you let us both go, we are of no threat to you. You have already won. You have infiltrated the Government, the Police, the Secret Services, and the army, everyone I might go to. I just want to go back to my ordinary life and let history unfold in whichever way it does.*'

'Very convincing' Satan acknowledged. *'You have been well trained for this eventuality'*. He went to the lever and held it in one hand, loosening the tramp's blindfold with the other. The tramp struggled and looked up with wild, startled eyes at the axe above his neck. He struggled violently to get free but it was futile.

'Don't kill him. Kill me' Kyle yelled valiantly.

Satan stopped and considered his options. *'That's very touching Mr Forster and I'd like to do that. Believe me! I'd like to see your head in that basket. Unfortunately, my orders are to keep you alive. Now I'm giving you one last chance to tell me everything.'*

'I would if there was anything to tell, but there isn't. I'm not a spy. I'm a pen-pusher from Wallsend. Let us both go and you will never come across us again. If I did go and tell someone about the 6th phase what good would it do without any evidence? You've taken my memory stick and my lap-top no doubt. You've searched my home for copies. I would be laughed at as a mad conspiracy nut.'

'I can't take the risk Forster' Satan said. *'I'm afraid if you can't help me then you can't help him'.*

The axe fell and severed the tramp's head from his body in one slice. Blood spluttered everywhere and the head thudded down into the basket. Kyle saw the fear in the tramp's eyes and was certain they were still moving after the head hit the basket. His body was life-less. His neck was a disgusting mess of torn sinews, blood and bone.

Kyle felt sick and speechless as he looked up at his tormentor, who was grinning with satisfaction. Satan fastened Kyle's blindfold again and left the room. Once more, Kyle was blind and alone but this time he was traumatised by the memory of Satan's cruelty and the loss of a good man's life.

*****

Kyle felt pathetic. He was weak, unshaven and naked apart from the stinking underpants he'd been captured in. He had been powerless to stop a man who had saved his life in Edinburgh get beheaded before his eyes. Satan seemed to be deliberately waiting until the hunger pains were unbearable before bringing him his paltry rations of bread and water with the occasional treat of fruit that was well past its sell-by date. It was crueller to keep him alive in this state than to move him into the guillotine, which stood next to him, a constant reminder of his dead friend.

He was mostly blindfolded, gagged and chained to the rack at both ends but he was given sufficient freedom to use an adjacent shite-bowl, to eat and to drink. Satan watched over all these activities with his nose turned up. Once Batman joined him and they had a heated debate about whether or not to kill Kyle. Satan was keen to earn his corn as an executioner. Batman wanted to keep him alive until he squealed or went insane. Neither considered letting him go.

Kyle found it difficult to call for attention when he was gagged. The sound barely made it across the cell no matter how hard he shouted. By the time Satan came in it was too late. Kyle had pissed in his pants.

'You disgusting pig' Satan said whipping his wet pants off and flinging them across the room. Kyle's hands were cuffed above his head so his privates were exposed.

'I thought you blacks were supposed to be well-endowed' Satan laughed. *'You're pathetic. I've seen more meat on a Linda McCartney sausage!'*

'Give me some dignity. Some fresh pants and a bed-bath' Kyle pleaded.

'You don't deserve dignity. You are a dirty black bastard.' Then he changed his tone to sound friendlier and asked *'Do you like football Forster?'*

'Yes'

'I should have let you have a game with us yesterday. It was un-even sides. There were 4 of them and only 3 of us. We lost 6:2. Still, it was hilarious. Do you know what we used as a ball?'

'I haven't a clue'

'That tramps head. There was blood everywhere. Once I had a shot from distance and the head hardly moved but one of his eyes went flying out of its sockets and landed in the top corner. I went running around the pitch with my shirt over my head. You would have loved it.'

'You're sick'.

'No, you are sick Forster. I'm as fit as a fiddle, but you are dying a long, slow painful death.'

Satan was right. Kyle was feeling ill. Every time he fell asleep he was woken by ghastly nightmares and visions. He felt like he hadn't slept for weeks and yet there was no rest in this hell-hole. The next time Satan returned he was accompanied by Batman and Robin. Kyle was stretched again to the point that his weakening bones cracked and a shot of pain left him screaming. Batman kept asking him the same questions over and over again. He wished he could make something up about being a spy working for an Anti-Illuminati organisation but he didn't know who to say he worked for.

Batman left the room in disgust, mumbling about waiting till the Chief arrived to decide what to do with Kyle. Satan sat on the bottom of Kyle's bed and spoke softly. *'You never told me Forster what a fit wife you had. A ginger tart with an ass to die for! I went round and paid her a visit last night just to put* her mind at rest. I told her you were spending some time in an asylum follow-ing a break-down and didn't want any visitors. She believed every word.'

'You saw Helen?'

'Oh I more than saw her. We got talking and she wanted a shoulder to cry on. I was only too happy to oblige and hear her tales of her useless, black hus-band who couldn't satisfy her in bed. I got a hard-on so I forced her up against the wall and kissed her. She fought and cried for me to stop but I could feel how much her tight fanny was crying out for a big, white cock so I just held myself firm against her and started moving up and down. Her mouth said no but her body said yes, yes, oh yes. She hardly resisted when I finally ripped her silk panties off and entered her from behind. I shoved it in one hole then the other and she was soon panting loudly. She ended thanking me for the best orgasm she had had in years.'

'I don't believe you'.

'Why not? Your hot, sticky ginger tart got filled with cream by a bloke at work didn't she?'

'You're not her type.'

'On the contrary, she loves it rough. She told me so. You were too gentle to excite her. She wanted a real man with a big, hard cock. If you were her type she'd still be with you Forster, but you lost her and now you have nothing.'

Kyle had never hated anyone as much as he hated Satan. He might be making it all up but Kyle couldn't be sure of anything anymore. Much to his surprise, Kyle managed to get some sleep before Satan's next visit.

'Forster' he laughed handing him some water. 'Are you missing your son?'

'Of course I am'.

'I thought you might be so this afternoon I thought I'd pick him up from school and give him a place on that spare bed. Would you like that?'

'You leave Nathan alone'.

'I thought that would get to you. You see, my theory is that you might have been able to keep strum and watch a worthless bum get be-headed but you wouldn't be able to sit there and watch your son's head drop into that bas-ket.'

'You bastard! Don't you get it? I've told the truth. There's nothing more to tell. I'd confess to anything to save my son, but there's nothing to confess.'

Satan turned the screws on the rack in frustration at the failure of his inter-rogation. Suddenly, there were steps on the stone floor and a friendly, well-spoken voice delivered Satan a rebuke. 'Satan. This is no way to treat a guest.

For god sake go and get him some fresh clothes while I help him off that awful contraption.'

Kyle wept with relief as the man freed him of all restraints and supported his head as he sat up. He could hardly move, yet alone run for freedom. He just sobbed like a baby and said *'Thank you'* over and over again. The man looked like Satan's polar opposite: small, fair, nimble and kindly. Satan returned with some clothes and a bowl of fresh water and left them on the stone floor without a word as the man cradled Kyle in his arms.

Batman came into the room with Robin and asked *'Do you need to see me Chief?'*

'Not yet', replied the Chief. *'Can you rustle Kyle up something to eat? He looks famished.'*

'Yes boss' Batman acquiesced and left the room.

'So you're the Chief' declared Kyle looking up starry-eyed at his host.

'I am indeed' said the Chief and he shook Kyle's hand. *'We really must move you somewhere more comfortable.'*

'I just want to go home' said Kyle.

'I know. You are not ready yet, but I'm sure you will be able to go home soon.'

Kyle could have hugged him but instead he cleaned himself up and dressed ready for his transit to a more humane prison.

Scene 9: Selling Satan

Cuffed and blindfolded Satan and an accomplice bundled Kyle into the back of a van and sped off to find him a new home. Satan kicked him in the balls as he bid his farewell by slinging him across the floor of his new room. Kyle could see enough through the blindfold to tell he was going to hate this place less than the last one. There was some light in the room and he could hear birds singing outside. There was the occasional distant sound of a vehicle passing and a flock of sheep in the fields. He even thought he could detect running water, possibly a nearby stream.

He was free to move around the room and his limbs revelled in their new-found freedom. He still had hand-cuffs and foot-cuffs so he couldn't walk but he could wriggle and crawl enough to discover the room had a proper bed and furniture with laminate flooring. Then he found a gap in the wall and bumped his head on an open door. Passing through the gap he was delighted to come across a toilet, basin and bath. His room was en-suite!

Suddenly he heard a car approaching and footsteps coming up the stairs. He prayed it was not Satan returning to take him back to his former prison. The door opened and a jovial voice greeted him:

'Welcome Kyle. How do you like your new home?'

'Much better thanks Chief', Kyle replied.

'Here, let me get you out of those cuffs and blindfold'.

Kyle felt a tear build up in his eye as he was finally set free of his chains and given back his vision. The Chief helped him to his feet. The first time he fell down, too weak to stand but the second time he steadied himself and managed to stagger over to the window. He was in a remote, stone-built cottage with fine views over the Cheviots. A farm track led away to a nearby farm and a footpath crossed the meadows to a beck running down the nearest hill.

'Beautiful view isn't it?' said the Chief.

'Yes. Where am I?' asked Kyle.

'Oh, come on! You don't expect me to tell you that, do you?' laughed the Chief. 'You are safe and you will be well looked after whilst you regain your strength. Then you will go home. You have this bedroom and bathroom. The rest of the cottage is out of bounds but a colleague will be living downstairs and you only need to knock on the door to get his attention'.

'Not Satan'.

'No. That thug has his uses but he is finished with you'.

'*Do you finally believe me when I tell you that I am on my own and not part of some plot to crush the Illuminati?*'

'*Kyle, I believe that the great courage and determination you showed finding out about us actually indicates that you are interested in joining us. You may have what it takes to be one of our senior executives. My task is to convince you to fight for us, not against us*'.

Kyle had a long hot soak in the bath and shaved. He felt almost human again. His new guard brought him a proper meal and asked him to call if he could get him anything else. Kyle called him once to test the theory asking if there was any chance of a newspaper. He came up apologising for only having the previous Sunday's paper. Kyle didn't mind. It was great catching up on the World outside and it was like having his own room service. He read about how interest rates had been slashed again to combat the economic downturn, car plants had been mothballed and President-elect Obama had announced a new fiscal stimulus package. Kyle had a good night's sleep for the first time in ages.

Kyle woke to the sound of a distant cockerel and a lost sheep calling for its flock. He found it easier to stand and walk about now and he cautiously tried the door. It was locked. He re-read the sports supplement, had another bath and dressed. After lunch, the Chief returned and asked him to complete an IQ test. Kyle thought it would be a useful guide as to whether or not he still had his wits about him after the mental torture that Satan had put him through.

'*I knew it*' the Chief proclaimed when he re-entered the room at dusk. '*Your IQ score puts you up there with the top 10% of the nation. With your brains and bravery you are just the sort of person the brotherhood needs.*'

'*I'm flattered but I don't believe in your elitist class system. I was horrified by the way the 6ᵗʰ phase talked about the unclassified as if they were pond-life.*'

'*I agree. The 6ᵗʰ phase was rejected at Bilderberg. The reason we were so determined to stop it leaking out was that it would do us immense harm if people really thought that was our plan. It wasn't. The liberals amongst us effectively argued against it and we now have a new plan, which is much more in line with the 12 pillars and less totalitarian.*'

'*Really?*'

'*Yes. The plan is still in draft but when it's finalised maybe I will let you see a copy*'.

'*I still can't see how people all over the World will turn against their democratically elected governments and let you just take over without a fight.*'

'*People are getting desperate. Democracy is just a concept. People worry more about jobs and security and food on the table than grand concepts. We will offer a solution because we control so much of the World's wealth and commerce that we can end the Credit Crunch as quickly as we started it. As*' an economist Kyle, you know that the western democracies can't afford the level of stimulus needed to get the economy booming again without drastic tax rises or savage spending cuts. We offer an economic alternative.'

'In America there is new hope that Obama will sort the mess out. They want to see him given a chance'.

'I hope we can convince Barack to join us. He is a very impressive man. He didn't come through the normal party machine like most Presidents so we've got work to do. However, many of those in Congress and in his administration are sympathetic so I think he might come round'.

'And if he doesn't?'

'That would be a shame. We might have to wait until he fails before launching our take-over. The public disillusionment will be more conducive than ever if a great hope of salvation fails.'

'I thought you were going to takeover in January, before he gets sworn in'.

'We need to be ready by January 2009 but if I was a betting man I'd go for April 2010. The World will be on its knees by then and Obama's honeymoon will be well and truly over'.

'You are definitely not going to assassinate him then?'

'Well, I'm not Kyle. I don't believe in violence. The brotherhood is a broad church. Satan would love to have Obama's head and half the people who voted Republican would probably agree with him. I cannot guarantee that he will escape an assassination attempt but I hope he does. We just have to be ready for every eventuality. We have been waiting hundreds of years for this great day to come and we are tantalisingly close now.'

With that he left. Kyle felt a warm feeling inside. The Chief seemed a very amiable, genuine guy and he had rescued him from a hellish existence. Maybe, the Chief and his co-conspirators were the right people to lead the World after all.

The next day the Chief brought a lap-top into the room and said as he booted it up that he had something Kyle needed to see. He inserted a DVD and pressed pause. 'This was taken at one of our meetings on Wall Street last year' he said by way of introduction.

The meeting started with a group of Gordon Gecko type characters talking bullishly about how much control they had over the World's financial markets. There was a knock on the door and a PA brought a new delegate to the table. Kyle was astonished to see it was his brother Dan. Dan shook hands brashly and shared typically smooth banter with the bankers. Then they all sat down and debated how they would bring about the next Wall Street Crash and allow the Illuminati to take control.

The Chief stopped the DVD and ejected it. He said nothing but looked at Kyle for a response.

'*My brother belonged to the brotherhood?*' Kyle uttered disbelievingly.

'*Yes. He was a good man. Tragically, he didn't get to see the fruits of his labour. He was very proud and when his bosses found out he had been responsible for their collapse they sacked him. He couldn't live with the shame of being found out. He thought he'd covered his tracks. It's all very sad.*'

With that the Chief put his arm round Kyle.

'*You can finish your brother's work. He believed passionately in a united world with no war or famine, where everyone who could work did work and international disparities in income for similar jobs were eliminated. He had the brains and bravery to risk his career engineering the conditions that would make a New World Order. Kyle, I want you to agree to join us. Do it for Dan.*'

Scene 10: Paranoid Android

Kyle didn't feel like a candidate for the intellectual elite. His mind felt like it had short-circuited with confusion. A few days ago he was being tortured by the satanic cult that had kidnapped him; now he was contemplating joining them and helping them take over the World!

The Chief was so kind and dignified and he had faith in Kyle. The Chief and Satan were like the Jekyll and Hyde of the Illuminati. He spoke passionately about everything and clearly shared Kyle's idealism. Sure, the Chief was radical and many of his ideas had roots in the sixth phase; compulsory international service for the young unemployed, a greater focus on preventing first-time criminals re-offending and diverting resources from defending borders to defending the Planet. However, the emphasis was on reducing human suffering and thinking globally; not on elitist social engineering.

The Chief also reached out to Kyle in a very personal way. During his 20's both Kyle's parents had died of cancer. By championing science over religion and squeamish morality, Illuminati scientists had found a cure for cancer. In time, stem cell research and genetic medicine could eradicate most life-threatening diseases and birth defects. The Chief explained how millions of lives are being lost while the World differed over scientific ethics. Currently, even after new treatments were approved it took decades for them to become widely available because drug companies would patent their products and restrict supply to inflate prices. The New World Order would prevent the tragedy that Dan experienced of being orphaned by the scourge of cancer. No wonder he had been a willing recruit.

Four days after the Chief had rescued him, Kyle knew he was physically well enough to return to the outside World. Plans had been made. His family and employer had been briefed that he was to be released from a psychiatric hospital. A doctor had visited Kyle and prescribed him benzodiazepines, a tranquillizer known on the street as wobbly eggs. One task remained; an interview with the Chief.

'*Come in Kyle*' the Chief said as he was escorted to a downstairs office at the cottage. '*Have a seat*'.

'*Thanks*'.

'*How are you feeling?*'

'*I'm much better thanks. The pills have calmed me down and made me less worried about what's going to happen in the World. I'm sleeping like a baby*'.

'*Good. You have had a really difficult time. You separated from your wife, your brother committed suicide, you saw a man shot dead in front of your* eyes and you became paranoid that a sinister cult was out to get you. You really needed help and I'm glad we rescued you when we did.'

'It didn't feel like a rescue when Satan had me on the rack!'

'No. I'm sorry about that. I've clarified boundaries with him.'

'Am I free to go now?'

'Yes. Your chauffeur is waiting to take you home. You will be blindfolded and cuffed for the journey and then set free. However, I hope it won't be the last we see of you. Your IQ test was remarkable given your state of mind. I meant what I said about you joining us.'

'I'm flattered but I really don't want to become involved. Like you said, I've been through a lot. I just want some peace and quiet now.'

'I understand. What we are planning is dangerous. You have shown great courage but more danger is not what you need right now.'

'No'.

'Well Kyle I guess it is goodbye'. The Chief rose and shook Kyle's hand. A guard instantly appeared, blindfolded Kyle and led him to the waiting car. He felt numb and surreal. He was not as excited about going home as he thought he would be. In many ways he was apprehensive about being left alone to care for himself and unsure how his friends and family would react to his sickness.

As the car left the bumpy farm track and hit smooth tarmac he asked his driver if he had missed Christmas.

'No' replied the driver. 'Today is only the first of December sir'.

Clearly, his captivity had seemed longer than it was.

Back at home, he shut all the curtains although it was not yet dusk and sat in silence for a while unsure what to do. Suddenly, he heard footsteps on the drive and someone fiddling with the front door. Kyle curled up in a shivering ball behind the sofa as he had done as a child every Saturday tea-time when the daleks were on TV. The intruder retreated. Kyle investigated and breathed a huge sigh of relief when he saw the free paper stuffed through the letter-box.

Kyle's phone rang. He stared at it suspiciously and could not bring himself to answer. He wasn't up to conversation. In fact, he wasn't up to much. He started opening the pile of post inside the front door but found it hard work and switched on the TV. He could not concentrate and it was on more as background comfort than viewing material. He jumped again as his cuckoo clock announced it was 4.00 p.m. and he remembered he was due to take his next pill in an hour.

Kyle had terrible nightmares that night. Images of his torture at the hands of Satan were everywhere. He dropped off into deeper and deeper sleep only to be woken by increasingly intense nightmares. The next morning he felt exhausted and didn't even consider work. He missed the calming voice of the Chief and his knowing smile. His trembling hands made him spill his corn-flakes and he decided to have his next pill an hour early to steady the nerves. He found it hard to separate the reality of his life from the nightmare of his dreams and wondered how long he had been in a trance. Maybe he would wake up properly soon and find himself still in bed with Helen and hear Nathan watching TV downstairs.

Dazed and confused Kyle ventured out to the supermarket. He saw Helen in every pretty girls face and Satan in every man the girl was with. He got some rations and a newspaper and returned home to microwave a meal for one. The phone rang again and this time he was brave enough to answer.

'Hello' he said.

'Kyle? Is that you? You sound odd!' It was Elton John.

'Yes. Who is it?'

'Elton mate. Are you all right? We've been worried about you. You haven't answered your mobile for weeks'.

'Oh. I've been away. I haven't been feeling myself but I'm getting a little better each day'.

'So you haven't been kidnapped by a mad dictator then?' Elton laughed.

'I needed some time away. That's all. I forgot my phone. I'm back now'.

'Anyway, I know its short notice but the lads are meeting up for a pint tonight. Are you up for it?'

'Sorry. I'm busy'

'Oh well. Look after yourself mate. See you'.

'Bye'. Kyle cried as he put the phone down. How did Elton know he had been kidnapped he asked himself? Also, was it a test to see if he was going to blag about the sixth phase? He suspected Elton John of being an Illuminati member, what with his Round Table links and all that. Could he trust any of his friends? It was safest to say nothing: nothing about the Books of the Illuminati, the kidnapping, the torture or the murder of the man who had saved his life. He couldn't face torture again. He would rather die.

Briefly Kyle did look at the pack of pills and wonder what would happen if he swallowed the lot. Then he thought of Nathan and their game of football on the waste-land in Wallsend. He didn't want to leave his son fatherless. He wanted to be respected and not laughed at as a crazy man who cowardly took his own life rather than confront his illness. He lay on the sofa and watched TV, eventually dozing off about nine and not waking up until midnight.

When he retired for the night he smothered his ears with the pillow to drown out the sounds of a car alarm going off nearby and an owl in the trees. The wind was accelerating and the tree creaked. Kyle was certain it was going to come crashing down through his window. He visualised a masked man following it through the window with an owl on his back and a gun in his hand. The owl then transformed into Satan and he was once more in the rack, being stretched beyond his 6 foot 2 frame. Then he fell into a deep, soothing sleep and all the problems of the World seemed to drift away.

He woke to find the sun shining and the Chief looking down at him from the heavens with his friendly smile. '*Every day you are getting better Kyle*' he reassured him. '*I am your friend. The brotherhood will always look out for you*'.

Kyle wanted to believe but just before he had been blindfolded and led away from the Chief's hospitality he had seen something that disturbed him greatly. Lying on a shelf in the hall was the envelope he had placed his IQ test in. It was unopened, just as it was when he had handed it to the Chief to mark.

Act 4: Weathering the Storm

Scene 1: A Friendly Face

It was a drizzly December day and Kyle sat debating whether or not to get out of bed when the phone rang. It was Kyle's boss, making a valiant attempt to appear concerned. After exchanging the predictable pleasantries about Kyle's health he cut to the chase:

'I know your sick-notes got another week to run but we would really like to see you back. If you are feeling better, how about returning to work on Monday?'

'Ok. The longer I leave it I guess the harder it will be to go back.'

'Absolutely! My door is always open if you find it's too soon or want to discuss going part-time for a while.'

'Thanks'.

'See you Monday then?

'Yes. See you Monday.'

'Bye Kyle'.

Kyle knew his boss's door was not always open. In fact, he looked deeply disturbed whenever anyone knocked on it without an appointment and the *'meeting in progress'* sign was almost permanently on display. He also knew that there would be a pile of work waiting for him, a deluge of e-mails to wade through and his boss would turn blue with panic if ever he asked to go part-time. Still, maybe he needed work to take his mind off things and give him a reason to get out of bed.

Kyle got dressed and got the metro into town. He got lost in Fenwicks and felt a panic attack coming on as he fought his way through the slow-moving traffic of old ladies armed with carrier bags. All the escalators seemed to lead up and he found the crowds oppressive. He ultimately found an exit and stepped out into the elegant thoroughfare of Northumberland Street. He passed the buskers, the queue of excited kids waiting to see the famous Christmas window display and the newspaper vendors and felt reassured by the familiarity of their shrill shouts of *'Chronicle, Chronicle'*. He stood outside the entrance to the World's biggest Marks and Spencer by the hot chestnut seller and considered his options.

Kyle decided to escape the hustle and bustle of the City Centre and go to the park for his lunch, grabbing a peanut butter and banana stottie en-route. The sun peeped out from behind the clouds as he cut through the University quadrangle and headed towards the floodlights of St James Park. Between the football ground and the Royal Victoria Infirmary, where 15 years ago Nathan had been born, was Leazes Park. He sat by the boating lake and ate his lunch watching the world go by.

A little boy was happily feeding the ducks, whilst his proud mother looked on. Kyle recalled many a time he had taken Nathan here to do the same and calculated that it must be nearly a decade since he had last done so. Over the lake he noticed a lady sitting down on a bench eating her lunch, huddled up under a big coat to keep warm. She looked like Helen. When he finished his lunch he got up and walked round the lake towards her, expecting to see her turn into a stranger as many had before her. However, to his surprise he realized that it was his wife and she was alone.

'Helen? I thought it was you! I was just having my lunch over the other side of the lake.'

'Hello. I heard they let you out. How are you feeling?'

'I'm much better thanks. How are you?'

'I'm feeling really old. I've just been to the RVI to find out about a face lift. I'd love to have one done but I think I will have to stick to the Botox injections. It isn't cheap!'

'You don't need anything. You are gorgeous, Helen.'

'No, I'm not. They must have put you on the funny pills. Look at all these lines. There seems to be a new one each morning. Honestly, do I look middle-aged?'

'No. You still look really young for your age'.

'There you go – for my age! Thanks a lot!'

Kyle could not win this argument. Besides, now she had drawn attention to the fact, Kyle thought Helen was showing more signs of her 40 years on planet Earth than he had previously noticed. She was still very pretty but she looked strained and her cheeks were sinking. Kyle quickly changed the subject:

'How's Nathan?'

' Fine. Have you had any ideas what you are getting him for Christmas?'

'No. I hadn't thought about it.'

'Well, there's a surprise! You've been out 3 days and you haven't been in touch with your son. Have you forgotten about us?'

'Can I take him out tomorrow? Maybe we can come here for a kick-around.'

'Bloody football! That's all you men think about. Well, that and the other!'

'Shall I pick him up about 11?'

'OK. I better get back to work now. See you tomorrow.'

Kyle sat for a while watching Helen trudge back into town. It had been a strange reunion; two strangers in a park. 20 years ago they had come to this park and frolicked on the grass in the summer. Kyle recalled how stunning Helen looked and how they couldn't wait to ravish each other, so much so that they ended up making love in the bushes. The bushes were still there but Helen, his first true love, was long gone.

*****

Kyle woke about 7 and looked at the clock. He went to the loo and returned to bed listening to the wind. Next thing he knew he heard distant church bells and the sun was beaming through his curtains. He looked at his watch and jumped up.

'Shit!' It was half past 11!

He texted Helen to say he was running late. She was already in her car when he got to Wallsend and she drove off at high speed without a word. Nathan was upstairs in his room on the PC. There were no hugs for Dad, no cries of '*I miss you*' just a grunt of '*what?*' when Kyle opened his bedroom door.

Kyle waited downstairs and about one o clock Nathan appeared in his Newcastle shirt and torn jeans and walked with his Dad to the waste-land. They had ruled out Leazes Park as the grey clouds were closing in and it wouldn't be light much longer. It was freezing and much muddier than last time they had played. The pitch contained a few iced-over puddles and Kyle struggled to keep his balance. He also felt incredibly unfit.

They didn't exchange many words but Kyle could tell the afternoon had meant a lot to Nathan and that meant a lot to him. A few flakes of snow fell as they got back home and Nathan run straight upstairs for a warm shower. Kyle opted for a long, hot soak, whilst he waited for Helen to return.

At about half four she sent him a text saying she was heading back from her Mums and Kyle could leave if he wanted so Kyle bid farewell to his son and returned to Gosforth. That night he had a glass of single malt and sat looking through an old photo album. Lost in nostalgia he missed the start of Match of the Day. In fact, he didn't see much of it as he soon fell asleep and woke up at the sound of the familiar theme tune announcing it was all over and it was time for bed.

Kyle had a long lay-in on Sunday morning. He wrapped up warm and braved the frosty pavements to get a paper and read more about the gloomy state of the World economy. He exchanged some texts with the 2 Johns and assured them he would join them on the next lad's night. He was pottering around in the afternoon when the doorbell rang and he congratulated himself on going to open it without the slightest hint of trepidation. Maybe, he was getting better!

He was astonished to open the door and see Rachel smiling coyly in a thick winter coat with specks of snow on it.

'Hi Rachel! That's a surprise!'

'How are you Kyle? We've all been really worried about you'.

'I'm much better thanks. Come in. You look freezing.'

'Thanks', said Rachel stepping out of the cold.

Rachel had little, delicate features but a lovely big smile and an expressive face that changed from shy and concerned to relieved and friendly within seconds. Kyle took her coat and showed her to the living room before going to the kitchen to make coffee. As he did so, he admired how her figure was beautifully sculpted by the tight, indigo denim of her jeans. Kyle remembered that Rachel took it black with no sugar and she smiled as he entered the room, touched by his memory. She was sitting in the arm-chair near the fire and Kyle sat opposite her on the sofa sipping his milky coffee.

Rachel wore a short, loose, bottle-green top that revealed an inch of white skin when she sat up straight between her top and her jeans. Her waist was so tiny that Kyle wanted to wrap his large hands around it and see if he could squeeze it enough to reach all the way round and link fingers. Kyle noted how Rachel ran her fingers through her mousy hair every time she put her cup down and he found her nervous gestures attractive.

'Everyone sends their love', she said. *'They are looking forward to seeing you tomorrow. To tell you the truth I think they've been struggling without you. Even Sam has had to work hard'.*

'I'm sure there will be a mountain of problems to come back to'.

'Are you sure you are ready to come back to work Kyle? You shouldn't rush these things'.

'Yes. I will be fine Rachel'.

Kyle paused and something about her warmth and demeanour told him he could trust her. It was a surprising and deeply satisfying revelation.

'Rachel. I haven't actually been in a mental hospital. You know I told you about the Illuminati and you warned me to stay away. Well, I wish I'd taken your advice because they kidnapped and tortured me.'

'I did wonder'. Rachel's face immediately turned from conviviality to concern before resting on compassion.

'At the Director's wedding bash I overheard him taking to the Deputy Chief about the New World Order. It sounds like they are both involved and they mentioned a big-wig from Darras Hall who had a secret copy of the Illuminati plans. I broke into his house, copied a file across and next thing I know two heavies had broken into mine and there's a gun pointing in my face.'

'No!'

'Yes. I was blindfolded, gagged, my arms and legs were locked in metal cuffs and I was kept in a dark basement on a bed that doubled up as a rack. A guard called Satan interrogated me about what I knew and who I was working for and tortured me. I even had to watch those bastards be-head the tramp that had saved my life in Edinburgh before they eventually realized that I was an innocuous nobody.'

'What did they do then?'

'Their boss came to see me and apologised. He was really canny and took me to a cottage in the Cheviots, where I was well-treated and nursed back to health.'

'I see. How long were you there?'

'I was only in the cottage for a few days. I must have been in the dungeon for two or three weeks. It was hell.'

'I bet it was. And the Illuminati let us all think you'd gone insane and been locked up?'

Kyle smiled. He was right to trust Rachel. Her question implied that she believed him and didn't believe he had gone nuts. He finished his coffee and looked at her in the eyes for the first time since she arrived. He felt a strong desire to kiss her small lips and hug her narrow frame. He was disappointed that although he was wildly aroused there was no physical response in his loins.

'Kyle, did you see a doctor when you were held prisoner?'

'Yes. He gave me these pills to calm me down. They seem to work although they make me a bit dozy'. Kyle got up and showed Rachel the jar of wobbly eggs.

'Dozy? You must be getting back to your old self' Rachel laughed.

Kyle laughed too and it was a beautiful feeling.

'Seriously but. I think you should stop taking those things. They are highly addictive and can really play tricks with your mind. If you feel you need help

see a proper doctor. Don't rely on one the Illuminati provided. It's in their interests to sedate you.'

'I'd never thought of that. Still, the doctor seemed genuine and it was after the Chief had taken me to the cottage'.

'You speak very fondly of this Chief'.

'Yes. He was a true gent and actually agreed with a lot of my beliefs. If he is in charge we have nothing to fear from the Illuminati'.

'Nothing to fear?' Rachel looked cross. 'Any organisation that uses torture and be-headings in this day of age sounds like one I fear very much.'

'The Chief didn't know that was going on. He was very sorry'.

'I'm sorry Kyle but it sounds like classic good cop, bad cop to me. If he was in charge then he was responsible for your torture, whether he licensed it or not.'

'Maybe you're right Rachel' Kyle considered. He then told her about the IQ test and the unopened envelope. As he did so, he tried to subtly make out the shape of her breasts under the short top but it was too loose and his glances too brief. However, he did notice her belly ring as she stretched and looked outside at the weather.

'I'm going to have to go now Kyle' Rachel said as she got up and went to her handbag. She took out a pen and wrote down a number. Kyle hoped it was her home number or maybe a mobile.

'This is the number of the Welfare Officer who deals with post-traumatic stress. She is really good. I think you should make an appointment Kyle and take things easy tomorrow. Don't let them work you too hard and come and see me if you want a natter. I'm really pleased you're getting better'.

'Thanks' Kyle said taking the note, relishing their first physical contact as he did so. Rachel did up her coat and said goodbye. She did not kiss him but her smile was full of compassion. He watched her brush the snow from the windscreen before driving off. Was she just a really nice girl showing kind concern or did she fancy him? Don't be silly he told himself. She is 29. I am 42. Still, there was no longer any doubt that he fancied her and it was great to see a friendly face.

Scene 2: Back to Normal?

Kyle looked at himself in the mirror. He felt strange wearing a suit again. Did he look strange? He combed his black hair and took a deep breath. *'Well, here goes'* he said to himself and he set off to work.

'Welcome back' said Sam as they emerged from the car park together and she gave him a big hug. *'Are you ok?'* she said sweetly. He was getting sick of that question, but he appreciated her warmth.

It wasn't too bad work-wise. He thanked the team for keeping things under control whilst he was away. Everyone was too polite to mention where. There were about 200 new emails but he managed to get through them all by lunch-time and at least half of them could be deleted with the most cursory of reads. He was summoned by his boss for the obligatory return to work interview straight after lunch and when he got back to the office he was amazed to see Sam and Donna deep in concentration on work.

He was beginning to get very tired and agitated and felt dizzy when he stood up to go to the loo. He knew what he needed but he remembered Rachel's advice as he opened the tube of pills. She was wise beyond her years and he knew he was already feeling withdrawal symptoms. He carefully split one pill in two, popped one half in his mouth, the other in his pocket and flushed the remaining pills down the loo.

He had a visitor when he got back to the office in the very shapely form of Alicia. All smiles and pig-tails she was telling Sam about her dishy new boyfriend. *'How's it going Kyle?'* she asked softly. He briefly described his first day back at work and she made lots of *'ah'* noises and ended with *'bless you'*. She was very sweet and very sexy but she spoke to Kyle like she was talking to a slightly backward child. Then she left wriggling her bum in a tight skirt and clattering her heels along the corridor.

The physical attraction made him think of Rachel and when he finished his coffee he went to find her office. She was sitting looking serious and professional in a familiar pin-striped trouser suit, her hair in a neat bun. She looked surprised to see Kyle and beckoned him in as she continued her conversation on the phone. She had a delightful accent, lyrical and intelligent. She expertly described the profile of a rape suspect to the inspector on the other end of the phone and fiddled with a pen as she did so.

'Sorry Kyle. There's been another rape in Killingworth. It sounds like the same guy as last month. What can I do for you?' she enquired when she eventually put the receiver down.

Kyle was disappointed by her formality. *'I just wanted to say thank-you for yesterday. I'm taking your advice. I've come off the pills and arranged to see the Welfare Officer tomorrow afternoon.'*

Rachel's formality broke with a delicious smile. *'Cool! You need someone to talk to Kyle. You've made a good decision.'*

'It was very good of you to think of me and come round to my house'.

'No problem. How has your first day back been?'

'Better than I feared but I'm really tired now so I'm having an early finish'.

'Good. You do that. It will get a little bit easier every day.' With that, Rachel's phone rang again and as she reached to get it she said *'Sorry Kyle. I will catch you later in the week. It's manic in here today'.*

'No problem. Bye Rachel.'

Rachel lifted a hand to wave as she answered immaculately *'Rachel Woods speaking'.* Kyle left the room and returned to the office to find Sam already packing up to go. It was five to four. Oh well, he thought, things are getting back to normal!

*****

The Welfare Officer was a terribly twee lady in her forties with no discernible accent. She made Kyle feel very relaxed as she talked clearly and slowly about all the experience she had dealing with trauma. She had dealt with police officers who had seen their colleagues killed, watched scenes of horrific violence and cruelty and been intimidated by gangland thugs. *'Nothing will shock me'* she laughed.

'Want to bet?' thought Kyle who had already decided that as this was confidential and a form of therapy he would tell the truth about his leave of absence. It took about 15 minutes of jolly chat and form filling before the Welfare Officer put on a serious face and asked Kyle to describe, taking as much time as he needed, what had happened to him that led to him seeking help.

She hardly raised an eye-brow as he re-told the story of his kidnapping and torture but every now and again she interjected encouraging noises and phrases like *'go on'* and *'you are doing really well'* mixed with the occasional *'golly!'*

When he finished she paused, made some notes and took off her glasses. *'You have done the right thing coming here. Coming here was the most difficult step but it is also the most important step to getting better.'*

Kyle nodded. He did feel better for getting it off his chest.

'Have you anyone at home you can talk to; a wife or a girlfriend?'

'No. I live alone. I recently separated?'

'Any children?'

'One. He's 15.'

'It must be very hard for you. I'm sorry.' She paused and sipped some water before asking Kyle to describe how he felt.

'I feel numb and kind of weird. I'm always tired and I have these frightening visions and nightmares. I see people I know in stranger's faces. I want to be alone but I get lonely and I think everyone's laughing at me and pitying me and nobody would believe me if I told the truth. They all think I've been in a mental hospital and I guess they are scared I might go off the rails again.'

The Welfare Officer was like a nodding donkey as Kyle described his feelings and when she finished writing she looked up from underneath her glasses and said *'these are very common feelings and perfectly normal reactions for someone who has been through trauma. How are you sleeping?'*

'Well, like I said, I'm having lots of nightmares and visions and sleeping a lot but it's disturbed sleep so I wake up tired'.

'Are you taking any medication?'

'I have been taking benzodiazepines but I've come off them. A doctor prescribed them when I was in captivity and I'm not sure I can trust him.'

'You should see your GP. You might need a milder tranquilizer or a referral for counselling. You should also have your blood pressure checked. How has coming back to work been?'

Kyle described his first two days back and she nodded enthusiastically again. She asked short, open questions and let Kyle do most of the talking.

'What about friends? How have they reacted?'

'Well, its early days. I wasn't ready for a night out but one came round to see me on Sunday and that felt good'.

'You need to make the effort to get out and see your friends, even when you don't feel like it. Friends are crucial to your recovery. It's at times like this that you find out who your true friends are. What about your sex-life. Do you have a partner?'

Kyle wasn't expecting this one and blushed as he explained quietly that he hadn't had sex for over 6 months. His embarrassment increased as she asked how often he masturbated. He wasn't sure what the normal answer was so he veered on the side of caution and said two or three times a week.

'That's good' she said. *'It is important to release any pent up frustrations'.* Kyle felt better and more able to talk freely about his experience in captivity and his fear over the New World Order. She nodded a lot but didn't seem especially shocked or even that interested in the revelations. Eventually, she looked at the clock and said *'I'm sorry but our hour is up. Would you like an-*

other appointment?' Kyle was surprised how quickly the hour had gone and how therapeutic just talking had been so he booked another appointment and returned to his office.

Scene 3: Live and Let Live

Just when Kyle's life was returning to normal and memories of his encounters with the Illuminati were fading he received an unwelcome reminder. He was in town completing his Christmas shopping when his mobile went off and a chilling voice said *'Kyle, its Batman. Meet me in John Lewis coffee shop in half an hour'*.

How did a blind man know he was in the City Centre and thus able to get to the planned rendezvous within half an hour? Was he being watched? Kyle checked himself for electronic tags and then thought how ridiculous he was being as he had not discovered anything when he had undressed, showered, bathed or changed clothes. Still, it was eerie.

Kyle liked John Lewis. He preferred to call it Bainbridge's, the name of the Geordie philanthropist that established the flagship department store. It was employee owned so all the profits went back to the employees rather than greedy shareholders. It shared this noble practice with the national John Lewis Partnership so it made sense for them to be taken over but Kyle was still cross when they rebranded the Newcastle store as John Lewis. Judging by the crowds flocking there in the midst of a global recession, it was not just an altruistic alternative to capitalism, it was a commercial success story.

Batman and Robin were already waiting in the coffee shop. He had a large latte' and a Danish pastry and was reading something in Braille. Robin looked up knowingly as Kyle approached but Batman was still focused on his reading.

'Batman. You wanted to see me' said Kyle.

'Ah, Kyle. Thanks for coming' said Batman, offering a hand-shake and a chair.

'The Chief wanted to make sure you were fully recovered from your illness.'

'That's good of him. Tell him I'm doing fine, thanks'.

'We have a regional meeting coming up. Some of the finest brains in the North will be there. Are you sure you don't want to come? You are very welcome.'

Kyle thought about it. He was tempted, not so much by the *'if you can't beat them join them'* mantra but by his eagerness to find out who the finest brains in the North were. Then he thought about how dangerous his associations with this brotherhood had proved to date and decided it was best for his health to decline the invitation.

'Thanks for the offer, but I don't want to get involved. I just want a normal life from now on.'

Batman was a good poker player. He never showed a flicker of emotion. He didn't try and persuade Kyle to change his mind. Instead he finished his coffee and Danish pastry, making small talk about Christmas and the state of the economy. He didn't wait for Kyle to finish his own beverage. He got up, shook his hand and stated *'I guess this time it really is farewell then. We won't be seeing each other again. I wish you well Kyle. Come on Robin, let's get a taxi.'*

Kyle sat pondering the meaning of this strange encounter. His overwhelming conclusion was that Batman was setting him a trap. If he has said yes to the meeting, he was still a threat and needed surveillance. His decline was a signal to cease monitoring Kyle and turn to more serious threats to the Illuminati. He had made the right choice but part of him wished he could have gone to the meeting and found out who was involved in the conspiracy and whether they were as benign as the Chief or as belligerent as Satan!

*****

One of the good things about returning to work after stress is that you can ask for what you want and your boss is afraid to say *'no'*. Bosses have to be so careful not to trigger a set-back and be deemed responsible for you returning to the sick-bed. Thus, when Kyle found out his boss was going to a presentation called *'The demographics of crime in a recession'* Kyle confidently asked to replace him.

'There's only one place for our department Kyle' his boss said softly.

'I'm really interested to learn how the data we produce can be used to prevent the socially disadvantaged turning to crime. Please could I go in your place?'

Kyle's boss rubbed his chin as he thought this over. *'Ok Kyle, but get me a copy of the slides'.*

In fact, there was only one reason why Kyle was so keen to attend this presentation. It was being given by Rachel Woods from criminal psychology!

Kyle got a front row seat, which wasn't difficult because as normal the first few into the room immediately went to the back of the room. Rachel appeared oblivious to Kyle's presence. She was wearing a black pencil skirt, black tights and a buttoned white blouse and she looked like a waitress at a top bistro. She also looked flustered and nervous, an unnatural performer to a crowded room of important people. Kyle realized that she was struggling to work the projector and he considered stepping forward to boldly save the day. However, what if he couldn't work it either? That would be counter-productive! Whilst he was contemplating his dilemma, a knight in shining armour from ICT entered the room and solved the problem to little Rachel's relief.

Rachel began timidly and someone at the back asked her to speak up. Kyle delivered him a hard stare. She gradually grew in confidence and the content was immaculate. Rachel clearly had a passion for what she was talking about and that eventually came through in her delivery. It was useful to. It did show

how demographic data that Kyle's section collated and verified can be used to profile those at risk of turning to a life of crime for economic reasons. Partnerships of Police, Social Services and Youth Workers could prevent this happening.

Although the blinds were down, the setting sun beamed in through the gaps and lit up the presenter, making it difficult to focus on the screen. At least that was Kyle's excuse, because he could not help but notice the shape of a white bra visible through Rachel's white blouse. The contours of her breasts were visible for the first time and unless she was well-padded, her breasts were reasonably full and perky for such a small girl.

At the end of the presentation Kyle went up to Rachel and said:

'That was brilliant Rachel. It really made me think my work is of value. Thanks.'

Rachel blushed. *'Thanks Kyle. I hate doing these things. I get really nervous'.*

'It didn't show. You were very professional'.

'I don't think they could hear me at the back'.

'That's their fault for sitting there. There were plenty of spare seats further forward. I could hear you perfectly'.

'I went on a presentational skills course recently and they told me I was too quiet. They also taped each of us doing a 5 minute presentation and played it back. It was horrible. I didn't realize what a strong Geordie accent I have. I will have to go to elocution'

'You have a beautiful accent Rachel. Don't change it whatever you do. Anyway, research suggests that intelligent, female, Geordie accents are amongst the most popular nation-wide and that's why there are so many call centres around here'.

'I thought it was because the labour was cheap and there was a back-lash against Indian call-centres'.

'Well that as well. Can I get you a drink?'

'That would be nice. I can't stay long but. I'm going out tonight with a friend to the Tyneside Cinema'.

Their conversation felt so natural that Kyle's request didn't feel like he was asking Rachel out, which he would have found embarrassing. There just seemed to be a chemistry there; a meeting of minds. Rachel drank diet Pepsi because she was driving. Kyle thought one pint won't hurt, but wondered after ordering it if Rachel would disapprove. If she did, she didn't show it. The time went far too quickly. They talked about cinema, books and music and found their tastes well aligned.

Kyle downed the residual half a pint to walk Rachel to her car and gave her a peck on the cheek as he said goodbye. She looked shy but pleased and Kyle watched her drive away with a growing desire in his heart. Back home he followed the advice of his Welfare Officer and had a wonderful wank, followed by a cool shower to calm his seething hormones down. He knew the simmering cauldron inside him meant something. He felt like his beating heart was bathing in a warm Jacuzzi. Was he was falling in love with Rachel Woods?

*****

Kyle had two Friday nights to look forward to. Tonight he was strolling up Claremont Road to the North Terrace and a re-union with his mates. Next week, it was the works Christmas party and Rachel would be there. Then he would break up for Christmas and New Year. Helen had agreed that he could spend Christmas day with her and Nathan so he wouldn't be on his own and he had got tickets to a couple of Newcastle's games in the festive period.

One Word was standing at the bar and offered a predictable greeting as Kyle approached with a big smile.

'Pint?'

'Cheers, One Word. I'll have a pint of OP please.'

One Word ordered and asked '*OK*?'

'Aye. It will take a lot more than being shot at, pushed down some steps, kidnapped, tortured and divorced to get me down'

One Word laughed and handed Kyle a delicious foaming pint of dark ale.

'God that tastes good' said Kyle as Elton arrived and slapped him on the back, simultaneously to demanding a pint of lager from One Word.

'So, what the fuck happened to you mate?' asked Elton and Kyle re-told the story of his kidnapping for the first of 3 times that evening. Everyone believed him, although some thought the story was embellished with tales or torture and be-headings, which seemed a bit far-fetched. They were all genuinely relieved that Kyle had recovered from his trauma and had declined Batman's invitation to the Illuminati meeting.

'If those pills made you dozy I'd hate to see what they'd do to One Word' laughed Mattie.

'*Bastard!*' said One Word.

'Maybe he's been on them for years' suggested Elton.

'Aye. That would explain a lot' agreed Mattie.

Changing the subject, Kyle noted his disappointment that the sexy student bar-maid wasn't on this evening. They all agreed and Mattie suggested she had probably gone home to Mummy and Daddy as the students broke up for Christmas today. Elton broke into a tirade about lazy students sponging off the state, which provoked a reaction from Kyle. Kyle explained how all they got now was loans and they provided a huge boost to the local economy. It got quite heated and Mattie decided he needed to intervene:

'Come on lads. One thing we can all agree on is that the number of students in Newcastle improves the quality of totty no end. That barmaid was stunning and she had a fantastic pair of bobby dazzlers'.

The tension was diffused with nodding consensus. Kyle reflected on how he had enjoyed Elton provoking him. Everyone had been tip-toeing around him for weeks. The heated disagreement had felt good. John Medburn then asked Kyle about his love-life and whether or not he had had any luck with the lovely Alicia. Kyle described his date at the Director's wedding bash and nobody sounded surprised at the disappointing outcome.

'So, is Alicia a free agent then? Have you given up on her and left the road clear for the charms of Elton John?' enquired Elton optimistically.

'No. She's met someone new. It sounds like she's really into him'.

'I bet he's really into her right now. Lucky bastard!'

'Have you got your eyes on anyone else Kyle' asked Dobbo.

'Maybe', said Kyle with a twinkle in his eyes.

'Go on. Who is the poor girl?' teased Mattie.

'There's a criminal psychologist called Rachel who I went out for a drink after work with. She's lovely but I'm not sure if she just wants to be friends or not.'

'Howay! A lass doesn't go out for a drink with a bloke unless she's interested in him Kyle' said Elton.

'What's she like?' John Medburn enquired.

'She's a complex character. I've known about her for years but not really known her as a person or thought much of her to be honest. She always seemed a bit aloof, quiet and serious. She always looked wrapped up in her work and prim and proper, neat and tidy. She always wore a suit and thus you kind of looked at her as a criminal psychologist rather than a single girl. However, recently I've got to see another side to her. She's warm and funny and very down to earth; not at all stuck up. She drinks pints, likes rock music and wears a belly-ring. She's been a Goth and a punk and she has a wild side that she keeps under wraps at work.'

'Never mind all that. Is she fit?' asked Elton.

'*Well. She's very petite. Only about 5 foot 2 at the most. And she's very slim. She's got a narrow back and a tiny waist. However, she's got curves and I think she's very pretty in a quirky sort of way. At first, I thought she was very mousy. Her hair is a mousy colour, her skin pale, her features small. However, now I see all the beauty spots and freckles on her skin and her blue eyes look bigger than they used to and I guess she's grown on me*'.

'*Has she got nice tits?*' Elton asked more directly.

'*I'm more of an arse man than a tits man Elton and she has a fantastic arse. She looks great in jeans and tight skirts. It is a real peach. I'm not sure about her tits yet but she's certainly not flat- chested.*'

'*Age?*' asked One Word.

Kyle laughed. '*She's only 29 but she's very mature. She's not all callow like Alicia and I don't think she's seeing someone or been with anyone for ages*'.

'*Sounds great*' said Elton putting his arm round Kyle. '*Go for her son. Give her one for me.*'

The conversation turned to football and the growing crises at St James' Park. '*I think we are going down*' said Dobbo.

'*Don't be daft*' said Elton. '*We may be crap but there have got to be 3 worst sides than us. The Baggies are down and then there's the Mackems and the Smoggies.*'

'*My money is on Hull. They are falling like a stone*' said Mattie.

'*Yes, but they only need couple more wins and they're safe. They must be on about 30 points already and we are on 20. I think we could get sucked into it if we don't get some players fit soon,*' proclaimed Kyle.

'*They said Leeds were too good to go down and look what happened to them*' added Dobbo. '*It's harder for teams that don't expect to be in a relegation battle to survive. Teams like Bolton and Stoke are experts at battling relega-tion. It's more of a culture shock for players like Michael Owen and Damien Duff.*'

'*It's the foreign mercenaries that worry me*' said Elton. '*They couldn't care if we go down or not as long as they are drawing their fat pay packets and splashing their cash down the Quayside.*'

'*You have got a point*' said Kyle. '*If we did go down we could be in serious financial trouble because we attracted several foreign players by offering ri-diculous wages and long-term contracts with no get-out clauses if we got rel-egated. If we get relegated we won't be able to off-load them and we won't be able to afford their wages. We might have to buy out their contracts in lieu of a transfer fee.*'

'Let's not talk about it. It's depressing. It is nearly Christmas everyone. Have you heard about the time Roy Keane set his dog on Santa?' asked Mattie.

'No' all replied expectantly.

'Yes. He was worried in case Santa was giving him the sack'.

'Oh God Mattie that's terrible', said Kyle, but he was still laughing a lot more than he would have done six pints earlier.

Scene 4: A Snowy Night on the Metro

It was the Friday before Christmas 2008 and it was frigging freezing. Even Geordies were digging out woollies and coats before they headed off to office parties and festive drinks. Kyle knew from experience that not much work was done on the morning of the Xmas lunch and his Boss allowed him to work from home.

He donned his best jeans and a new casual shirt, splashed on some after shave and tried 2 or 3 jackets and coats before settling on one that was a compromise between comfort and warmth. As he waited for the metro to Central Station he wondered if he should have just gone for warmth as the wind was bitter and the sky ice blue.

The Copthorne Hotel is a classy establishment situated right on the Quayside with fine views of the Tyne Bridges from its river-facing rooms and panoramic indoor pool. The leisure club is a popular haunt of Tyneside's rich and famous and the cuisine is highly regarded. However, Kyle knew that wherever they went for Christmas Dinner the numbers involved made it impossible for the chefs to conjure up the culinary delights they provided the rest of the year. Instead, the emphasis was on presentation to disguise the paltry portions. He expected each dish to look like a work of art and taste like it had just come out of the microwave.

Then there was the Chief Executive's Young Mr Grace speech to look forward to. Annually he took the microphone to tell everyone what a very good job they had done this year. Kyle wondered what he would say if one year they had been really crap, crime had doubled, the inspectors had slated them and a major corruption enquiry had been launched. He would probably say something like *'it has been a very challenging year but I still think we've done really well.'* Kyle suggested to Sam as she pulled a face *'he probably thinks its motivational but we'd be much more motivated if he just said lets skip the speeches and go and get pissed. The beers are on me'*.

The sound of crackers and party whistles, chatter and laughter filled the dining hall as the free wine flowed and the guests looked forward to hitting the town. They were sat in large round tables, one for each section with name-plates just in case anyone felt rebellious and tried to scupper the seating plan. Kyle looked around the other tables and eventually spotted Rachel sitting in a huddle of psychologists. She was sipping cautiously at a large glass of red wine and not yet wearing a party hat. Kyle was just about to remove his when he noticed her smile and don a pink crown.

There seemed a long wait for coffees and the wine had run dry on Kyle's table but Sam and Donna came back with a bottle they had commandeered from ICT and topped everyone's glasses up. Kyle noticed the first people get up and split into those heading home or for some last minute shopping and those ready to hit the bars. He was concerned the psychologists might leave before he had finished his wine, but they all seemed to be in deep conversation, probably analysing the rest of the guests.

Kyle was torn between his duty to stay with his team and his desire for Rachel's company. It was still early; twenty past 3. However, on the Friday before Christmas, Kyle knew the bars would already be packed. He asked who was up for a drink on him at the nearby Quayside Inn. He chose this large Weatherspoons partly because of its size and proximity and partly because the drinks were half the price of all the other trendy establishments along the waterfront. Unsurprisingly, Sam and Donna were the only two on the table to join him and they both moaned about his choice of watering hole. Kyle knew they would want to hit a trendy bar but he was the team leader and it was his round so Weatherspoons it was.

When he got back with their drinks he estimated that about 40-50 of those at the dinner had chosen the same pub and as at least half of the diners would have headed off home or to the shops the odds were good that Rachel would be here somewhere. They mingled with HR and Kyle tried not to drool too visibly at Alicia in her figure-hugging bodice and mini-skirt with more bronze skin visible than fabric. She must be freezing he thought, but she seemed immune to the cold.

As Kyle reached the end of his pint, Sam announced that her, Donna and Alicia were off to a bar that Kyle hadn't even heard of. He declined their invitation to join them and also their offer of a pint. He wished them all happy Christmas and got a peck on the cheeks from Donna and Alicia and a passionate embrace and kiss on the lips from big Sam. He felt like he'd been hit by a juggernaut as her huge jugs hit him at full throttle and her lips knocked him off balance.

Kyle wandered around the Courtyard and confirmed that Rachel was not there. He went inside and searched, stopping for a chat with a couple of people as he did so. Just when he was about to give up and go to the bar he spotted her with a couple of colleagues and a couple of uniformed imposters who Kyle recognised from CID. They had managed to corner her round a table and there was no room for Kyle.

Rachel wore a black, low-buttoned, silk top, a tartan mini-skirt and black tights and shoes. Her long, dark hair hung forward over her white skin and she sported understated, Celtic jewellery. The tight top was buttoned tantalisingly to reveal just a small bit of cleavage but enough to suggest it might be the tip of an ice-berg. Colin tapped him on the shoulder as he watched her brush her hair on either side of her slender shoulders.

'Can I get you a pint Kyle?'

'Cheers Colin. I'll come with you and choose one.'

Kyle knew there was plenty of time for romance and he didn't want to embarrass himself by making his dishonourable intentions too obvious. It was five to five and the night was young.

Kyle joined Colin's jovial group standing in a circle all with pints in hand. The talk alternated between work and football, safe ground for a group of blokes in a Weatherspoons. Kyle kept an eye on developments around Rachel's table and while one of Kyle's group left to get the next round in, the psychologist sitting next to Rachel got up and put his coat on. However, before Kyle could think of an excuse to leave Colin's pals and sit beside his heart-throb, one of the CID blokes blatantly left his side of the table and shuffled up uncomfortably close to Rachel. *'Bastard'* thought Kyle. The uniformed lot have their Christmas do tomorrow. He shouldn't even be here!

Kyle resumed a conversation with Colin becoming increasingly concerned he might have a rival for Rachel's affections. The CID bloke was more her age and very cocky. Kyle thought his next pint tasted a bit off and Colin suggested they headed for the more intimate Cooperage across the road. Kyle hesitated and then accepted, thinking it might be an opportunity to suggest an escape route for Rachel. The question was did she want one?

When he noticed Rachel was nearing the end of her pint, he hovered around her table for a gap in the conversation and said *'Hi Rachel. We are off to the Cooperage. Would you like to join us?'*

Her sparking eyes lit up as she replied *'Hi Kyle. I was just thinking the same thing'* and then turning to her drinking companions added *'shall we go across the road?'*

The 2 CID blokes couldn't get out of the chairs quick enough to join Rachel, Kyle, Colin and 3 of Colin's mates head for the Cooperage. One of the group got the round in whilst Rachel went to the loo. There was one table left by the roaring fire but only two chairs and a stool. Ignoring protocol, Kyle went and sat down. The other 6 blokes stood looking at the two vacant seats, knowing they should offer Rachel one of them. When she returned she sat next to Kyle and Colin took the stool. Kyle noticed the green eyed monster in the face of the CID man and the two coppers moved away for a private conversation near the bar. Kyle checked his watch. Seven thirty and at last I've got Rachel's company, he thought.

*****

'I thought you were a Guinness drinker' Kyle said admiring Rachel's choice of beer.

'Sometimes I like Guinness and sometimes real ale, always a dark one mind. I'm not keen on the pale ales.'

' Most of your generation seem to be into lager'.

'I'm no spring chicken Kyle. I'm going to be 30 next year.'

'I wish I was only 30'.

'You can't be much older. What are you? 35? 36?'

'Keep going!'

'37? 38? You are never 40?'

'42 I'm afraid'.

'Never! Well, you look great for your age Kyle'.

'Thanks Rachel and you look great for your age too'.

The pub was packed now. Another big party had come in and jostled their way to the bar. However, Kyle felt like they were the only two there. He was so impressed with little Rachel. She was on her fourth pint on top of the red wine and she still sounded sober and articulate, although more confident and flirty than normal. She spoke so much sense on every subject and yet did so with grace and modesty. Her pupils had doubled in size and she looked closely in Kyle's eyes whenever he spoke. Her outfit was sexy but refined.

'I like your top. It suits you' said Kyle.

Rachel thanked at him and said she liked the Japanese kimono print on it and had got it from a small shop in High Bridge. As she did so she pulled at the silk and smiled shyly, seemingly aware that it opened up a gap between the top two buttons for Kyle to briefly glimpse a lacy black bra cradling two mounds of white flesh. Surely, he thought, Rachel is flirting with me. I'm not imagining it, am I?

They discussed the impact of the recession on crime and agreed that they had to prepare for the success of recent years in bringing crime down being reversed as people got desperate and drug and drink use increased.

'Speaking of drink use' Kyle said *'can I get you another pint Rachel?'*

Looking at her half full glass Rachel said *'I shouldn't but go on. Christmas comes but once a year'.*

As Kyle was at the bar there was a loud cheer and a blast of icy air. A man came staggering in with snowflakes on his coat. *'It's only bloody snowing'.* A spontaneous chorus of White Christmas followed and several people went outside to confirm that the flakes were real and not an especially impressive stunt by one of the bar-owners.

'It could be a White Christmas' said Kyle as he returned with the drinks noting with satisfaction that the CID men had left.

'I hope so. We haven't had one in years. There seemed to be loads when we were bairns' Rachel replied.

'*Well, there was one in the mid 90's I remember*'.

'*Aye but Kyle I was a bairn in the mid 90's*'.

They laughed and Rachel patted Kyle's thigh as she said '*sorry*'.

'*Don't tease me Miss Woods*' he laughed pushing her jokily and lingering as he patted Rachel's thigh. Colin and his mate Sammy sat down on two stools opposite saying '*mind if we join you?*' Kyle shook his head although he did mind really.

The conversation turned to favourite kids TV programmes and happy childhood memories as the Pogues and Kirsty McColl sang a '*Fairy Tale of New York*' on the stereo.

'*I love this song*' said Rachel singing the lyrics quietly as she gently rocked to the music. '*You have great taste*' Kyle said and joined in the singing, leaving the other 2 feeling a bit out of it. When it finished Rachel gulped her pint down and got up saying '*my round, what's youse lot having*'. She was just beginning to slur her words but she had downed six pints and some wine and she was tiny.

'*God she's got a lovely little arse*' Colin said as they watched her go to the bar.

'*I know*' agreed Kyle.

'*I think you might be in there mate*' Colin added leaning forward.

Kyle went to the bar to help Rachel with the drinks. When they sat down he felt confident enough to move closer to her so their arms and legs occasionally brushed against each other and there was no resistance from Rachel. Sammy told a joke. Kyle didn't get it, but Rachel found it hilarious so he pretended he did get it and laughed too. As she rolled back laughing raucously she again patted Kyle on the thigh, not once but twice. The second time Kyle kept her hand there under the table and squeezed it and she squeezed back. The electricity rushed through his veins.

Colin asked Rachel if she wanted another drink. '*No. I'm going for the Metro now before we all get snowed in*' she said. Colin turned to Kyle next '*A pint for you Kyle?*'

'*No thanks Colin. I've had enough. I will make sure Rachel gets her metro*'.

'*Very noble of you*' said Colin.

*****

The snow was falling fast as they staggered back to Central Station to catch the Metro and neither had especially thick coats or jackets. At the top of the steps, Kyle put his arm round Rachel as she skidded a bit laughing sweetly

149

and as she didn't complain he kept it there and then they held hands as they got to the station.

'*I'm freezing*' she said squeezing Kyle's hand.

'*Here. Take my jacket*' he offered.

'*Don't be silly. You've only got a shirt underneath*'.

'*I'm not cold. I'm burning with alcohol. I insist*'.

When they got to the platform Kyle said '*You've been to my house but I don't know where you live Rachel.*'

'*I live in a little apartment in Ponteland, not far from work,* ' Rachel replied, her teeth chattering. '*I get the metro to the end of the line at the Airport and then get a taxi for the last 3 miles.*' With that, their metro arrived and they staggered into the end carriage. They sat, still holding hands, with Kyle dying to kiss her. She wiggled out of his jacket and returned it to him.

'*What made you become a criminal psychologist*?' Kyle enquired, noting his own words were slurring now.

'*I've always wanted to be a detective. I studied criminology at Uni and really enjoyed the criminal profiling bit. I love my job. My boss is retiring soon but I'm not sure I'm ready for promotion*'.

'*Rubbish. You would charm the pants off any interview panel.*'

'*I don't do charm, Kyle*'.

'*Rachel, you charm people without even knowing it*'.

This was the moment. Their eyes locked and they moved their faces closer, so close that Kyle could feel Rachel's alcoholic breath on his skin. He kissed her lightly on the lips and she kissed back. They parted briefly before Kyle cradled her small face in his large arms and moved in for a deep, passionate kiss. Oblivious to all around them they kissed and rubbed noses and rolled tongues for at least five minutes.

'*Wow*' said Kyle beaming with satisfaction as they parted and Rachel now hot with passion took off her jacket and smiled back at Kyle. He went back in to kiss her and she leant forward toppling him back and leaving her giggling. He gripped her waist and confirmed his fingers didn't quite stretch round as they kissed again, this time Rachel leaning back against the train window. Rachel probed deep inside Kyle's mouth with her tongue and he moved his hand down to stroke her sexy thighs. He felt a strong erection as he discovered soft skin and silk. Sweet little Rachel wasn't wearing tights at all but black stockings and suspenders. He sighed with pleasure as the train jolted into the next station.

Kyle looked out to see the sign '*Wansbeck Road*'. '*Shit, I've missed my stop*' he said.

'*Oh well. It looks like you will need a taxi at the airport as well*', Rachel laughed. They resumed their kissing and Rachel's hand moved inside Kyle's jacket and shirt prompting him to move his hand up Rachel's blouse and cup a breast in his hand through her lacy bra.

'*Wait*' said Rachel removing Kyle's hand and standing up.

'*Shit, I've over-stepped the mark*', thought Kyle. '*I've just fondled a work colleague's tits on a metro train. I could get reported for this.*'

However, Rachel was not cross she was checking that the only other person left in their carriage was pissed and asleep. Her hands trembled and she rocked unsteadily as she started to unbutton her blouse. Kyle watched her transfixed, dying to help as she struggled with a button. Slowly Rachel peeled off her blouse and placed it on her jacket. A diamond ring lit up her concave, porcelain stomach and her pert breasts rose majestically above a lacy, balcony bra. There was no padding, no under-wiring. She needed neither. Nervously she reached behind her and undid her bra strap, removing it in one smooth movement.

Rachel stood before him topless as the train came into another station. She giggled and turned away from the window covering her chest only to reveal herself again when she realized the platform was empty. Kyle pulled Rachel into his lap and sucked her nipples until they were both erect. He cupped one breast in each hand and they fitted like a glove. They kissed again and Rachel undid the buttons on Kyle's shirt as he felt her bottom beneath the silk of her French knickers.

The sleeping drunk stirred and Kyle turned to look at him but Rachel turned his face back towards her and with a resolute look calmly undid her suspender belt and rolled down her soaking knickers. She folded them up and placed them in her handbag and as she turned to do so Kyle lifted her skirt and caressed her sexy, naked bottom. Initially she giggled and tried to pull her skirt back down but then she stood straight and allowed him to closely examine this work of art, kissing her gently on each bum cheek.

Suddenly, she turned and Kyle could see her clitoris up her skirt like a juicy, swollen berry and it was too much to bear. He pulled her towards him, her tits swinging into his face and he bit them as she reached inside his pants and pulled out his throbbing cock. She straddled him and placed him inside and they rocked to the rhythm of the train. Kyle held Rachel's' skinny waist as she writhed and thrust hard up and down in his lap. He kissed and sucked and bit her tits and her breathing became deeper and her movements faster. Suddenly the train pulled into a station and Kyle's dam broke. A torrent of semen shot up through Rachel, releasing seven months of pent-up frustration.

However, Rachel was relentless. As the train started up again she got faster and faster and her moans and breaths louder and louder. Kyle gripped her sexy bum and was hard again. *'Yes'* she said feeling his size growing inside her. The metro seat creaked beneath them as she sapped every ounce of energy and the driver slammed on the brakes. They were coming into the Airport terminus and Rachel was determined to get her satisfaction. She came the second the train stopped. There was a little scream and a warm flow around Kyle's cock and she stopped gasping for breath moving gently round and round as their breathing returned to normal.

The drunk woke up and stared in disbelief at the lovers. Rachel quickly reached for her bra and blouse and dressed as Kyle tucked himself away. The drunk stood up and fell back down again shouting *'It's Christmas!'* and laughing insanely. Kyle and Rachel laughed as they finished dressing and got out of the train into the snowy night. Kyle felt like all his Christmas's had come at once.

Scene 5: Rachel's Regrets

'I can't believe we just did that' declared Rachel as they waited in the airport taxi queue.

'I know that old gadgie looked like he thought he was dreaming'.

'Aye. Let's hope he thinks he's been dreaming in the morning'.

'Still the fear of getting caught made it even better. You were out of this world Rachel Woods.'

Rachel looked belatedly bashful. *'You can stay the night if you want to share a taxi'* she offered.

'Thanks. I'd love to. Do you know it's seven months since I last had sex?'

'It's probably even longer with me. I guess we both couldn't wait any longer', Rachel laughed.

Rachel's flat was in a modern, two-floored block with a communal front door leading to a green and walkway. It was small but perfectly formed, just like its owner. *'I'm sorry about the mess. I wasn't expecting guests'* she said as she led him though the living room to the kitchen. *'Coffee?'* she asked.

'Just a glass of water please.'

'Actually, that's a good idea.'

'It will seem so in the morning'.

Rachel found Kyle a spare toothbrush and invited him to go to the bathroom first, whilst she flicked channels on the TV. When he came out Rachel had already changed into a night-shirt and hung her clothes, including those from her handbag neatly on the back of a chair. As Rachel cleaned her teeth Kyle examined her underwear. She wore a 32C bra and the damp, black French knickers were size 8-10. Rachel called out and he quickly put her knickers down: *'I'm going straight to bed. Feel free to go through and make yourself comfortable.'*

Kyle entered the bedroom to find it scattered with the remnants of hasty preparations for a night out. A hairdryer, several alternative skirts, a vanity case; all delightfully feminine. He climbed into the comfortable double bed as he heard Rachel come out of the bathroom and do a tour of plugs, locks and lights. She switched out the bedroom light and placed some glasses and a contact lens case on the table on her side of the bed. As she lifted the bed to climb in her expressive, little face looked embarrassed. Kyle followed her gaze and realized that on the table on his side of the bed stood a large, black vibrator and a used wipe. She stretched to retrieve the vibe and hide it away saying *'close your eyes Kyle'* but it was too late. Giggling profusely, Kyle grabbed the dildo and started teasing Rachel with it. He held it above his head and grabbed her round the waist as she reached out for it, kissing her passionately.

Rachel returned the kiss and they knelt on the bed trying to kiss each other as tenderly as possible. Then Kyle lifted Rachel's night-shirt over her head. She was naked underneath and the moonlight shone through the slim gap in the curtains and lit up her slim body. He moved round and kissed the back of her neck. She moaned softly and lay on her belly propped up by the pillow to expose the incredible curves of her rear profile. Kyle switched on the vibrator and tickled her feet. *'You're ticklish'* he said in response to her giggling. He moved it up her legs, over the mountain range of her butt and down into the valley of her back as she waved her lower legs in the air and held the rest of her gorgeous body still. Kyle moved the vibrator to her inner thighs and like a gymnast Rachel moved up on to her fingers and toes so her bum was in Kyle's face and it was easy to plunge the vibrator deep inside her from underneath.

After much moaning and thrusting, Rachel removed the rotating and vibrating toy and Kyle inserted the real thing. Kyle delighted at how tight Rachel felt from this angle. Rachel delighted in how much bigger Kyle felt from this angle. They both climaxed quickly and within seconds of each other as if one orgasm was the echo of the other.

They lay for a while kissing and then Rachel got out of bed and walked naked through the living room to the bathroom. He heard the sound of the shower and ever the environmentalist Kyle decided to save water and share her shower. He stood for a few seconds observing how beautiful her little body looked through the glass of the shower cubicle and felt a warm rush of blood. He got in the cubicle and pushed her face-first against the opposite side. She sensed his hard cock in the small of her back and rose on tip-toes to allow him to enter her from behind.

'Wrong hole' she said as he penetrated but Kyle was too turned on by the tightness of her arse to stop now and the warm water acted as a lubricant. He screwed himself inside and came for a glorious third time. *'You are so sexy Rachel'* he said kissing the back of her neck again. They dried each other and Rachel said sweetly *'can I go to sleep now'*?

'Yes' Kyle laughed and he slept feeling ten feet tall and floating on air. Seven months with no sex and then three times in one night! *'And after about eight pints worth of alcohol – what a stud I am'* he thought.

*****

Kyle smiled as he worked out where he was and how he ended up there. He could hear Rachel in the kitchen and slung his boxers on before joining her.

'Morning' he said wiping his bleary eyes. *'Sleep well?'*

'What with your snoring? It was like sleeping next to a foghorn!'

'Sorry Rachel. It must have been the booze.'

'I've just put some toast on if you want some and there's fresh coffee in the percolator'.

'Great! How are you feeling?'

'Rough. Here you go' said Rachel handing Kyle a coffee. 'Never again' she added and Kyle hoped she was talking about the heavy drinking and not the sex.

'Are you not having any breakfast Rachel?'

'I've already had mine thanks'.

Kyle sensed a cooling of their relationship as he looked out of the window at the thin layer of snow and ice and sipped his coffee. Rachel did look a far cry from the gorgeous sex-pot of the previous night as she dried some pots wearing baggy jeans, long t-shirt and spectacles. She mopped her brow with some cool water and swallowed 2 painkillers.

'Thanks for letting me stay Rachel', Kyle said as he buttered his toast.

'No problem. I really ought to have a tidy up today but I need some fresh air. I will probably walk to Sainsbury's and get some cleaning stuff and some Resolve.'

'I guess I better get the bus back into town', Kyle stated hoping Rachel would tell him not to rush off.

'I'd give you a lift but I reckon I'm still over the limit'.

'No problem honey. I will make a move in a minute'.

They kissed on the doorstep and wished each other happy Christmas. In the bus, Kyle remembered that he hadn't got Rachel's number and he hadn't even made a mental note of her flat number. Thus, he would be reliant on her contacting him, which wasn't ideal. He had a slight hangover but after his night of passion he felt on top of the World.

*****

Christmas came and went and Rachel didn't contact Kyle. Between Christmas and New Year he went looking for her flat in Ponteland. He eventually found what he thought was hers but there was no answer on the door. He waited for a while in his car but he was coming down with a dose of man flu so he soon gave up. The man-flu also meant he wasn't up to his planned attendance at John Medburn's New Year party down the Quayside. He managed to see the New Year in quaffing whiskey on his own and went to bed as soon as Big Ben's chimes had finished.

He was still far from 100% when his holiday finished but he was determined to go to work in order to see Rachel. He went along to her office at about 11 and found her sitting in a long, grey skirt, black boots and a purple jumper looking at a map on the wall with pegs mapping crime scenes.

'Happy New Year Rachel! Did you have a good one?' he asked, moving in to kiss her. She turned and only offered her cheek.

'Yes. It was fine thanks. How was yours?'

'Christmas was ok. I went round to see Nathan open his presents. New Year was crap but. I came down with man-flu'.

'Oh dear! Are you feeling better now?

'Nearly there. It's good to see you again. I didn't have a number to keep in touch.'

Rachel looked embarrassed. *'I'm sorry Kyle. I'm snowed under. I'll catch you later'.*

Kyle was troubled as he went back to his office. It appeared that Rachel had regrets about their night of passion. Maybe she only went with him because she was pissed and when she sobered up she was ashamed at what she had done. There was the 13 year age difference, the fact danger seemed to follow Kyle around, the fact he was still technically married. There were lots of plausible explanations. However, she felt so right for him and he wanted her so much.

The next day he decided to go to work early and wait for her in the office car park. He didn't have to wait long.

'Rachel' he shouted, stepping out of his car. They got a coffee from the vending machine and sat in the empty canteen.

'Rachel, do you regret what happened at Christmas?' Kyle asked directly.

Rachel shook her pretty head and said *'No Kyle. It was great. We are both single and we both needed it. However, I like to keep my work and private life separate. Do you understand?'*

'Aye. That's a relief. I was thinking you might have used me for my body'.

'You wish!'

'You know, it's not just lust with me Rachel. I do love you, you know.'

'You are a lovely bloke Kyle but I'd like us to just be good friends.'

'Is it the age difference?'

'No. That doesn't bother me. The last relationship I had was with someone at work. I had to put up with all the gossip and bitching and I felt awful when he turned out to be a bastard. I'm not saying you might turn out to be a bastard, but I just don't want to go down that road again. It complicates things and I like my work too much.'

'I read that more people meet their life-partners at work than in pubs and clubs.'

'You need to take things slowly Kyle. You aren't even divorced yet and here you are talking about new life-partners. It scares me. I really have to get back to work now.'

'Rachel. Can I have your mobile number?'

Rachel thought for a few seconds and then said with a confusing nod *'I'd prefer not to if you don't mind Kyle. Let's keep things professional.'*

Kyle's heart sunk and he placed his feverish head in his hands. Love could be so cruel and it felt like he had been given the perfect Christmas present only to have Santa send the bailiffs round to re-possess it.

Scene 6: Financial Melt-down

Kyle phoned in sick the next day. His man-flu had got a second wind and his heart had lost the will to fight it. He watched a satellite news channel and absorbed for the first time the extent of the financial melt-down:

- around 20 banks, insurance companies and financial institutions around the World had folded;

- at least three times that number had been bailed out by the State;

- shares had tumbled with the FTSE down by a third in a few months;

- the stock market collapse had wiped millions off pension and endowment funds, destroying the retirement plans of ordinary people;

- house prices had fallen by 20% from their peak, trapping millions of home owners in negative equity;

- mortgage arrears and re-possessions had reached record levels;

- new lending had plummeted and the extent of security or deposit required had become prohibitive;

- although base rates had fallen at their fastest ever rate the majority of loan rates had barely changed;

- many car plants had been mothballed as stocks exceeded demand;

- Governments had started printing money to get people spending again;

- all the major economies were contracting with horrendous forecasts for 2009; and

- UK unemployment had returned to the high levels of the previous Tory Government.

'*Happy New Year*', Kyle said with an ironic voice as he switched the TV off in disgust. He looked out of the window at the quiet, sedate streets of Gosforth and let off some steam:

"They say you can't have too much of a good thing. They are wrong. Everything loses value with frequency. Some football fans are so spoilt with success that they are depressed if their side goes a whole season without a trophy. As a Newcastle fan without a single meaningful trophy in my living memory I would be in heaven if we won just one. Everyone agrees winning is great, but if it happens too frequently it is simply dull.

Economic growth is the same. It is the fuel which keeps us in work, provides the revenue for public services and allows us to enjoy an improved standard of living. God how we miss it now it's gone! But we all became drunk on success, drowning in a sea of crazy credit and even crazier bonuses. Our economies grew too fast, choking our streets with second cars and draining the Planet of resources. After every night of binge drinking, a hangover follows and the world economy has been on one hell of a bender.

Freedom is another virtue prone to excess. The American Constitution is built around freedom. It is a universal principle of human rights. Wars are fought over it and rivers of blood flow defending it. By the 1980's it was treason to argue against greater freedom. Bankers, brokers and executives demanded freedom to do what the hell they liked and amazingly they got it. They claimed they were strangled by red tape and regulation. It was all bloody inconvenient having to obey rules, implement controls and account for decisions. Deregulation was the panacea and concepts like risk management and internal control were barriers to success.

How many children would go to school if they had the freedom to choose? How many men would be rapists if they had the freedom to rape? Taken to extremes, freedom destroys societies. It breeds selfishness and irresponsibility. That is what happened when we deregulated. Millionaires became billionaires playing poker with our money and when their luck ran out it was you and me that paid their debts.

Even today we hear our commercial and political leaders talking about lifting the burden of audit, inspection and regulation. Surely, we need tighter and better supervision and control, not less. Have we not learnt from two decades of growing fraud, corruption and negligence in the de-regulated private sector? Standards of governance and accountability in the heavily inspected public sector have improved exponentially.

Rachel told me about an interesting psychological experiment. 100 people were asked if they would inflate their travel claims if they knew they weren't checked. 25 said they would. The same 100 people were asked if they would inflate their travel claims if they knew 25 were already doing it and getting away with it. How many said they would? The answer – 75! Freed of control, in a climate where the cheats were prospering three quarters of us would commit fraud.

Wealth creators were heralded the heroes of the boom. Heroes for creating wealth for themselves! Surely, the real heroes are the tax inspectors, benefit inspectors and government auditors who protect the public purse, catching the cheats, deterring the tempted and improving efficiency. If this is red tape, let's make it stronger. Let's mark the boundaries and catch the strays. When they cut through the fence in search of gold in the hills they endanger us all and yet we never learn. We keep shooting the sheriff!"

The Illuminati understood the importance of regulation only too well. Paradoxically it was one of their 12 pillars, but they campaigned vociferously for de-regulation. They knew that freedom from effective supervision and control was all that was needed for human nature to destroy democracy for them. They didn't need to dominate politics like they did in the States. All they needed were a few key leaders and advisers selling de-regulation and the gullible politicians would be caught in their trap. They couldn't believe how quickly greed and selfish risk-taking spread throughout the World from Beijing to Baltimore. They just had to sit back and wait for the bubble to burst.

By January 2009, the natives were restless. Millions had lost their jobs, their pensions, their homes and their faith in the integrity of the professionals that they employed to look after their money. They were outraged to hear of the huge bonuses awarded to failed risk-takers. They were baying for the blood of corrupt or negligent billionaires. The time was right for the New World Order.

Batman was in triumphant mood as he addressed a sympathetic assembly of the rich and famous. At one point he was heckled by a couple of members who thought there must be a better way than causing pain and suffering to so many people. Batman said Einstein was right; everything was relative. The conventional way to overturn democracy was through war, which killed thousands and was worse. He got a standing ovation.

However, Batman wasn't finished. He played on his disability with a deeply personal account of how he had lost his sight as a UN peace-keeper in Uganda. He had then spent decades raising money for disabled charities and scientific research, only to find one project investigating a potential cure for blindness was killed off by government spending cuts. He lived in hope that diverting spending from warfare to research would one day restore his sight. It motivated him every day and he was willing to die fighting for a better world. This time the ovation lasted three minutes.

Meanwhile, Kyle was doing something he had never done before. He was having a pint with One-Word. One-Word didn't do twosomes. He drank in packs, where his frugal conversation was less of an issue. However, he had sent a text asking if anyone could meet him tonight because he had just received a redundancy notice and needed to get pissed. Kyle had been the only one available. It had only taken one look at One-Word's forlorn face to remind him to get his own problems into perspective.

'*How are you coping One Word?*' asked Kyle handing him a pint. '*I imagine you must feel awful.*'

'*Shite*' replied One Word and that was about as far as the conversation went.

Scene 7: Heads up

Kyle took the rest of the week off sick. He just couldn't face the dark mornings of early January; not when he was still sniffing and sneezing and feeling totally drained. He felt better over the weekend and went to 'Wet n Wild' with Nathan. However, when the alarm went off on a cold, dark Monday Morning it was desperately hard to flick the cosy covers off and get ready for work.

There was a mountain of e-mails awaiting him but by half past ten there was just one left unopened. It was from morourke@edinburghuniversity.co.uk; which mystified Kyle. He opened it and shivered as he read:

Hi Kyle,

It's Dougie from the brotherhood. I'm using a colleague's e-mail address because I'm sure I'm being monitored and I don't want to put you in danger again. I fear for my life.

A close friend of mine at Yale was murdered at the weekend. He had evidence that the President-elect was going to be assassinated at his inauguration by white supremacists. The brotherhood had decided it was best not to stand in their way. My friend had a reliable contact in White-House security and was going to brief him. He told me his name and posted me the evidence. It arrived the day after his murder.

I understand you are no longer being watched. You are the only man left that I can trust to use the evidence well. There are many good people who have the power and will to stop this crime but they need the evidence. It gives details of the plot and names the conspirators. If you want to help, please respond with a simple 'yes' and no other words to this e-mail account. I will be on the Edinburgh to London train arriving at Newcastle at 13.35 on Saturday. I will be between coaches J and K. I will pass you a parcel out of the door and continue on my journey.

Be brave,

Dougie.

Kyle read the e-mail several times looking over his shoulder and shielding the screen. He printed it down, put it in his pocket and deleted it, fearing that it might self-destruct. He opened the paper in the loo and checked the date. *'Phew'* he said as he saw it had been sent the previous day so it was next Saturday that Dougie was referring to. Kyle had vowed to stay out of Illuminati business, but the Chief had lied to him. He had assured Kyle that Obama would be safe and the day of reckoning would be delayed if they couldn't persuade him to join. He had heard nothing from Rachel since their early morning coffee. *'What have I got left to lose?'* he asked himself. He returned to his desk and sent a single word message to the mystery e-mail address.

It said *'yes'*.

*****

The train was on time and Kyle followed it along the platform so he stood between coaches J and K. The door opened and a long queue of travellers dismounted. Then a slightly shorter queue of travellers got on in their place. Kyle stood in the doorway, waiting for Dougie to appear and drop him a parcel. He wore a long flashers mackintosh with deep inside pockets, ideal for hiding things in. It was the first time he'd wore it in six years; well, since he got told he looked like a flasher in it!

The guard slammed the door shut and looked down the platform. *'Howay Dougie'*, Kyle said under his breath. The whistle went and still no Scotsman with a suspicious package. The sound of the central locking clicked and the train began its journey south. *'Shit'* said Kyle aloud. He went for a coffee to ponder the possibilities. There was a chance Dougie had missed the train so Kyle checked the board for the next arrival from across the border. It was only half an hour.

The same thing happened with the next train and the train after that. Finally, Kyle resigned himself to the fact that Dougie had either got cold feet or been found out. He had no evidence to take to the White House and no names of the people he could trust. He would just have to hope the assassination plot failed.

Back at home Kyle watched Soccer Saturday on Sky TV followed by a live FA Cup 3rd round tie on BBC1. He had a couple of beers and soon dozed off in front of the television. He was woken by the phone at half past eleven. He trembled as he answered it, imagining a call from Dougie's kidnappers warning him off.

'Hello' he said tentatively. There was no answer and after a few seconds the caller hung up.

'Wanker!' said Kyle and went up to bed via the loo. He stripped to his boxers and brushed his teeth, swearing again at the sight of blood from his gums. He didn't even bother to switch the bedroom light on as he yawned and stretched his way towards his bed.

His duvet looked like it had already been slept in as Kyle removed his watch and placed it by the bed. He turned and lifted the duvet. He sprung back.

'Shit.....Holy shite.......oh my God....No!' he left the room and went downstairs for a wee dram.

Still dripping blood all over his pillow lay Dougie's severed head. It was a ghastly reminder from Satan that Kyle needed to stay out of Illuminati business or his head would be next.

The single malt clarified Kyle's mind. He wouldn't mention his connection with the deceased but he had to ring the Police. This was a whole new ball game and he just had to hope he wasn't regarded as their prime suspect.

Scene 8: Don't Leave the Country

Kyle cursed his curiosity. Just when he had finally managed to escape from his violent nightmare, he gets one arcane e-mail and walks right back into it. Now he was in a police cell under suspicion of murder. He knew the law. The Police would have to charge him by 6.00 tonight or let him go and they had no evidence. However, he had it on good authority that by that time, the elected President of the World's most powerful nation would be shot dead, quashing the hopes of a generation and plunging the planet into chaos.

A drunk in an adjacent cell had been insulting him for the last hour. Kyle had tried to rise above it and ignore him but his patience finally cracked:

'Will you fucking shut up you pissed prick' he yelled.

There was silence for about two minutes and then a shout:

'I'm still here monkey-fucker.'

Kyle checked his watch and tried to work out the time differential with Washington DC. It was a pointless exercise because he couldn't remember the time of Obama's inauguration and even if he was released on bail he was hardly likely to be very credible, whilst he remained a murder suspect. A voice from the cell opposite called out of the dim light.

'Don't look so glum mate. It's a cruel world. Shit happens.'

'Thanks for that', Kyle replied.

Kyle retreated to the corner of his cell and sunk his head in his hands.

'I can still see you arsehole!' shouted his cell-mate.

*****

'Wake up Forster. You have a visitor' said the PC.

Kyle sprung into life. Maybe it was one of his mates, or Rachel or even Helen. Unfortunately, he was to be disappointed. It was the Director from work.

'God, you look terrible' he said when he saw Kyle being led hand-cuffed to see him.

'I thought I needed to become one of our statistics' Kyle joked.

'This is no laughing matter Kyle. You work for Northumbria Police and you are being held on suspicion of murder. This is hugely embarrassing. The Press have already heard a rumour. You know how our place leaks like a sieve.'

'I know but all I've done is report a crime. You would have done the same if a severed head turned up in your bed.'

'The point is a severed head wouldn't turn up in my bed!'

The Director paced up and down the room before continuing:

'In the last few months, a man was shot dead within feet of you, you fell down some steps drunk and cracked your head open, you took a month off work with mental health issues and now you just happen to find a head that some poor bastard had mislaid turn up in your bed. Kyle, you must be a very unlucky man.'

'You said it'

'So it's all a coincidence then? You are clean as a whistle?'

'Yes. I am.'

'Kyle. I've been to see the HR Director this morning and I've got to hand you this. You are suspended on full-pay for a month, whilst we launch an internal investigation into your suitability for your current role. Of course, if you get charged and don't get bail it will be irrelevant. However, I've heard that's looking unlikely based on what they have on you to date. You know? I haven't made up my mind if you're incredibly unlucky or incredibly lucky'.

'Put it this way. I wouldn't ask me for a racing tip'.

The Director smiled and shook his head as he left the Police Station and Kyle was led back to his cell. Another four hours passed. Kyle waited for shouts of astonishment as news of the crime of the century crossed the Atlantic but there were none. In fact, it was pretty quiet. Even his neighbour had got bored of insulting him.

Suddenly, there were heavy strides in the corridor and a Constable led him to an interview room, where a colleague was waiting. There was no tape, no introductions and no apology. It was short and sweet.

'We've had the results of the DNA test back from the lab. There was none of your DNA on the body part. There were traces of another person's DNA who we have not been able to identify. It's not yours and it's not the victims. Have you any idea whose it could be?' the man quizzed.

'No. I told you. I don't even know the victim, let alone who killed him'.

'OK, you are free to go without charge. Collect your belongings from the desk and enjoy your enforced leave. However, we will probably need to talk to you again about this case. You remain a suspect. Please don't leave the country Mr Forster.'

Scene 9: Climate Change

Kyle could not believe how warm it was when he walked to his local for a swift pint. It was mid-winter and it was mild enough to drink outside. The mid-day sun had brought office workers out for a stroll along Gosforth High Street and many had dispensed with both coats and jackets. He sipped his pint in the urban beer garden and watched the traffic file past on its way into Newcastle. There had been some crazy weather in recent months. Some of the worst flooding in living memory, tornados in Wolverhampton, snowstorms in Bognor and now this!

He overheard a conversation about global warming.

'The thermometer in my Audi said 17 degrees this morning. 17 degrees in January! I tell you, if this is global warming I will have some of this'.

The other person nodded. *'My mate in London said it reached 22 degrees yesterday'.*

Kyle imagined them happily reclining on deck-chairs and supping their ale whilst the sea lapped around them and a sick polar bear floated past on the last fragment of the polar ice-caps. *'Yeh. Great this global warming'* he scoffed.

Kyle knew the Illuminati were right on climate change. Economic competition had made controlling greenhouse gases that were devouring the o-zone layer, upon which life on Earth depended, virtually impossible. There had to be concerted and co-ordinated international action. Europe had a good record. In ten years recycling rates had gone from about 5% to 25% and use of public transport had grown again after decades of decline.

However, Bush's America went on spilling its guts out on the planet with no consideration for anyone else and the developing countries thought why should we bother if the richest country in the World doesn't give a fuck about global warming?

Talking of Bush; his most presidential performance came in the dignified transfer of power to his successor. President Obama was sworn in without any reports of an assassination attempt. He had made a typically brilliant speech and immediately set about righting the wrongs of his predecessor. The recession on both sides of the Atlantic was gathering pace but at least Obama brought hope that something might be done to halt the slide.

Kyle wanted to rejoice in the election of a black President but he could not be sure that Obama was still on his side. Had he been won over by Illuminati promises of peace and prosperity? Why else would the planned assassination attempt have been cancelled? There was a chance the liberal voices within the brotherhood had forced a change of plan or maybe the plotters had been rumbled. Kyle hated not knowing, but he remained a murder suspect suspended from work so he no longer had the inclination to play detective.

A robin landed in the beer garden, looking confused by the unseasonal weather. Its chest was more light orange than red and it was spoilt for choice with the crumbs in the beer garden. It flew off when an old man came and sat down at Kyle's table.

'Canny day!' he remarked.

'Aye. It's beautiful'.

'You off work?' asked the old man.

'You could say that. I'm suspended whilst they clear-up some mix-up.'

'A misunderstanding like?'

'Aye. A misunderstanding.'

'My son is only working 3 days a week now. He works at Nissan you know in Sunderland. Terrible this recession. He reckons if things don't pick up soon they might shut the plant and piss off back to Japan. Terrible this recession!'

'Aye'.

'He's got two young bairns you know; and a wife and a mortgage. He can't survive long on half wages. He's been to the bank asking for a mortgage holiday, just whilst he gets himself straight like. They told him to piss off. And you know what gets me. It's our bank. We own it and it still won't help a hard-working man keep his house and feed his bairns. These bankers want stringing up.'

'They have a lot to answer for'.

'Aye. You are right lad. They have a lot to answer for. A lot to answer for them banks, ' the man said laughing and nudging Kyle in the ribs.

Kyle finished his pint and bid the old man goodbye. He felt a bit at a loss for what to do so he went to the library and casually read some literature on the Illuminati, politics and economics. He didn't find out anything especially new but it passed some time and he didn't want to go down the slippery slope of getting pissed in the middle of the day.

*****

One day blurred into another as he kept his nose out of mischief and tried to find things to pass the time without spending too much money. He figured that there was a strong risk of him being dismissed at work even if he was cleared of murder. It was not a good climate to be looking for work so he might need to live frugally for some time.

He was ironing a shirt and listening to the radio when the phone rang. It was Northumbria Police. They had arrested a suspect for Dougie's murder based on a DNA match with an ex-con. Kyle was in the clear. He made a few calls to let people know and uncorked a bottle of red to celebrate.

The next day was mild but extremely windy and he felt like he was being blown along the High Street when he ventured out for holiday brochures. He went for a couple of pints to browse through them, this time in the comfort of a cosy lounge with a real log fire crackling nearby.

Back home, he was making tea when there was a knock at the door. He turned down the heat on the hob and went to answer it.

'*Hi Kyle*' said Rachel. She was wrapped up warm in a coat that buried her, but her beautiful smile was all the warmth that Kyle needed.

'*Rachel. Come in. Long time no see*'.

'*Yes. I've been really busy at work. It's been manic. I heard about your run-in with uniformed. I take it, it was Illuminati related?*'

'*Aye. Come in. I will tell you all about it.*'

Kyle turned the oven off and boiled the kettle. He told her all about the e-mail from Dougie, the assassination plans and the horrific scene in his bedroom. Rachel listened intently and put her arm round Kyle as he finished his tale. He kissed her gently on the lips and she returned the favour but removed her arm and backed away when he moved back in for more.

'*Rachel. I don't understand. One minute you're sleeping with me and the next you are pushing me away. I don't get it.*'

'*Well if you think I'm sleeping in your bed after telling me about finding severed heads under the duvet you can forget it!*'

'*We could go to yours.*'

'*Kyle. Let's just take things one step at a time. You remember what I said about relationships at work*'.

'*Yes and look how much I love you. I get myself deliberately suspended just so you can go out with me*'.

Rachel laughed. She had a soothing, feminine laugh befitting of a petite girl. She sipped her coffee whilst she thought about her next contribution to the conversation. Kyle waited patiently.

'*I'm no Bond girl Kyle. If we go out, I want to be sure I'm not going to end up in a gun-fight, a car chase or a shark pool. I like my adrenaline rush but a cup of coffee in front of Coronation Street isn't so bad either.*'

'Rachel. The way I feel about you, I could live in some totalitarian super-state quite happily as long as we were together. I wouldn't do anything to put you at risk.'

'So you've no interest in meeting someone in Government who knows about the Books of the Illuminati then?'

'Rachel, are you teasing me?'

'No. My brother Nick works as a political advisor in the Cabinet Office. He wants to meet you urgently.'

Scene 10: Pimlico

Nick Woods was the rising star of New Labour. At 26, he had already made himself known to two Prime Ministers. After reading politics at Sheffield he got a job with a political think-tank where his sharp mind and youthful exuberance quickly came to the attention of left-leaning MPs. He was head-hunted for a new job in a growing team of spin doctors that worked within the Cabinet Office and provided the Cabinet with fresh ideas and an alternative outlook to the conservatism of senior civil servants.

As the train headed South, Rachel told Kyle about the time her brother had met Tony Blair in Downing Street.

'It was shortly before Tony Blair finally handed over the reins to his old friend and adversary Gordon Brown. Tony had called a meeting of spin doctors and civil servants to consider ways of leaving a legacy that would cement his place in history. The PM entered the stately room and fourteen wise men and women stood to attention round a rectangular, walnut table. There were two spaces. The PM sat in one of them at the head of the table and began the meeting. The other belonged to Nick, who was new to his job and running late.

Tony had just finished going round the table seeking introductions when the door opened and Nick entered wearing jeans and a Newcastle United shirt. Fourteen soberly dressed souls turned open-mouthed to stare at the audacious late-comer. Half of them were thinking that a protester had somehow managed to evade security and gatecrash their important meeting. The other half were thinking that the career of the Cabinet Office's latest recruit was over before it began.

Before the murmur had died down, the PM had got up and walked round the table to shake Nick's hand. 'I don't think we've met he said'. 'Nick Woods' replied my brother shaking Tone's hand enthusiastically and describing his recent appointment. 'Well Nick, said the PM: I like your shirt but its last season's kit. I hope we pay you enough to but this season's soon'. Fourteen ambitious souls muttered under their breath what a jammy bastard this strange interloper was. In a few seconds he had made more of an impression on the PM than they had managed in a few years.'

'Wow. What an amazing story' said Kyle, warmly aroused by the sound of Rachel's voice. *'Your brother certainly has some bottle!'*

He couldn't help thinking of the last time they were together on a train. There was no chance of a repeat performance. The train was packed and Rachel was wearing tight jeans rather than stockings and suspenders. Kyle thought she looked stunning and he wondered why it had taken him so long to truly appreciate her beauty. He was doing his best to just be friends but it was difficult when images of her naked body and raging orgasms kept occupying his lonely mind.

He asked Rachel what Nick thought of the 2 PMs. She described how they were polar opposites in terms of personality but incredibly close in terms of politics. The success of New Labour's landslide election victories and popular first term owed much to the interesting dynamic and tension between the two men. They complemented each other perfectly. Where Tony was lacking, Gordon excelled and vice-versa. Nick thought that either could have made a great PM providing the other was at their side. Unfortunately, they both wanted the top job and when Gordon finally took over he was left brooding and isolated, whilst Tony earned a good living on the international debating circuit.

Kyle remarked on how Tony also happened to leave office just before the greatest economic crises since the 1930's. Rachel nodded. *'Yes. There were plenty of advisors warning that the bubble was about to burst so Tony took great pleasure in handing Gordon a poisoned chalice. Tony had a great sense of timing and political nous. Gordon lost all of that in his increasingly bitter lust for power.'*

'Does your brother think either of them are Illuminati?' Kyle enquired.

'You will have to ask him that' answered Rachel as the tannoy signalled their arrival at Kings Cross and people began to collect their belongings. Kyle was keen to meet Rachel's brother. He had a feeling they would get on just fine.

*****

Rachel had promised to ring her brother when they got out of the tube at Pimlico. They found a quiet side-street away from the hustle and bustle of Vauxhall Bridge Road and she started to dial. Kyle sat on a wall and watched the world go by. There were sharp businessmen in sharp suits, Rastafarian dudes with ghetto blasters and woollen hats and lost tourists trying to find their way to the Tate. It was a warm day in early February and the passers-by painted a colourful scene of life in a twenty-first century metropolis.

Kyle turned to an imaginary audience in the near-by square and reflected on London:

'London is like marmite. You either love it or hate it. I guess that's because there is so much of it to love or to hate. Other British Cities share its mixture of sprawling council estates and leafy suburbs but London does it by extremes. There are no half-measures in London. Cocooned in their millionaires rows and squares or middle-class avenues there are thousands of Londoners who wouldn't want to live anywhere else. In fact there are so many that feel this way that London house prices have grown exponentially to the rest of the country with families fighting in the avenues for each property that hits the market. Once they have made it on to the London property ladder they look

smugly down on the rest of us, safe in the knowledge that if ever they sold up and moved outside the M25 they will have made a fortune.

However, they are only one half of London's story. Half of the capital's population live in rented accommodation with no chance of ever being able to join the property owning classes. They are not all poor. Some of them are earning above the national average income and yet they still can't get a mortgage for a two bedroom terrace in Peckham. They are part of a disgruntled generation, many of whom came to London from abroad or the provinces seeking a better life and ended up trapped in as much poverty as they left behind. They despise the property developers who are continually snapping up £200K bargains in working-class areas and flogging them on at huge profits to wealthy new-comers. Areas like Notting Hill and Islington, which were once affordable have become exclusive and areas like Clapham and Stoke Newington that were once cheap have been gentrified to appeal to home-owners and price out the riff-raff.

I dislike London's inequality and distorted property market. My heart goes out to the desperate people living in a high-rise jungle of grime and crime. I pity the home-owners, who survive in a prison of long working hours, after-work drinks and a frantic battle to balance two jobs with childcare and a mountainous mortgage. I know of friends that moved to London after they graduated and made a fortune. They earn twice as much as me but still have less disposable income and less leisure time. They moan constantly about overcrowded commuter trains and stressful jobs. Young, ambitious Geordies have turned into middle-aged Reggie Perrins. It is all very sad.

If I did have to move to London for work I would aspire to live somewhere like Pimlico. It embodies all that is best about London and seems immune from the class struggle of many areas. All walks of life live in Pimlico and it is impossible to tell the council flats from the wealthy pads. It has an equalitarian culture all of its own.

Look over there you have a scruffy black kid, whose mere presence on a street corner would terrify the residents of Kensington. He is deep in friendly conversation with a neighbour in a suit with a gleaming BMW parked outside. There are contrasting cultures living happily beside each other in a melting pot of diversity.

Pimlico has other benefits. It is in walking distance of Westminster and the City Centre, it is close to the river and Victoria station and the Victoria Line gives it good access to Kings Cross and the North. The houses are beautiful. They are mostly three-story with small, neat front gardens and steps leading up to black front doors and down to basements. Most are flats, but some are vast Georgian houses with million pound price tags. They are all well-kept and clean and there are dozens of leafy squares where residents can come and relax on sunny days, well-away from the fumes and the chaos.

If London was more like Pimlico, I would understand its attraction. As it is, I much prefer Newcastle. Newcastle has a similar variety of amenities, culture, *entertainment and beautiful architecture but within a much more compact area. It also has a clear sense of identity and pride shared by all its citizens, rich and poor. There is warmth about Newcastle that welcomes a stranger in and buys them a pint. In London, outsiders come and go inconspicuously and they tend to cling together looking for safety in numbers amongst fellow immigrants. There are Irish areas, West Indian areas, Australian areas and now even Portuguese areas. If London was as good as Newcastle they would want to embrace it and become cockneys, not change it to make it more like the places they left behind.'*

*****

Nick lived in a gorgeous basement flat in a splendidly symmetrical square. He welcomed his sister and her guest enthusiastically at the front door and said *'Perfect timing. We are just about to start'.*

He led them to an airy dining room with views out through net curtains on to the square and a large oak table with a candlestick centrepiece beneath an imposing chandelier. At the other side of the room was a large portrait of Earl Grey of Newcastle, famous for being the author of the Great Reform Bill and liking a lemony kind of tea. Kyle and Rachel were introduced to two other guests.

A stout, scruffy Texan bounded across the room and intercepted them. *'Hey guys. I've heard a lot about you both. I'm Ed Falconbridge from San Antonio, Texas. I'm a freelance journalist who has been investigating the dark side of American politics since Watergate. All the politicians over the pond know me and respect me, but most of them wish I'd bugger off and leave them alone.'*

'Quite an introduction Ed' said Nick with a sense that he had just had the limelight stolen from him. *'Now this is Wendy Harpole. She had a top job in the City and was fired when she blew the whistle on some insider dealing. Wendy got a job as a Treasury Advisor under Gordon Brown and became concerned about the influence of big business and bankers over public policy.'*

Wendy was a forthright looking lady in her 50's with glasses and a lean, hungry look. She looked like she would speak little but end up winning any argument. *'Pleased to meet you'* she said with a business-like smile before returning swiftly to her seat.

'OK. I declare the first meeting of the Illuminati Resistance open' Nick began with authority and a touch of pomposity.

"First, let me introduce myself. I am Nick Woods. I am a political advisor to the Cabinet. I have top level access to the PM, his circle of advisors and to senior civil servants. I have a reputation for speaking my mind, so please don't be offended if I do so today. I remember on my first day in my new job I had the pleasure of meeting the doyen of spin-doctors Alastair Campbell. After listening to me ranting and raving about the injustice of some anti-terror laws I

heard Alistair turn to a Minister and say 'Who the hell does that Geordie kid think he is?' I took that as a complement."

He looked around the table and was comforted to find his guests were hooked on his every word.

"This is the agenda for today. Firstly, we need to remind ourselves why we are here. Secondly we need to share what we know about the Fifth and Sixth phases. Thirdly, we need to agree an action plan. So, why are we here?' He paused dramatically and poured some water from a jug before continuing.

'The free world is in danger. The Illuminati have infiltrated every bastion of power and wealth. They have among them some of the richest men in the world and they know that especially in a recession money can buy you anything. I used to believe there are some things that money couldn't buy. Working in Westminster soon destroyed that notion. After all, try telling a lady of the night that you can't buy love. Every phone box for miles is plastered with stickers refuting that claim. The Illuminati have more than wealth and influence on their side. They have science. Most of the world's top scientists are members and they have kept back many of their greatest inventions to give the brotherhood a technical advantage over the opposition. If anyone doubts the Illuminati have the capacity to take over the World and rule it as they please then please leave now.'

Nobody moved. Nobody spoke. They all waited patiently for their confident, young host to continue.

'The Illuminati have succeeded in bringing down the global economy. They are now starting on a new campaign aimed at disgracing the political establishment further. Over the rest of this year you can expect a campaign of shocking revelations about politicians expense claims, corruption and scandal on a scale never seen before. By the end of the year people will be desperate for change. Any change! Any movement disassociated with the main political parties based on a broad coalition of eminent people will find a receptive audience. The Illuminati will claim to be part of a coalition to clean up politics and rebuild the economy and they will be welcomed with open arms. They won't be properly scrutinised. They control the media so they will be heralded the world over as saviours.

In country after country they will demand and achieve through political and financial pressure a new election with them standing on an anti-democratic ticket. They will use democracy to get elected and then end democracy by establishing a one-party system with a senior management team running the country through a series of regional offices. In other countries, they will use military strength and mass protest to seize power rather than obtain it democratically. The result will be the same. By this time next year, there will effectively be a global management team, a global army of secret police to maintain law and order and no longer any way of removing them from office.

I think we all know that there is a bitter power struggle within the Illuminati between right-wingers and liberal idealists, which has delayed their plans and led to a more gradual transfer of power. However, make no mistake there are dark forces behind the brotherhood. Who will win the day? Well, of course, it will be the men with the most money and power. These men have a right-wing agenda that will be like George Bush with brains. Many within the brotherhood are only now starting to understand the dangerous spiral they have started, but the secret police are already operational. Don't be in any doubt. We are risking our lives just meeting here. Rebels and doubters have been murdered, beaten-up, kidnapped and tortured and silenced in medieval ways.

Within Government, there are many good people wanting to resist the New World Order, but they are scared. The Illuminati are ruthless and unforgiving and they are everywhere. Politicians don't know who they can trust in their own parties. Civil servants, army generals and secret service heads are similarly unsure what side their colleagues are batting for. There are enough good people to stop the Illuminati ever getting to power in Britain but there are not enough brave ones. I called you here today because I think you have the guts to stand up for what you believe in. Ladies and gentlemen we can make history together. Please raise a glass to the resistance!'

Act 5: The Resistance

Scene 1: Batman Takes Flight

Rachel apart, every member of the resistance brought something new to the Pimlico meeting. Kyle brought first-hand experience of the lengths the Illuminati were prepared to go to in order to preserve their secrets. He was also the only person to have read all six of their books. Wendy revealed the Illuminati were orchestrating a new wave of financial panic to offset the impact of economic stimulus.

Ed spoke loudly and at great length about how the US Government and big business had been in bed together for years and no individual, not even the President, was powerful enough to resist the Illuminati influence on all the major institutions. He didn't seem to have much evidence but he spoke with such conviction it seemed impossible to believe that he was talking bollocks.

Nick brought the most knowledge to the table. He knew of at least one member of the Cabinet and one member of the shadow Cabinet who were setting aside party interests to campaign for a New World Order. He could not name a single senior politician that he could say with 100% certainty was 100% clean! He had heard that the sixth phase had been postponed in the light of the American presidential election and an assassination attempt had been considered.

The Illuminati planned to give Obama a six months honeymoon before undermining him with a negative press campaign, allegations of left-wing connections and a sniff of corruption. That is if their efforts to persuade him to join the brotherhood failed. Nick had seen a paper by an American political scientist that suggested America remained a deeply conservative country that had elected Obama because of his leadership qualities, not his politics. The more policies he tried to implement, the more unpopular he would become.

Kyle found the meeting fascinating but he was frustrated that when it came to the action plan he had little to contribute. Before they blew the whistle they needed more information on who they could trust and who might be part of the conspiracy. Nick, Wendy and Ed all had networks to exploit to glean information. Kyle was suspended from work and he couldn't see him getting much information on the New World Order from One Word!

When they left the meeting Kyle noticed Rachel seemed especially quiet.

'*You seem quiet Rachel. Is everything all right*?' he asked.

'I always seem quiet around my kid brother. He can talk for England!'

'Yes. He's a canny bloke but he likes the sound of his own voice.'

'I don't know why Nick invited me really, apart from me knowing you, I mean. I felt like a spare part. I didn't have anything to contribute and I don't do politics. I prefer to put my faith in people I know personally rather than people I hear about through the media.'

'I know what you mean but this is different. Think of all the people that lost their lives fighting for the right to vote, opposing fascism and defending freedom and democracy. We owe it to them not to let the Illuminati win.'

Rachel smiled and looked at the pub that stood between them and the tube station.

'I could murder a pint' she said.

'You read my mind' replied Kyle, returning the smile.

They both went for a pint of Poacher's Dick. Rachel pulled a face as she tasted it.

'What's it like' asked Kyle.

'You taste it. I think it might be off'.

Kyle had a sip and confirmed it tasted rancid. As he tilted the glass, bubbles of sediment floated upwards.

'I'll take them back' he said decisively and he rejoiced at the approving look from Rachel. He knew that if he hadn't been with her he probably would have drunk up and not caused a fuss but somehow he felt it his duty to defend his princess from stale beer.

'That looks better' Rachel said as he returned with two pints of Young's Winter Warmer. *'Did you tell him his Poacher's Dick has gone off?'*

'Aye. I felt it safest to go for something local and not named after someone's dick.' Kyle said as he sat down. He waited for Rachel to taste it and she smiled approvingly.

'That's gorgeous: sweet but not too cloying. You can taste caramel and bitter orange.'

'Aye! That's spot on. Have you ever thought of becoming a beer taster for CAMRA Rachel? You have one hell of a discerning palate.'

'No. I'd like it too much. I'd end up with a beer belly'.

Kyle laughed. He couldn't imagine Rachel with a beer belly if she drunk 10 pints a day. She looked very skinny in her black boots, tight jeans and oversized Green Day t-shirt. She had foam on her soft, pink lips and Kyle wiped it off and gazed into her deep, pretty eyes.

'So apart from being drop dead gorgeous and liking pints of bitter and rock music what else makes you irresistible to us alpha-males?' he asked in the style of Jeremy Paxman. *'I suppose you are going to tell me you're a big football fan!'*

'Well. I did use to love football. I used to go with my brother and stand in the Gallowgate.'

'No'. Kyle wanted to make love to her right there in the pub.

'Yes. I'm a right tom-boy. I used to prefer a kick-around with the boys to playing with dolls any day. I enjoyed the atmosphere and I also liked seeing athletic men in shorts. Rudi Gullit was my favourite; I was chuffed when the Toon appointed him as manager and devastated when he got the sack. I also liked David Ginola but then everyone fancied Ginola.'

'So when was the last time you went to St James?'

'Oh. It was years ago. Keegan had just left as manager and things weren't the same. Besides, by then I was much more into music. To be honest by the time I was a teen-ager my football posters had been replaced by a shrine to Damon Albarn. I thought he was gorgeous and I found the Brit-pop scene really exciting.'

'That doesn't sound like a tomboy; posters of pop-stars and admiring footballer's thighs.'

'Being a tom-boy doesn't make you a lesbian Kyle.'

'Rachel. You are too feminine to be a tom-boy. You are kind and gentle and petite and you have all these girly gestures. You are beautiful.'

To Kyle's surprise, Rachel leant over and kissed him firmly on the lips.

'Thanks' she said and she returned to her pint, looking genuinely touched by Kyle's earnest flattery.

*****

On the way back Kyle had tried to convince Rachel to go to the following week's meeting of the resistance but it was to no avail. He had even offered to pay her rail fair. Rachel was adamant that she had nothing worthwhile to contribute and she didn't fancy spending every weekend going backwards and forwards to London. Kyle found it difficult to make her out. She obviously liked him. She obviously fancied him. They were both effectively single. Why should one bad experience with a previous partner and work-colleague deter her from dating him?

He was so deep in thought on this very point that he got off the metro at the Haymarket when he had intended to go on to the Monument. It was a lucky break. As he started to walk down Northumberland Street he noticed a blind man crossing the road with his dog and heading up Ridley Place. *'Fucking hell! The caped crusader himself! '*. He chuckled and then followed Batman from a distance.

Robin led Batman into a travel agent and after checking the coast was clear, Kyle followed. Kyle browsed through some brochures whilst listening intently to Batman booking a flight and ordering some currency. He was booking a flight to Cairo for four people. Kyle did not recognise the other names. However, he was quite evasive at the agent's affable questions, just stating that his trip was for business rather than pleasure.

Kyle wrote down the times of the flights. Batman immediately dialled a number on his bulky mobile and Kyle overheard him say:

'Ok Chief. You out again? Anyway, I just wanted to say the flights are booked for the times you asked for. There was no problem. I'm on my way home now but give us a bell when you get the message and we can discuss the details. Cheers'.

Kyle felt relieved. He now had new information to report back to the resistance. He wasn't going to feel like a spare part. He also might be able to combine business with pleasure. He had been thinking for some-time about a break in the sun. Maybe he was destined to go to Egypt.

Scene 2: Paparazzi Chase

Whilst Kyle was observing the caped crusader book a flight, Ed was sitting in a turbo-charged car outside one of New York's most salubrious hotels. His photographer Pedro was at the wheel, because much to Ed's annoyance he was still banned from driving.

Ed had more contacts than Spec-savers. One such contact had told him of a meeting in this hotel between the son and heir to one of the richest business empires in the World, a Russian oil tycoon and a banker who was advising the President on the Credit Crunch. He suspected all 3 of being senior Illuminati plotters. Indeed the famous American dynasty had been linked with the Illuminati for a century and Ed had always believed in the motto: *'There's no smoke without fire.'*

He was not the only member of the Press lying in wait for their prey. The Russian was under investigation for tax evasion, corruption and a host of distinctly capitalist sins. However, he was a long-standing friend of the American tycoon and their play-boy antics were a source of fascination for journalists, especially when politicians were embroiled in them.

He got out of the car and went for a chat with an old buddy from the Washington Post.

'Hey Jules you faggot. How's it hanging?'

'Just fine Ed. How are you?'

'I'm still banned from driving and getting sued for maintenance from two different women but apart from that I'm on top of the world.'

'So what's the score with this hotel meeting? Are there dodgy deals going on inside or are they drinking the hotel bar dry?'

'Probably both if I know those bastards. I'd like to be a fly on the wall. My information is that they are part of a global conspiracy that would make Watergate seem like second page news.'

'You are not still going on about the USA being run by a coalition of bankers and politicians planning to take over the world are you?'

'You will be sick that you turned my story down when I finally nail the bastards I tell you'.

'Ed. Not everything is sinister. You've lost credibility. That's why you haven't been employed for years. You can't tell me that you don't regret pushing the whole conspiracy thing too far; that you enjoy being freelance'.

'The best decision I've ever made Jules. Being a wage-slave isn't for me. Look, I'm going to check out the back of the hotel'.

'OK Ed. See you buddy'.

Ed only got half-way round the corner at the rear of the hotel when he saw the bodyguards emerging from a rear entrance and a limousine waiting with its engine purring.

'Shit' he said and run as fast as his little fat legs would take him back to his car.

Pedro flung the passenger door open for him and revved up the engine. Ed jumped into the car as it started to head off, too out of breath to speak but pointing where Pedro should head. Another car followed them with a photographer leaning out of the window. The rest of the press realized what had happened too late to play any part in the Paparazzi chase.

*****

Ed's car gained on the limousine and he tried to identify the passengers but the windows were blacked out. The limo weaved in and out of the Manhattan traffic and the two press cars followed in its slip-stream. It went through a red light and Ed closed his eyes as he saw a garbage truck slamming on the brakes. He felt his neck violently twisted to one side and then the other and sensed the car leave the road before thudding down and regaining its course and speed.

When Ed opened his eyes he saw that they had managed to escape with a bit of wing damage but the other press car had ploughed straight into the truck, leaving a pile of smoke and twisted metal.

'Shit' he said looking behind him. Turning round he noticed there was now a car between theirs and the limo. *'Out of the way faggot'* he yelled, gesturing out of the window. However, by the time they managed to overtake the *'faggot'* their quarry was two blocks away and turning out of view.

'Step on it. You drive like a girl Pedro' Ed yelled.

It was no good. By the time they turned the corner the limo was out of sight.

'Where to now boss?' said Pedro calmly.

'Get on the freeway and see if we can pick them up' Ed replied in a voice that suggested he knew it was a lost cause.

They accelerated to 90 miles per hour but the limo was still not in sight. Ed was just about to tell Pedro to abort the chase when a bullet went through the rear windscreen and narrowly missed his head.

'*Son of a bitch*' Ed exclaimed, turning to see that the hunter had become the fox. A car was hot in pursuit with a black guy leaning out of the passenger window holding a pistol. Pedro didn't need telling. He put his foot down and watched the dial go over 100. Up ahead there was congestion filling both lanes. There was not enough time to brake. Pedro swerved the car off at the junction allowing the incline of the slip-road to help the car brake and avoid a collision.

Ed turned round hoping the gunman's car had gone on careering into the stationery traffic ahead. It hadn't. They were still being followed and this time they were in slow moving traffic. A second bullet whizzed past them as they turned into a side-street searching for free road to aid their escape. The screech of wheels indicated the chase was still on.

After the next junction the gunman withdrew his weapon and closed the window. Their car began to slow down and took a turn into a side-road. '*What the hell*?' said Ed and the blue flashing light of the NYPD answered his question.

'*Looks like it's my turn to lose my licence* Boss' said Pedro pulling over.

'*Great isn't it. They don't go after the dude shooting at us. They prefer to book us for speeding. Dick-heads!* ' Ed moaned.

*****

There was a last minute change of venue for the next resistance meeting. Ed had been detained in New York. Thus, it was switched from Nick's flat to a Westminster office block with video conferencing facilities. Ed described his car chase vividly and eventually Nick interrupted him:

'*Can I stop you there Ed? Apart from confirming that a meeting of three prime suspects took place in New York, did you actually find anything new out?*'

'*No. I guess I didn't*', Ed admitted.

Wendy had nothing new to add either so the stage was set for Kyle and his tale of Batman's flight to Egypt.

'*Great. Well done Kyle*' Nick said. '*I have it on good authority that there is going to be a huge Illuminati Conference, where all the nominated Executives and Chief Executives and the interim management team get together and plan the 6th phase. It's like Bilderberg times ten. All I was missing was where and when the conference was going to be.*'

'*Cairo here I come*' said Ed via VC drowning out Kyle who had just began to speak.

'*You were going to say Kyle?*' prompted Kyle.

'*Oh. Just that I would like to go to Nick*'

'*Well let's think this one through. I can't go. I'm too well known to British politicians. My presence would be hard to explain. Ed, your presence as a freelance journalist is no problem. Why wouldn't a journalist cover a meeting of the rich and famous? Kyle, I'm not sure about you mate. You are well-known to the Illuminati in the North East. You might be at risk.*'

'*Not if I go as a tourist to see the sights and just happen to liaise with Ed over there.*'

Whilst Nick was thinking about this Wendy intervened. '*I don't fancy going myself but why don't Kyle and Rachel go, as a young couple on holiday. They won't look conspicuous and unless the North East Chief happens to see Kyle they won't be in any danger*'.

Kyle liked that idea but added a note of caution. '*I will have to talk to Rachel. I'm not sure she will be up for it. I think she wants to stay out of all this.*'

Nick laughed. '*Don't worry about my sister Kyle. She's tougher than she looks. I will have a word with her and explain you are to keep away from the conference venue and just provide back-up to Ed*'.

Nick was right. Rachel rang him for the first time and at last he had her mobile number. She was obviously very tempted by a holiday in the sun and a chance to see the pyramids. She was still reluctant to get involved but she was also excited.

'*So shall I book us some flights and a hotel?*' asked Kyle. '*I will pay and I will choose a decent hotel with a twin room or two singles if you'd prefer*'.

'*OK Kyle, but I will pay my share and you can book us a double as long as you promise not to snore!*'

Scene 3: Every Cloud!

Kyle remembered his brother's motto as he booked a hotel in Cairo for a fortnight's time. *'Every crisis is an opportunity'* Dan used to say. Dan used it to express his positive outlook on life as well as his penchant for snapping up cheap assets that he could later flog off at a profit. Dan had always been an unlikely candidate for suicide as he was a glass half full sort of bloke. Kyle decided you never could tell how people would react when all their hope was snatched away from them and what they believed in turned out to be an illusion.

In February 2009 the World was entering its darkest phase since the Second World War. Hope was thin on the ground. Even the most bullish of financial analysts were resigned to a deep, world-wide recession. The pessimists were forecasting a financial Armageddon, in which whole countries went bankrupt unable to finance the huge debt they had taken on to prop up the banks and stimulate the economy. Shares were incredibly low and still the market was sluggish. Scarcely a day went by without a fresh announcement of redundancies.

It was not a good time to face the prospect of dismissal from work. Kyle couldn't understand why the inquiry was still going ahead. He had been cleared as a murder suspect and another man was behind bars. However, he was still suspended and now had to face a grilling from the HR Director, his own Director and the Deputy Chief Constable. He couldn't decide if it was a conspiracy to punish him for his resistance to the New World Order or bureaucracy gone mad.

However, there was a silver lining to this grim background. After a few weeks of uncertainty his relationship with Rachel was back-on. She was still coy and wanted it kept under wraps at work but she had agreed to wait for him outside the inquiry and go for a drink afterwards. They were also sending regular texts and Kyle saved the first to arrive with two kisses as a treasured souvenir.

Kyle couldn't wait to spend some time with the woman he loved under the warm Saharan sun. A text came through from Rachel as he lay looking out at the wild weather blowing in from the North Sea. He scrambled for his phone knocking his lap-top from the bed as he did so. There was excitement with every text, tinged with the anxiety that she might have changed her mind and decided not to go to Cairo with him.

He smiled as he read the message:

'Hi Kyle, have u booked the hotel? Love Rachel. XX'

*****

Kyle's hopes that the inquiry was some sort of administrative hoop his employer had to go through were soon crushed. After asking Kyle to outline that he was totally in the dark about why the head of a complete stranger turned up in his bed the Deputy Chief Constable weighed in with:

'Our information suggests differently Kyle. We were really hoping given this second chance you would come clean. Lying to a police officer is a serious offence for someone who owes their living to the Police Authority. We need to able to trust you and the information you supply. I'm not sure we can'.

Kyle asked *'What does your information say?'*

The 3 inquisitors looked at each other and the Deputy Chief continued with a deep frown:

'We have a sworn statement that you did know the deceased. Allegedly, you procured drugs from him in Edinburgh on the afternoon of your accident. Your normal supplier felt the deceased was muscling in on his clients, dealt with the rival and sent his head as a gruesome reminder of the penalty that faced those that crossed him. '

'The drugs certainly explain your erratic behaviour Kyle' added his Director.

'We understand that you have been through a very upsetting time and can offer you much better ways to get over your pain and sense of loss than drugs' offered the HR Director.

'However, it does not alter the prospect of criminal charges. Your lie hampered our investigation. It amounts to perverting the course of justice' the Deputy Chief insisted.

Kyle was silent throughout these interjections. His brain was working overtime, weighing up the options. The truth was not one of them. Two of his three inquisitors were members of the Illuminati. It was better to admit to being a mendacious druggie than a continuing danger to the New World Order.

'You know as well as I do that the sworn testimony of a murder suspect is unreliable. What evidence have you got to back up these allegations?'

'Kyle' said his Director disapprovingly. *'We have obtained CCTV footage of you meeting the deceased in Edinburgh. The image is not clear but it looks like some sort of deal takes place in the pub and the identity of the two participants is not in doubt.'*

Kyle sighed. He was on a sticky wicket.

'OK, I admit it. I have been using weed to get through the pain of my divorce and the loss of my brother. I was in the pub and the stranger might have been the victim. He looked vaguely familiar but I met him once for a few minutes to get some weed and I couldn't be sure it was the same person when his head

turns up on my pillow. I didn't lie. I just wasn't sure it was him and didn't want to bring up my drug habit.'

'Thanks Kyle' said the HR Director making some notes.

The Deputy Chief was less satisfied. *'I've been a police officer for 30 years and I have never heard of a user travelling 100 miles to buy weed.* I reckon we are talking something stronger.'

'We clearly need to talk about this among the 3 of us and let you know the outcome' concluded the HR Director.

Kyle left in a daze, unsure if he was to face criminal charges and unemployment and dreading both. Rachel held his hand as they walked to the pub with him repeating every word of the inquiry.

She sipped on a pint of Guinness and reassured him. *'I don't reckon they will want the embarrassment of charging you. They will look bad in the press. Imagine the headlines if the man responsible for crime figures is convicted of lying. I reckon you will get a written warning, a wrap across the knuckles and be let back to work within a couple of weeks.'*

Rachel was right. A letter arrived three days later. He was not going to be charged. His suspension would only last until the end of the month, subject to an occupational health assessment and a drugs test. It was a written warning regarding his inappropriate behaviour and he would be re-asseseed in April to confirm he had mended his ways and his work was up to scratch.

Scene 4: Drinking in the Last Chance Saloon

Kyle was just on his way out for a Saturday night on the town with the lads when his mobile went off. It was Nick Woods ringing from his Pimlico flat. He sounded uncharacteristically deflated.

'It looks like time is running out Kyle' he said with the tone of someone fishing for reasons to be contradicted.

'Why do you say that?' Kyle challenged.

'I've just come from a meeting at the Cabinet Office. There's a plot to overthrow the PM and set up a cross-party coalition government to tackle the economic crisis. A huge scandal is about to break that will lead to mass resignations and put pressure on both party leaders to step down. If they refuse, there will be a leadership challenge.'

Kyle wanted Nick to name names but he knew he wouldn't so he enquired *'And the link to the New World Order is?'*

'The two plotters are two of the Illuminati leaders in this country. They play at being political foes but are really old friends with a lust for power and connections to the rich and famous all over the world. They are both booked on flights to Cairo. They are both Bilderberg veterans. They are both ruthlessly ambitious.'

'So the economic downturn is a smoke-screen for a coalition that will take this country into the New World Order by the back-door?'

'That's about it. Political advisors on both sides are trying to get the leaders to sack the plotters but neither has the bottle. Firstly, it's all hearsay and they want hard evidence. Secondly, Brown's leadership is so fragile that he can't risk a Ministerial sacking.'

'I'm surprised that Cameron doesn't act. The polls suggest he will win the next election anyway.'

'The Tory plotter and Cameron are old Etonian buddies. Telling him to sack his old school-friend is like telling Caesar to sack Brutus.'

'He won't believe the soothsayers until the knife is in his back?'

'Yes! If we are going to stop this we need to act quickly. Beware the ides of March!'

'Are you sure this hearsay evidence is reliable?'

'You can never be sure but I've heard the whispers from very different sources; reliable sources. The thing that bothers all of us is the old chestnut that

we don't know if the men at the top are sympathetic to the New World Order or not. They may be playing a clever game. They may be putting out these rumours to flush out opposition. That could be the real reason for not dealing with the plotters. The plot might not be against Brown and Cameron but against the democratic process that elected them'.

'Do you think that is likely?'

'Kyle, I really don't know. Some days I think that there's no way Gordon would be an Illuminati leader. Other days I see how cosy he is with big business, bankers and tax exiles and I think it makes sense. I wish I knew but I don't and his inner circle is untouchable. They are the only ones he trusts and in return they are exceedingly discrete.'

'Maybe we will find out in Cairo'.

'I hope so. I think it could be our last chance!'

* * * * *

There was a depleted gathering at the Crown Posada. One Word couldn't afford to go out because of his impending redundancy. John Medburn was on a date with his mystery girlfriend. Elton John was working. He never worked Saturday nights but ostensibly the economic downturn had finally started to hit the painting and decorating business and he could no longer afford to turn work down.

It was a sombre gathering. The Toon had lost again and relegation was looking possible. Dobbo was full of woe, but not just because of the sad demise of Newcastle United.

'I had to carry a body out of a fire in Arthurs Hill last night' he said solemnly.

Even Mattie couldn't think of something witty to say in response to that and he respectfully kept quiet whilst Kyle prompted him to develop his story.

"He was an old miner who turned to drink when Maggie Thatcher shut the last of the pits. He moved to Arthurs Hill when his wife died a few years ago and he used to stand outside the brewery breathing in the fumes. He got nicked once for stealing a keg and trying to roll it back up the hill to his maisonette. We got a referral about a year ago from Social Services. He was an alcoholic, chain smoker, living alone and was showing early signs of dementia. I went round there and spent an hour with him giving him a home fire safety check. We fitted a smoke-alarm and warned him of the dangers of smoking in bed.

Three weeks later we responded to a 999 call. He'd set fire to his kitchen and it was quite a mess when we got there but he'd managed to stagger out and just went to hospital for a precautionary check. He was so pissed he could hardly speak. I was angry with him for taking the battery out of the smoke alarm that I'd installed, but I could tell it was going in one ear and out the other. Anyway, I fitted a hard-wired alarm and hoped that would be it.

We got to his house within 5 minutes of the call last night, but he was long dead. He'd got back from the pub and decided to cook but obviously fallen asleep on the sofa buried in a pile of lager cans, fag-ends and a dirty duvet. The smoke alarm was ripped out at the wall. A neighbour said he'd smashed it with a sledge-hammer when it woke him up one night. In fact, it had alerted him to setting his bed on fire. The alarm's reward for saving his life was getting smashed to a pulp for 'making his head ache worse and waking the neighbour's bairn'. I guess he was a casualty waiting to happen but it's the first time I've carried a dead person out of a fire and it choked me up.

Amongst the burnt out ruins I found a tin box that had survived the fire. In it were his prized possessions. A wedding photo dated 17/4/61, a photo of him at the coal-face with his son in the early 80's and a ticket to the 1955 FA Cup Final".

Kyle put his arm round Dobbo as the big man wiped a tear from his eyes. *'I will get you a whisky chaser'* said Mattie and went to the bar. Dobbo had almost finished his pint by the time Mattie returned with a double whisky.

'Were you chatting up the bar-maids again?' asked Dobbo.

'No. Have you seen the state of her? She looks like the back of a fire engine. No, I was chatting to this bloke at the bar who knows someone whose friends with Shearer's gardener. He reckons Shearer has been offered the manager's job!'

'Was he pissed?' asked Kyle

'No. Straight up! He reckons it's a done deal'.

'Why would Shearer want to leave his cosy TV job to take over that bunch of over-paid, work-shy tossers?' asked Dobbo.

'He's a Geordie. He turned Man United down to play for the club he loves. He'd jump at the chance to save us from relegation?' explained Mattie.

'Aye. I can see him being tempted, ' Kyle acknowledged. *'if we go down he won't get the blame and if we stay up he'd be the Messiah'.*

'He will be the only manager with a bar named after him at the ground', Dobbo noted with a marginally brighter tone.

Mattie laughed. *'First King Kev, then Sir Bobby, then Special K again and now Shearer. If he fails who will be the next Geordie Messiah, Ant or Dec?'*

They all laughed and drank away the blues. Kyle had never seen the tiny pub so empty on a Saturday night before. The credit crunch must be biting, he decided. However, recalling his conversation with Nick, considering the prospects of relegation and sensing the impact the credit crunch was having on his friends he felt like his whole world was there; drinking in the last chance saloon.

Scene 5: Airport Disco

The flight left Heathrow for Cairo at six in the morning. Kyle had offered to book an airport hotel but Rachel pragmatically agreed that it would be a waste given that they would have to get up and check in at 4 in the morning. Thus, they planned to crash out in the departure lounge and get some kip on the plane. They arrived at about 11 and found a few people already laying claim to the silver metal benches but plenty of room for two more travellers.

'They could have put some padding on the seats' Rachel said frowning at the cold, hard metal.

'I don't suppose they want to encourage sleepers' replied Kyle emptying his rack-sack and yawning at the thought of a restless night.

They sat down and listened to some tunes on their I-pods. Only the frequent tannoy announcements disturbed the music. There were plenty of disparate groups coming and going in the first hour, flying off to all parts of the globe but with the same ritual of emotional farewells and excited queuing. The cleaners were hard at work, a security guard paced up and down and the shutters went up on some retail outlets. After midnight the hive of activity died down and people started to bed down. Rachel returned empty-handed from a tour of the duty-free outlets and Kyle went to have a look as much to pass the time as to find something to buy.

When he emerged from the shop he noticed a group of travellers had set up camp on the seats opposite theirs and one of them was standing ogling Rachel. Kyle felt a primitive urge to deck him but a security guard was nearby looking desperate for some action to make his job worthwhile. Rachel was laughing and seemed to be lapping up the attention of the young man with designer stubble and baggy jeans.

He turned and offered his hand to Kyle with a warm smile and a glint in his dark brown eyes. *'Hi. I'm Nial'* he said in a genial Irish accent. *'I was just telling Rachel about the time I slept here on the way to Bangladesh and slept so well I missed my flight.'*

'Kyle' Kyle said shaking his hand but sending *'fuck off and leave my girlfriend alone'* vibes back as he did so.

'Nial is a UNESCO voluntary worker Kyle. He is meeting up with the rest of the volunteers here tonight to fly out to Mozambique in the morning where they are going to dig wells and install a fresh water supply' said Rachel sensing her partner's jealousy.

'I see' said Kyle hoping Nial would leave them alone.

Nial was undeterred. *'Here, won't you two gorgeous Geordies join us in a night-cap?'* he said and before they could respond two cans of Guinness were thrust in their direction. Rachel had caught a second wind and Kyle didn't want to be the party pooper so he found himself moving across to the party of volunteers and joining in their engaging conversation.

Initially, there were 7 in their party but by 1 o clock there were 20 of them, equally divided between Brits and Irish. The Guinness was flowing and the crack was good. Nial was the life and soul of the party and he produced a guitar and started to strum away requests. Kyle tried to think of a notoriously hard tune to prove the fallibility of this charming imposter but everything suggested he played brilliantly. As they drunk more, the chemistry between Rachel and Nial became more palpable.

Kyle didn't know how to react. Here he was being invited in warmly and given free alcohol by a group of morally faultless people more of Rachel's generation than his own and he felt threatened and unable to relax. They were so cool and he was so uptight that the situation was uncomfortable. He looked on as Nial taught Rachel a few chords lingering as their fingers touched on the strings. Am I being made a fool of? Kyle thought but there was nobody to ask apart from Nial's burgeoning fan club.

He needed a piss and yet he was reluctant to leave Rachel and Nial alone. Eventually he could cross his legs no longer and he hurried off to the gents. One of Nial's mates followed and stood beside him at the urinal.

'Don't worry about Nial and Rachel' he said with a voice that sounded home-sick of County Limerick. *'Nial is like that with all the pretty girls but he's never unfaithful. He has a beautiful girl back home in Dublin who he's totally devoted to and he wouldn't cheat on her, if he was invited to an orgy with Girls Aloud'.*

'Thanks', laughed Kyle.

'I'm not saying he wouldn't go mind, just as a spectator you understand and you know what the horrible thing is? It's the fact that they know he's unobtainable that makes the pretty girls keen.'

'Rachel certainly seems to have fallen for his blarney'.

'Don't worry about it mate. I've seen Nial's willy. He's hung like a lepricorn. A big black stallion like you has nothing to fear'.

Kyle zipped himself up embarrassed by the attention that Nial's cordial friend had paid to his genitals but simultaneously flattered and relieved. He enjoyed the rest of the airport disco even singing along to *'Whisky in the Jar'*. Rachel seemed reassured and less flirty. By half past two, most of the party were asleep. Kyle and Rachel were back on their bench huddled up together and kissing quietly.

'That Nial is quite a character' Kyle declared.

'*Aye. He said I had a lovely bone structure*' Rachel responded slurring her words slightly.

'*That's male-speak for I want to get into your knickers Rachel*', Kyle said kissing her on the forehead.

'*You're not jealous are you Kyle?*'

'*Why would I be jealous? He's got the wit of Dave Allen, the looks of Pearce Brosnan, the guitar skills of the Edge and the compassion of Bob Geldof. What have I got to be jealous of?*'

'*You know, you scored as well.*'

'*What?*'

'*It seems that Nial's mate Christian took a bit of a shine to you. Did you not realize he's gay?*'

Remembering their conversation in the urinals, Kyle shuddered.

'*Don't worry*' said Rachel. '*I will make sure he doesn't pounce on you in your sleep.*'

This time their kiss was long and passionate and Rachel's tongue penetrated deep inside. She fell asleep on his lap and he listened to the soft sound of her nocturnal breathing. He felt far too uncomfortable to get any sleep, but he daren't move in case he woke her. She looked so peaceful and her nubile, petite body kept him deliciously warm. She murmured when the tannoy sounded rudely but did not wake. He covered her ears to help smother the sound.

Eventually Kyle realized he was the only person still awake in the whole terminal and looking down at Rachel and running his hands through her soft brown hair he felt like the luckiest man alive. He couldn't move his hands to wipe the tear rolling down his cheek and dropping on to Rachel.

'*I love you Rachel*' he whispered in her ear and he meant it so much he didn't care if anyone saw his tear of heard his confession. He thought back to one of Nial's sing-along guitar numbers and the lyrics seemed appropriate. It may be the end of the world as he knew it but as long as Rachel was with him he would be fine.

Scene 6: Cairo or Bust

The weary tourists trudged through the tunnel out into a crescendo of noise and confusion. Like sprinters out of the blocks, taxi drivers raced to intercept them shouting *'taxi'* as if their lives depended on the fare. One of them shoulder-charged another out of the way and tried to grab Rachel's bag. Kyle fought him off with a firm *'no'* and stood tall between the diminutive taxi driver and the equally diminutive Rachel. Meanwhile, another taxi driver had crept up on the blind side and was saying *'English? I speak very good English. You want taxi'.*

Rachel was looking flustered and Kyle decided that they weren't going to be left in peace to debate the transport options.

'How much to Giza?' he asked the taxi driver who had boasted about his linguistic skills.

'Yes. Come with me. Giza. Yes, Giza this way' said the driver either ignoring Kyle's question or revealing weaknesses in his claim to be a fluent English speaker. *'Giza'* he kept repeating as he took their bags triumphantly. His rivals were already competing for the next tourists through the gates.

The taxi sped off through the dust with the sound of middle-eastern music beating out from the antique stereo and the *'lucky eye'* mobile swinging hypnotically across the dashboard. With his passengers safely on board, the driver understood Kyle's question regarding the fare much better and uttered a number of Egyptian pounds that seemed frighteningly large. Whilst Kyle struggled with the currency conversion the driver came back with *'about twenty English pounds'*. The guide books suggested £15 but Kyle wasn't too bothered until Rachel nudged him whispering *'it's actually about £28!'*

It was pointless arguing. The taxi was entering the sprawling Cairo suburbs and the noise of bleeping horns and shouting street traders drowned out conversation. The traffic swerved indiscriminately between lanes and the drivers used the horn as a substitute for indicators. Suddenly the taxi braked in the outside lane of the dusty highway leading to a flurry of expletives, arm gestures and angry blasts of the horn. A donkey laden with fruit was being walked down the outside lane of the highway by two men in Arabic dress.

Kyle could feel his heart beating fast as the taxi jerked into life again the driver turning to shout at the donkey owners rather than looking at the road ahead. The traffic was moving slowly now with five congested lanes on each side of the carriageway and pedestrians weaving in and out of the traffic like slalom canoeists riding white water. One youth battered the taxi's bonnet aggressively as the taxi driver just avoided running him over and then he continued crossing the road oblivious to the traffic. There were crowds everywhere jumping onto an endless succession of minibuses and unofficial taxis that slowed down to walking pace to allow passengers to squeeze on and off.

About half the men and three quarters of the women wore Arabic clothes and many looked frail and stressed. The side-streets were a maze of sand, concrete and graffiti with tatty market stools and the occasional camel. Kyle hoped this was downtown Cairo because if it wasn't he wanted to go home already. Rachel pointed out the Nile as the taxi sped across the bridge and headed towards the pyramids.

The taxi driver said the name of their hotel enthusiastically. '*Yes. Is it far?* Kyle asked.

'*No. Not far*' the driver said smiling and swigging at a tepid bottle of mineral water. Even in February, Kyle could feel the Egyptian heat and he mopped his sweaty brow. The driver turned up the air conditioning and checked the name of the hotel again. '*Ah*' he said nodding with delight. '*Not far*' he added turning to Kyle.

'*Concentrate on the bloody road*' Rachel whispered to Kyle and squeezed his hand.

Five minutes later the driver did a u-turn. Kyle and Rachel looked at each other anxiously. This was not a good sign. They were heading back away from the pyramids towards the Nile. The driver pulled in at a scruffy looking hotel and got out of the taxi. Kyle could see him and a perplexed old man exchanging frantic hand signals at the side of the road. Ultimately he got back into the taxi and said '*Ah. Hotel*' but the name was lost in a blast of horns as a car had broken down in the third lane and was being push-started by a posse of pedestrians.

Soon they were travelling back the other way again. '*No wonder it's £28*' said Rachel. She was looking stressed and exhausted and Kyle asked the driver if he knew where he was going. With one hand at the wheel, he reached into the glove box with the other and pulled out a street map handing it to Kyle. It was all in Arabic and completely useless to him. The driver thudded down on the brakes and leapt out with the engine smouldering in the mid-day sun. Kyle handed him the map and he went to ask someone in another hotel reception. Then it was back down the other way again, the driver nodding and smiling relentlessly. He pulled up again and went into another hotel reception. Kyle was losing the will to live and Rachel looked angry. The driver came out beaming and opened the boot. Kyle looked at the name of the hotel. It was theirs!

Kyle paid the driver when he gently put the bags down on the marble floor beside the reception desk. The driver's expression looked like a wounded puppy as he stood re-counting the money. After a few embarrassing seconds he looked up at Kyle and said directly '*tip?*'

Kyle did not have the energy to argue. He gave him some loose change which the driver thanked him for but looked disappointed by. The audacity of him, thought Kyle. He spends half an hour driving up and down, obviously clueless as to where our hotel is, almost crashes a dozen times and then expects a tip!

'Welcome to Cairo' said the smartly dressed receptionist.

*****

After changing and showering Rachel and Kyle enjoyed a cool drink by the hotel pool. Most of the guests were elderly tourists soaking up the afternoon sun and reading trashy novels. The hotel courtyard was an oasis of calm in this frantic city and Kyle could feel the stress dissolve as they lay in the deck-chairs. Before long, the impact of his sleepless night caught up with him and he dropped off to sleep on the comfy, padded deck chair.

When Kyle awoke, Rachel was nowhere to be seen. He searched around for a note but there was no sign of her and his watch said half-past four. The sun was hidden behind the hotel and the air was cooling rapidly. He went back to their room but there was no sign of her so he found his phone and switched it on. There were two messages. The first was a voice-mail from their Texan ally.

'Kyle you faggot. Hope you and Rachel got here safely. I've been busy watching the summit guests arriving. Meet me at the entrance to the pyramids light-show tonight at 7.30 for a de-brief' said Ed.

The next was a text from Rachel: *'Gone exploring. I didn't want to disturb you. Love R. X'*

The text was only sent at half-three so she hadn't been gone long but Kyle was worried about her exploring the mean streets of Giza on her own and he rang her to make sure she was ok.

'Where are you?' he asked.

'Just outside your room' she laughed. *'Will you open the door I've got my hands full of shopping?'*

That night Ed and his photographer ordered a bottle of wine at a table with distant views of the ancient pyramids. The distant sound of classical music and commentary competed with the chatter of the diners.

Ed reeled off the list of guests he had spotted arriving at the desert resort at the end of the pyramids road. Many of them were strangers to Kyle and Rachel but Ed had an almost encyclopaedic knowledge of the World's rich-list and announced them like chart entries. Sheikh what's-his-name is no 31 in the rich list, then there's King so-and-so who is 70th and that Russian oligarch who is a mighty no 21. There were politicians too. Kyle had already guessed Britain's representatives and he got bored by the number of US senators Ed rattled off with a mixture of relish and contempt.

Ed quaffed his wine with large gulps and took a deep breath. *'You'll never guess who the guest of honour was!'*

'Go on' said Rachel indulging him.

'Well dear. Take a look at this' he said snatching the camera from round his photographer's neck.

'It's a big limo with an American flag, a chauffeur and two indistinguishable passengers' she said with a shrug.

Ed was cross. *'Use the zoom button'* he said rather obtusely.

Rachel zoomed in and the image was very blurred but she thought she recognised the faraway look in the eyes of one of the passengers. *'Is that President Bush?'* she asked.

'Ex-President Bush if you don't mind' Ed replied smugly. He then retold the story of how security patrols had removed them from their hide-out close to the resort entrance and they had sneaked back across the desert and took the photos with a telephoto lens. They knew someone important was about to arrive by the fact that nobody was allowed within 400 yards of the complex and then this convoy of limo's arrived with armed police on mopeds up-front.

'Did you manage to speak to any of the guests?' enquired Kyle.

'Yes, but they didn't speak to me. One senator greeted me with something like fancy bumping into you here Ed but that was about it. However, I did bribe a guard to tell me that the place is completely booked out to the summit and he has never seen security like it. He reckons there are about 300 guests from all over the World and no press are allowed in'.

Ed topped up his glass and shrugged. *'I offered him 1000 US dollars and he still wouldn't budge. It's unusual over here for bribes not to work. The Arab looked petrified and yelled for a colleague so we bid a hasty retreat.'*

'It's an appropriate place for an Illuminati summit' said Rachel.

Ed looked at her like he thought she really shouldn't be bothering her pretty little face. *'What are you on about Miss Woods?'*

'The pyramid is an ancient Illuminati symbol. So it is appropriate they should choose the only hotel in the world with a decent view of the pyramids'.

'How do you know that?' asked Kyle impressed.

'I probably saw it on TV or read it in a book. I don't know' Rachel said modestly.

'Well, I don't know about symbols but I do know that with a guest list like that the Illuminati mean business. We just need to find out what the fuck they are talking about in that desert fortress of theirs', Ed declared.

They all thought about little else over the meal but if there was no way of getting into the complex or getting the guests to talk there didn't seem to be an answer. They agreed to meet again for dinner the following night. Ed and his photographer would stake out the hotel again in case there were any more comings and goings. Kyle and Rachel would visit the pyramids as tourists, something both were looking forward to.

Back in their air conditioned hotel room Rachel yawned as she climbed into bed in some pink pyjamas beside the naked and expectant Kyle. He placed his hand round her waist and squeezed her hand before moving it up beneath her top to feel her left breast.

'Not tonight Kyle' she said firmly. *'I'm knackered'*.

Kyle turned over throbbing with unquenched desire. Thoughts of George Bush calmed his ardour. It seemed incongruous that a staunch Christian with strong views against stem-cell research would support a movement based on science defeating religion. However, he was relieved that Obama and Brown had not been implicated. It didn't prove their innocence but it meant there was still hope. With that thought he listened carefully and confirmed what he thought he had heard. Very softly, and as quiet as a mouse, Rachel was snoring.

'Hypocrite' he whispered kissing her hair.

Scene 7: In the Shadow of the Pyramids

Ed was back in his desert spy-hole at the crack of dawn.

'*Well, blow me*' he uttered into his binoculars as he focused on the gates. In the pivotal spot where he had stood the previous morning and been forced away by a zealous guard was Hank Walters of the Tribune.

'*Come on. We've got company*' he told his cameraman and the two of them set off across the sand.

'*You are a day late Hank. They all arrived yesterday*' Ed called.

'*Ed. Good to see you*' Hank replied as he turned to shake his hand.

'*So! Have you finally accepted I'm not nuts to warn the world about global conspiracy or have you just travelled half way round the world to take the piss out of me*?' Ed enquired.

'*Go on then? Indulge me! How's an economic summit of political and business leaders connected with the New World Order?*'

Ed told him the basics and added the odd name to wet Hank's appetite but kept much of what he knew back. Hank was listening but he was not taking much in. He was used to conspiracy buffs and fed up with all the time dissipated on red herrings. He used to respect Ed as a serious freelance journalist, but lately he felt he had lost his marbles.

'*Ed. I'm sorry to be the one to break this to you but this summit is to discuss a co-ordinated response to the credit crunch. There's no hidden agenda. I've known about it for months. The only secret has been where and when it would take place. The secrecy is because there was intelligence suggesting a possible terrorist attack; not because they've anything to hide.*'

'*Why then is ex-president Bush the guest of honour? Barack Obama showed more interest in the credit crunch than Bush even before he took the Oval Office. Economic summit my arse!*'

'*Bush accepted the invitation before the election and decided to use it to wave goodbye to the world stage. You know as well as I do Ed that the real business will be done at a much lower level. Bush is just here as a figurehead, not to make decisions or advice on economics, thank God*!'

'*OK. Why won't they talk to journalists? Why did an armed Guard drag us from this very spot yesterday? Even bribes don't work. Why can't I even get a copy of the agenda if it's not hidden? I've covered lots of world events and this is different.*'

'The terrorist threat is much higher here. That's why it's different. Egypt has its Islamic fundamentalists and there have been several bombings. The only mystery for me is why they chose such a risky venue.'

'Have it your way. Just be prepared to look stupid when the truth is exposed'.

'Ed. You told me that last month when you told me Obama was going to get shot at his inauguration. Now I really would have looked stupid if I had run with that fanciful story! No wonder you can't get an interview. You've lost all credibility.'

Kyle and Rachel decided to take a camel tour of the pyramids before the sun got too hot. There were no shortage of offers but it was extremely difficult to negotiate with people that spoke so little English. Briefly, Kyle toyed with the notion that this was one argument for the New World Order. However, he soon decided that the hassle made life colourful. Rachel was looking colourful today. She wore a vivid top with all the colours of the rainbow splashed on haphazardly. Her tight white trousers shone like a beacon to focus Kyle's glare on her arse as she expertly mounted the camel and rode away across the white sand. She wore a red ribbon in her bunched hair and a trendy pair of ray-bans.

Kyle was rather less gamely as his camel rocked him from side to side and swayed his head to shake away the flies.

'Keep up' laughed Rachel looking back.

'You've done this before' replied Kyle.

'I used to go horse riding as a kid.'

'That's a bit girly, being into horses. I thought you were supposed to be a tom-boy.'

'I had a friend who was crazy about horses and spent all her time at the stables. I just wanted to get out in the country and ride and couldn't see the fun in grooming and shovelling shit but each to their own.'

The pyramids and sphinx were spectacular and made good photo-shots. Rachel was full of energy and bounded about the ancient monuments oblivious to the dry heat. Kyle bought an over-priced bottle of cold water and sat admiring the view. His mobile rung and he got there in time to hear Ed's Texan drawl.

'Kyle. Can we bring forward our meeting this evening? I will have to skip dinner. I've arranged dinner with a press colleague and a Senator from the summit and hopefully I will get something to prove this whole thing has not been a wild goose chase.'

'Sure. What time do you want to meet?'

'*5.00 back at your hotel? It won't take long as there's not much to report I'm afraid.*'

'*Ok. See you later Ed*'.

'*What's the matter*' asked Rachel jumping down from an ancient stone wall.

'*I don't know. It was Ed and he sounded like he wanted to go home. He wants to meet us at 5 at our hotel because he's got a dinner date with someone from the summit.*'

'*Well that's good isn't it?*'

'*Aye, but it was how he sounded. It was like he'd given up.*'

*****

'*I can't wait to get out of this shit-hole*' promulgated Ed, without the slightest regard for who might over-hear him. He was annoyed at the price of the bourbon he had ordered at Kyle and Rachel's hotel. '*I can get it cheaper in the States and yet the average wage here is a few dollars a week. What a rip off!*'

'*Have you had a frustrating day?*' asked Rachel.

'*Whilst you guys have been seeing the sights I've been standing outside the gates of a hotel watching pretty much nothing happen all day with some arsehole who thinks I've escaped from the loony bin.*'

'*I guess that's a yes*' laughed Kyle.

'*The only high point was when Senator Shaw from Georgia came out for a fag and waved away the guards to have a few words with us*'.

'*Did you learn anything new?*' asked Rachel.

'*No. He backed up Hank's story that this is all kosher; an economic summit with extra security because of a terrorist threat. When I told him the press restrictions were like nothing I'd ever seen before he apologised and invited us to dinner at the Cairo Hilton.*'

'*Do you believe him?*' quizzed Kyle.

'*Well if he doesn't spill the beans after I've showered him with free booze then I will be on the first plane out of here tomorrow. I'm not having another day like this one.*'

'*It does seem strange that yesterday they wouldn't let you near the delegates and today a delegate is able to arrange dinner with you*', Rachel commented.

'*According to Shaw it's because they had kept things so secret they didn't expect any press to be here and when they found they'd been rumbled they didn't know how to react. The Egyptians didn't have a strategy in place for dealing with the Press so they took a safety first approach.*'

'*I still don't buy it*' said Kyle. '*There is too much co-incidence about Nick's information, Batman flying out here (hardly an economic guru) and the secrecy about the summit. The discussions are about power and not economics.*'

When Ed left Rachel proposed '*Shall we have dinner here tonight? There's an Egyptian show on with belly-dancers, fire-eaters and local music, whilst you dine. It sounds canny.*'

'*OK. Just because Ed's having a bad time there's no reason to stop us enjoying ourselves.*' Kyle acquiesced.

Scene 8: Propositioning a Belly Dancer

The sound of traditional music drew Kyle to the window and he observed a small gathering of diners in the courtyard and an old Egyptian strumming a large stringed instrument. A child was breaking the 7 pm curfew and swimming in the moonlight whilst an attendant took pool samples with a large net. There was no sign of a belly dancer but the wine was flowing and there was a lot of activity around the bar and the adjacent kitchen.

Rachel shouted out from the bathroom for him to pass the mosquito repellent and he obliged through the narrow gap in the doorway, her delicate hand fumbling for it through the gap. She had been half an hour and Kyle could not see why she couldn't have just gone out as she was as he had been admiring her all day. Five minutes later and she opened the door, still brushing her long brown hair. There was a perfectly timed round of applause from the diners and Kyle said *'Your fan club like your outfit'*. She was very modestly dressed and made up, considering she'd been in the bathroom for over half an hour. She wore a knitted, lilac top with a buttoned v-neck and a long, patterned skirt. A silver necklace hung over her white skin and only the subtlest of lipsticks and blusher were evident.

'You look beautiful' Kyle remarked.

'Don't be silly. I'm white as a sheet' said Rachel unconvinced and checking her handbag.

Partly to re-assure Rachel just how much he fancied her and partly because he was absolutely gagging for sex, Kyle jumped on her pushing her on the bed.

'I thought you were hungry' Rachel said getting up and pushing him away.

'I am. Hungry for you' Kyle said.

Rachel looked distinctly unimpressed. *'Men! You've all got one-tracked minds.'*

'Not true. Just now, whilst you were getting ready I was wondering if they had Sky Sports, ' Kyle replied hoping humour would dig him out of the hole. She smiled in partial forgiveness, got up and opened the door.

The service was slow but the food fresh and satisfying and the carafe of red wine much better value than Ed's bourbon. Kyle decided he needed clarification on the status of their relationship. Rachel fascinated him, but she also confused him. He felt as if Rachel couldn't decide whether he was a friend or a boyfriend. Kyle decided Venus must be a very indecisive place as men were never troubled by such procrastination. On Mars, once you had decided to sleep with someone you were either in a relationship or it was time for the friendship to end.

Rachel opened up about her previous relationship with a CID officer. *'I didn't even fancy him at first'* she explained. *'He had a legion of fans but to me he just looked dead ordinary, although I did notice he had a fit body. He worked out a lot and was all biceps and hair gel. He made it obvious he fancied me and after I rejected him he suddenly became all soft and romantic, besieging me with texts and e-mails and even writing me soppy poems and letters. He'd come over as a macho, alpha-male to everyone but showed this softer side just for me and he kind of wore me down.*

Like you, he was recently separated and he used to tell me how his wife didn't understood him and he'd never been as much in love with her as he was with me. It was all very flattering and all my friends kept egging me on, telling me how sexy he was and how lucky I was to have him drooling all over me. Eventually, I agreed to date and we got on well. He was really charming and not as full of himself as I had imagined. I didn't sleep with him for at least a month and during that time he sent me flowers and texted me about ten times a day. The texts got increasingly rude, referring to what a lovely body I had and how horny I was making him and it made me feel good.

One night I put on a short skirt and a sexy new bodice and watched him ogle me all evening. He walked me home and we had a cuddle on the doorstep and I could feel how much I turned him. When he walked away disappointed I took pity on him and called him back. He run back as fast as his legs could carry him and we did it on the stairs.

We were inseparable after that and I let him move in for a time but then suddenly he announced he was going back to his wife. I was gutted. I tore up all his love letters, deleted all his texts and donated the sexy lingerie that I had seduced him with to a charity shop. After that I vowed never to date another work colleague or another married men. So you can see why I'm wary of you!'

Kyle felt so much better for his knowledge, kissed her hand across the table and promised her he was never going back to Helen and he would look for another job if she didn't feel comfortable working with him. Rachel told him not to be silly but she looked like a weight had been lifted from her slim shoulders. Kyle had been so deep in conversation that he hadn't even noticed the belly-dancer begin her routine.

'Don't you find it incongruous Rachel that Islamic culture deems it unethical for girls to show the slightest glimpse of flesh and yet one of their eldest traditions is for semi-naked girls to gyrate around the floor and get notes stuffed down their cleavage'.

'You are right. I've been covering myself up since I got here out of respect and then you look at her dressed like a Latvian lap-dancer. I might get out the shorts tomorrow.'

'If you do that, we might not get out of the hotel room' said Kyle immediately regretting his candour. However, this time, Rachel smiled back shyly.

The belly dancer approached Kyle and wiggled her cleavage in front of him. She was pretty, petite and dark-haired and her skin felt firm and warm as he slotted a fiver into her bra. He turned and looked at Rachel as the dancer gyrated away to the next table and sensed a silent jealousy in her blue eyes.

'She's gorgeous' Rachel said watching her dance.

'So are you honey' Kyle said. *'I really do love you, you know'*.

'I know you do' Rachel replied. This was not the answer Kyle was fishing for.

They finished their drinks, paid the bill and returned to the room. Kyle offered Rachel first use of the bathroom but she said *'no you go first Kyle. There's something I've got to do. I won't be long.'*

When Kyle came out Rachel had left the room so he sat up in bed reading the guide book to consider options for their final day in Cairo. Ten minutes later, Rachel still hadn't returned. *'Come on Rachel. She's impossible that girl'* he said under his breath and picked up the phone to ring her. He put it down again deciding that it might be another own goal to come across as checking up on her too soon. Another ten minutes went by before he heard the door open and he looked up to see who would come round the corner. At first, there was nobody and he wondered if it had been a good idea given his recent past to have climbed naked into bed with the door ajar.

Then Rachel appeared round the corner wearing the belly-dancer's costume. She looked shy and apprehensive but it fitted her perfectly. The sound of the folk music was still audible from the courtyard and Rachel began to gyrate gracefully to the music. She slowly peeled off the bra and Kyle reached for her swinging breasts. It seemed ages since their Christmas party coupling and it was all he could do to hold back the dam before entering her. She didn't seem to mind. This time, the sex was a gift to him and she pleasured him with more grace and style than in his wildest dreams.

*****

Kyle woke briefly and admired Rachel's sexy naked torso beneath the cotton sheets. She was sleeping soundly so he did not wake her and before long he must have fallen to sleep as well. When he awoke there was no sign of her. He slipped into some shorts and pulled the curtains to check the weather. It was overcast but the sun was burning a hole through the cloud as it rose above the buildings. He noticed a note on the table. *'I've gone to see Ed for breakfast. I didn't want to disturb you. R. XX'.*

Kyle smiled. She's no wall-flower that girl he reminded himself, impressed by her gumption. Rachel returned whilst he was in the shower. He came out with a towel wrapped around him and asked if Ed had any news.

'No. I was worried in case he might be flying out this morning and it was lucky I went round because he got nothing out of the Senator last night and was preparing to go, but I changed his mind.'

'How did you do that?'

'Well, you know last night when I went to see the belly dancer?'

'Actually, I thought you had packed the costume yourself to entertain me'.

'You wish! I paid her 100 pounds.'

'Don't take this the wrong way baby. You looked sensational and I had the time of my life but 100 quid to hire a costume. She ripped you off'.

'No. That was only part of it. You see she is entertaining the summit guests at the closing dinner tonight. I paid her 100 pounds to seduce one of the delegates and steal some conference papers for us. I said you would pay her another 100 if she came up with anything worthwhile'.

'Rachel. You are amazing. I hope Ed was impressed.'

'Yes. He knows which senator to target and is going round to see the belly-dancer later to return the costume and give her the low-down.'

Kyle laughed with delight. '*You're not just a pretty face Rachel*' he stated and pulled her down on the bed. This time she did not resist. They kissed each other all over as he unzipped her shorts. When he went to remove his hand she stopped him and adjusted the position, kissing him harder and breathing deeply. He got the idea. It was time to return the favour from last night and within a few minutes she was frantically writhing on the bed sucking every ounce of pleasure out of her potent orgasm.

Scene 9: The Blue Nile

Kyle and Rachel decided to get a local bus into Cairo and visit the Egyptian Museum. The taxi drivers outside the hotel returned to their cabs disappointed and watched them prepare to cross the road to the bus stop with *'they will never do it'* expressions. The Giza traffic was relentless; five lanes in each carriageway and vehicles of all shapes, sizes and velocity. Buses and unofficial taxis made up one in three of those vehicles hogging the curb, slowing down whenever a local indicated they wanted to jump aboard.

Five frustrated minutes passed when Rachel squeezed Kyle's sweaty hand. *'Follow me'* she said and stepped out into the road behind a frail, old local bravely crossing the road. Her instincts proved reliable. The old man expertly negotiated the crossing, with Rachel and Kyle following in his slip-stream.

The highway conquered, their next challenge was getting a bus to central Cairo. All of the destinations were written in Arabic and none of the locals spoke English. Kyle asked a couple of drivers *'Egyptian Museum?'* and *'Central Cairo?'* They shrugged or shook their heads and Kyle got back off before the vehicles sped away. Eventually he said *'we are going to have to just jump on and see where it takes us'*. Rachel looked unconvinced but she nodded and moved closer to the curb.

The bus driver looked at Kyle like he was an imbecile when he asked *'Cairo'*. Rachel said *'I guess it would be like a foreign tourist jumping on a bus in Clapham and asking London?'* There was standing room only on the bus and the locals seemed astonished to see tourists aboard. The fare was coppers but it was easy to see why tourists preferred the relative safety of a cab ride. Just before the bus reached the Nile it veered off to the left. Kyle looked at Rachel and said *'I don't like the look of this.'*

The bus stopped at the Zoo on the western fringes of the City and then turned back into the shabby suburbs of downtown Giza. Ultimately, it stopped at a bus station almost as far from their destination as when they had embarked. All the passengers got off. A donkey almost knocked Rachel over as she turned around to get her bearings and she looked irritated. *'I knew we should have got a taxi'* she said.

Kyle sprang into action, frantically searching the bus station for someone who spoke English. Eventually he found a boy about 9 or 10 who declared proudly *'I speak good English mister.'* He nodded at the mention of the Egyptian Museum in Central Cairo and went off towards a kiosk in the corner of the bus station beckoning Kyle to follow. The young boy had a lively conversation with the man in the kiosk and there followed lots of pointing, chin-rubbing and arm gestures. He emerged triumphantly with the direction: *'One-One-Zero'*. He led Kyle and Rachel to the stop and stood patiently, signalling that Kyle's thanks were not the expected reward for his endeavour. Kyle produced a tip, equivalent to the bus fare he had paid and the boy skipped away, clasping the money like a treasured possession.

Bus number 110 did take them to Central Cairo but when Kyle and Rachel dismounted in a bustling, old square they could not see the Museum. A young man standing nearby asked *'American?'*

'No. English' Kyle replied emphatically.

'Good. English are our friends' the local beamed shaking Kyle's hand. He added *'Are you lost?'*

'We are looking for the Egyptian Museum.'

'Ah! You want the Egyptian Museum? Come with me. I will show you.'

They followed briskly as he engaged Kyle in friendly conversation about Newcastle United and the time he had visited London. Suddenly, he stopped and said *'Please come inside. You look very hot and thirsty I offer free drinks.'*

They entered a sweet-smelling perfume shop and were immediately led through to a back-room where an elderly lady greeted them with a warm smile. The young man served them with a cool Pepsi Max, whilst the lady smothered Rachel in perfume testers. *'I'm sorry but I don't want any perfume'* Rachel explained sweetly. *'We just want to go to the Museum'*. The lady smiled back. She obviously didn't speak English. Kyle called the young man back to explain. He looked offended and said *'but the Museum is closed for siesta. It opens again in half an hour. You not like our perfumes?'*

'No. It's not that. Your perfumes are lovely but you told us you would show us the way to the Museum and not a shop' Rachel replied assertively. The young man's demeanour changed and he spoke to the old lady in Arabic. She came back with a few words of English *'Special Offer. Half price.'* Rachel looked at Kyle and said *'I do quite like this rose one'*.

'Ok. If I buy this half-price will you take us straight to the Museum?'

The young man couldn't wait to wrap the perfume up and take Kyle's money. Kyle noted that the bottle was much smaller than the one Rachel had been shown but he didn't have the energy left to complain. When they got to the Museum there was only an hour and a half left till closure and there was no evidence that it had ever shut for a siesta.

*****

Meanwhile, the World Summit was reaching its conclusion. The final speeches were delivered and the guests departed to dress for the formal closing dinner and a chance to un-wind from the taxing business of taking over the World. Ed winked as the belly dancer nervously entered the hotel complex and was briskly searched by a rough security guard. Ed felt relieved that he had changed his mind about wiring her. He had expected a thorough search but not one quite as intimate in broad daylight!

The delegates were all well-oiled by the time the belly dancer was enticed on to the stage. There were plenty of lurid comments and whistles as she started to dance. Her target was easy to spot. A US Senator with a paunch and steamed up glasses sat at one of the tables closest to the stage, his tie dangling half-way down his chest. He leered and rubbed his sweaty palms as she went to his table and performed a personal routine. As he stuffed dollars down her cleavage, she whispered in his ear and he went visibly red but after a slight hesitation nodded enthusiastically.

Back in his hotel room she ordered him in a sultry accent to undress and lay on the bed. She tied his hands to the wrought-iron headboard. *'I love power. It makes me so horny'* she said. *'Tell me how powerful you are and how you are going to save the World.'*

He did not need much encouragement. Here was a beautiful, slim 20-something brunette who was practically naked and the only reason she had selected a fat, fifty-something American for no-strings sex was his power and wealth. It made sense to him and he needed to use this asset to get what he desperately wanted. After all, she was just a poor Egyptian girl, who spoke broken English. What threat was she to the New World Order?

He confessed that the economic summit was a front for something much bigger. He told her that by the end of the year there would be a single Government responsible for the whole World and he would be one of the Leaders. He told her that that the New World Order would prevent war and famine and cure a series of economic and medical ills. Naturally, he exaggerated his own part. He felt stiff and ready by the time she blindfolded him and let him caress her naked body.

The belly-dancer kept him talking and waiting whilst she surveyed the room for evidence. The delegate pack was just as Ed had described and easily accessible on a dressing table. It just squeezed into her hand-bag. *'Order me champagne'* she said. He acquiesced and when room service arrived she intercepted it at the door and popped the cork. She poured it down his throat and over her tits, which he rubbed with glee. He was at breaking point and a mixture of hands and lips brought him to orgasm before she had to suffer the indignity of penetration. She feigned disappointment and dressed saying *'I wanted big, powerful man; not one who comes too quickly'.*

'Sorry. Please untie me' he muffled struggling with the knots and the gag.

'No. You suffer now' she said and left the room, hoping she wouldn't be searched on exiting the hotel. There was a taxi waiting. It was past midnight and the guard merely checked her papers and waved her through. She had earned the extra 100 pounds that she was about to receive from Ed. The toughest security in the World was no match for man's basest weakness.

*****

Rachel and Kyle had dined in the verdant Zamalek district on the West Bank of the Nile. They walked back towards the Centre to catch a taxi back to the hotel pausing on the bridge to admire the view and suck in the warm, night air. The Nile was wide and peaceful, its indigo waters lapping gently against the pretty boats moored to either bank. On the East Bank there were numerous disco boats with colourful lights, a variety of Western and ethnic music and crowds of young people out enjoying themselves.

As they walked on down the East Bank, Kyle reflected on how familiar this scene was. Sure, half of the beautiful, young girls present were veiled but they still stood kissing passionately by the water's edge in the same way as the young did every Friday and Saturday night on Newcastle's Quayside. Young love was a common language and a beautiful one.

He longed to kiss Rachel and they paused again at the top of some moorings. She felt the same way. He pulled her close, kissing her passionately and feeling the weight of her breasts against his chest. They were practically conjoined in a passionate embrace for the next hour. *'Rachel. I love you so much'* he declared.

She looked back at him, her eyes blue as the Nile and for the first time she uttered those magic words. *'I love you too Kyle.'*

Scene 10: Feeding Back

Back in Nick's Pimlico flat the resistance considered the implications of the delegate pack they had just perused.

'You've done brilliantly' proclaimed Nick. *'This is the evidence we needed. I propose taking this to the PM as soon as possible.'*

Wendy was sceptical. *'I think it's still too risky. We don't know Brown is clean. I recognize some of the business names on this delegate list and they have the PM's ear. The fact that he was not present does not prove his innocence'.*

'I agree' said Ed. *'The first law of journalism is the only person less trustworthy than a politician is another journalist'.*

Nick was annoyed. *'I'm sorry but trust is our only hope. If we give in to fear and suspicion we are bound to lose. We have a paper here confirming my information about a coalition government for the UK. There is no way a PM would surrender power to a coalition, especially after all the years that Gordon has waited to get the top job. I'm telling you, he is being plotted against and this is the evidence he needs to act.'*

Wendy stuck by her opposition to breaking cover. *'The PM has to hold an election next year. There is no way he can win outright given the polls and the recession. Maybe a coalition is his best hope of keeping power but he is keeping out of the plot in case it all unravels. I think we need to keep this information close to our chests until the plotters break cover.'*

Nick was speaking quickly now, his adrenaline-fuelled Geordie dialect causing Ed some difficulty in translation. *'Bollocks. Lenin once said you can't have a revolution without the conditions that make a revolution possible. We now have those conditions. The global recession is at its deepest. The Illuminati have to act. We now have conclusive proof that they will act and we know the names of the main conspirators. We must not keep this information from the leaders that are being plotted against, just because of some paranoia that they could be implicated. We owe it to our country to tell our elected representatives.'*

Ed stated *'I don't know. I'm passionate about democracy but I smell a rat. Can't we find a politician who isn't connected to any of the Cairo delegates and go to them first?'*

Nick got up and walked around the table thinking. He stopped by Kyle. *'What do you think Kyle?'*

'I think that what we are doing is very difficult. We are trying to guess the mind-set of a man that none of us really know. Is Gordon Brown a likely supporter of the Illuminati? I only know what I hear in the media and with due

respect to Ed I know that can be unreliable. I think we need a professional; someone whose job involves getting inside the minds of criminals and identifying the likelihood of suspects being guilty. We are lucky to have your sister here with us today. I suggest that we go with whatever Rachel thinks.'

Four heads turned towards Rachel, who had been quiet throughout the meeting. They all knew Kyle was right. She may have been an unwilling participant in the resistance to date; but now their future rested on her narrow shoulders.

Rachel began her report nervously. *'I think we need to look at Brown the man, not Brown the politician. He strikes me as an indecisive, risk-averse man. He is a loner who desperately wants to please but can't seem to guess the public mood, leading to a series of embarrassing u-turns. He trusts very few people and keeps his thoughts close to his chest. He is intense, intelligent and thoughtful. He likes to study ideas in detail and not rely on instinct. Snap decisions are not his forte. He has a strong sense of destiny and a conviction that he is the man to lead his country and single-handedly steer us out of recession. He is a religious man with a strong code of morals but he believes that the end will justify the means to an extent. It is deciding where to draw the line that he finds so difficult.'*

Rachel stopped and sipped some water. None of the guests spoke but Ed coughed and took in some water as well. Rachel continued once he recovered.

'I think he is very unlikely to be part of a world-wide conspiracy. He is too much of a loner. He doesn't trust people unless he knows them well. He would hate the idea of being subservient to some greater power, where decisions were taken by international committees. He would rather be a big fish in a small pool than a small fish in a big one. In short, I think he would rather fight on when others have lost faith in him than cling on to power through a fractious coalition.'

'Thank you Sis' Nick exclaimed. *'So you agree that we can trust the PM?'*

'I didn't say that Nick. I just think he is not part of this particular conspiracy.' Rachel corrected him.

'Well. That's good enough for me. I would add that I know Brown politically as someone who is Euro-sceptical, an economic control freak who fought the European Exchange Mechanism with passion. I don't see him as someone likely to sign up to an international economic policy, which he has very little influence over. He would rather resign.' Nick's certainty was impressive. *'Does anyone disagree that I should seek an audience with the PM?'* he asked.

Nick looked at Wendy and Ed. Wendy was still and silent. Ed looked like he was about to say something and then just shrugged. Kyle placed his hands on Rachel's black-stocking clad thigh under the table and looked around the table.

Nick stood up tall and looked down on his elder accomplices. '*OK comrades. I think we should all meet the PM and let him see a copy of the delegate pack. I will arrange it immediately.*'

Act Six: The New World Order

Scene 1: Prime Minister's Questions

10 Downing Street is a tardis of a property. Behind its famous black door lies a maze of corridors, offices and reception rooms. In one such room, decorated with oak panelling and oil paintings Kyle, Rachel, Nick, Ed and Wendy waited patiently for their 3.20 audience with the Prime Minister.

'You can almost smell the history of this place' declared Kyle. Rachel's reply was drowned out by the Westminster chimes of the imposing grandfather clock as it struck three, seconds ahead of Big Ben.

'What's the plan, guys?' asked Ed when the chimes stopped.

Nick answered with a detailed account of Downing Street etiquette as if he had been here far more than the six times he actually had. All agreed it was best for him to take the lead to ensure that their conspiracy tale had the stamp of Cabinet Office approval.

At 3.25 a grey-haired lady in a bottle green suit entered the room and introduced herself as a Downing Street civil servant.

'I'm sorry but the PM has had to take an urgent phone-call from President Sarcozy and he has asked if you would meet his senior advisor on terrorism and home security instead. Would you follow me please?'

'Hey. Wait here. We came here to see the organ grinder, not the monkey' Ed protested. *'The future of the world is at stake. How do we know we can trust this guy?'*

The civil servant pulled a face like she had just come out of the portaloo at the end of the V Festival.

'The fact that you are here proves how seriously the PM takes the threat and he only delegates such matters to people he can trust implicitly.' She lengthened her stride and marched down the corridor in disgust.

'Well that's me told' Ed whispered to Nick.

The official knocked on a door at the end of the corridor and a big booming voice barked out *'Come In'*. She immediately turned from scary official into a mousy minion as she uttered *'Sorry to bother you Sir but this is the deputation to see the PM about the Illuminati threat'.*

'*Ah yes*' he said with Churchillian authority and re-adjusting his glasses that he had been peering over. The introductions over, he sat back in a big leather chair and said '*so. You have information about the Illuminati that might be of interest to us. Please tell us everything you know and how you came to know it. The PM has told me to give you as much time as it takes. He is deeply concerned.*'

Nick Woods gave a superb account of the plans for a New World Order, the coalition government in the UK and how the five guests had come to meet and form a resistance. The mandarin was not easily impressed. At times he conveyed discouraging grunts and frowned with a mixture of scepticism and impatience. However, his mood changed when Nick produced the Cairo summit pack.

'*How did you get this*?' he asked leaning forward and putting his glasses back on briskly.

'*We bribed a belly dancer who was performing at the summit* ' responded Nick.

'*Mind if I take a copy*' he asked with his finger already hovering over the button to summon his PA. The PA came in and agreed pleasantly to take a photocopy and bring in tea and biscuits. Obviously, they were going to be staying longer than the 10 minutes that they had been reserved.

*****

'*This is quite a dossier Mr Woods*' the Mandarin said. '*Do you want a job in MI5? Some of our top agents have failed to come up with this much information. Thank goodness this illustrious list of conspirators does not include our little French friend or I would have to interrupt the PM, which is never a good idea.*'

'*Do the names on the list surprise you*?' Nick enquired.

'*Some of them do. It is the extent of the Illuminati infiltration world-wide that worries me. We had it down as an American plot with a few power-brokers in each major country tagging along. This really suggests international influence that crosses ideological and ethnic lines far more than we imagined.*'

'*I agree. You will have noticed the delegates include a Cabinet member. Do you think he is out on a limb on this or could other Cabinet members be implicated*?' Nick probed.

'*I also noticed a prominent member of the Shadow Cabinet was in attendance. It confirms our information that there is a cross-party bid to topple the PM. I won't go any further than that.*'

'*Is the plot likely to succeed*?' Nick added.

The mandarin shrugged and sat back in his chair. *'I never make predictions in politics. However, the mass media can make or break a Government. It is clear from this guest list that the Western media are dominated by Illuminati members. It won't require much effort on their part to make the PM the fall-guy for the desperate state of the economy and champion the coalition as the panacea.'*

Ed had been silent too long for his own comfort. *'Ok so we are in deep shit. How are we going to scrape it off our shoes?'*

The PA came in with the refreshments and as she exited the Mandarin called after her for five copies of the Official Secrets Act to be brought in. He paused for a few seconds after the door shut behind her before continuing quietly:

'I will discuss that in private with the PM. Your job is done in getting this information to us. For your own safety you now need to slip back into obscurity and let the experts deal with the problem. You must promise not to breathe a word of this conversation to anyone. I'm sure you don't need me to tell you just how high the stakes are.'

'That's all very well' complained Ed, *'but how do we know you will act quickly. There's no time to waste.'*

'You have my word as a member of Her Majesty's Government'.

'Bullshit' replied Ed. *'You're a politician for God's sake'*!

Nick intervened: *'Hold on Ed. We are all on the same side. We have placed our trust in the PM and his Office and we have to trust them to take whatever action is expedient.'*

The Mandarin stated *'Nick. On your way out, ask my PA to arrange a meeting between the PM, you and me. There are some sensitive issues that we could do with your input on.'*

Nick glowed with recognition and turned to the others promising to represent them at the meeting. After the guests had signed the Official Secrets Act, the mandarin asked if anyone had any more questions. Wendy asked some financial questions that clearly weren't his area of expertise and he bluffed his way through the response. Kyle asked how confident he was that President Obama could be trusted. Again the answer was evasive. *'That's one of the issues that we will discuss at the meeting with the PM'* he replied.

Rachel didn't say a word throughout the 40 minute duration of the meeting. However, on the walk back to Westminster tube station she told Kyle *'that was a waste of time us being there. Nick should have gone alone really.'*

'I don't know about that. It's not every day you get to see inside Downing Street. It's a shame we didn't get to meet the PM but' Kyle replied.

'*Number 10 is just a house and Gordon Brown is just a person like you and me Kyle'* Rachel shrugged. '*I wouldn't want to be a celebrity for all the money in the World. Just imagine having everything you wear, everything you say, everything you do scrutinised. It would be like going on Big Brother and never getting evicted*!'

Kyle laughed and kissed her hand. '*Don't worry honey. If our part in saving the World makes us famous, I think your brother will hog the headlines.'*

Scene 2: Diplomacy

Unlike his sister, Nick Woods loved the limelight. He dreamt of being adored. Sometimes he was the idol of the Gallowgate, kissing his badge as 50, 000 Geordies celebrated his latest goal. Other times he was strumming a guitar and singing his own songs to thousands of hysterical music fans. He also harboured secret dreams of being elected Prime Minister and changing the world before retiring to the Northumberland coast. He entered politics partly because he was angered by inequality and injustice and partly because he didn't have sufficient talent to make it as a footballer or a rock star.

Nick knew that his political prowess would be useless without a profile. Nick remembered the Cabinet Office meeting where allegations of an Illuminati plot to take over the World were first mooted. The consensus of opinion was to question its authenticity and not waste time on rumour and speculation. However, Nick saw it as an opportunity. He estimated that there was a 90% chance he would be wasting his time investigating it. However, that meant there was a 10% chance that he could discover something that could give him a higher profile than half the Cabinet. It might even save Labour from almost certain defeat at the next General Election. It would then only be a matter of time before the kingmaker became King.

Nick cleared his diary and told his peers that he was working on an urgent project directly to the PM. Suddenly, Westminster was rife with conspiracy theories. Information that politicians and civil servants had been sitting on through fear of ridicule started landing on Nick's desk. The jig-saw was starting to take shape.

Nick's high spirits were dampened by a late night phone call from Texas.

'Nick. It's Ed. What the fuck is your Government playing at?'

'What do you mean Ed?'

'I mean that we go and tell them about a clear and present danger to the free world and they say well the PM might have a slot free the week after next.'

'Ten days is remarkably quick for an advisor outside the PM's inner circle to get a meeting with him. In any case there will be lots going on behind the scenes. I am getting useful information all the time'.

'Thanks for keeping us in the loop buddy!'

'I'm sorry Ed but the resistance has done its job. It is now the Government's job to take whatever action is required'.

'I don't trust your Government any more than mine. Politicians are either dishonest or negligent. Either way it's the same result. That meeting at no 10 was crap.'

'Have you any better ideas?'

'I've been making enquiries and I've found an editor of a US daily that is prepared to publish my story upon receipt of the original Cairo delegate pack. Once published, there will be an international outcry and the New World Order will be strangled at birth. I need that pack Nick.'

'I'm sorry I can't give you it'.

'Fuck off! You weren't even in Cairo. I set the whole thing up and it's down to me that we knew which senator to seduce. Now give me the god dam file. '

'I'm very grateful but we agreed that I would present my evidence to the PM and leave it at that'.

'We never discussed what would happen if the British Government hadn't got a clue what to do about it. You Brits still think of yourselves as an Empire. Wake up and smell the roses! You are a small island not a World power. You can't achieve anything without US support. We need to go to press in the US and flush the bastards out.'

'You just want a good story.'

'I've got a great story but I was a fool to trust you with the evidence. I took a copy of course but the editor wants the originals or the deal's dead'.

'This is a delicate international incident that needs diplomacy. I can't risk a sensationalist piece of journalism blowing the whole thing.'

'Well fuck you!'

With that Ed put the phone down. Nick was seething and paced up and down to let off some steam. As a political advisor he relied a lot on instinct and his instinct told him it would be foolish to go to Press in a single newspaper, especially in the country that was the cradle of the New World Order. The establishment would close ranks and rubbish the story and the UK Government was unlikely to upset the White-house by claiming they believed the conspiracy theory. Besides, he hated being sworn at.

When he had calmed down Nick rang his Sister. Rachel quickly sensed the disquiet in Nick's voice.

'What's the matter Nick? You sound upset.'

'I've just been speaking to Ed. He told me to fuck off.'

'Why?'

Dominic Varadi

'He wants the original delegate pack to run a story in the States. I said no.'

'Did you explain why?'

'Yes but he thinks us Brits won't be able to do anything without the US. I told him how sensitive the whole thing was but he wouldn't listen.'

'Did you lose your temper?'

'No. He lost his temper. I told you. He told me to fuck off.'

'Ok Nick but I know you've got a temper on you as well. I think you should sleep on it and call him back in the morning and apologise.'

'Me apologise? He's the one that should be apologising.'

'Maybe but the stakes are too high for us to fall out. Ed might decide to start mouthing off all that he's learnt and do more damage than if he did get the story.'

'You are not suggesting I give him the pack Rachel?'

'No. Suggest a compromise whereby he gets the pack if the PM doesn't act on the information when you meet him. His inaction would be a better story. If all goes well and he does act we will keep Ed in the loop so he can have the World exclusive once it's all resolved.'

'I don't know Rachel'

'Nick. Put yourself in Ed's shoes. You have the chance to make the biggest scoop of your career. Then a foreigner comes along, takes the evidence from you and casts you aside. You would feel pissed off wouldn't you? He needs to feel he still has a role in saving the World and something to be gained from being patient.'

'I don't want to have anything more to do with him Rachel. Did you know he didn't even vote for Obama? He calls himself a liberal conservative, whatever that is and says McCain would have made a great President.'

'He's a journalist Nick, doing his job. You are a political advisor doing your job. You both need to put personal feelings and political differences aside and work together.'

'I know but it makes me sick that we are all in this to save the World and he just wants to make a quick buck.'

'I'm sure that's not his only motive just as I'm sure you've recognised the career opportunities this could open up for you'.

'Ok Rachel. I will ring him but I'm not grovelling. Thank you Sis.'

'Take care, Nick'.

'*And you, Rachel. See you*'.

Nick swallowed his pride and made that phone-call. Ed was bruised but gradually came round to Rachel's suggestion. The resistance were united again thanks to her diplomacy.

Scene 3: Out of the Frying Pan!

It was a glorious day and Kyle decided to walk into Newcastle across the Town Moor. The daffodils were waving gently in the crisp breeze and the hills were dotted with joggers, kite-pilots and model aeroplane enthusiasts. Kyle was in a buoyant mood. Firstly, because he had finally received confirmation that he could return to work next week and secondly because he had a date with Rachel lined up tonight.

His battle with the Illuminati had so taken over his life for the past six months that he had not been on a proper date since he left Helen. Previous excursions with Rachel had been through work or the resistance. It was refreshing and thrilling to be meeting her without ulterior motives. Kyle had promised to get two tickets for an Indie band that Rachel liked. He hadn't heard of 'Modern Works' but their musical tastes were well-aligned so he trusted Rachel's commendation.

Kyle was relieved that the governance of the world was no longer his responsibility. He stopped to stroke a dog that barked playfully at his heels. Its owner called the pet sternly and it dashed away down the footpath. Kyle wondered if Nick would ring him after his meeting with the PM. As he reached Exhibition Park his phone rang. It was Helen wanting him to have Nathan tonight.

'Sorry. I can't. I've already got plans' explained Kyle.

'Have you forgotten you've got a son?' Helen complained. 'He never sleeps over at your place. If it wasn't for football you would never see him.'

'He's 15. He doesn't need baby-sitting any more. He's welcome to come over any time but I won't be in tonight.'

Helen put the phone down. She had a knack of making Kyle feel guilty and spoiling his good moods. It was as if her depression was contagious and she intentionally passed it on down the phone-line every time Kyle had the audacity to feel content.

He secured the tickets without a problem and received another call on his way back to Gosforth. This time it was John Medburn suggesting a birthday bash on Thursday. This call left Kyle in better spirits but he half expected Helen to ring back asking if Nathan could sleep over on Thursday instead. She didn't and thoughts returned to his date with Rachel.

Rachel parked at Kyle's and they got the metro to Central Station together. She wore blue jeans and a white t-shirt and they went for a pint in the Centurion and on to the Forth, although remembering she had her car parked at Kyle's, Rachel opted for a coke in the latter. 'Shit. That means she doesn't intend to sleep over' thought Kyle. He teased her about how good his pint was but she was wise to the tactic and laughed it off.

Kyle fought his way across the sticky floor to the bar and procured a pint and a half of Guinness. *'I can probably dance off a half'* Rachel had conceded. She was true to her word. At the Indie disco, which followed the gig, Rachel moved with the grace and rhythm of a Russian gymnast and the attitude of an anarchist.

Rachel knew as many words to the tunes as he did and they challenged each other to guess each song from the intro before the other did. Rachel won 6-5. Kyle claimed to have let her win. The finale led to the whole dance floor obeying the command of Tim Booth to *'sit down next to me'* with every chorus. Kyle was merry rather than pissed as they waited in the cloakroom queue. Rachel dropped her ticket and bent down to collect it.

'God Rachel, you have got a fantastic arse' Kyle remarked earnestly and he reached out to pinch it. She coiled up like a cobra and snapped *'Piss off Kyle'* as she collected her jacket and made for the exit. Kyle made haste after her.

'Rachel' he called perplexed.

He caught her up by the taxi queue and put his arm round her but she shook it off and said *'get off me'*.

'What's the matter?' Kyle asked.

As she shuffled forward in the queue Rachel turned to Kyle and said *'you are always going on about how sexy I am and it's annoying. You make me feel like a piece of mea*t'.

'That's ridiculous'

'Why?'

'Well for one thing I'm a vegetarian.'

Rachel was not amused. She asked if anyone in front was going to Gosforth. They weren't.

'I'm sorry Rachel. Most girls would love to be told how tasty they are all the time'.

'So you're an expert on female psychology now are you?'

'Come on Rachel. It's silly to waste money on a taxi. Let's get the Metro. We don't even have to sit together if you don't want to'.

They just made the last Metro and Rachel sat opposite Kyle but ignored him throughout the journey. She couldn't wait to get in her car and drive off back to Ponteland. Kyle's good mood had enjoyed a short life. He was tossing and turning all night and not for the reasons he had envisaged that morning. He felt a huge injustice. He had ended up paying for most of their holiday in Egypt and the tickets to the concert. He had never even heard off the band but had gone for Rachel's sake and yet one slightly lewd comment is enough to send her home in a strop.

The next morning Kyle concluded that he loved Rachel too much to become a misogynist and he would have to swallow his pride and make amends. He sent her some beautiful flowers with a message that read:

'To my sweetheart Rachel, I love your mind most of all. Sorry for upsetting you. Love Kyle. XXXX'

She rang him to thank him for the flowers, which she said were lovely.

'I'm sorry I was in such a mood' she said *'it is my time of the month'.*

Kyle breathed a huge sigh of relief. However, she continued *'I'm not sure we should go on seeing each other. I think we both want different things in life and maybe last night was a sign'.*

'What do you mean different things?' said Kyle despondent. *'I would be happy with anything in life as long as I'm with you Rachel.'*

Rachel sighed. This was hard for her but she needed to say it. *'Kyle. I'm 30 soon and I want to meet someone who can give me children'.*

'So you're dumping me because I've had the snip?'

'I know it's cruel but I've only just realized how much I do want a family. It's better to call it quits now don't you think?'

'I can find out about a reversal.'

'You've got a grown-up kid and you don't want any more. I'm sorry Kyle. You're a lovely guy even if you do get on my nerves sometimes.'

'Here we go. Kick a man when he's down. Why do I get on your nerves? Do you think I'm shallow?'

'No. If anything you are too deep. You are kind and generous and interesting but can be a bit pompous and condescending. You need to be less opinionated and understand that women can make their own mind up about things. Don't be upset.'

Kyle was extremely upset. He could scarcely speak and eventually they agreed to give their fledgling relationship a break and think things over. He stood staring into space and watching the rain drops cascade down his window frame. His optimism evaporated and the house felt lonely as hell.

Scene 4: Friends Re-united

'How can someone say they love you one day and then dump you the next when you haven't done anything wrong?' Kyle complained to his captive audience in the pub.

'That's women for you' said Elton John. *'They are as fickle as Boro fans. Take my daughter. I finally give in and bought her a Boro kit. A few weeks later she gets sick of following a team doing even worse than the toon and unable to fill a 30, 000 capacity stadium and says she doesn't support them any longer. I congratulate her on realizing there's only one big team in the North East and then realize she's switched her allegiance to fucking Man U.'*

'I'd rather have a Smoggie for a kid than those cockney glory hunters' Kyle confessed. There followed a vociferous debate on the better of two evils. The debate didn't extend to Sunderland. *'I'd have to divorce my kids if they started following the Mackems'* said Elton.

'Talking of Sunderland, I've applied for a job there' revealed Mattie. Observing the gasps of horror he added *'we've been put on a four day week and had a pay freeze imposed. I can't afford to pay my mortgage if I don't change jobs.'*

'Still Sunderland', exclaimed Elton.

'I worked there for a few years' Kyle added *'and I wouldn't go back for any amount of money. It's a dump'*

Mattie said *'It's not all bad. Like any city, there are parts to avoid but it has its good areas.'*

Elton scoffed *'tell me one good thing about Sunderland'.*

'Well' said Mattie. *'The metro; you can get to Newcastle in 25 minutes'.*

'I hope your new job isn't with the Mackem tourist board' laughed Kyle. *'Come to Sunderland. You can get to Newcastle within 25 minutes!'*

The conversation turned to music and Dobbo and Mattie recalled the time they went to the Leeds Festival and it was unusually dry and sunny. On the Sunday morning Dobbo sensed a business opportunity and stood out in the camp-site with a placard offering a free sun oiling to female passers-by. Mattie charmed a few customers but Dobbo wanted some quality control so Mattie wrote on the reverse of the placard *'sorry; oil reserved for fit women'* allowing his pal to turn the placard round whenever he didn't fancy the opportunity.

'I'm sure Rachel wouldn't appreciate me laughing at that' declared Kyle.

Mattie decided not to go down that road again and asked Dobbo if he remembered he'd got so wasted he couldn't see when they had returned to the camp-site on the Saturday night.

'I wasn't that bad' insisted Dobbo. *'It was pitch black'*.

'Dobbo man, when we couldn't find our tent you went up and asked for directions only to find you were talking to a wheelie-bin with a black sack on top.'

'You really should get a sight test mate' added Elton. *'once at the match you got Alan Shearer and Shola Ameobi mixed up'*.

'Come on. It was a crowded penalty area down the Leazes End and you can't blame me for not believing that Shola had scored a scorcher.'

'I hear U2 are touring this year. Will you be going?' Kyle asked Mattie.

'Kyle, I can hardly afford to feed myself and they're charging £80 a ticket. I've loved U2 since I was a bairn but I feel like ringing Bono up and saying hey Bono. You can stuff your Joshua tree up your arse!'

'There wouldn't be room' laughed Elton John. *'He's been up his own arse for years!'*

The conversation turned to John Medburn's birthday and the onset of middle-age. John challenged everyone to a down-in-one and as usual he trounced the opposition. He then went to the bar with Kyle to get the next round in.

'Do you think Rachel and you are finished?' John asked.

'I don't know mate. I think she's great. We get on so well together. There's a real chemistry between us and conversation is so easy. She is intelligent and down to earth and has similar tastes.'

'And she quite literally goes like a train'.

'Yes. She is a little sex-pot and you would never have guessed it because she's so shy and reserved most of the time.'

'That's what six pints of Guinness can do to a good Catholic girl. You should advertise the stuff. Guinness is good for your sex-life!'

'Aye, it must be the iron.'

'Well I hope you work it out. I wouldn't lose hope. She's bound to have doubts if she's getting broody and you're as seedless as a Satsuma.'

'Cheers John. How's your love-life going?'

'It's going ok. We've broken up a couple of times but the getting back together is almost worth the upset. Sometimes you don't know what you've got till you lost it.'

'*One thing Rachel said bothers me. Tell me honestly do you think I'm pompous?*'

John laughed. '*Are you sure you want an honest answer? Well, you can lecture people sometimes and come across like you know better and everyone else must be really thick.*'

'*So the answer's yes!*'

'*The good thing about mates is they make allowances for each other's weaknesses. Wives and girlfriends expect their partners to change. In my book that's why so many seem to end up disappointed.*'

Kyle nodded. '*Careful. You are beginning to sound like me!*'

Scene 5: Capital punishment

'You're late' said the sharp-dressed man in the silver Jaguar as a skinhead in a suit jacket and designer jeans climbed into the passenger seat in the pub car park.

'If I was late you would no longer be here' replied the skinhead.

The driver ignored the rebuke and produced a bulging envelope from his jacket pocket.

'The price has increased. I need an extra grand up front and ten grand on delivery, ' the skinhead sneered looking around for unwelcome spectators.

'We had a deal'.

'This is heavy-duty stuff. The risks are too great for 50 grand.'

'I've only got an extra £70 on me' the driver said scanning his wallet.

'I will take that as a down-payment'. The skinhead pointed at the driver's Rolex.

The driver reluctantly removed his watch and handed it to the skinhead, who further upset his partner in crime by examining it in case it was a fake. Satisfied, the skinhead placed the watch on his wrist and counted the bank notes in the envelope.

'Same time, same place tomorrow' grunted the skinhead and opened the car door.

The driver leaned over to shut it and called the skinhead *'don't screw up'.* The skinhead gestured with his fist without turning round and disappeared round the corner of the pub.

*****

Kyle survived his first day back at work. The worst bit was getting out of bed at the crack of dawn. It took him until noon to stop yawning. Unusually, he found himself looking forward to the next round of coffees and making more than his fair share.

Back in Gosforth, he kicked off his shoes and collapsed on the sofa. He looked at the time and seeing it was almost bang on six he switched on the news. Spring had arrived but the green shoots of economic recovery were notable in their absence. He remembered what he had learnt from the Cairo dossier. Soon the Illuminati were going to release an unprecedented series of political scandals to the Press. They had got hold of information on MP's expenses that they hoped would wreck Parliament far more than Guy Fawkes could have done with twice the dynamite. The planned disclosure in the summer would have been mitigated by civil servants blacking through sensitive information. However, the Illuminati had the full uncensored register and it was political dynamite.

Kyle wondered how Nick had got on today with the PM. He hadn't heard anything and realizing that the rest of the news was full of the usual fodder of knife crime and celebrity bashing his curiosity got the better of him. He dialled Nick's number but his phone was switched off so he dragged himself to the kitchen and stuck a meal for one in the microwave.

*****

Nick had left his Pimlico flat with an hour to spare before his meeting with the PM. It was only a twenty minute walk but it was a lovely morning and he fancied a leisurely stroll along the Thames. He passed a gang of youths arguing by a bus stop and turning saw one of them punch a black kid in the ribs. He went back and remonstrated with the offender, undeterred by the torrent of abuse he received. The black kid thanked him and moved away.

After crossing Vauxhall Bridge Road and entering a quiet avenue leading to the Tate he became aware of someone following him. It didn't surprise him. Youths didn't take kindly to being disciplined in front of their peers and as long as he kept in public view all he could expect was another mouthful. He quickened his stride and took the first side road down towards the busy Milbank.

The road took him through the grounds of Chelsea Art School and the presence of crowds of students milling about reassured him enough to stop to tie his laces. As he got back up, a huge shadow raced across the tarmac towards him. His heart leapt and he turned to admonish the larger than expected delinquent, hoping that the size of the shadow was a trick of light.

Nick's face fell. A blade flashed beneath his belated defence. He crouched. He fell. The students screamed. The blood gushed out across the tarmac. Nick panted his terminal breath and his eyes froze as he saw a middle-aged skinhead fleeing the crime scene.

Kyle came back into the lounge with his supper on a tray. The newsreader said *'There was another fatal stabbing in London today, but it seems the criminals are getting ever more daring. This one happened in the City Centre, just yards from the Thames, in broad daylight. Caroline Jones reports'*:

'Shortly before 11 o clock this morning this art college in Pimlico, close to the Tate Gallery was the scene of a gruesome stabbing. A man in his 20's had stopped to tie his shoe-laces when a middle-aged skinhead run up and stabbed him in the stomach before fleeing the scene. An ambulance arrived within five minutes but the man was pronounced dead. The students that

witnessed the assault are being treated for shock and receiving professional counselling. Police are said to be following a number of leads but as yet the criminal is still at large. Anyone with information is urged to ring this number.'

At that moment Kyle's phone rang but before he could get to it, the news reporter had returned to the studio and the presenter had added an update. *'News just in the Police have named the victim as 26 year old Nick Woods, who was a political advisor at the Cabinet Office.'*

Kyle could scarcely speak as he picked up the receiver. He heard a distraught Rachel on the other end of the line saying *'Kyle, Kyle. Are you there?'*

Scene 6: Funeral

Nick died on a cold, cloudy day in April 2009. It was a day that transpired to be a Magna Carta for his grieving sibling. Rachel had been prepared to end her romance with Kyle and return to single-life. It was difficult because she did love Kyle and she knew that her feelings were more than reciprocated. However, she was certain deep down that it was the right thing to do.

However, Rachel could not bear to sleep alone that night. She craved to be cradled in Kyle's strong arms. Her grief needed sharing and Kyle was in the right place at the right time. She packed an overnight bag and waited by the window. Kyle arrived punctually and opened his arms for Rachel. He was just as she had hoped; strong and silent.

Suddenly the future seemed a long way away for Rachel. In any case, grief eroded her broodiness. Kyle understood his role and took strength from her fragility. He was a rock and Rachel quickly realized that at this stage in her life she needed to cling to him like a limpet.

It was disconcerting for Rachel. She once told a friend that she would never give her heart away again because becoming dependent on a man was the road to ruin. For a relationship to work both partners must be capable of getting by without the other. Dependence on a partner puts an impossible strain on relationships and the romance is poisoned by the fear of ending up alone. However, these were exceptional times. She had lost her kid brother. It was no time for rules and theories. She agreed to stay with Kyle until the funeral and with each day that passed it became harder to imagine going back to her empty flat.

Kyle asked Rachel if she would like to visit the scene of her brother's murder and leave some flowers. She said she would so he took the afternoon off work and drove her all the way to London, five hours there and five hours back. It helped. There were dozens of flowers marking the spot on the tarmac at Chelsea Art College. The students had respectfully left the shrine undisturbed and even a few Newcastle shirts and scarves lay in honour.

Rachel met a friend of her brothers and the two of them went to Nick's flat. Kyle waited at the friend's house at Rachel's bequest. On the way back to Newcastle, they stopped at a service station on the A1. They had a midnight coffee and a stretch of the legs and Rachel thanked Kyle for his understanding. Kyle explained that he too had lost a younger brother recently, so he knew what she was going through. Before continuing on their journey Rachel opened a hold-all and pulled out a replica strip.

'This is the shirt that Nick was wearing the day he was introduced to Tony Blair. He would have liked you to have it.' She smiled for the first time in days as Kyle proudly tried it on and thanked her with a passionate embrace. Ra-

chel fell asleep as they passed the chimneys at Ferrybridge and woke up as the car crossed the Tyne Bridge.

'*We're home darling*' Kyle said warmly. The lights twinkled on both banks of the Tyne down below and up above the stars mirrored them, guiding them back to Gosforth.

*****

The mourners gathered under a leaden sky. Newcastle's West Road Crematorium was located half-way up a steep bank shielding the City from the wind and rain that lashed in from the North Pennines. Dressed in black, Kyle and Rachel met friends and relatives outside the Chapel of Rest and received a succession of condolences. Kyle noted how well Rachel was holding herself together, although the anguish was written all over her strained face.

There was a murmur of approval as the doors opened and the guests found sanctuary from the wind and drizzle. The turnout was impressive and some of the latecomers had to stand at the back of the Chapel as one of Kyle's work colleagues delivered the eulogy. Kyle learnt new facts about his dead friend. Nick's happiest memories related to swimming with dolphins and whales, which he experienced on a family holiday and then took up as a hobby. It led to membership of Greenpeace and several trips to disrupt whaling fleets and seal culls. He had always been an activist, willing to fight courageously for his beliefs. The eulogy made no reference to Kyle's belief that this courage cost him his life.

The colleague concluded by revealing that Nick had spoken to him just days before his death and told him what song he would like played at his funeral. Again, he made no inference that Nick's death was politically motivated and he knew he was in grave danger. However, his poignant pause allowed a murmur to drift down the aisles.

Nick's coffin slid away from view to the deliciously appropriate sound of Glasvegas and their anthem to a young life cut tragically short '*Flowers and Football Tops*'. A lady burst into tears and went dashing out of the Church and suddenly the floodgates opened as the roar emotion of the song penetrated the hardest of souls. Kyle comforted a sobbing Rachel, whilst trying to hold back his own tears. Images of Nick leading the resistance flashed through his mind. He also saw the War poster from his student days, with the single word '*Why*?' and felt a potent blend of anger and confusion fester inside him.

The rain had stopped when they left the Church. Wendy was first to approach Rachel as she wiped the tears and stared into space.

'*I'm so sorry for your loss Rachel. Your brother was a great man. I'm sure he was destined for great things.*'

'*Thank you Wendy*', Rachel replied and then she asked the question that everyone had been afraid to ask. '*Do you think the Illuminati killed him?*'

Wendy hesitated and then said. *'Come with me. There's someone you should meet.'*

Standing chatting to Nick's work colleagues was the top mandarin they had met at Downing Street. Wendy did the introduction and left. His name was Ralph and he ushered Rachel and Kyle away.

'Ralph, *I need to know who killed my brother'* Rachel said bluntly.

'I understand that and I can assure you HM Government is giving full co-operation to the Police to catch the assassin.'

This did nothing to appease Rachel. *'How do I know the Government were not complicit in his death? He was stabbed on his way to meet the PM.'*

'Yes, but the meeting was far from secret. He let word of his meeting and its purpose spread around the House. We know that there are enemies of democracy on both sides of the House. It seems probable that they ordered his death to stop him passing further information to the PM.'

'What further information?' Rachel sounded incredulous.

'We will never know. Eye-witnesses said that he was carrying a large envelope bulging with paperwork when he was stabbed. When he got to hospital it had disappeared. He told me the day before his death that he was compiling a dossier of information that would blow the PM's mind when he met him. He never mentioned anything to you?'

'No' said Rachel.

'It may seem like we have done nothing with the information that you brought us from Cairo but I assure you we have. Here is my card, if you think of any other way in which you can help us.' Ralph handed his card and bid farewell.

'I'm sorry I got you into this' Kyle told Rachel as they wandered away. *'If we hadn't met, you wouldn't have got your brother involved and he might be alive today.'*

'Thanks Kyle but I think he was already involved.'

'Maybe but you wanted to stay out of it and let history take its course. I should have listened to you Rachel. This is all too heavy.'

Rachel cleared her throat and spoke firmly. *'That was before they killed my brother. They will live to regret that. I will make sure of it.'* She looked Kyle straight in the eye and added *'so are you in or are you out?'*

Scene 7: Race against Time

Kyle groaned as the alarm clock woke him from his first decent slumber of what had been a long night. Rachel had been restless. She was up and down like West Bromwich Albion for drinks of water, calls of nature and God knows what else. At about half four Kyle heard her go downstairs for the fourth time, only this time she didn't return and Kyle was finally able to get some sleep. He found her curled up on the sofa with a sleeping bag.

'*What are you doing there?*' Kyle asked yawning.

'*I'm sorry. I couldn't sleep and I thought I'd disturb you less down here*'.

Kyle kissed her softly on the forehead and went to turn the kettle on. He stretched and looked out at the early morning mist. He turned as he sensed Rachel behind him.

'*I think I might have a way of finding my brother's killer*' she said.

'*Don't you think we should leave that to the Police*' Kyle asked.

'*Oh yeah; like you got the Police involved when you got kidnapped and tortured you mean.*'

'*Ok. I take your point. What's your idea?*'

'*We know from eye-witnesses that Nick had a large envelope when he was stabbed and none of them saw what happened to the envelope. It was not recorded in the register of his property when the ambulance arrived at hospital. It had mysteriously disappeared.*'

'*So you suspect the paramedics?*'

'*No. They travel in two's so it would have required collusion. Moreover, they couldn't have arranged it so their ambulance attended that particular 999 call. Two nurses signed the patient's property register within half an hour of him being admitted to St Thomas's. It must have been taken in that half an hour window. The most likely culprit is the pathologist.*'

'*Or a doctor or porter or anyone that had access to the morgue in that time?*'

'*I thought of that but something else occurred to me in the night. Most of Kyle's friends from London were at the funeral but there was one notable exception. He was good friends with a pathologist at St Thomas's called Nigel Prior. I met him once. He gave me the creeps. He was full of slimy comments. Then he told some gruesome tales from the path-lab as if they were funny and name-dropped about his celebrity friends. Trust me; he took Nick's envelope, which means he probably knows the killer.*'

Kyle considered the issue as he poured the coffee and looked into her deep blue eyes. *'Let's get on the first train to London'*.

*****

'I'm afraid Mr Prior is on annual leave today Miss Woods' the receptionist at St Thomas's said putting down the phone. Rachel explained her relationship to the diseased and how a treasured possession had gone missing. She suspected Nigel Prior might have taken it for safe keeping. She asked for his home address.

'I'm sorry but I can't give out staff addresses under any circumstances'. The receptionist was good.

'Please can you just confirm that he was on duty when my brother was admitted?' Rachel pleaded. The receptionist went away. Five minutes later she returned and called Rachel to the desk.

'Yes. He finished his shift immediately after your brother's admission and has been on leave since.'

'Thanks' said Rachel looking at Kyle and rushing out of the hospital.

'Where are we going?' asked Kyle.

'Nick's flat. I have a key. Knowing Nick, I'm sure he will have an up to date address book.'

Rachel was right and within an hour they were knocking on a door in Roehampton. There was no answer. An old lady came out of the house opposite and shouted across the road:

'Excuse me. Mr Prior is on holiday. May I help?'

Rachel explained her predicament.

'Oh come in and have a cup of tea' the lady replied. *'Nick was a lovely young man. He visited Mr Prior on many occasions. In fact he was only here the day before...'* She couldn't bring herself to mention the murder and instead said *'Did you know Mr Prior well?'*

Rachel bluffed. *'Yes. We are old friends. Mr Prior went to Cambridge with my Dad.'*

'Whilst you have your tea I will go over and have a look for this envelope. I have a spare key to go in and water Mr Prior's plants whilst he is away.'

As soon as she shut the front door Kyle turned to Rachel and said *'Your Dad never went to Cambridge!'*

'He did once. He saw Newcastle play at the Abbey Stadium'.

Kyle laughed. Rachel looked apprehensive. '*I can't see Nigel Prior leaving an envelope of political dynamite lying around for a nosey neighbour to find. What should we do?*'

They sipped their tea and searched for inspiration. Kyle stood up and went to the window. The lady had left Mr Prior's door ajar and he briefly considered trying to sneak inside to hide until she had gone. Then he noticed a small parcel addressed to Mr Prior on the lady's window sill. Underneath it was a hand-written note, which said '*Mr Prior*' and then a four digit number: 2505.

'*What do you think of this?*' Kyle asked holding up the note and shrugging. Rachel came to the window. She looked at the note and then across the road to see the lady locking up Mr Prior's. '*It could be the alarm number*' she said pointing at the box on the front of the house. Kyle was busy looking at the parcel. It was from Sky TV. An idea came to him. He carefully slid the seal open and found a bill inside for the installation of Sky Plus together with a welcome pack. The front door opened and Kyle quickly put the bill in his pocket and re-sealed the package.

'*I'm sorry Miss Woods. I searched the house and couldn't find your envelope. I tried ringing him on his mobile but there was no answer and I've got to go out soon*' the old lady said entering the room.

'*Oh well*' Rachel sighed. '*Thanks for trying. I will give him a ring on his mobile tonight.*' They left and started to walk back to the bus stop. At the end of the road Kyle stopped and said '*as soon as neighbourhood watch goes out I'm ringing for a locksmith. If you pretend to be a dizzy wife whose locked herself out and show this bill he should break the lock for you and then you can try the alarm number.*'

'*What if it's not an alarm number?*' Rachel enquired.

'*Your instincts have been right so far. I think it's worth the risk.*'

It was at least two hours later when the lady finally left her house. The plan worked perfectly. The alarm number was right. The locksmith suspected nothing, although he wasn't best pleased that Rachel had to write a cheque for his £120 charge. He added another £20 on '*to cover the VAT and inconvenience*'. Kyle quickly found a safe in a bedroom cupboard and tried the alarm number. It worked and he reached inside for an envelope, calling Rachel from downstairs.

To Kyle's dismay there was no envelope and nothing obviously incriminating. He picked up the most unusual item. It was an audio tape. Rachel took it to play on a hi-fi she had seen in the living room. Kyle continued his search for the envelope.

'*Kyle*' Rachel yelled from downstairs. He hurried down in response to the excitement in her voice. She pressed '*play*' and they listened together to a taped conversation in hushed tones. The recording crackled but the words were clear and chilling and the voices recognizable.

'Ok. You agree we will never win Obama and Brown round and they are a threat to the New World Order?'

'Yes but if we are patient they will be hounded out of office by an angry electorate wanting solutions to massive debt and unemployment. Give it a year maximum and then we move.'

'I know that's the plan but do you really think the management team will not reward us if we got rid of Obama and Brown now? We will be heroes. We might even get a job on the management team. I fancy Chief Executive of Barbados!'

'We might be heroes to the brotherhood but the public might not welcome the assassination of their democratically elected leaders, credit crunch or not'.

'You haven't been listening. My contacts in the CIA can make this seem like an act of Islamic Fundamentalist terrorism. There will be nothing to link the assassinations to us.'

'Ok. I will get the information you need. One other issue before you go. I've just come from a meeting with Nick Woods. Have you heard of him?'

'The name's familiar. Is he a MP?'

'No. He's a political advisor but he knows a lot about our plans and is spreading rumours around the House. You might want to have him silenced.'

'OK'.

With that, the tape clicked and went dead.

Kyle broke the silence. *'We've got to get to Downing Street quickly. The PM is due in Washington tomorrow to meet Obama. If they are going to kill them both, tomorrow's the day!'*

Rachel rung Ralph in the taxi and he gave her an address in Whitehall to head to. Kyle checked his watch. It was four o'clock and the rush hour traffic was already building up. He tapped his fingers impatiently and cursed every red light. Rachel leapt out of the taxi in Whitehall whilst he paid the bill. She was already in reception asking for Ralph.

Ralph listened to the tape expressionless. He immediately dialled a number and left a message. *'Jim. I need to get a message to Gordon urgently. He is to cancel his meeting with the President. If he goes ahead with the meeting we have a red-risk scenario.'*

'*I only hope he gets it in time*' Ralph said. He then rung another number and said calmly '*get me the White-House*'. A few seconds later he added '*Is that the White-House? This is Downing Street. We've had reliable intelligence about a terrorist attack tomorrow if the PM meets the President. For security reasons I'm afraid we must cancel.*' There followed a heated debate. When Ralph put the phone down he looked stressed for the first time.

'*I'm not sure if they can be trusted to get the message to the President*' Ralph stated quietly.

'*I have an idea*' said Rachel. Kyle and Ralph looked at her and willed her to share it.

'*We need to get news of the assassination plot and the wider Illuminati conspiracy to as many people as possible around the World as quickly as possible. The solution is simple. We use the internet. The Illuminati's greatest invention could be their downfall.*'

Ralph and Kyle looked at each other. The irony was beautiful. The enemy had invented the web to spark revolution but the same web could be used to trap them and scupper a plan that had been centuries in the making. Kyle laughed and hugged Rachel. Ralph was immediately on the phone. There was no time to waste.

Scene 8: Breaking News

Big Ben struck six times. Rachel read her You-tube posting and attached various papers from the Cairo conference and the assassination audio file. *'Here goes'* she said and pressed the button. She called it *'the credit crunch conspiracy'*. Within seconds the hit counter illustrated that someone somewhere in the World knew their secret.

She turned her attention to the social networking sites. Twitter, Face-book, My-space and others provided fertile ground to sow the seeds of conspiracy. A vociferous debate soon commenced between believers and cynics regarding the authenticity of the documents and recordings. Someone in Sweden set up an on-line vote on the issue.

Meanwhile Kyle and Ralph were working with an IT guy on a posting to the UK Government's official site. Kyle stated *'this will prove the sceptics wrong'* as Ralph submitted the posting for approval. The IT guy put the phone down and said *'it's been successfully transmitted but it won't go live until 9.00 tomorrow morning.'*

Big Ben struck seven times. Rachel's You-tube posting now had 2, 464 hits. She was finding it difficult to keep up with all the questions on the social networking sites. One bloke from Hong Kong wanted to know if betting on horses would be allowed in the New World Order. A lady from Spain said she couldn't believe how gullible people were, taking such an obvious hoax seriously.

The door bell rung and Ralph went to answer it. Kyle looked nervously out of the window but couldn't make out the visitor. He breathed a sigh of relief when a timid looking man in a grey suit entered with a lap-top. He was a Government press-office employer. With Ralph's help he set about drafting a press release. The IT chap transformed into a PA and fielded dozens of calls.

Big Ben struck eight times. The hit counter now read 9, 206. *'Not bad for 2 hours'* remarked Kyle.

Rachel was less impressed *'the future of the planet is still getting fewer hits than a clip of a cow falling into a river that was posted about the same time.'*

The guy from the Press Office created another posting with the title *'Obama assassination planned tomorrow'* and put a link in it to Rachel's posting. Within minutes the hit counters had gone crazy, turning over too fast to read the numbers they contained. Kyle turned on the TV and switched between the news channels. There was still no coverage.

'You do realize three quarters of these channels are run by Illuminati support-ers' said Ralph. He looked exhausted but the adrenaline was still pumping through Rachel and Kyle's veins.

'Look' said Kyle. The Breaking News banner on the BBC quoted Reuters reporting a White-House denial of a Presidential assassination plot. *'Lying Bastards'* said Kyle and slumped in a Chair watching the news.

'A coffee would be nice' declared Rachel typing assiduously away. Kyle got up and made a round of teas and coffees. As he brought out the beverages on a tray the news cut to a CNN interview with a senior White-house aid.

'I can assure you the President's life is not in danger and nor is Prime Minister Brown's. I understand Mr Brown is not feeling well so he has pulled out of today's meeting with President Obama. As always we must remain vigilant against terrorism but the state of alert has not changed. This ridiculous scaremongering plays into the hands of the terrorists.'

The interviewer asked the aide to comment on internet speculation that there was a conspiracy by leading statesmen, bankers and entrepreneurs to take over the World and solve a credit crunch problem that they had created in the first place.

'Really; I thought CNN was a respectable new channel not a vehicle for crazy conspiracy buffs.'

'Have you seen the evidence posted on You-tube? It looks authentic.'

'Hitler's diaries looked authentic.'

'So you are certain the story is a hoax?'

'Of course it's a hoax'.

And that was that. Big Ben struck nine times. Ralph's Whitehall office was still frantically busy but the mood was now lugubrious. The CNN denial had knocked the stuffing out of them. The hit counter had reached six figures but it now seemed meaningless. What good was it that people were reading about the credit crunch conspiracy and the assassination if they didn't believe them?

When the phone rang they all jumped. It was the PM for Ralph. Ralph left the room to take the call in private.

When he returned he looked worried. *'He wants to pull the press release until we're certain the evidence is authentic. Apparently a voice expert over there reckons the conspirator isn't who we say he is. He doesn't want egg on his face if the whole thing turns out to be a hoax.'*

There was nothing on news at ten on the conspiracy or the assassination. The press guy and the IT guy left and Ralph offered Rachel and Kyle a sofa-bed in the building. He left for his own home at about twenty past eleven and they fell asleep with the TV on quietly in the back-ground.

'Look at this Kyle' Rachel asked when she logged on the next morning.

A banker who had been an Illuminati member had broken rank and revealed further secrets on You-tube. He told how the entire banking and credit system came within days of collapse in autumn 2008 until the economic stimulus and bank rescue packages initiated by Gordon Brown saved capitalism. He posted minutes of finance meetings showing how banks were deliberately starving the World of credit to facilitate the New World Order. The combined hits were now almost 200, 000 world-wide.

Just as Kyle was packing the sofa-bed up, Ralph entered the room smiling. He was carrying a copy of the Guardian. *'It is front-page news'* he said. There was an article describing how its bitter rival the Daily Telegraph was due to publish details of the Cabinet's extravagant expense claims that could bring down the Government. The Guardian alleged that the confidential information had been stolen by a leading Illuminati member.

Rachel showed Ralph the banking revelations. *'It's coming together'* he agreed.

At half past eleven, the PM finally cleared the Press Release and the official web-site posting. The official confirmation of the conspiracy sent shockwaves around the World. Entire internet platforms crashed at about one as the Illuminati's greatest invention creaked at the seams. President Obama and Gordon Brown held separate press conferences. The President broadcast from the Oval Office. Gordon Brown chose the Statue of Liberty.

Over the next six hours no fewer than seventeen high-profile conspirators were arrested in the UK alone. Ralph cracked open a bottle of champagne and the cork hit the chandelier.

'We've done it' beamed Kyle. *'The Geordies have saved the World!'*

Scene 9: Alnmouth

Legend has it that when Queen Victoria's royal train headed north of Newcastle en route to Balmoral she insisted they opened the curtains so she could appreciate the beauty of Alnmouth Bay. In May 2009 the view was still breathtaking.

A cool blue sky merged with a royal blue sea on the horizon. The gentle waves caressed miles of golden sand that blended effortlessly into lush green dunes and a championship golf course. To the North, a fine Norman keep stood imperiously guarding the secret kingdom. To the South, a row of brightly painted houses, all in different colours looked over a sheltered harbour and creek. Alnmouth's isolation helped keep its treasures secret. Even most of the tourists that flocked to nearby Alnwick to see Harry Potter's castle usually passed it by. Only Kyle and Rachel disembarked at Alnmouth station as the train headed on to Scotland.

There were a few people in the High Street browsing in the pretty shops or making their way to the golf course. However, the beach was deserted, safe for a man walking his dog and a distant flock of seagulls. Apart from its isolation, the other deterrent to tourists was the weather. A frequent sea fret meant that the weather in Newcastle or Edinburgh was not always a reliable guide to that on the Northumberland coast. When there was an Easterly breeze, the coast could be bitterly cold and the sand could blow off the dunes. It was not normally a place for sun-worshippers but Kyle loved it and so did Rachel. Alnmouth was raw nature, unadulterated by the excesses of modern living.

Moreover, today the sun was strong, the breeze docile and the sky clear. Rachel took off her cardigan and wrapped it round her slender waist as they walked hand in hand across the sand. The warmth of the sun blessed her milky white skin and she relished the sweet taste of salty sea air. Kyle sensed the warmth of Rachel's hand in his and rejoiced in the comforting buzz of a mind at peace with itself for the first time in a year.

It was one month to the day since the news broke of the Illuminati plot. In that time remarkably little had changed in the World. Kyle shuddered to think how it might have changed if they had not acted when they did. After the initial flurry of arrests there was a world-wide consensus to avoid a witch-hunt and to forgive those involved in the greatest conspiracy of all time. There was a deluge of denial from those suspected of Illuminati links. Some politicians quietly exited the stage to spend more time with their families. Some bankers and top executives took early retirement with golden goodbye payments to keep them in caviar and truffles. Credit eased a little bit and the green shoots of economic recovery started to burst through. Job prospects remained bleak as redundancy processes worked their way through to their sorry conclusion.

Kyle forecast it would take another year before the economy fully recovered and unemployment started to fall again, but recover it would.

The public soon tired of stories of sinister cults and financial sabotage. In any case, they had a new focus for their anger. The Daily Telegraph published its leaked dossier on MP's expenses. For weeks, their cover story dominated not just political debate but the debate of ordinary people from Lands End to John o' Groats. At a time of recession, MPs were billing us for cleaning their moats and building duck-houses. The most shocking aspect of the revelations was the complete lack of contrition from the MPs themselves. It seemed that on planet Westminster they actually believed they were hard done by earning more than twice the national average wage and having to account for what they claimed as expenses.

Gordon Brown had made much of how he had saved the world by revealing the Illuminati secrets and stopping the greedy banks going under and losing all our money. However, his limp presentation and a hostile media dampened the expected Brown Bounce in the polls. The media made much of Brown's delayed action and his attempt to then steal the thunder from the real heroes that had died or faced torture fighting the Illuminati. Worse still for Brown, the Telegraph's revelations on expenses spent the first week concentrating almost entirely on offenders within his Cabinet and stole his thunder. By the time the shadow Cabinet were exposed as being equally guilty, the shock-value of the daily scandals had diminished and polls suggested Labour was hurt much more than the Tories by the scandal.

There was much for Kyle to be depressed about. The high hopes of New Labour seemed to be dying a long, slow painful defeat. Even Alan Shearer's appointment as manager couldn't save Newcastle United from relegation and the Crown Prosecution Service had dropped an investigation into Batman's kidnapping and torture of Kyle through lack of evidence.

However, Kyle was happy. Rachel had decided to stop rationalising about the obstacles to their romance and enjoy the present. They were high on the elixir of love and the drug made them feel invincible. Rachel had shunned publicity and pushed Kyle forward as the hero that the Press were searching for. She told Kyle modestly that she had just come along for the ride whilst he endured a series of life-threatening adventures fighting the nefarious enemy. Kyle tried reasoning with her that ultimately her brilliant mind had saved the day but that just embarrassed Rachel and he knew better than to push her into the public spotlight.

Kyle was lined up for a series of interviews, photo-shoots and advertising campaigns. Rachel declined all such invitations but helped her boyfriend negotiate the media frenzy that had engulfed him. Alnmouth was the perfect antidote for this frenzy. It was tranquil and sublime and there was not a journalist in sight.

*****

Kyle rested his head in the dunes and watched a jet-plane leave tracks in the sky. Rachel was lying on her flat stomach asleep, her head resting on the rise of the dune. Kyle watched her brown hair blow gently in the breeze and her firm, petite body rise and fall slightly with her breathing. Her t-shirt had risen up her back to reveal a slither of white skin before the blue denim of her jeans. Kyle sat up and admired the view. He concluded that the curve of Rachel's bottom was better than anything in the Louvre. He observed a distant trawler bopping up and down on the North Sea. An excited child giggled with pleasure as he explored the rock-pools with bucket and spade.

Kyle turned to address an imaginary audience on the sand:

'The World is full of beauty but we are blinded to it. We have become so cynical, so negative that we have forgotten how to enjoy what nature has bequeathed us. As children, we took pleasure in the simplest things. Now many of us have been programmed to believe that we can't afford to be happy. We spend our lives chasing the riches only to find they were here all along as free as the air we breathe.

The Beatles said that all you need is love. They made millions proving otherwise but that simple message should not be forgotten. Think back to the intoxication of your first true love. Of course that state is ephemeral but the joy it brought can get you through the darkest hours and give you hope of a better tomorrow. Happy memories provide an umbrella in a storm. If you have loved once then you can love again. You need the courage to give your heart again, make compromises without resentment, not expect too much and appreciate your loved one for what they are, not what you dreamt they would be.

There is a lot of hope before us. Human beings have come such a long way in such a short time. We just need time to evolve emotionally and catch up with the pace of technology. The triumph of human spirit can overcome almost anything. If we really put a man on the moon are you really telling me we can't find a way to appreciate the beauty all around us? I grew up, as most black men did, with a chip on my shoulder. Generations of slavery and abuse conditioned me to see discrimination in every misfortune and suspect the worst of people. However, if America can elect a black President then it is time to forgive and move on.

We must trust our instincts and our friends and ignore the cynics. Tales of a broken society sells papers but it destroys souls. One day we will break free of the media conspiracy that has chained the human spirit. We will realize that we live in a much better world than our parents and grandparents did and all the evil that is reported is not new; it has always gone on, without the coverage that it gets today. The more we are told our society is broken the more broken it becomes. We have to break out of the vicious cycle and take strength from the warmth and kindness of our friends and loved ones.

I have been tested more than most of you ever will be. In the last year I have lost my wife, my brother, my best friend's brother, for a time my job. I have been kidnapped and tortured like a medieval prisoner. I have been shot at and witnessed unspeakable scenes of sexual depravity. Am I bitter? No, not any more. I have found new love and new hope. I have great friends that stuck by me through thick and thin and a son I am proud of. My story is a lesson to the Prozac generation. When Obama asks can we be build a better society where more of us enjoy the fruits of happiness? I say yes we can!'

Scene 10: Epilogue

Kyle was as proud as a peacock. At 3.00 p.m. he would stand on the City Hall stage and be given the freedom of the City. He had no intention of invoking the freeman's right to graze cattle on the Town Moor. However, the thought of being recognized in the same way as his heroes Kevin Keegan, Alan Shearer and the recently deceased Sir Bobby Robson made him feel taller than the 6 foot 2 inches that he actually was.

Sir Bobby died last week after a long battle with cancer. The dignity of the knight's final year was typical of the man and a refreshing contrast to the self-obsessed demise of a z-list celebrity earlier in the year. Sir Bobby was an ebullient example to us all. Rachel had persuaded Kyle to do a Calvin Klein photo-shoot at 2.00p.m. , donating the proceeds to Sir Bobby's cancer charity. Initially, Kyle resisted saying there was no way he was going to mince around in his underpants just an hour before his moment of glory. However, the appeal of the £50K cheque to Sir Bobby's charity swung it.

Kyle read the speech he had composed on Alnmouth Beach to Rachel. It was a special moment; the first time he'd read any of his secret speeches to anyone and a dress rehearsal for the acceptance ceremony.

'What do you think?' he asked apprehensively.

'It's fantastic' Rachel said. *'President Obama himself couldn't have written something better.'*

Kyle blushed. Rachel's praise meant the world to him. However, she continued *'I'm not sure this afternoon is the right time for such a speech but'.*

'What do you mean?'

'It's just I think most of the people there would prefer something lighter; less high-brow. That's just my opinion.'

'So you think I should dumb it down? It might not be what the people want but it's what they need Rachel. I have a once in a lifetime opportunity to get my message across and you think I should just say thanks and how proud I am!'

'I don't know Kyle. Maybe you should ask Mattie'.

They were meeting Mattie for a pint at one to calm Kyle's nerves. Kyle knew Mattie had the gift of the gab but Kyle was upset that Rachel thought he might be able to deliver a better speech than him.

Mattie read the speech in the beer garden of the Carriage without any emotion. He put it down and picked up his pint of Old Speckled Hen.

'Well' Kyle said impatiently.

'I think it's very you Kyle' Mattie said when he'd taken a big sip of ale.

'What the fuck does that mean? Do you like it?'

'To be honest I think its shit. You are planning to meet an adoring crowd with a speech about how stupid they all are and how they need to stop being so miserable and negative and start appreciating the World around them. You really know how to win friends and influence people don't you Kyle.'

'I don't think that's what I'm saying'.

'That's how it comes across. They want a speech that's more Mohammed Ali than Barack Obama. You have to adapt what you say for your audience Kyle. Trust me'.

Kyle was despondent. *'I think Mattie's right Kyle'* added Rachel.

'Oh so you think its shite as well!' Kyle commented.

'No. It's great but it's not the time or place for it.' Rachel put her arm round Kyle.

Mattie took a big swig and then asked Kyle to consider something like this:

'Thanks for this award. I'm overcome to be in the same company as my he-roes; people like Keegan, Shearer and Robson (pause for applause). I don't know how an ordinary Geordie from Wallsend ended up in this position or if I really deserve to be standing here addressing such a huge crowd. I will let you into a secret (pause to wet appetite for Illuminati revelations). The other day I had a call from Mike Ashley. He said Kyle you sound like the sort of hero I need to get Newcastle promoted and get me my money back. I said Mike I know I saved the World but you can't expect me to save the toon! (pause for laughter).

Seriously, I am truly honoured to receive the freedom of the City I love so much from you the best people in the World (pause for more applause). It is especially significant to receive it a week after the sad death of Sir Bobby Robson. He was a true gentleman who taught me the importance of enjoy-ing life and living every minute like it's your last. Sir Bobby (looking to the heavens) I salute you. (pause for more applause). I dedicate this award to Sir Bobby. Thank you.'

'Wow' said Rachel. *'Did you just make that up on the spot?'*

Mattie was looking at a sullen Kyle. *'Don't you see that going down better mate?'*

Kyle shrugged. *'I don't know. Don't get me wrong. It's a great speech but it's very you Mattie.'*

Rachel had finished her pint and was looking at her watch. *'Don't you think we should be moving?'* she asked. It was quarter to two.

'OK, here goes!' and the three friends headed off to the City Hall. There was already a huge crowd gathering and they had to negotiate a posse of photographers, journalists and autograph hunters as they located the stage door.

Kyle was ushered through by a camp man in a loud shirt. The cameras were set up at the back of the big stage and huge velvet curtains hung down from the ceiling separating this side-show from the main event due an hour later. The bright lights and nerves combined to make Kyle hot and sweaty and he struggled to hear his instructions above the music. He glanced to the side of the stage. Rachel and Mattie had been joined by Elton John, John, Dobbo and One Word.

Kyle went over to them. *'Bloody hell! What are you lot doing here? This is embarrassing enough.'*

'I wouldn't miss it for the world' laughed Elton. *'Kyle posing in his pants! I wet myself just thinking of it.'*

'Lucky Calvin Klein don't want you then' said Mattie.

'I don't think Elton's beer gut is quite what they are looking for' laughed Kyle.

'Howay. Your no Brad Pitt yourself mate' Elton retaliated.

'Have you thought which acceptance speech you are going to deliver?' asked Mattie.

'No. I'm going to play it by ear' Kyle said looking nervous again.

'Well good luck mate' said Mattie. *'Just imagine the applause and relax and you will be fine'*. He slapped him on the back and offered his hand *'No hard feelings?'*

Kyle shook it. *'I hope not'* he said. *'At least not until the Calvin Klein shoot has finished!'*

'Good luck Kyle' said One Word with uncharacteristic verbosity.

His friends whistled as he stripped to his underwear. The poster design was already agreed. He would appear holding a big globe with the strap-line *'I saved the World wearing Calvin Klein.'*

They laughed as he was instructed on the correct pose and coerced into flexing his muscles. The camp man handed him the globe. He felt extremely embarrassed but the thought of his dead mum and dad and Sir Bobby willing him on from Heaven soothed him.

'*Um let's make it like you are breaking free from your torturers*' said the camp man. Suddenly Kyle was tied up in fake chains and blindfolded and gagged. He was instructed to pose as if he was breaking free from his chains through brute force. He sensed the camera flash again and again and sensed the camp man was enjoying this rather too much.

'*Is that it*?' he shouted through the gag.

'*Just a mo*' replied the camp man.

Meanwhile, Kyle's home phone was ringing. It switched to the answer-phone and the voice of a Jewish New Yorker was recorded:

'*Kyle, I'm Lucas Barowski. We met at your brother's funeral. Your brother rang me shortly before his death. He sounded very agitated. He told me that he had found out that top bankers were colluding to bring the World's economies down and now he had been fired he wanted to reveal all. To my eternal regret, I told him he'd been drinking and to ring me when he'd sobered up.*

The next morning I heard he'd committed suicide. I thought nothing of it at the time. I knew how much his job meant to him. However, when all this Illuminati stuff blew up I started digging. Now I've found a prisoner who confessed to pushing Dan over his balcony. Please ring me back when you get this message. I plan to run the story tomorrow but I want to clear it with you first.'

Suddenly, the music changed to '*Local Hero*' the song that Newcastle United enter the fray to. As the music stopped Kyle was aware of a commotion. He removed his gag and blindfold.

Ahead of him his mates were in hysterics patting Dobbo on the back. Kyle looked to his left in horror. The velvet curtains had opened and a packed City Hall were laughing and whistling at him. At the front of the stage the Mayor was aghast. The Calvin Klein crew had left and the clock showed 3, half an hour later than his watch.

He looked at his friends again. The bastards had set him up. He turned back to his audience to deliver his speech and wished they were imaginary. They were all too real. There was no way he could deliver a deep and meaningful speech now. Searching for some words of wisdom conducive to his predicament only one word came to mind.

'*Shit*!'

The End

Lightning Source UK Ltd.
Milton Keynes UK
25 November 2009

146716UK00002B/129/P